HELL

IS

OPEN

HELL

IS

OPEN

GARD SVEEN

Translated by Paul Norlen

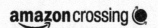

Text copyright © 2015 Gard Sveen
Translation copyright © 2017 Paul Norlen
All rights reserved.

Previously published as *Helvete åpent* by Vigmostad & Bjørke in Norway in 2015. Translated from Norwegian by Paul Norlen. First published in English by AmazonCrossing in 2017.

Published by AmazonCrossing, Seattle

www.apub.com

Amazon, the Amazon logo, and AmazonCrossing are trademarks of Amazon.com, Inc., or its affiliates.

ISBN-13: 9781503943919
ISBN-10: 1503943917

Cover design by Faceout Studio

Printed in the United States of America

But fear not for me, my friend, for I have already seen
Hell open
standing.

PROLOGUE
NOVEMBER 1988

For unto us a Savior is born, thought Tommy Bergmann.

He glanced through the windows of a house that stood close by the road. There was light in the middle window, a solitary golden Christmas star beaming out into the winter darkness.

Just in front of the house a dark-clothed figure was leaning over; he didn't appear to have noticed the car. Bergmann's partner, old Kåre Gjervan from Trondheim, stopped the car and put it in neutral. The man turned his head slowly in their direction. They looked furtively at each other, the men in the patrol car and the dark-clothed man. The windshield was covered with sleet. Gjervan turned on the windshield wipers. The figure by the roadside stood motionless, looking straight ahead into the sleet; even his dog stood as if frozen, staring at the two beams from the headlights, the sleet falling to the ground, as if the world was nothing but a snow globe and there was no evil in it. Even many years later Bergmann fantasized that right then, in that little pocket of time, he'd opened the car door and run the other way, back to the city, run until he was completely out of breath.

Kåre Gjervan swore quietly to himself, just as he'd done at the gas station at Mortensrud as Bergmann grabbed the portable radio when the call came through from Dispatch. There was less than an hour left on their shift, but Bergmann was bored and didn't want to wait for another car to report in. Unlike old Gjervan, Bergmann was only twenty-three, and he was eager to experience something on duty, not just count down the hours like Gjervan, who couldn't wait to get home to his wife and kids.

Gjervan pounded his hand a couple of times on the gear shift. The sound of his wedding ring made a metallic sound.

"Get the old man and the dog into the car," he said.

Just as Bergmann opened the car door, the man on the roadside started moving toward them and slid into the backseat.

They drove for several minutes through the darkness until they'd left all the houses behind and only dense black forest lay ahead. At last the forest road ended, dissolving into nothingness. It was as if they'd arrived at the ends of the earth. Only the headlights that lit up the spruce trunks showed that the world existed beyond the car. The wet dog, an innocent Labrador, cocked its head when Bergmann turned around and looked at them. Black blood was still caked on its nose. The man in the backseat sat quietly and stared out the windshield.

"What were you doing in the forest?" said Bergmann quietly.

The man did not answer.

Kåre Gjervan adjusted the rearview mirror and studied the man who had called the emergency number from one of the houses down by the main road.

"I'm telling you," said the man in the backseat. He paused, then closed his eyes. "This is the Devil's work."

Although the beam from the MagLite was powerful, darkness enveloped them. The spruce trees were so dense that Bergmann thought the sun wouldn't penetrate their depths on even a bright summer day. Gjervan carefully put one foot in front of the other, but kept an even pace as he ventured deeper into the forest. The caller was already well ahead, the dog pulling him along as if he were a dogsled. Bergmann fell behind a few steps and tightened his grip on his MagLite until the fine waffle pattern was embossed in his hand. There was a squishing sound under his feet. Ice-cold water had seeped through his military boots, and a faint odor of rotten earth rose up around him. He sped up to catch up with Gjervan. When he reached him, he heard a voice call out from farther in the forest.

"Here!" called the man with the dog. It looked like he was having a hard time holding it back. Bergmann tried not to imagine the worst.

"Oh, help me," he whispered to himself a minute later. "Dear God, you must help me."

The two men in front of him had stopped up ahead by a dense cluster of spruce trees. Gjervan slowly angled the MagLite away and waited a few seconds, as if he wanted to collect himself. Bergmann stopped on the narrow path a few steps behind him. The caller worked to restrain the dog as Gjervan bent over and removed what looked like branches and spruce twigs. He stood up quickly and took a couple of fumbling steps backward. His flashlight fell to the ground. Bergmann gripped his more tightly and took the last few steps up to the two other men.

Even in the white light from the flashlight, and even though she'd been lying there for days, she was easy to recognize from the police bulletin. Kristiane Thorstensen lay in two taped-up garbage bags that someone had tried to cover with branches and moss. The dog had torn open the top part, and her head was visible. The bags had torn in a few places, and it appeared that the birds had been after her too. But her face seemed untouched. She was bruised, but looked better than Bergmann had feared. Gjervan leaned down and carefully touched the baptismal necklace she wore around her neck. Bergmann closed his eyes and tried to tell himself that she had surely died quickly.

When the crime scene investigators arrived and pulled the garbage bags aside, all hope of a quick death disappeared.

She was so mutilated that he could no longer believe that there was anything but evil on earth.

He was unable to take his eyes off the left part of her chest.

He heard one of the CSIs mumble, "Trophy hunter," and quietly swore a death sentence over the man who had done this, after which he was in no shape to understand anything other than Gjervan's arm over his shoulders before everything turned black.

They drove back to the city in silence. Gjervan stopped at the Shell station again and parked the car in the same place as before, in the dark on the side of the building. He picked up the portable radio and called Dispatch. In a quiet voice he said simply, "Address," and waited until the man at Dispatch understood what he meant. As always, there were plenty of journalists listening to the police radio, but Gjervan evidently didn't want to give away this particular bit of information. Then he asked for the name of the minister in Oppsal parish, and asked Dispatch to call the person in question. *Why did he do that?* thought Bergmann. What was done was done, though. He knew that the first pack of hyena-like journalists was already on their way.

He studied Gjervan's hands as he took notes. They were just as steady as if he were sitting at home on a Sunday evening writing Christmas cards. A claw seized Bergmann's chest. He was twenty-three years old and had never seen a dead person—much less one that had been murdered—before tonight. *And now,* he thought. Now he was going to meet the parents who had lost their child.

"Do you want anything to eat?" said Gjervan, opening the car door.

Bergmann shook his head.

"You have to eat."

He shook his head again. He stayed in the car with his eyes closed and tried to control his breathing.

It turned out that they would have to be content with the interim pastor in Oppsal parish this first Sunday of Advent. He had no car, so they picked him up at Abildsø, where he lived in a basement apartment rental. He wasn't much older than Bergmann, and on the way up to Skøyenbrynet, the street in Godlia where the dead girl's family lived, he tried to talk about Kristiane, asking in a quiet voice if she didn't go to Vetlandsåsen Middle School and play handball, as if she were still alive.

"It's not easy to believe in God," the pastor said barely audibly. "When something like this . . ." It seemed as if he had run out of words.

As the car turned toward Skøyenbrynet, Bergmann caught himself wishing they would never get there. When Gjervan stopped the car in front of the Thorstensen family's red house, it occurred to him—and the thought frightened him—that they had nothing more to offer the family than this, three guys in a Volvo patrol car: himself, just out of the Police Academy; a deathly pale interim pastor who looked as if he regretted his faith in God; and old Kåre Gjervan. If it hadn't been for him, they would have nothing to lean on.

Bergmann thought he glimpsed a face in the kitchen window as he walked along the leafless hedge toward the front door. If it hadn't been for the fact that the outside light was on, the house would have looked abandoned. His mind flitted to the fact that he was less than a mile from where he himself had grown up. But this was another world, a realm of prosperity he would probably never experience. A world that in a few seconds would never be the same again, that would be in ruins with a single press of the doorbell.

As they stood on the doorstep, he stared at the sign on the door. It was a ceramic plaque that one of the kids—perhaps Kristiane herself—had made in grade school. Big blue glazed letters read, "Here live Alexander and Kristiane, Per-Erik and Elisabeth Thorstensen." Now they would have to take it down. Kristiane would never come home again. She would never stand on this doorstep and think that the sign was childish.

He spotted an Advent candleholder on the kitchen table through the kitchen window. One candle was lit. Bergmann thought it seemed absurd to light an Advent candle when their daughter was missing. But what did he know? Maybe it was a way to cling to normalcy, the hope that she was still alive. He heard the dull sound of the door to the entry porch being opened. Bergmann swallowed heavily, and his pulse raced. He caught the gaze of the interim pastor, who looked even paler than before—if that was possible—in the light from the outdoor lamp over the front door.

All three took a step back as the door opened. A man came into view in the doorway. Gjervan cleared his throat as the man in the door scrutinized the three men on the doorstep.

"Per-Erik Thorstensen?" said Gjervan in a quiet voice.

The man barely nodded.

Gjervan cleared his throat again.

"Yes?" said Per-Erik Thorstensen in a cracked voice. His eyes were already filled with tears, as if the sight of the uniforms and the pastor's green parka told him all he needed to know. Nevertheless there was a hint of hope in his voice—that the three men on the doorstep came bearing good news, that a miracle had taken place on this first Sunday of Advent.

Cautious steps could be heard behind Thorstensen as a woman came down the stairs from the second floor. She stopped in the passageway inside the entry porch with her hands to her face.

"I'm sorry," said Gjervan.

A shiver passed through Bergmann as the woman began to scream. It seemed as if she was never going to stop.

He was only able to make out four words from the hysterical sounds.

"It's all my fault."

She said it over and over again: "It's all my fault."

Her husband took a few fumbling steps backward.

Without turning around he said, "Elisabeth, Elisabeth."

She just screamed louder behind him, until it seemed physically impossible that she could keep it up. Thorstensen leaned back against the wall in the passageway, knocking over several framed photos on a chest of drawers as he did so. The sound of splintering glass mixed with Elisabeth Thorstensen's screams. Gjervan went over to Per-Erik and took him by the shoulders.

Bergmann exchanged a quick glance with the pastor. They studied each other for a moment before Bergmann noticed that it had suddenly become quiet in the house. Apart from a weak, desperate sob from Per-Erik Thorstensen, who was now leaning against Gjervan's uniform jacket, silence had fallen. Bergmann walked inside, and Gjervan nodded toward the kitchen, which was to the left of the hall.

Bergmann walked across the large Persian rug in the hall toward the kitchen, where the sound of utensils clattering to the floor could be heard. He stopped in the doorway. The Advent candle flickered on the kitchen table. A Christmas star was on one of the kitchen chairs, ready to be hung up.

Elisabeth Thorstensen was kneeling on the ground. She raised her head and stared apathetically at Bergmann. For a moment he was unable to move. He studied her facial features and was almost certain he'd seen her before, long ago. An image popped up in his mind. For a second or two he saw it clearly. She was young, standing in a long corridor, reaching her hand out to him.

He tore himself away from the train of thought.

"Don't do it," he said, nodding toward her right hand.

She pressed the big kitchen knife harder against her wrist. He saw that blood had already started to trickle, but that she still hadn't cut completely across the artery.

He took a cautious step into the room. The pine floorboard creaked under his military boot.

"Don't touch me," she said quietly. "Don't touch me, you pig."

Without a sound she pulled the kitchen knife forcefully across her wrist. Bergmann had time to think that it was good she didn't cut along the tendons, down into the flesh. The tendons were severed, but the blood wasn't pouring out. He crouched down in front of her, but not before she managed to cut herself again. He took a firm hold of her right wrist, which hung limply. She seemed suddenly drained of energy, and her fingers let go of the knife immediately. Bergmann tossed it across the floor.

He pressed his big hand hard against her thin wrist, a chaos of white cuts and black warm blood oozing out between his fingers. Her head sank toward his leather uniform jacket. She pressed against his neck; he put his free left arm over her back and tried to call to Gjervan, but not too loud. Kåre must have understood the situation, as somewhere behind him Bergmann heard Gjervan's voice barking out short commands. He picked out the words *ambulance, Skøyenbrynet*.

He tightened his grip on her wrist and swept his gaze across the kitchen counter. A dish towel was only an arm's length from him. He tried to get up, but Elisabeth Thorstensen held him back. He let go of her wrist; he had to put the towel in place as a compress. She raised her right hand to his face, so pale that she looked as if she would soon faint.

"My child," she said. "I will never see my child again."

PART ONE
NOVEMBER 2004

1

He knocked the alarm clock to the floor as he reached for his phone. It was Leif Monsen, the duty officer at Kripo—the Criminal Police. Tommy Bergmann had no great confidence in Monsen. He was infantile, an obvious racist and politically well to the right of Genghis Khan. But when it came to crime scene descriptions, Monsen was worth listening to. No one in active service had seen more than he had. And when he said a crime scene was ghastly, there was no reason to doubt it.

Though Bergmann heard the words *duct tape* and *knife*, *hammer* and *blood*, they barely registered, as if they weren't real. It was the words that followed that made him wake up properly.

"I don't see how it could be possible, but it must be the same man," said Monsen. His voice sounded desperate for a moment. "I've sent a car up for you."

As Bergmann hung up, he heard the sound of a diesel engine and a car braking quickly. The bedroom lit up with a blue flashing light.

The light on the roof of the car painted the walls in Oslo's Svartdal tunnel. The driver pressed the siren button on the midconsole, as a car at the end of the tunnel was straddling two lanes.

"So you're Bergmann," said the young uniformed officer in the passenger seat. Bergmann grunted in response. This was not the time to start a conversation. Besides, for the first time in his life, he was unsure what the kid was referring to, how far down in the system the rumors had trickled.

He had no time to think further before the car stopped outside the building entrance on Frognerveien. Two patrol cars and an ambulance were blocking the street. The flickering blue lights from the three cars flashed on the wall of the apartment building. A uniformed officer stood by the door, his ears red from the cold; the temperature had gone down considerably during the night.

Monsen's voice rang in his ears on his way up the stairs: "It's ghastly down here, Tommy."

Bergmann kept his eyes on the deep-red carpet that ran like a snake up and over the steps and tried not to imagine what he would encounter in the apartment.

The metallic smell of blood wafted out the open door. Another uniformed officer stood out on the landing, looking like he was about to throw up at any moment.

Leif Monsen walked over to Bergmann as soon as he stepped inside the apartment. It looked like any old apartment on the West Side—three contiguous rooms, walls painted white, a maid's room behind the kitchen. He guessed that in reality it was a transitional apartment for high-end whores.

"She's still alive," Monsen whispered. He repeated it, his voice sounding almost eager: "She's still *alive*."

Monsen was subdued. That was unusual.

"Who called it in?"

"We don't know. Unregistered prepaid card. A man simply called in and said that a woman, or *girl*, had been found killed in this apartment. He thought she was dead. Damn, the caller may have seen the bastard who did this."

Damned technology, thought Bergmann, only now looking at the clock. It was four thirty in the morning. He heard footsteps out on the landing. It was yet another EMT team. They ran through the hallway, almost knocking Bergmann and Monsen down as they headed into the bedroom. They were followed by Georg Abrahamsen with a colleague from Forensics in tow, and finally Fredrik Reuter, who appeared to be on the verge of a heart attack after the trip up the stairs.

Abrahamsen forced his way into the bedroom with his camera. Bergmann, Monsen, Reuter, and Abrahamsen's colleague from Forensics—Bergmann could never remember his name—all remained standing silently in the dark hallway. A minute later, Abrahamsen reappeared. He'd been thrown out of the bedroom, and a brief quarrel arose. Reuter intervened to stop it.

"I have to know what position she's in," said Abrahamsen as he was pushed across the hall by a massive EMT.

"They're trying to save her life, if that means anything at all to you, Georg." Reuter appeared to have gotten his resting pulse back. Abrahamsen loosened his grip on the camera.

Reuter went back into the room with the two of them and evidently worked out an amicable arrangement; or at least so it seemed, as Abrahamsen remained in the bedroom.

After putting on shoe protectors and a hairnet, Bergmann spent the next five minutes walking around the apartment. He started in the kitchen, which appeared to be completely new. The modest contents of the cupboards appeared to confirm his initial impression that the apartment was used for quite different purposes than a residence. A few plates and long-stem glasses, wineglasses, champagne in the refrigerator. Nothing edible. The countertops were bare; the perpetrator might have taken anything that could lead them to him, but that seemed unlikely. He cast a glance out the kitchen window toward the back courtyard. A lamp shone down by the entryway into a couple of windows. The curtains in the bedroom had probably been drawn, and there was almost certainly a lightproof blind or something like it as well. For a couple of seconds everything seemed completely hopeless. As if this winter would be the last one, that there would never be another summer.

He shook his head as Reuter came into the room with two patrol officers and Halgeir Sørvaag. Reuter had a bundle of forms in his hands.

"Neighborhood canvass," he said.

There were sounds in the hall, and a stretcher came into view. Bergmann went to have a look at the slight woman—no, *the young girl*—with the oxygen mask over her mouth. The blanket they had placed over her was already drenched with blood. Remnants of duct tape were visible on her wrists, and her eyes stared stiffly up at the ceiling, as if she were already dead. Four or five EMTs and a doctor followed the stretcher, one of whom held a bag of blood, another securing the cannula that was inserted in her forearm. God only knew what she looked like under the blanket.

Bergmann felt a shiver down his spine, and his whole body shook uncontrollably for a moment. The sight of the girl made him feel that all this was his fault—that he was to blame for everything that had happened to her.

Everyone in the apartment paused while the ambulance personnel left the apartment, listening until there were no more sounds in the stairwell and the curt commands to and from the ambulance service had died away.

The quiet did not last long.

One of the neighbors started screaming frantically on one of the floors below. She had probably seen the stretcher being carried down the stairs, the blood transfusion, the young white doll face.

Just like Kristiane, thought Bergmann.

"I need to take a look at your pictures," he said to Abrahamsen, who handed him the camera. He clicked over to the display screen. How young could she be? She had to be one of the youngest prostitutes in the city. Bergmann felt an almost uncontrollable fury rise inside him.

If—no, *when*—he got hold of the man who had done this, and the men who had brought this young girl into the country (because he was quite sure she wasn't Norwegian), he would pound the life out of them with his own hands.

She must have been tied up by her wrists against the headboard on the bed; at least that's what it looked like. The tape over her mouth had been pulled off and hung slackly from her cheek. It would take him many weeks to forget what the rest of her looked like.

"Fucking bastard," he said to himself. He had to walk around the room a few times and catch his breath. He was on the verge of pounding his fist into the wall, splintering the double doors with his skull, and kicking down everything that was in the white-painted room—chairs, dining room table, a TV, a bookcase.

He went into the bedroom last, after all the others had already gone in, as if the situation were more dangerous for him than for them.

A large double bed occupied the middle of the room. Sure enough, remnants of gray tape hung from the wrought iron posts at both the head and foot of the bed.

"It was me and the first uniformed officer who cut off the tape," said Monsen. His eyes looked sad under his white hairnet.

Halgeir Sørvaag never asked anything of anyone, which was perhaps why he was the one they all turned to. Without a moment's hesitation, he went down on all fours and began minutely examining the room. Bergmann scanned the room for an overview. He sensed that the perpetrator had been taken by surprise. He didn't know how, but that must have been what happened. Monsen must be right, the perpetrator had been interrupted before he could finish his work.

"What did the caller say?" He sought Monsen's gaze.

"You can listen to the log, but he didn't say much."

"I think he was surprised," said Bergmann. "Someone who shouldn't have been here entered the apartment. The caller may even have seen the killer."

"She's still alive," said Reuter. "And I'll be damned if that girl doesn't survive. Then we'll get him. She can probably identify him."

"Amen," said Monsen. His eyes shone a moment, as if he was having the same thought as Bergmann: only the Old Testament could deliver justice in this case.

Bergmann left the room to Abrahamsen and Sørvaag. He couldn't stand to be there a moment longer. If there was anything to find there, they would find it.

He took Reuter with him out into the adjoining room.

"It's the same man," Bergmann told him. "He must have been triggered by all the recent news about the Kristiane case. Wasn't that the way the girls were killed? Isn't that what you've always told me? You were part of the investigation."

"But that man should be Anders Rask," said Reuter. "And he's locked up at Ringvoll."

2

The traffic appeared to be blocked for good on Majorstukrysset. An endless row of cars sat in both directions on Kirkeveien. The Route 20 bus tried to nudge its way into the massive line, but didn't even make it out of the bus stop in front of McDonald's.

Although November had barely begun, a fine layer of snow was settling over the city. Bergmann sensed it was going to be a long winter.

"Wouldn't it be nice if I told you there was something to blame it on?" said the voice behind him.

Bergmann didn't answer. He just sat silently on the windowsill. He had done a lot of talking over the past few months. Today he couldn't bear to. The past twenty-four hours had been bad enough as it was.

"On a father you've never met, who theoretically may have been violent? On a mother who systematically made you feel guilty and punished you for showing any emotion?" Viggo Osvold was trying to focus his gaze, though he was shaking rather severely. "The causes are one thing. You can't do anything about them. The question is: How can you live with them? And then, how can another person live with you living with them?"

"Hege never saw me cry. Have I said that? Not really."

"You just wanted one more chance? Is that what you mean?"

"Yes."

"Why should she have given that to you? Would you really want to be with a person who'd given you chance after chance? After ten years?"

"Eleven. But no. The answer is no."

Osvold breathed heavily through his nose. He took off his glasses and shook his head almost imperceptibly, as though to suggest that Bergmann hadn't made an iota of progress over the last few months. He might have been thinking deep down that little other than medication would help.

Bergmann had still not managed to give him a proper answer to his question: "What do you feel along with the aggression? Do you feel small, afraid, rejected, wounded, alone, proud, sad?"

"All of that," he'd answered. "A child. I'm just a child again."

Osvold always followed up with the abuse, the eternal abuse. Beatings, rape, incest, and homicide were all basically the same. "All abuse of women is about power. Did you feel powerful when you hit her? Or impotent?"

"I don't know." Bergmann had no better answer. Osvold had nodded, raised his eyebrows, and made a kind of grimace, the start of a sympathetic smile. He had been reluctant to give Bergmann a tentative diagnosis, even in response to direct and repeated questions. A diagnosis would tell Bergmann that he was sick, which he could use as a crutch: *I'm sick, therefore I hit.*

"You're functional," Osvold always said. "For that reason I don't want to give you a diagnosis. Maybe later, we'll see."

Bergmann peeled off five two-hundred-kroner bills.

Osvold picked up his gold pocket watch, which lay on the coffee table in front of him, between a box of Kleenex and an orchid that had seen better days.

"I have to go," said Bergmann, picking up the *Aftenposten* from the desk. He showed the front page to Osvold.

The psychiatrist put away his folder. His life, his messiness. In fifteen minutes it would be another crazy person's turn—someone else whose life was so out of whack that it would be nearly impossible to straighten it out in the course of a single lifetime.

Bergmann should have been down at police headquarters with everyone else, but Reuter thought the therapy sessions were more important. Besides, there wasn't anything more he could do right now. So he'd been subjected to forty-five minutes on the couch with Osvold. The first act belonged to the technicians, as Reuter liked to say. It was the opposite of the theater. The killing first, followed by the technicians. Then the second act could begin. The final act was merely the undramatic joining of separate tragedies tangled up in each other.

Much like his own life.

Hege had reported him for domestic violence early in the fall. Her new husband had gotten her to do that. The penalty range was three to six years.

Surprisingly, it had been something of a relief. He didn't for the life of him want to go to prison—and he certainly didn't want others to find out what he'd done—but when the report appeared on the table, it was like coming out of the closet. Something inside him wanted her to show her strength. He wanted Hege to say, *I'll crush you if I want to.*

Osvold thought this was positive. *Very* positive, he had even ventured to say. The problem was the trigger points. Bergmann had trouble putting those into words. Explaining his actions. They hadn't yet gotten to his feelings, but maybe that wasn't so bad. He didn't know if he still had any.

Hege had dropped the charges when he said he was willing to go into therapy. At headquarters only Reuter and the head of Human Resources knew about it. But he was sure it had leaked out anyway. Not to the entire staff, but to a couple of important decision-makers. Which would effectively prevent any career advancement if he didn't start brown-nosing. He was on the waiting list for Alternatives to Violence, where men like himself surely belonged, a fellowship of men who beat women. Maybe he would continue with Osvold too. In a strange way he liked the cross-eyed guy fairly well.

"One slip-up, and you're out on your ass," Reuter had said to him. "You can't even be a rent-a-cop with a gas pistol on your hip. And if Hege gets you convicted, you'll get three years. You've admitted you're guilty. We could have filed a case against you. We *should* have filed a case against you. If you end up in prison, you're dead, you know that? They're going to beat the living shit out of you in there, Tommy. Break every bone in your body. I should have done it myself now that I think about it."

3

He walked all the way down to the victim's apartment on Frognerveien. The long line of exhaust-spewing cars eventually faded away.

A semblance of normalcy returned as he approached the entry doors. The events of the night before flickered in his mind's eye for a few seconds—the flashing blue lights, the uniformed officers, the knowing looks of the ones who'd seen the badly injured girl.

The ambulances, the patrol cars, and the police tape by the entry doors were all gone by now. Only two crime scene technicians were still at work inside the apartment.

He pounded on the door and put on a pair of shoe protectors. In the bedroom the bed had turned black. How much blood had she lost? How many times had he stabbed her with the knife? Struck her with the hammer that still lay on the floor? But there was not a single fingerprint; the man must have worn gloves, probably latex. Though the knife was gone, they deduced that it was a medium-sized weapon with a four- to five-inch blade. He felt physically ill at the mere thought of having a blade like that stuck in his body. The girl had been stabbed in such a way that she wouldn't die of the stab wounds themselves, but from the loss of blood. Even so, the perpetrator had struck enough of her vital organs. It couldn't be avoided on such a small body.

He moved his eyes to the remnants of duct tape on the headboard. She'd been taped to the bed—with tape over her mouth as well—when Monsen and the first patrol arrived.

But it was the same method, he thought. Most of it added up. Reuter, who'd worked in the eighties as a rank-and-file investigator, had grudgingly acknowledged that this murder attempt was more or less identical to the six homicides Anders Rask had been convicted of in the nineties. The hospital reports indicated that the prostitute had the same methodical knife and hammer injuries as the six other girls. It was likely that the only reason he hadn't begun the trophy collecting—the removal of body parts, as if he were a self-appointed Aztec priest—was because he had been interrupted. If he'd had time to finish, there would have been no doubt.

The first girl, in Tønsberg in 1978, had lost the little finger on her left hand; the other girls had each lost one of the other fingers; and the sixth and last one had lost the thumb on her right hand. After that Rask set about removing their female organs in a way that Bergmann tried to think about as little as possible.

The only thing that was certain was that Anders Rask could *not* be behind this homicide attempt. He was confined to the Ringvoll Psychiatric Hospital and had recently been trying to get his case reopened. It was equally certain that whoever had tried to murder this young girl knew about the methods Rask had employed in his six homicides. Although every detective and crime reporter in Oslo knew perfectly well how the murders had been committed, the verdict—including all the specifics of the murders—had never been published, out of consideration for the victims' survivors. Either they were facing a copycat—a Rask admirer who was among the few who knew all the details of the old murders—or perhaps Rask was wrongly convicted and another man had committed the murders and was at it again. Or else the Oslo police were facing an even greater nightmare: there was a connection between Anders Rask and an unknown perpetrator on the outside, a perpetrator who operated just the way Rask had.

Bergmann couldn't take any more. The only thing that kept him going was that the defenseless young girl might have seen the face of the man who'd tried to kill her.

4

Bergmann went back to the front door of the apartment, which had been open when they arrived the night before.

He stood on the landing and tried to reconstruct the night for himself. The perpetrator had probably rung the bell outside the building. He may have met the girl at the strip club Porte des Senses, but more likely he'd responded to an ad on the Internet. If they could only identify who the girl was, they could launch a legitimate investigation. But there was no computer or phone in the apartment, no address book, not so much as a single scrap of paper anywhere.

He walked slowly down the steps to the two big wooden entry doors, painted white, that led out onto Frognerveien. The doorbell was unmarked. The apartment was owned by a Norwegian company, which in turn was owned by an Estonian company. The CEO of the Norwegian company was a Norwegian businessman by the name of Jon H. Magnussen. He spent 183 days a year in Cyprus and could only be reached through his attorney, who supposedly had no knowledge of the apartment.

Bergmann studied the remnants of the fingerprint powder that lingered on the doorbells. He didn't even know why they bothered. *He stood here,* thought Bergmann. With a bag or a suitcase, or maybe a backpack. He must have kept his tools—the knife, the hammer, and the duct tape—hidden somewhere.

They had searched for a man early this morning—one who they had captured on a surveillance camera walking up Cort Adelers Gate, away from Porte des Senses toward Drammensveien—but he had no bag, suitcase, or backpack. Perhaps he simply lived in the vicinity. Maybe it wasn't the perpetrator at all.

He pushed open the door and started back up the five flights of stairs. What did someone think who went up such a stairway, carrying a knife and a hammer and a roll of sturdy duct tape?

Bergmann remembered the semihysterical voice of the caller. *A young man,* he thought. Her pimp, or perhaps an errand boy who was supposed to pick up her money for the big boys. So this kid showed up in the middle of the night, perhaps he took a cut for himself by sleeping with her; every jerk outdid the last in the prostitution industry. Regardless of who the caller had been, he had arrived unannounced. Either the door was open, or the person in question had their own key.

The young man must have gotten the shock of his life when he walked into the apartment. Bergmann couldn't bear to think about what he'd seen for long.

But he also could have seen the perpetrator. He must have. Bergmann had listened to the audio log at least ten times that morning: "Hurry up, you have to hurry up. She's dying. She's dying!"

The call was registered at 3:47 a.m. It came from a phone with an unregistered prepaid card, which might mean that the caller was somehow connected to the girl. The voice had no accent. He was clearly not Eastern European.

The call didn't give Bergmann much to go on, but it could mean that there were two people who had seen the perpetrator. That said, they couldn't protect the caller if he didn't report himself. But he'd probably gotten out of there faster than hell. There were bloody tracks out in the hallway, which suggested that the man had followed him.

But the girl was still alive. She was their gold now.

He stopped on the fourth-floor landing. The young couple who lived there had already been questioned. They hadn't heard a thing—which was perhaps not so strange considering that the girl's mouth was taped shut. They had also firmly denied knowing anything about the type of operation that went on above their heads. He'd nonetheless felt that the young newlywed and mother of a small child had wanted to tell him something more.

He decided to ring their bell. But before he pressed the doorbell, his phone rang. Halgeir Sørvaag announced that he would leave Oslo University Hospital immediately if Bergmann didn't come and relieve him. He was too old to work for free, he said.

Bergmann hurried back down the stairs. He'd have to talk to the couple in the apartment tomorrow.

If the girl in the hospital woke up, one of them had to be there. It was their only chance.

5

She woke up to the sound of someone calling her name. The room said nothing to her. She'd dreamt about her again. That she went upstairs to the second floor of her house in Skøyenbrynet. Half-muffled sounds could be heard across the dark passage. The two of them in her bed. The scream.

Where are you, mother?

I'm here, Kristiane. So far away, like I always was.

The usual disappointment washed over her. It was Peter's young voice from out in the kitchen.

"Mom?"

"I'm resting," she whispered. She didn't have the energy to shout. After a while he appeared in the doorway. He entered the room and turned on the reading lamp.

"Why are you lying down here in the office?"

"Get me a glass of water," she said. "Will you?"

He turned around without a word. Closed the door. She knew that he'd understood for a long time that she didn't have any more love to give. She knew that he'd probably started to despise her for something he couldn't even put into words.

Her head felt heavy as she got up. She could have taken a valium or two, but wanted to wait. The weak light from the reading lamp cut deep into her skull, down into the spine and out into the small of her back.

Her hands trembled as she picked up the *Dagbladet* off the desk. She'd heard the news in the taxi from the Radisson hotel. When she got home, she sent Rose out to buy all the papers. Reluctantly she had sat down and spent half the day reading news websites.

The police want to contact this man, it said. There was a grainy picture of a man in a black coat crossing Cort Adelers Gate in the direction of Drammensveien. His face was hidden by a NY Yankees baseball cap.

The picture had been taken at 1:59 a.m.

She knew that he went to clubs down the street. She used to get turned on by the thought. And the cap. He wore that kind of cap at the cabin. Sometimes in the city as well.

When had he come to the Radisson hotel?

She barely remembered. She hadn't gotten home before nine o'clock. Rose said that Peter hadn't asked about where she was. That morning, Rose had woken him as she usually did, made breakfast, and packed his lunch. Once in a great while Elisabeth Thorstensen got up and drove him to school herself, but only if the weather was bad or she wanted to feel like a normal mother. Normal? Normal mothers don't think that way about their twelve-year-old son: I had you to forget.

And now I hate you.

Shut up, she said to herself. She heard Rose and Peter talking together out in the kitchen. She laughed at something he said, in a way that suggested she might be a bit taken with him. A thirty-year-old Filipina housekeeper charmed by a twelve-year-old boy. There were days when Elisabeth wasn't sure if Asgeir was even Peter's father. Peter resembled Alex. One accident triggered by another.

One day I'm going to cut you, she thought. *Really cut you.*

Her eyes were filled with tears.

Don't grow bitter. Wasn't that what she'd been told? Bitterness would only lead you into the abyss.

Would that be so wrong?

Just to let go.

6

By the time the taxi finally stopped in front of Oslo University Hospital, a thick layer of snow covered the ground. Bergmann had ended up with a Dane behind the wheel. He'd never experienced snow in November, even though he was from Hjørring. "Welcome to Norway," Bergmann had said. The Dane had driven so slowly that the prostitute might have died on their way to the hospital. But getting a ride in a police car was out of the question. Though only a dozen people at headquarters knew which hospital the girl was in, that was already too many in Bergmann's opinion.

The sound of John Coltrane's *A Love Supreme* stopped abruptly as Bergmann slammed the car door shut. He watched the Mercedes's red taillights until they faded in the blowing snow, which had a sickly yellow cast in the glow of the streetlights.

He considered it a miracle that the EMTs and the ER doctors had managed to keep her alive all night. She'd been on the operating table for nine consecutive hours, and Bergmann prayed to a god he no longer believed in that she would soon be able to talk.

It must mean something that she'd come out of this with her life intact.

He allowed himself two cigarettes outside the entrance. He didn't know how long he would be in there.

The reception area was empty as the sliding glass doors closed behind him. No one sat behind the front desk, but he heard subdued laughter coming from inside the nurses' office just beyond it. White lamella curtains blocked the view into the room—and, he assumed, the view out. He turned and studied the ceiling and walls. The only visible cameras were the two positioned over the sliding doors. They each covered a sector of the reception area, but once you headed down one of the long corridors to the right or left, you would be out of sight of the camera lenses.

There were plenty of stories of junkies who wandered down hospital corridors in search of morphine and anything else they could get their hands on. That they hadn't considered this with regard to the young girl was more than Bergmann could understand. It would only take one unfaithful employee at the hospital for the truth about the girl's location to end up on the front page of the city's newspapers. If that happened, even a guard in the reception area and a policeman outside her room wouldn't be enough.

"Hello," he called out toward the nurses' office. The laughter subsided.

A young woman stuck her head out. She looked embarrassed for a moment, but appeared to recover quickly. A guard appeared behind her.

Her expression turned serious, and Bergmann wondered whether she and the guard thought that he was the murderer who'd come to finish what he'd started.

"Is this the way you keep an eye on things?" said Bergmann.

"No, we're keeping watch," said the guard as he walked around the counter and started patrolling the lobby.

You're wasting my time, thought Bergmann, but he said nothing.

He scanned the large reception area and studied the small compact guard as he walked toward the entrance doors. *If the man who killed these girls shows up here, you'll be dead too.*

7

He headed down the long corridor, and instead of taking the elevator up to the third floor, he took the stairs. Midway up, a bad feeling came over him. He leaned over the railing and looked down toward the basement, where the orderlies wheeled patients from one ward to another. The dead were taken to refrigerated storage down there, and pathologists sliced into murder victims—with the blessing of the prosecutor. Hadn't they suffered enough already?

Bergmann stood for quite a long time staring through the narrow rectangular opening into the basement. How long had he been inside the hospital? And he'd only encountered two people—the nurse and the security guard. How many other entrances did a hospital like this have? The whole arrangement was dangerous, wasn't it?

The murderer knew that the young prostitute was so badly injured that the police were unlikely to take the chance of transporting her any farther than necessary. And if he was familiar with the hospital system, he knew that Oslo University Hospital was the safest place to take a badly injured girl of unknown identity.

Bergmann had tried to convince Reuter that Oslo University Hospital was too obvious, but his words had fallen on deaf ears.

Increased staffing was also out of the question. There was no budget for it, and Reuter couldn't work magic.

A door slammed behind him, but when he turned around no one was there.

He heard a door being opened farther down the corridor, and a male nurse appeared. He walked toward Bergmann, extending his hand.

"Kristian," he said, but Bergmann didn't really register his name, and he didn't think he said his.

A woman's voice buzzed in his head. At first he couldn't place it. Then it came to him.

It's all my fault.

So many years ago.

The doors leading into intensive care opened automatically. The walls were ash gray, as if they'd seen too much sorrow and death.

"She's at the far end," said Kristian.

"Okay," said Bergmann. He'd already spotted the armed uniformed officer sitting outside the door at the far end of the corridor. Halgeir Sørvaag stood before the officer, holding forth about one thing or another.

Bergmann didn't like Sørvaag, but he was a capable bastard, he would give him that. He was the one who'd found a matchbox from Porte des Senses back at the apartment on Frognerveien. Milovic, the gangster who ran the place, had been promised amnesty by Chief Public Prosecutor Svein Finneland if he cooperated. They figured she was probably one of his girls, who'd been brought to the country in a container, and surely no more than fourteen years old. But Finneland didn't give a damn about that. He wanted to get hold of the man who'd committed the murders Rask was convicted of. He was convinced it was the same man. Bergmann was not equally certain.

He greeted the men and showed his ID to the uniformed officer, a burly man from Majorstua police station.

Sørvaag took his leave with a couple of grunts.

"You should have one in the chamber," Sørvaag said to the uniformed officer, then smiled to himself.

Idiot, thought Bergmann. But he had a point. In an encounter with what might be the country's most dangerous man, you only got one shot.

"She's in here," Kristian said, as if Bergmann still hadn't realized that.

He looked in through the safety glass. The room was darkened, apart from a faint light at the far end where the girl lay in her bed. How old could she be?

"I want to go in and see her," he said.

"I think that—"

"You heard what I said." Bergmann turned toward Kristian and jabbed him with his index finger. The uniformed officer stood up tentatively.

"And you sit down," Bergmann said to him. "I'm not the one you should be on the lookout for."

"But—"

"Get hold of the doctor on duty, Kristian. Otherwise I may make a few calls around town, do you understand? And then I can't guarantee that you'll ever work in this city again."

Kristian returned only a minute later with a woman about Bergmann's age, though it was possible she'd already turned forty. He thought he'd seen her before, on a previous case, but couldn't remember which one.

"I would really like to see her."

The doctor's gaze moved past him toward the room where the young girl lay.

"She's very weak. We're probably going to put her in an induced coma, but you may already know that. We've been evaluating her closely; the last hour has been better."

Two nurses appeared in the doorway to the nurses' station.

"Isn't anyone in there with her?"

"We're registering the slightest movement," the doctor said, looking straight at him now.

"Even if she talks?"

She nodded.

"*Has* she talked?"

"Yes. Somewhat. Incoherently. The policeman who was here today couldn't make anything of it. And, I must repeat, she is very, very weak. She's practically hovering between life and death. She lost a critical amount of blood, even though she—"

"Someone should be sitting with her at all times." Bergmann didn't have time to listen to this doctor. In situations such as this one, every word was crucial. He would give anything at all for a scrap of information. He pulled a voice-recognition Dictaphone out of his pocket and held it up to the doctor.

"It will be this or me."

After several minutes, the doctor finally gave in, though due to the danger of infection, he would have to put on shoe protectors, a hairnet, a mouth mask, and the same green coat as the doctor. The doctor said flat out that she didn't want to lose her because of an unwashed policeman with a cold. In her condition, even the slightest infection could kill her.

Bergmann studied himself in the mirror in the nurses' office. The room smelled sterile, and the poster advertising the wine raffle next to the mirror seemed completely out of place. His mind flitted to Hege, for whom this was commonplace, who stood like this every day. He wondered whether he would ever get over her.

He put on the hairnet and leaned toward the mirror. In the harsh light there seemed to be no end to the circles around his eyes. He took hold of the mask and thought that the girl would surely die of shock if she woke up and he was the first thing she saw. He felt a moment of panic at the thought of sitting by her side for two or three hours, desperately hoping that she would wake up and say something definitive.

If that could lead to justice, then it would be worth it.

The doctor led him in silence back to the room. Bergmann exchanged a few words with the uniformed officer. Though he was a big burly man, Bergmann knew that nothing would stop the perpetrator once he got there.

He was led into the room. The girl lay in a big hospital bed. He'd never seen anything like it before. He tried to count how many hoses she was connected to, but grew lightheaded at the sight of her. She wore an oxygen mask over her mouth, and a wobbly hose linked it to the oxygen supply behind the bed. The EKG machine gave off a green glow. He followed the numbers and diagrams with his eyes. It was like something out of a sci-fi movie he'd seen a few years before—the title of which he couldn't remember—where half-dead girls lay in a kind of comatose state and predicted murders before they were committed.

That was how he felt just then. That he could predict everything that was going to happen. He knew why the attempt had been made on the girl's life. And he knew that he was the only one who could find the man who'd done it. Because Rask was still in prison, and because Rask had given the interview in *Dagbladet* three weeks ago, in which he said that perhaps he hadn't killed Kristiane after all. The five others, yes, but not Kristiane. Maybe not.

When the doctor left, he nearly collapsed into the chair by the side of the bed. He studied the girl's face, feature by feature. In the weak light, she looked vaguely Slavic, and he was sure for a moment that she was just like the girl in his dream, the girl with the doll-like face. Her skin was white, drained of color, almost transparent.

Her head jerked. Bergmann jumped back in the chair.

Her eyeballs started moving beneath her thin eyelids. Her mouth opened slightly, and his gaze flew to the EKG on the other side of the bed. Her pulse had risen, her blood pressure too.

Suddenly it was over, as quickly as it had begun. She stopped moving, her pulse fell, she exhaled heavily and then fell back in what seemed like a quiet morphine-induced state of calm.

The door opened behind him, and the doctor cast a long shadow across the floor. She studied Bergmann and the girl a moment, then went over to the EKG machine. She cocked her head, pressed a button, and a few seconds later a printout emerged from a printer alongside the apparatus.

"Did she say anything?" she said, turning toward Bergmann.

He shook his head.

"She's had some similar awakenings over the course of the day. Yes, she woke up for a minute or so earlier, but it was impossible to make contact with her."

That's why I'm sitting here, thought Bergmann, but he merely nodded in response.

The doctor bent over the girl and placed her hand gently on her forehead. He followed the movements of her long fingers, the broad wedding ring on the ring finger, as they stroked the girl's light hair.

"She's not much older than my middle daughter." The doctor smiled sadly at him, as if there was nothing she could do other than stroke the half-dead girl's hair and pray to higher powers that she would survive.

"You look like you could use some sleep," she said, patting him lightly on the shoulder. Several minutes after she'd left, he still felt the warmth from her hand.

He had an almost irresistible urge to take the girl's hand and hold it. He felt his eyes getting moist, then chastised himself for being a sentimental pig. He closed his eyes and touched the little hand carefully, so that he didn't touch the cannula.

After half an hour he felt his own breathing fall into the same rhythm as the girl's. A couple of hours later, he fell asleep on the chair. He was wakened by the doctor, who was crouched in front of him with her hands on his shoulders.

"Let's find a room for you," she said.

He barely remembered being transported to a bed in a vacant two-person room. The last thing he saw were white snowflakes against the window, as they melted and trickled down the glass.

8

The music from the first act of *Swan Lake* always made him so damned sentimental. It was as if Tchaikovsky knew exactly which buttons to push. The melodramatic first scene, followed by the two waltzes that reminded him of a time that he would never get back, when his daughters were little and went to ballet school and appeared in Christmas performances. That was before he became a consultant and clinical director. Before craziness became his career.

Arne Furuberget picked up the remote control and turned off the music. He'd had his legs on the desk for so long that the blood had left his feet. With great effort he got them down to the floor. His legs tingled painfully for a long time, until the blood returned. He wondered what it would be like to wake up in a straitjacket.

Furuberget started walking in circles in the dim office; only the green library lamp indicated that there was still life in the office so late in the evening. He took a deep breath and tried once again to shake off the feelings of guilt, working up a certain professional distance to his personal life. He strode over to the CD player and put the Russian music back on. Then he poured himself a straight vodka and stood by the windows that faced toward Lake Mjøsa. He drained his glass in one gulp and reminded himself that there were no breath tests in this place. A few lights in the courtyards below the clinic were all he could see between the sheets of sleet. Otherwise it was pitch black out there.

He heard a faint scream some place above him. No one else would have heard it, but he had developed a sixth sense for these almost supersonic outbursts from patients.

As if by intuition, he called the nurse on duty.

"Are you still at work?" she said.

He didn't reply.

"What do you think about increasing the dosage?"

He liked to query the foot soldiers. It made them feel a little more important than they were. *No,* he thought. *They* were *important.* More important than he was, weren't they? They were the ones who were in the trenches twenty-four hours a day. Not him. As a rule he went home at four o'clock. He would arrive the following morning and read the reports and case records, see some of the patients for therapy, and look over the protocols the various teams worked by.

The nurse told Furuberget what he already knew—that it was Johansen, the accountant from Kirkenær, shouting on the floor above. His psychosis was intensifying, and evenings were worse than mornings. Always muttering something about wolves wanting to kill him, he lived in a kind of parallel universe.

They agreed that Johansen's current dose of Trilafon was sufficient. Although Furuberget knew that an increase wouldn't do him any harm, he nonetheless decided to wait. Johansen was as far beyond cognitive therapy as you could get. Maybe after Christmas, if higher powers cooperated.

"We can revisit the situation after Christmas," Furuberget mumbled, then smiled dejectedly at his own pessimism. He'd just seen this situation far too many times before. Once a patient was as lost in his own mind as Johansen was, there was almost never a way back.

He looked at the clock on the wall. It was starting to get late, and he fleetingly regretted having come back to work after leaving for an early dinner with his wife. While she was in the middle of an after-dinner nap, he'd suddenly felt compelled to return to Ringvoll.

The feeling that he'd made an irreparable mistake would simply not go away. Furuberget knew perfectly well that he had encouraged Anders Rask to have the conviction in the Kristiane case taken up again. Rask had said as much, just as suddenly as he had admitted to the murders many years ago: "I wasn't the one who killed Kristiane."

And now an attempt had been made to murder a new girl in the same manner. He'd confirmed the perpetrator's method with his old rival and colleague, the psychologist Rune Flatanger, who worked with the Criminal Police. The only detail that had been lacking was the cutting off of the little finger on the girl's right hand, but the perpetrator probably just didn't have time. Although Furuberget and Flatanger had disagreed about many things over the years, Flatanger had given him the information he needed. The community was small enough that they had to help each other, especially where Anders Rask was concerned.

The thought—or more correctly, the gut feeling—was unavoidable: if Furuberget had rejected Rask's indirect plea for help reopening the case earlier in the year, the girl would not be hovering on the brink of death today. Only one thought was worse, which was what compelled him to come back that evening. Had Rask made a fool of him? And even worse: Did Rask have contact with someone on the outside? Someone who planned to help him finish what he had started in 1978?

He sat down at his computer and printed out Anders Rask's correspondence from the past year. Furuberget personally read all the letters that were sent to the thirty patients on the maximum-security ward, out of concern for both their own mental health and the society they might one day return to. On rare occasions he would let a letter be sent on to the patient. The most monstrous rapists and killers—each one more psychotic and schizophrenic than the last—received mail weekly, not only from people who hated them and threatened their lives, but also from women who would do anything at all for them.

The women provided both their address and telephone number. For many of the inmates, this information could prove to be much too great a temptation, or compulsion if you will, when they got out. The admirers may have been signing their own death sentence without knowing it. That said, the majority of the patients on the ward would never have a chance to execute the crimes they dreamed of committing against these women. They were simply so sick that their lives would end behind the hospital's barbed-wire fence.

But Anders Rask had always been a mystery. And his many years in the ward had not made him any less mysterious. Strictly speaking, nothing about his conduct inside the walls of the hospital suggested that he would remain there indefinitely. His violent fantasies had largely subsided in recent years, and proper medication kept the psychosis in check. It seemed that the voices in his head were gone.

If he'd ever been psychotic in the first place.

Over the course of the past forty years, a few psychiatric patients had slipped beneath Furuberget's radar. Though it was not something he wanted to admit publicly, it was indisputably true. It was almost impossible to identify the nearly perfect psychopaths. They could be your best friend and better actors than you would find on any stage. But they would never have confessed to six murders just like that. That was only the beginning of the mystery of Anders Rask.

He thought of the letter that he had let through.

The sender was anonymous, he remembered that. Though the contents were cryptic, they seemed harmless. Rask had received a number of anonymous letters over the years, and Furuberget had passed all of them on to him.

I have to read that letter again. He had thought it was from one of Rask's many admirers when he read it the first time. Could it be from the person who had actually killed these girls? Or one of Rask's co-conspirators? Rune Flatanger at the Criminal Police had told him that they couldn't rule out any possibilities at this time, and that no connection had been found between Rask and the person who had tried to kill the girl on Frognerveien.

He found the date of the letter he was searching for. The "From" box in the electronic subject field was glaringly empty. In the comment field it said, "Undated letter, date from postmark on the envelope." He studied the date. March 22. A Monday, wasn't it? Postmarked Oslo Mail Terminal. He didn't know that much about the post office, but assumed that the letter was placed in one of the mailboxes in the vicinity of Oslo Central Station, right by the mail-sorting terminal. This meant that the sender lived or worked in Oslo. Unless he'd gone into the city and mailed the letter there, with the intention of misleading them.

The only thing he could be certain of was the date.

The letter had been postmarked a little more than a week after Rask's attorney had gone to *Dagbladet* with the news that his client had retracted his confession. He hadn't killed Kristiane Thorstensen after all. The following day, the newspaper had featured the request for reopening the case. The following Monday this letter had been sent to Rask. Furuberget figured that the letter writer must have thought about it for a few days before writing and mailing it.

It could be a coincidence, of course. But Furuberget had a special sense for such things. He was a man of science, but sometimes he could feel when he had made a fateful error. Twice he had released patients who were healthy according to standard psychological metrics, even though he knew deep down that they were dangerous. It had gone wrong both times. A murder and a grotesque rape. Now Anders Rask had taken the first step toward release with the Kristiane case. If he won, the others would be in jeopardy. All the patients knew that the evidence in their own cases was equally inadequate.

The letter, thought Furuberget again. *That damned letter.*

He only had six months left until retirement, and now he found himself in a quandary. He knew that he should let it be, turn a blind eye to this situation and leave it to his successor, but he was no fool; he knew that if he did such a thing, his conscience would ruin his final years here on earth.

Should he have realized that the man who tried to kill the girl last night was the same one who had written to Rask? It was a wild notion, so wild that only a patient on the maximum-security ward would even have thought of it. Nevertheless, Furuberget found himself unable to ignore it.

He knew that Rask had a folder that contained all his correspondence.

There was only one thing to do.

Tomorrow, when Rask was at the workshop, he would go into his room and find the letter.

Either Rask had committed all the murders himself, or he had been used by someone who was close to him. But there was a third alternative: that two of them had been involved in the murders—and the other one was still at large.

He had an idea that he should have had long ago. Was it possible that Anders Rask communicated with the other person by letter, and that person wrote to him anonymously? Why hadn't he considered that possibility before?

Because no one had killed anyone in this manner since Rask had been arrested.

Furuberget searched for Anders Rask in the "Sender" field in the mail archive. Then he printed out a list of all the letters he had sent since 1994.

9

The sound of the snowplow blade broke the silence, and its orange light flickered through the curtains. Then everything turned quiet again.

Already so much snow. The thought was almost unbearable.

Elisabeth Thorstensen sat up in bed and glanced at the digits on the digital clock radio. She reached for the vial of valium. Her regular doctor had prescribed it after she collapsed at the store. In front of the newspaper rack.

How many do I have to take?

There weren't enough to be able to end it all.

Take one to sleep? Who cared about sleeping?

She got an old lover—an anesthesiologist at an Oslo clinic—to prescribe Seconal for her. But it was far from enough, since she was only allowed one red capsule at a time. So once a week, she took her pill and slept for a full twenty-four-hour stretch. That would have to do.

Her voice, she thought. That was the very worst. That she wasn't able to summon her voice.

"Kristiane," she whispered out into the darkness. Each syllable a song of its own.

She told herself that if she just lay quietly enough, she would be able to remember her voice. "I'm home!" coming from down the hall. The bag dropped on the floor. The shoes she never took off. The squealing and laughter from her room, full of friends. Her own fingers through the thick curls, the salty hair after a day in the sun at Kragerø.

Sometimes she fell asleep during the day and heard steps on the stairs. Her steps. The disappointment grew greater every time she discovered that it was only Peter.

As she got up, her nightgown fell to the floor. For a moment she thought that someone else had taken it off her. "No," she whispered. "I'm alone." She stood naked in front of the mirror. The swelling around her wrists and ankles had gone down a bit. Some bruises were left, that was all. He liked it rough, and she'd always given him what he wanted. She was born to do that—to be powerless—but sometimes he had crossed the line. That had all been a long time ago. Last night, he had been worn out, old.

Those were the kind of men she attracted. Or to be more precise, the kind of men she wanted. That was probably what had attracted them to each other back in the day. Plus and minus. She had wanted to be minus. A damned minus.

Asgeir no longer touched her, so that wasn't a problem. Or rather, she was the one who didn't touch him. She put her hands around her breasts. They were still nice, but it had been expensive—just like the rest of the discreet cosmetic interventions she'd had done. She'd promised herself eternal life on the outside. If Kristiane stood in the door one day—if she ever came back—she wanted to be just like she had been then.

Kristiane is back, she thought. If I leave this room, she will come back.

She walked quietly past Asgeir's room. The low rumbling coming from in there filled her with contempt. The way he still loved filled her with contempt. As if she were made of porcelain. He didn't want to sleep with her—or more correctly, was no longer able to sleep with her. It was as if he'd given up any effort to be a sexual being. But he would still behave like a caring husband till death do us part, even if he knew perfectly well that she slept with other men. He hadn't even asked where she'd been last night. Didn't hear her phone ring during the evening. Or that she'd pulled out of the garage.

Asgeir was so easy to fool that it was hardly even exciting.

She dug out a bag of panty liners from the back of the medicine cabinet. *The way an alcoholic hides bottles,* she thought, smiling at herself in the mirror. She made a slightly bigger opening in the plastic packaging and shook out the two razor blades she'd placed there.

She carefully pulled the edge of one razor blade across the scars on her wrist. The skin was still thinner there than on the rest of her forearm and always would be. A shiver of phantom pain cut through her, as if she'd opened the artery again.

She got up fumbling from the floor, almost fainted over the sink. The sight of her pale face in the mirror scared her. It slowly turned into Kristiane's, and she held her hands to her mouth so as not to scream. Then, the very thing that had happened so many times that she should have known better happened.

Kristiane stood behind her, in a long row, as if she was a Russian nesting doll that had been disassembled. Naked, the way she'd been in the pictures from the autopsy. She'd insisted on seeing them. Screamed when she did. It was the biggest mistake of her life.

No, not the biggest.

Snakes grew out of Kristiane's mouth, and blood streamed out of her eyes. She appeared to scream at Elisabeth, but didn't make a sound, apart from a faint rumbling. Finally the pale dead face turned into a vipers' nest. The snakes spit blood at the mirror and grew bigger, eventually striking her on the neck and licking her back with their hissing forked tongues.

Elisabeth scratched her face so hard that the marks would be visible in the morning.

"Away, away, away," she whispered. She'd had these dream visions thousands of times. Why couldn't she learn to live with them? Kristiane wasn't dangerous. She had never been dangerous.

I have to dare to turn around.

She slowly turned around.

No one was there.

The dozen or so ghosts of Kristiane who had been standing behind her were gone. On the floor were bare tiles. There were no bloody footprints like the ones she'd seen a few days ago. No black snakes crawling over her body.

"It's only your imagination," she said to the room.

Why did that damned newspaper have to print those pictures of her? Why did they have to write about her? It was as if she had been killed all over again in front of everyone, in front of the whole country, a naked little girl, mutilated, scared and alone.

She tore off a long length of toilet paper, which she then wrapped around the razor blades. Then she left the bathroom and headed downstairs. She stopped halfway. There were no steps behind her. Kristiane wasn't following her. *Don't follow me tonight,* she said to herself. *Please, not tonight.*

She picked up that day's *Dagbladet* in the office and went into the kitchen. There were still embers in the fireplace. Maybe Rose had smoked under the hood. Or Kristiane.

Stop, you sick creature. Stop.

She paged through the newspaper. Asgeir had cut out the pictures of Kristiane. She ran her fingers across the square holes. Then she unwrapped the toilet paper and picked up one of the razor blades. She cut across the face of the byline picture of the reporter, Frank Krokhol, the one who always had to write about Kristiane. Then she cut a slit across his throat.

She walked upstairs as if sleepwalking. She stood in the darkness outside Peter's room for a long time. Somewhere in the distance she heard the snowplow rumbling along. Like thunder. For a moment she was certain that she would never hear thunder again. That this would be her last winter.

She pushed open the door to his room. The big room was far more than he needed, the sleeping, spoiled boy.

With careful steps she moved across the floor. He hadn't pulled the curtains, and his face was visible in the soft glow from the streetlight. For several minutes she sat on the edge of his bed and listened to his heavy breathing, her fingers gripping the edge of the razor blades, one in each hand.

At last reason won out.

She kissed him on the cheek and whispered, "I'm sorry." Even though he was twelve and had the body of a fifteen-year-old, Peter still slept the innocent sleep of a child. She pulled the coverlet over his shoulders and gently stroked his hair.

Down in the office she turned on her computer. The bluish light was reflected in the windowpane, and she quickly pulled the curtains closed.

The murder attempt on Frognerveien was still the top story on *Dagbladet*'s website. She pressed her finger against the screen, right on the eyes of Frank Krokhol, an old byline picture in which he looked younger than he did today.

Attempted murder of prostitute last night. Her condition is serious, life-threatening injuries. Taken to a hospital in the Østland region. The police did not want to release further information at this time. They would like to make contact with a man who was seen on Cort Adelers Gate at about two o'clock Thursday morning.

Elisabeth enlarged the screen image, but it only made the picture of the man with the cap and dark overcoat look fuzzier.

It didn't matter. She knew it was him. It couldn't be anyone else.

She'd gone to the Radisson hotel, just like she had in the old days. But he hadn't arrived until three o'clock in the morning. Or was it four? She was unable to remember.

No, she thought. *No. Not just him.* It must be something worse. Something far worse. He'd looked at her back then. She knew everything about such looks. He'd watched Kristiane since she was twelve or thirteen. With the same desire that he'd looked at Elisabeth.

Had she been blind to certain things? The way her own mother had been? Had they both been after her?

But worse, she thought.

No, he wasn't that old back then.

Had she carried something so dreadful inside her?

If they hadn't sold the house, she could have gone up to the room and checked. It *was* her hair. She couldn't mistake Kristiane's hair. It really was.

That Saturday, she thought. *November 1988.*

When did she leave? When did she come back?

She closed the screen on *Dagbladet*'s website and searched for the police hotline in the Yellow Pages. With weightless steps she walked down the hall to the landline phone. She held the scrap of paper in her hand carefully, as if it were a newborn infant, as if it were Kristiane herself in 1973.

She entered the first few digits. Then she hung up.

Why should I speak up?

It wouldn't bring her back to life.

It wouldn't give her any peace either, because she had never said anything back then.

What could she say? They would just send her back. For satanic irony.

Rask? It had never been Rask.

Rask. What a laughable idea.

She groped her way farther down the hallway, as if she were in an unfamiliar house in pitch darkness. The door to the guest bathroom opened, and she tumbled across the threshold.

She started to smile, studied her own face in the mirror. She got uglier and uglier.

"I was always more beautiful than you," she said to her reflection.

The next thing she remembered, she was standing in the entry, with her coat on. Black eyes. Kristiane's voice filled her head—at least what she thought was her voice, a thin girl voice, like a preschool girl. She went slowly upstairs. Into her bedroom. Screamed. Had she screamed?

Kristiane had no room here. It wasn't her house.

She would soon learn that they no longer lived in Skøyenbrynet. She had a new husband, a new life; she had for a long time now.

She had to pee, but didn't dare go into a room with a mirror. She knew that Kristiane would be standing behind her again.

She screamed loudly before she fell to the floor.

She was still lying on the floor when Rose came in. Rose got down on her knees beside her.

"Elisabeth," she said quietly. "It's all right, Elisabeth."

"Not a word," said Elisabeth apathetically. "You mustn't say anything to Asgeir. Promise me that. He'll send me back. I can't take it, okay?"

Rose stroked her forehead. She promised, just as she promised every time.

"Don't quit. You must never quit."

Rose undressed her in the bedroom, until Elisabeth was standing completely naked before her. Rose held up one of her arms and studied the bruises.

"Who is doing this to you?" She stroked Elisabeth's forearm.

Elisabeth shook her head.

"Don't ask me about it. Ever."

"You should lie down now," Rose said, leading Elisabeth over to the bed. She left the bedroom door ajar just as much as Elisabeth wanted.

Elisabeth kept herself awake until she heard Asgeir's alarm clock ring at six thirty. Then she started stroking herself to the thought of *him*. She hadn't even showered since Saturday. And no one would ever get to see the bruises.

I do everything for him, don't I?

10

A voice caused him to wake up. Bergmann stifled his own scream. He gasped for breath and felt goose bumps rise on his skin. He shivered as he recalled the dream. Not the one he usually had—the one with the doll-faced girl in the forest, in which he never reached her in time—but something worse. Much worse. A dream in black and white. He was lying in a casket. At the last second he threw his arms up and kept the lid from being closed over him.

He looked around the room, his breathing still so heavy that he barely managed to get air down into his lungs. The room was much too large for him to feel secure. All was silent. The only thing he could see were the snowflakes outside the window.

He turned on the lamp on the side table. The clock on the wall showed it was two in the morning.

Was he in the ICU? No. He didn't think so, but he couldn't remember exactly, even if it had only been an hour or two since he was brought here. He didn't even remember what day it was. He could hardly recall why he was here at all. He lay there for a while, turning from side to side. He should have turned off the lamp, but it made him feel safer to keep it on. It was the first time he'd ever dreamed that he was going to die—and buried alive to boot.

He heard a sound in the corridor, the first noise since he'd woken up. A door opening, followed by electric door closers equalizing. Then cautious steps, wasn't that it? The steps stopped right outside his door. For a moment he was certain that the door was pushed open an inch or two; he could see a little strip of light appear on the floor.

He tried to hold his breath as he sat up in bed, preparing to throw himself down on the floor. *The water glass,* he thought. *I'll break it and shove it into his throat.*

He sat that way for perhaps as long as a minute, breathing quietly in and out of his nose.

At last the door closed.

He went over to the door as quietly as he could. He held up the glass and opened the door.

Glanced first to the left, then to the right.

Nothing.

Only a seemingly endless corridor with bottle-green flooring and an equally long row of wash lights in the ceiling, every other one turned on. He turned his focus back to his breathing. With dream-like steps he went back into the room and carefully closed the door. He wasn't sure whether any of it had really happened or if it was simply his imagination.

For a while he remained standing by the window. It was snowing more heavily now. A few cars were driving west, and he followed them with his gaze. He thought about Hege, who lived somewhere around here, in Blindern. He was no better than the man who at this moment was hunting for the girl in the ICU. He wasn't. Then he thought about Hadja. She was the only person for whom he'd felt anything since Hege left. They'd had a flicker of a relationship last summer before he'd withdrawn without giving her a reasonable explanation. He excused himself somewhere deep down. There was so much she didn't know, so much he never wanted—or could never bring himself—to tell her.

"Someone else has to save you," he said. "I can't do it."

He fell asleep again.

The next thing he knew he was being shaken by the shoulder. A dark-skinned nurse was standing over him.

He thought he was still dreaming.

Once again he looked right into his own face in the dream; he was the one who was trying to beat the little doll-faced girl to death. The image of the bloody body crawling away from him mixed with the sight of the nurse. For a few seconds he couldn't grasp what was dream and what was reality.

The young woman before him said a few words. She spoke in the dialect of the south coast; it was as if summer came out of her mouth. He was going to ask where he was, when he finally managed to register what she was telling him.

"She's awake."

He stuffed his shirt in his pants as he followed her down the hall. When she held her key card up to the door at the end of the corridor, it seemed to take the lock ages to open. He tore open the door as soon as the lock emitted a clicking sound, and they ran down the stairs to the floor below. The nurse was several steps ahead of him when they reached the doors to the ICU. He was gasping for breath as he hurried after her down the corridor, half-blinded by the strong light of the ward. A crowd of people stood outside the nurses' office, and he recognized the doctor from earlier in the evening. She met his gaze. Her eyes were narrow and wreathed by dark circles; she looked as though she'd aged in just a few hours. She was speaking with a male colleague and her expression was even more serious than before.

Bergmann tried to hear what they were saying, but couldn't quite catch their rapid exchange.

"Sorry to interrupt you."

"You can go in," said the male doctor, older than himself, as he studied Bergmann from head to toe.

"Is she talking?"

"Incoherently. I don't understand a thing. She's speaking another language. Sounds Slavic, but I don't think it's Polish."

"Quick," said Bergmann. He pushed a nurse aside, headed into the nurses' office, and rushed to put on the coat and hairnet. The two doctors then led him into the girl's room. The light in there was stronger than it had been the night before, making it harder to read the measurement devices on the other side of the bed. The girl was slowly writhing from side to side. A nurse he hadn't seen before was bent over her, holding her hand and stroking her forehead.

"There now," said the nurse. "There now."

For the first time Bergmann thought the woman doctor looked bewildered. The girl started whispering, then kept interrupting herself with small moans of pain. She seemed to be trying to stay calm, unless she was just so doped up that she was in no condition to speak.

He thought he saw blood under the bandages on her torso, but he knew he could be mistaken. She'd pulled down her blanket. But yes. Upon closer inspection, it looked like her wounds had started bleeding again. He clenched and unclenched his fists. Deep down he knew that no surgeon could stop her internal bleeding.

The girl started speaking more loudly, but still incomprehensibly. He went over to the bed and stood alongside the nurse. The girl's eyes were still closed. She was whispering quietly now, so quietly that it was almost impossible to hear her. He pushed the nurse to the side and leaned down toward the girl.

She mumbled something even more quietly. He could feel her breath against his cheek. She already smelled of death and decay.

Just as he was about to straighten up a little, the hairs on his body stood up.

The girl opened her eyes and looked right at him. They were gray and already lifeless.

"Maria," she said quietly.

He shook his head.

She reached her arm out toward him, almost tearing out the cannula, but she didn't seem to notice. She took his hand and squeezed it. Her hand was so little that it disappeared in his. She mumbled another word before quietly repeating the name Maria. Then, again, this word he didn't understand. *Edel?*

No.

Without warning she screamed, "Maria!"

Bergmann was so shocked he let go of her hand and took a step back.

She sat up in bed and screamed louder than Bergmann thought a person could. The room filled with white and green coats. He staggered backward until he touched the wall.

Suddenly the screams stopped. The fragile body gave off a few twitches. After those thirty seconds of chaos, silence fell.

"Defibrillator," said the doctor. Though her voice was calm, Bergmann understood that she had no control over the situation. She looked almost helpless for a moment, then she recovered her composure. The two doctors exchanged brief commands. Bergmann glanced over at the medical equipment. Everything appeared to have flattened out. The girl's hospital gown was torn, and her bandaged body almost jumped in the bed.

He could do nothing but watch. Watch as they were losing her.

"We're losing her," the woman doctor said, confirming his worst fears before the doors to the operating room closed.

Bergmann remained standing in the corridor outside the nurses' office. He stood helplessly with his fist clenched around a scrap of paper he barely remembered having written on. He leaned against the door frame, pulled the mask off his mouth, and opened his hand. On the crumpled piece of paper it simply said "Maria."

"We're losing her," he said to himself.

He left the ICU, still wearing the white coat, hairnet, and shoe protectors, and stumbled up the steps to the floor above. He walked down several corridors but couldn't find his way back to his room. It was four thirty in the morning, and there was no one in sight. He eventually found a nurse and tried to explain that his police ID was in this room he was unable to find. She stared at the piece of paper in his hand. He was gripping it tightly, as though afraid of losing it.

His bubble jacket was still there, hanging untouched over the chair.

When the nurse left, he studied the door to the room. The door closer was fairly strong, with good resistance until about halfway, but it wouldn't have required much strength to open it a crack. He went out in the corridor and closed the door. Then he pushed it open, the way it had been opened earlier that night. He had to push to gain a clearance of a couple of inches. A gust of wind or low pressure could never have opened the door. Besides, nothing here could cause a draft. He pushed the door wide open.

Who was here last night?

Or had he been dreaming?

He decided to ask the nurse down at reception if anyone had entered the hospital earlier that night; there may even be a visitor list. She was talking on the phone while another nurse and an orderly stood by the reception desk.

He waited a minute or two, but she paid no attention to him. He knew perfectly well they didn't keep a visitor list. And even if they did, the man he was looking for wouldn't have signed in under his own name. But he could be found on the footage from the surveillance cameras in the reception area.

He closed his eyes and tried to clear his mind. He could use a little fresh air. "Maria! Maria!" was still ringing in his ears.

He decided to leave, to walk until he found a taxi, even if it took a while to track one down.

Just as the doors opened and he was about to go out into the massive snowstorm, he sensed that he ought to turn around.

The nurse was still on the phone, but she met his gaze, as if she had been waiting for him to turn around.

Then she lowered her eyes and continued her phone conversation.

11

There was light driving snow over Lake Mjøsa. The landscape seemed shapeless, as if it were an Impressionist painting whose details had been blurred.

Arne Furuberget finished off the croissant he'd warmed up in the microwave down in the hospital kitchen. The closest he got to the aroma of a big city was the vacuum-packed croissants at the supermarket Rema 1000. He could have worked anywhere in the world, but had ended up at this remote location in Toten.

At exactly five minutes to ten he broke up the management meeting and sent the rest of the group out the door. Rask would be taken from his room to the workshop at exactly ten o'clock, where he would work for two hours until lunch. That gave Furuberget three hours to search his room. It could go more quickly if he had help, but he couldn't take that chance. Searching for a letter he had already released was illegal.

He walked quickly up the stairs to the third floor. Once there he slowed down. His pulse was racing, but his breathing was regular. After a knee injury last year, he couldn't run as much as he used to, but he got out enough to keep himself in better shape than most people on the brink of seventy.

Outside the security passage to the ward, he went into the nurses' office and assured himself that Rask had been taken to the workshop. Then he asked the shift leader to give the order to turn off the camera inside Rask's room.

"No questions" was all he said.

Ole-Martin Gustavsen had worked at Ringvoll for twenty years and knew when to keep his mouth shut.

A young temporary nurse followed Furuberget over to the first door. Furuberget would have preferred to go alone, but that was such an obvious breach of conduct that it couldn't be done. The temp was tall and sturdy, which gave Furuberget a kind of comfort. Over the course of his long career in psychiatry, his life had been threatened more than once. He had simply dismissed those moments at the time, but that was back when the employees were always in a clear majority in relation to the patients. Budget cuts now forced them to operate right on the edge of what was safe. They only had funds for two employees along with one patient in the security ward. Furuberget knew that was on the edge of what he could permit, but what could he do? Neither he, nor the country's politicians, wanted uniformed guards patrolling the hospital, but sufficient funding for a safe workplace didn't seem to be a priority either. Soon there would probably be no money for self-defense training for new hires either.

Furuberget held his access card up to the optical scanner beside the door and entered the four-digit code. The two manual locks in the steel door then had to be unlocked within the next thirty seconds. Though he had his own set of keys, he let the nurse do the unlocking.

The temp held the door open, and Furuberget stepped into the camera-monitored passage. Once the outer door had closed behind them, the nurse relocked the two manual locks. Two yards ahead of them was another steel door, which could not be unlocked unless the first one was locked. Only a switch inside the nurses' office could unlock both doors at the same time.

Only, thought Furuberget. Occasionally he thought that the inconceivable might happen. That someone in there could press just that button. All the security ward's employees underwent a thorough background check, one that was even more rigorous than the patients' if that were possible.

It would never happen.

The corridor beyond the last door was empty. The room at the far end on the left was Anders Rask's, on the side of the building that faced away from Lake Mjøsa. Every quarter, Rask applied to change rooms for one with a view of the lake, but Furuberget rejected his bid every time. Fortunately he could use psychiatry as an excuse—it would be upsetting for the four patients with rooms facing Mjøsa to give up theirs—but Rask evidently knew that was a lie.

That was the way Rask was. He had never brought up the issue directly with Furuberget, only in the form of a letter through his attorney. But Furuberget felt sure that the room meant nothing to Rask; it was only a pretext to torment him. The big problem was that for several years now Rask had not fulfilled the criteria to even be housed in the security ward. He had been sentenced to psychiatric treatment because, according to the legal expert, he was psychotic when he committed the murders. But now, in 2004, there was little or nothing that indicated that he was. In theory he could have been transferred to an open ward on the basis of his exemplary conduct. It was only gut instinct that prevented Furuberget from accommodating Rask's wish to leave the secure ward for good. Some days, Furuberget suspected Rask of being the most calculating psychopath he had ever been exposed to, but he was reasonably sure that Rask's controlled facade would crack eventually. And if it cracked after Rask had been transferred to an open ward, the consequences would be insurmountable. If Rask were acquitted of Kristiane's murder, it would be even more difficult for him to prevent transfer to an open ward. And once he was on an open ward, he would be permitted to take leave. And if that happened, Furuberget knew that Rask would never return to Ringvoll again.

The corridor had just been mopped and smelled strongly of cleanser. The odor made Furuberget feel briefly nauseated. He opened the hatch in the door. A shiny plastic mirror was mounted up in the left corner, so that he could see the bed and steel toilet. Furuberget checked his watch. Three hours ought to be more than enough.

"I'll call when I'm done," he said to the temp. The door buzzed behind him, and the electronic strike fell into place, the little piece of metal that protected the world against Rask. Or maybe it was the other way around.

He went straight over to the wall-mounted bookshelf with rounded corners, which was filled with books on the top two shelves. It was rather paradoxical. The whole room was furnished so that there were no breakable or sharp objects. But the paper in the old Cappelen reference book was so sharp that Rask could have cut himself with it if he chose to. Furuberget had nonetheless let him keep both the reference book and the other books. Anders Rask was narcissistic enough that he would never kill or injure himself.

And now I'm going to find your damned letter, thought Furuberget.

He picked up a bundle of papers off the shelf and started rifling through them.

The letter wasn't there.

He paged meticulously through the folder where Rask kept his correspondence, neatly ordered by date. *There's just as much craziness outside these walls as there is inside,* thought Furuberget. Rask was convicted of the bestial murders of defenseless girls, and women were lining up to marry him.

He picked up the printout of the mail log that he'd brought with him and compared the letters and dates.

"No," he whispered.

The letter wasn't in there with the others. There could only be one reason why. *Rask predicted this,* thought Furuberget. Predicted that a new murder would take place. Maybe even initiated the whole thing by giving his attorney the message about wanting to reopen the Kristiane case. And he knew that Furuberget would be sitting like this, in his room, holding all his letters in his hand.

"That son of a bitch," Furuberget whispered to himself.

He took out the little notebook he kept in his pocket. He spent the next half hour drawing a sketch of the bookcase, the placement of the books, and the binders. Then he started tearing all the books out of the bookcase.

Now it was too late to turn back. He leafed through the pages of the roughly forty books—twice.

Nothing.

He picked up the first volume of *Kaplan and Sadock's Comprehensive Textbook of Psychiatry* and started to go through it again. Rask had a small library of psychiatric literature, all purchased with taxpayers' money. Furuberget often thought that it was only the physical, legitimized force and medications he prescribed to people like Anders Rask that gave him any advantage. If anything, Rask had better prerequisites for talking about psychiatry than he did.

He scanned the room. There weren't many other places he could have put the letter. He assured himself that the control light in the camera up on the wall was not shining red. Then he removed the bed linens, which were caked with Rask's sperm. He shuddered, but forged ahead.

The letter was nowhere, not in the pillowcase, not under the sheets.

He calculated how much time he had until lunch and decided he could just manage to take the stuffing out of the mattress. Once he started pulling the cover off the mattress, he thought about giving up. It was almost solidly attached.

And when he'd got the light-blue material off completely and absorbed the disappointment that the letter wasn't there either, he realized that he didn't have time to put the mattress cover back on again.

Time, he thought, looking at the mess on the floor. *Rask can't find me like this.* How long would it take to get that mattress put back together?

He let the cover be and decided to turn the bed on its side. It was made of metal, but the legs were hollow. After several minutes he managed to get the rubber stopper off the bottom of one bedpost.

He went over to the call button by the door. He wanted to call the guard, but stopped himself. Instead he went over to the chest of drawers and took out a bundle of clothes, freshly ironed from the laundry. Nearly identical checked shirts, underwear, and socks.

"Nothing," he said. "Nothing!" Then he picked up Rask's crazy clipping book. He had ordered copies from the National Library of all the newspaper articles about the six murders he was convicted of. Though he had thrown away a few of them, he had neatly pasted the rest into a big binder, the kind that Furuberget's daughters had used for school when they were small.

Someone pounded on the door. Furuberget's heart nearly stopped and he sat as if petrified with a thick red volume, *The Book of the Law,* in his hands. The book—which Rask had referred to several times in the past few years as his Bible—was written by a man who was, if possible, even more disturbed than Rask himself, an Englishman by the name of Aleister Crowley. Rask had often mentioned the book's opening line— "This book explains the universe"—to Furuberget, who, being neither an occultist nor sexually deviant, had refused to read it.

Only now did he notice the sweat under his suit, how it was trickling down from his scalp. A drop of perspiration fell onto the blood-red front cover and left a dark stain.

Medusa.

Hadn't there been something similar in that letter? Medusa's tears?

He took another book from the shelf and tried to leaf through it, but his fingers would not obey.

"Is everything okay?" The temp's voice sounded cold and surreal through the loudspeaker.

"Yes," said Furuberget.

"I just wanted to remind you that lunch starts in ten minutes."

"I need you to help me," Furuberget said quietly. He lowered his head, as if he were standing before an executioner who was waiting for him to expose his neck.

The door buzzed.

The temp's eyes widened.

Ten to twelve, thought Furuberget.

Maybe Rask wasn't hungry that day. Maybe he didn't feel like sitting and lecturing one of the three other inmates he was allowed to eat with.

"No questions. You've never seen this, okay?"

"Okay."

"What was your name again?"

"Fredriksen."

Not very imaginative, thought Furuberget. He decided at once not to renew his contract.

"We have to work quickly. I'm searching for a letter, but I'll be damned if I can find it." He tried to smile at the temp, but only felt himself grow even more desperate—another step closer to being a helpless old fool.

After restoring order and getting the cover back on the mattress with Fredriksen's help, he took one last look around. The room appeared to be the way it had been when he arrived.

"Not a word, Fredriksen," he said as they were in the process of letting themselves out.

Fredriksen held his gaze longer than normal.

"What is it about that letter?"

"Nothing."

The young temp laughed quietly, which only confirmed Furuberget's decision to let him go.

At home that evening he was in no mood to talk.

"I want to go away for Christmas," his wife said, picking at her meal. Furuberget ate with mechanical movements, as if he was forcing the food down.

"Did you hear what I said, Arne?"

He was trying to remember the text of the letter, but realized that he had to give up. At some point, you just have to let go—wasn't that what he was always telling his patients? Not the sickest ones, of course, but those who might have a tiny hope of one day returning to normal life.

"Christmas," he said. "You want to go away."

"Surprise me." She smiled in a way that reminded him why he'd fallen for her once upon a time.

His wife went to bed early, at nine o'clock. Furuberget stayed up and listened to Tchaikovsky. After two glasses of whiskey he was so sentimental that he started to cry. He thought about his daughters. Grown now, and then some, with children of their own, but to him, they would always be little. Then he thought about the young girl on Frognerveien, and about Kristiane Thorstensen. The five others.

"I mustn't make a mistake." He tightened his grip around the crystal glass, squeezing so hard that it almost cracked.

He fell asleep sometime toward morning, after having booked a two-week vacation to Langkawi in Malaysia. It cost an arm and a leg, but she would definitely be surprised. Although he felt determined not to let Rask win, he knew he must simply let this be.

Let it go, even if it would cost several lives. Although Pontius Pilate had hardly lived a good life, he had at least survived.

When he got in the car in the morning to drive to Ringvoll, he sensed there was more snow on the way.

"I'm just imagining things," he said to himself.

Few exercises were so pathetic as self-deception.

Anders Rask was a pedantic. He never would have hidden the letter—much less torn it to pieces and flushed it down the toilet at night—if he didn't have a good reason for it. A very good reason.

12

Bergmann took his eyes off the screen. He didn't know how many times they'd run the surveillance-camera footage. They could sit like that until Christmas without getting any closer to the answer. All they had were the images of a man walking from Porte des Senses up Cort Adelers Gate toward Drammensveien at 1:59 a.m. the same night the girl was almost murdered.

Or was *murdered,* thought Bergmann.

She was dead. She had died right before his eyes. And all they had were twenty seconds of film of a man whose face was completely hidden by a cap. And he could simply be a man on his way home. Though his actions may not have been completely innocent, it was entirely possible that he wasn't a killer.

Milovic, the owner of Porte des Senses, would not be linked to the young girl who was killed. Not even a verbal agreement with the chief public prosecutor could do anything about that. Milovic had stuck his neck out far enough as it was.

They hadn't gotten a single credible tip about the man in the cap. Just the usual doomsday prophets calling and talking nonsense. The only ones who could possibly recognize him must have been at Porte des Senses themselves. And they likely preferred to keep their mouths shut rather than admit that they'd been at an illegal club and spent the night doing things they shouldn't.

In a declamatory voice, as if he'd already given up, Reuter went through the case one more time. Times, places, interviews with neighbors. Repetition for the sake of repetition. They wouldn't get much further until they discovered the girl's identity.

Bergmann met the gaze of Susanne Bech, who sat across the table from him. She'd been watching the prosecutor, Svein Finneland, almost the entire time, with a strange expression on her face, as though she was struggling with her emotions but trying to act indifferent. She lowered her sad eyes and scribbled something on her notepad, then picked up her phone and stared at it for a long time, as if she'd received a text message she didn't understand. He speculated that she'd quarreled with her ex-husband, and that he'd struck a sore spot.

"What was it the girl said again, Tommy?"

"What?" said Bergmann.

Reuter pointed at him from his seat up by the screen. "Maria?"

"Yes, Maria."

"Nothing else?"

"Yes, one word. But it was impossible to understand. In another language, maybe Lithuanian, I don't know."

"Maria," Reuter said to himself. "We'll figure out what language she was speaking later today."

Bergmann pressed the "Play" button on the Dictaphone he had sitting in front of him.

The room was completely quiet for a few seconds. Then they heard some voices in the background, followed by the girl, mumbling quietly to herself, after which she said, "Maria."

And then the sudden scream.

Bergmann closed his eyes. He felt like he was being thrown against the wall again.

"Maria!"

The girl's voice seemed to frighten the whole gathering. She screamed as if she'd seen the Devil himself.

Reuter propped his chin in his hands and stared down at the table. He shook his head slightly.

Hanne Rodahl, the police chief, fiddled with her reading glasses. Bergmann saw that she was mouthing the word "Maria" to herself. Halgeir Sørvaag looked as if he'd just woken up. He should be awake, since he was responsible for the investigation. He whispered something in the police chief's ear. She frowned.

"What are you two whispering about?" said Finneland. He was in an even worse mood than he'd been earlier that day. He had taken a chance by making a deal with Milovic, and now it seemed to have led nowhere. Anders Rask had gotten the case reopened, and they had a new homicide on their hands. It could hardly get much worse for Finneland, a man with ambitions to take over the world if he got the opportunity.

"Rewind," said Sørvaag.

"Why?" said Reuter.

Bergmann picked up the Dictaphone and stopped it. The doctor's curt commands died away.

"Rewind. To before she says 'Maria,'" said Sørvaag.

Bergmann rewound.

The girl mumbled a word, but Bergmann couldn't decipher it.

"What is she saying?" said Finneland.

"Hush," said Sørvaag, holding up his hand. He grabbed the Dictaphone and rewound it again.

The room grew even quieter than before as the recording was played again. Two words, perhaps the same one repeated. Then "Maria," and finally the scream: "Maria!"

Sørvaag stopped the recording.

"Edle," he said. "I think that's what she's saying. Or am I the only one who's hearing that?"

"Maybe so," said Reuter. "I don't hear it. I don't even think the Criminal Police will get anything out of that recording, but God knows."

"It's just that I've heard that name, Edle Maria, some place," said Sørvaag.

"She doesn't say anything before 'Maria,'" said Finneland. He breathed demonstratively out of his nose. "In any event nothing I can make out."

"I think she just says 'Maria.' Or do you think it's possible she means '*Ave* Maria'?" said Reuter. "Jesus came out between the legs of a skinny little Jewish girl by that name, Halgeir. May be her mother or sister for all we know."

Finneland opened his mouth to say something, but evidently changed his mind.

"Yes," said Sørvaag. "But it's damned strange." He leaned forward in his chair, almost like an over-eager schoolboy who was about to tell his teacher a good story, but then forgot what it was.

"That was cryptic," said Finneland. Bergmann could clearly see the sweat rings on his shirt. The dark areas under his armpits grew every time he moved his arms. Finneland was thin and sinewy, with a boyish appearance, the kind of man who worked out six days a week with a pulse-rate monitor. *A man of which there's a dime a dozen,* thought Bergmann. There were more and more of his kind, a type that didn't exist when he started in this business.

"My first boss here in the building. You must remember him, Hanne," Sørvaag said, turning to the police chief. "Old Lorentzen, he was head of Homicide back then. I'm fairly certain he was the one who mentioned Edle once, maybe even several times. Or was it Edel? Ellen? This was in the seventies. As far as I recall, her middle name was Maria."

Finneland looked like he was about to run out of patience. Rune Flatanger had rolled up his shirt sleeves and jotted down some notes on his pad. Bergmann did the same himself. Much could be said about Halgeir Sørvaag, but he knew him well enough to take the man seriously.

"Okay," said Finneland reluctantly. "It sounds pretty off the wall, Sørvaag, but have the personnel file for this Lorentzen checked. Then we should be able to figure out where he worked, or if he's still alive."

"He died ten years ago," said the police chief. She nodded to Sørvaag to continue.

"Lorentzen, or Lorentz as we called him, told a few of us about a case involving a young girl up north somewhere who was killed in a pretty vile way. They never found the killer, and I recall him saying that he never forgot that case. I'm sure her name was Edle Maria."

"I think that's a long shot, Sørvaag. But I'll give it a try. It must be possible, damn it, to figure out if some Maria or other was killed north of the Arctic Circle. When was it this *Edle* Maria murder took place? Or was it Ellen?"

"I don't think it was Ellen. It must have been sometime in the sixties. In northern Norway, I think."

"Anyone remember any of this? It must have created some uproar."

"Norway was like two countries back then," said Flatanger. "Whatever happened north of Trondheim was of little or no interest down here."

"True enough," said Sørvaag. "Damn it, they weren't interested in any of us from up in Sunnmøre back then."

"So neither of you can remember the case?"

"No," said Hanne Rodahl.

"No one else?" asked Finneland. "Any bells?"

Flatanger threw up his arms. "Beats me," he said.

Finneland took a deep breath.

"We can't just go by our gut feelings." Finneland sighed dejectedly, as if Sørvaag were a child who never learned. "Find the personnel file for Lorentzen, Sørvaag. Then you can get back to us."

"Good luck, Halgeir," said Hanne Rodahl. "Maybe we're not entirely on the wrong track here then, huh?"

"It may have been that Marie was the middle name, when I think about it," said Sørvaag. "And not Maria."

Finneland barely managed to suppress a "Good Lord." He raised his arm and studied his pulse-rate monitor.

"We don't have time for this. Why should a fourteen-year-old girl from Eastern Europe scream out a reference to an old murder case from Jokkmokk?"

"Maybe the girl was just Catholic," said Sørvaag a little uncertainly and laughed at himself. Small beads of sweat had formed on his scalp. Bergmann followed one of them as it trickled down his forehead and landed on his eyebrow. He had just managed to get a handkerchief out of his old cardigan when Finneland gave him a piece of his mind.

Bergmann wrote on his notepad in big block letters: "MARIA. EDLE MARIA?"

13

Arne Furuberget thought that the patients might need therapy *after* spending time in the therapy room. The harsh light made the peach-colored walls appear sickly, like vomit, he thought. He'd spent an unreasonable amount of money to furnish the room a few years ago, and now even he couldn't stand it. The only extenuating feature of the room was that it faced toward Lake Mjøsa, which was bathed in sunshine just then, encircled by narrow snow-covered fields. The winter light was as sharp as it could only be in the Nordic countries, and such days made Furuberget think that there was no more beautiful country on earth. Why spend sixty thousand kroner on a Christmas vacation in Malaysia?

He turned his thoughts to the man before him. Anders Rask was looking down at his Crocs. The only thing he wanted to talk about today was the reopening of the Kristiane case. Nothing else seemed to interest him. Furuberget put down his pen and pad on the table between them and exchanged glances with the two male nurses. One of them was the temp, Fredriksen. Furuberget felt somewhat embarrassed about his encounter with him. He had lost control for a moment where that cursed letter was concerned.

Furuberget went up to the window and thought that Rask could grab the pen that was on the table, stick it in the nurses' necks, and then throw himself against the grate in front of the window.

"Why won't you move me to an open ward?" said Rask behind him.

Furuberget didn't reply. It was the first time Rask had asked him about it. *Something's cooking,* he thought. Something had happened to Rask recently.

"I think you're going to regret this," said Rask.

"Why?"

"I just want to be treated like a human being."

"You *are* being treated like a human being. Maria," said Furuberget. "What comes to mind when I say that name?"

He turned toward Rask.

"Jesus."

"Nothing else?" Furuberget smiled carefully.

Rask just stared ahead indifferently. "Why did you ransack my room, by the way?" he asked.

Furuberget tried to breathe calmly. How could he know?

"I didn't."

"Crowley was on the wrong side of the reference book. You made a mistake."

Furuberget decided not to answer.

"Did you make a drawing of the books' placement on the shelf?" Though Rask smiled, his eyes were dull and lifeless.

Furuberget hoped that he was able to conceal that he shuddered.

"You should have taken a picture of the bookshelf with your phone." Rask's smile widened, like a child's. "First you put *The Book of the Law* back wrong, and now you're asking me about Maria. Magdalena or the Virgin?"

He still has it, thought Furuberget. The letter. But he couldn't pursue it. He might already have ruined everything.

"What about Edle Maria?"

Rask's expression remained neutral. He appeared completely uninterested in the conversation.

"What would you say if I told you that I don't think you've killed anyone in your whole life?"

"That you're going to be slaughtered." Rask gave out a quiet, girlish laugh.

Furuberget closed his eyes. He had to concentrate so as not to sigh out loud. He felt a certain relief that Rask had finally revealed that he still had violent fantasies. On the other hand, it was the first time they were directed at him.

"It's been several years since you behaved like this, Anders. I can't recommend a transfer when you say such things. Even if you have all your cases reopened and are acquitted. Do you understand that? Why do you say such things?"

"Because you want to keep me in here until I die. For that reason you have to die first."

"Shall we finish up, Anders?"

"I didn't mean it."

"We're done."

Rask did not answer. He just sat there with a sad smile, as though content at having threatened Furuberget, but disappointed because he knew that now it would be more difficult for him to move to an open ward in the foreseeable future.

Furuberget turned over responsibility for Rask to the two nurses.

In the security passage he remained standing so long that the door had to be unlocked twice. He thought about the conversations he'd had with Rune Flatanger down at Kripo.

For two weeks he'd barely slept a wink.

The murdered girl had screamed "Maria." Flatanger had sent him the audio file. The girl had also uttered another word before "Maria." One of the policemen thought the girl had said Edle or Edel. Maybe

Ellen. He claimed to recall the name from an earlier case. But then he'd more or less dropped the matter, thought he'd remembered wrong.

But Furuberget knew he'd heard the name before. He just couldn't remember where. And it wasn't Edel or Ellen.

It was Edle. Edle Maria. One didn't forget such a special name.

Flatanger had asked him to bring up the name in his therapy session with Rask. Furuberget hadn't said a word about it ringing a bell somewhere in the back of his mind. It was just his luck. Just when he'd managed to put the business about the letter behind him, this name turned up.

He looked at the clock on the wall. The girl would be buried down in Oslo in an hour.

Back in his office he took out his calendar and drew an *X* over today's date. *Five months until retirement.*

He hoped that he wouldn't remember where he'd heard the name Edle Maria before then. That was the key, and he didn't know if he wanted to find it.

14

It was nearly impossible to smoke a cigarette outside. Bergmann turned up the collar on his jacket, as if that would help against the wind that threatened to cut his head off. But then again, maybe the Alfaset cemetery wasn't the place for a smoke anyway. He got back in the car and rolled down the window. His gaze was fixed on the white chapel. He tossed the cigarette aside after taking a few drags. The sight of the seemingly endless cemetery repulsed him. *This is the last stop,* he thought, looking out over the industrial-looking gray landscape. *One day I'll be lying here myself.*

But not yet.

Two or three cars were in the big parking lot, but he hardly noticed them. When he walked into the chapel, he saw only Frank Krokhol and a photographer from *Dagbladet*, both of whom had taken a seat in the front row, and the minister and the funeral director.

The sight was more depressing than he'd been prepared for. He knew that the girl in the casket was a fourteen-year-old who had run away from an orphanage outside Vilnius, and that her name was Daina. The only relative Kripo had managed to track down was an alcoholic aunt who had figured out that the cheapest alternative was to let the Norwegian government lower her niece into the frozen earth in Oslo.

The only consolation was the colorful painting on the back wall, painted by Modernist artist Jakob Weidemann. He remembered that his mother thought his work was nothing more than graffiti. The last time he was here was when she was buried. Though he told himself that was why he was so depressed, he knew that was a lie.

The minister nodded at him and Krokhol. Bergmann took off his jacket and set it between himself and the reporter, as if he wanted to establish a certain distance from him. He wasn't there out of the goodness of his heart, which Bergmann imagined he himself was. The homicide investigation had more or less dried up, to the point that he was ready to give up. No one had any leads on the man on Cort Adelers Gate; Milovic was keeping his mouth shut about the girl, his attorneys having stopped any attempt to pin him to her; and Finneland had checkmated himself after the amnesty agreement when Milovic delivered the film from inside the club. Finally, the personnel folder for the former head of Homicide, Lorentzen, had disappeared. Sørvaag's hopeless Maria track was just that—hopeless.

When the minister started preaching, Bergmann thought that he might just as well leave at once. *Make sure to get the poor child in the ground,* he thought. It was a relief when the bells rang.

Frank Krokhol stood up beside him and tried to look sympathetically at the minister. Bergmann stood up and turned to leave the chapel.

A woman dressed in black sat in the last row. Her hat concealed her face, making her look out of place, as though from another era, or a movie he'd seen once.

She got up slowly and opened the door.

Bergmann put on his jacket and followed her. He turned around and made sure that Krokhol wasn't following him. Krokhol was still standing with his hands folded before him, trying to appear as dignified as possible, so that the minister would give him some good quotes about the lonely funeral afterward.

The woman was already well ahead of him, heading up the hill toward the parking lot.

"Elisabeth Thorstensen," Bergmann said to himself. He stopped and let her go.

It couldn't be anyone else. For a second he had caught her gaze.

For a few seconds he was quite certain.

I've seen you before.

Before Skøyenbrynet.

He called Dispatch and got her cell-phone number. It rang four times before going to voice mail. He left a message explaining who he was, and that he would like to speak with her.

"It's all my fault."

Why had she said that?

PART TWO

DECEMBER 2004

15

Bergmann moved at a sleepwalker's pace and had done so for almost two weeks, ever since the Lithuanian girl was buried. They'd rarely had so little to go on. In addition, there was no worse time to be killed than in the last few months of the year. Overtime budgets had long since been used up, and sick leave was pouring in. Besides, there was no escaping the fact that an anonymous young prostitute from Lithuania was soon forgotten in smug, nouveau riche Norway. It was as if there was a tacit understanding that Daina wasn't one of them. And no one outside headquarters knew yet that she was most likely the latest in a long series of murdered girls.

The vaginal tests taken from Daina at Oslo University Hospital and the microscopic skin fragments removed from under her nails showed a DNA profile that could nicely match the profile that was found on Kristiane Thorstensen in 1988, and the next victim—another prostitute—in February 1989. The problem was that the old profiling system was so rudimentary that the profile fit 10 percent of all men. Nonetheless, when compared with the injuries Daina had sustained, it was probable that they were facing one and the same perpetrator. For that reason, it was also becoming more and more likely that Anders Rask was innocent.

But there was a lid on this information. Reuter didn't want to give away anything that might be of interest to the perpetrator, and Hanne Rodahl didn't want to frighten the inhabitants of Oslo right before Christmas, much less reveal the agency's hopelessly meager headway in the investigation. She hoped to be promoted to police commissioner sometime in the new year, so it was better to say as little as possible about what she called internally "an extremely unpleasant mystery." Though the press releases stated that "out of consideration for the investigation the police cannot provide any additional information," in reality such nonsense meant "we're fumbling blindly." Sadly, Daina's only hope for justice was that she had probably been killed by the same man who had killed six other girls starting in 1978. That was the only reason she was even still an agenda item for Bergmann, Sørvaag, and the rest of headquarters.

She was probably killed by the man who was supposed to be Anders Rask. But who couldn't be Rask. The man who had killed Kristiane Thorstensen.

Bergmann knew that if he found out who killed Daina, then he would find out who'd killed Kristiane and the others. But Rask was locked up at the Ringvoll psychiatric ward. And someone had committed an almost identical murder only a few weeks before. So that couldn't have anything to do with Rask.

Or could it?

As he started down the steps to the subway, Bergmann considered that Rask might be in the process of lulling the whole country into an illusion of his own innocence. Three or four Somali men jumped aside—the mere sight of him enough to make them afraid of being arrested—but he couldn't care less that they were openly bargaining over a gram of khat. As he continued down into the narrow tunnel, the cold from the street was gradually replaced by an intoxicating warmth from the row of underground shops. The heat had a deadening effect on him, and he felt how little he'd slept the past few weeks. Not even the ice-cold gust of wind down on the platform caused him to wake up properly. His peripheral vision seemed to have dissolved, and shadows glided before him, appearing suddenly from the side, before they disappeared again. Every sound was amplified and hard, almost metallic between the walls of his cranium. With every crackle in the loudspeakers, a nasal voice that reported further delays, he started, nearly reaching for an invisible pistol holster under his bubble jacket.

The platform was filled with people from every corner of the globe, dressed in multiple layers to guard against the steadily increasing cold. Resignation was written on their faces, as if they thought they wouldn't survive yet another winter. Bergmann had never thought of Oslo as the sort of city that stroked your cheek and whispered seductive words in your ear, but the past few weeks had been so fiercely cold that the city resembled a bombed-out war zone, in which people ran from building to building and sought shelter from underground subway stations like this.

He'd been to his first hour at the Alternatives to Violence offices in Lilletorget and felt completely empty, like the sort of gray concrete conduit that snaked through the satellite city. He didn't know whether he liked the therapist, but he'd been more open with him than with Viggo Osvold. Osvold was the sensitive one; he moved like a cat around warm porridge, cushioning his words in cotton. ATV was nothing like that. But he didn't want to stop going to Osvold. Although ATV could surely teach him to behave like an almost normal man, Osvold could reach deeper down. Bergmann had both feet stuck in a childhood that was nothing but a black hole. He had a vague memory of having lain somewhere a long time, perhaps for hours, alone, while he screamed. That was his first memory, and he couldn't have been very old. It came to him more and more often these days. At last he'd stopped screaming. Then he'd heard other voices and someone crying. Was it his mother? He didn't know, how could he know?

A black hole, he thought. And he could get no damned further without help. He understood that much at least.

Line 4 to Bergkrystallen finally appeared, shooting down the track like a dragon out of the black hole.

He stared at a picture of a woman in one of the ads on display between the platforms. She had long, wet hair and was dressed in a bikini; behind her was a Turkish sea, a palm tree, hot sand under her feet. A suntanned man had his arms around her. It was as far away from a late Monday afternoon in December at sixty degrees north latitude as you could get. As he looked at it, the woman's face blurred between the windows of the subway and morphed into Kristiane Thorstensen's. The doors opened, and Bergmann forced his way into the car. He found a place to stand closest by the doors and got a final glimpse of the smiling female model in the ad. "The days you remember," it said at the bottom. Kristiane had gotten no more days, no chance to head south in the middle of winter with the man in her life. How old would she have been today? He counted back. Thirty-two. No, thirty-one. And would she have looked like that? *Yes,* he said to himself. *Yes, that could easily have been her in the ad.*

Kristiane Thorstensen had been dead for sixteen years, and now she was everywhere. He saw her face wherever he looked. Even when he didn't want to look, his gaze was drawn toward a man who sat with his back to him, in the seat next to the Plexiglas wall, struggling with one of the advertising supplements in *Aftenposten.* As the man browsed the newspaper, Bergmann knew what was coming—he'd read the paper himself earlier that day.

The commission had made the decision right before the weekend: they had ruled in favor of Anders Rask and allowed the Kristiane case to be reopened. The newspapers couldn't get enough of it, and the television newscasts had gone overboard with speculation. There was hardly anything else on the radio.

"Who Killed Kristiane?" was *Aftenposten*'s headline. The obligatory ninth-grade class photo of her, dating back to the early fall of 1988, filled half the page. Bergmann felt a little surge in his belly and cursed himself for it. Every time he saw her face, he once again became the boy he'd once been, unhappily and unattainably in love with girls like her. She had a round face, borderline chubby, with curly hair. He thought that the boys had probably named her the "prettiest at school"—though not the "nicest"—and wondered whether she had had that undefinable *something* that blew the boys away and gave her more girlfriends than she really needed.

Yes, thought Bergmann, this was precisely how he imagined Kristiane Thorstensen. Simply by seeing her smile and her eyes— which seemed to glisten as they gazed toward the photographer—the natural curls and the little cleft in her chin, Bergmann knew that Kristiane was the kind of girl no one ever forgot. He wondered how many boys had heard her say, *I like you too, but as a friend, promise me you won't be sad, okay?*

He'd never had anything to do with that murder investigation, having just graduated from the Police Academy at that time, but God only knew how many hours he'd spent thinking about her in the years that followed.

He should have felt guilty because it was actually Kristiane's killer he wanted to find, not the poor Lithuanian girl's. At times it seemed as if he'd altogether forgotten the girl who was buried in a country her aunt couldn't afford to travel to, and who couldn't afford to bury her in her homeland either.

But he remembered only Kristiane. Not the poor faceless ones, but the privileged girl who had lived only a stone's throw from where he himself had grown up.

"Kristiane," he muttered, as if he were an old recluse talking to himself. He'd tried to forget her, repress her, banish her from his mind for the past sixteen years. He'd made a promise to her there in the woods.

A promise to a young girl who would never be more than fifteen years old that he would always be good.

He glanced over at the newspaper that the man in the seat beside him was reading. Her big eyes looked right at him. It was as if she were saying to him, *How could you?*

16

The living room floor was overflowing with newspapers. Every one of them was opened to the Anders Rask cases. One of them had a facsimile of an old two-page spread that read "The Monster" in fat bold type over an almost ten-year-old picture of Rask. The man who was convicted of Kristiane Thorstensen's murder had gotten the case reopened, and now the other five murders he'd been convicted of were in line. Rask's defense counsel, a young attorney from Gjøvik, had a three-page interview in *VG*, under the headline "Finds *No* Convicting Evidence." The journalists had plenty to say, but Bergmann couldn't blame them. The news was a gift to them. He'd read the commission's justification for reopening the case, and it was painful reading, almost a character assassination of the police, and Kripo in particular. It seemed as if an earthquake was gathering force under the trifecta of press, prosecutor, and court. Had they all been wrong? Was Anders Rask not the fiend they'd all agreed that he was, a beast that deserved to die a slow and painful death? Was he merely an assailant—bad enough, but no murderer?

Bergmann put a VHS cassette into the old player under the TV. The cassette was labeled "Rask September 1994 NRK." He hadn't watched the documentary about Rask for a few years—couldn't bear the sight of him—but he couldn't put it off any longer. He cleared the coffee table of the remnants of dinner, the butcher Anders Rask and food not exactly compatible.

Bergmann lit a cigarette and held it up to the TV screen, so that the ember hit young Rask right below his right eye. A clip from a 17th of May celebration in the early 1960s appeared on the screen. The quality of the color film and the fact that they could afford a movie camera at that time suggested that Rask came from a well-to-do family. But according to the filmmaker, Rask had grown up the child of divorced parents in Slemdal. His mother rented a little basement apartment, they were short of money, and Rask had presumably been seriously bullied at school at first but eventually got along fine. He did well at school and graduated with an education degree from the Eik campus in Tønsberg of Vestfold University College in 1979. Tønsberg was also where he found his first victim. He was completing his practice hours at Presterød School when he killed Anne-Lee Fransen, a spindly thirteen-year-old girl who'd been adopted from South Korea.

Bergmann fast-forwarded past the interviews with psychiatrists and psychologists. He knew their explanations all too well. Anders Rask was a classic example of an alienated, sensitive child, with an Oedipal and subsequently pathological love-hate relationship with his mother, who had struggled with rather extensive mental problems and been hospitalized several times herself. It was also made clear that Rask's father had abused the two daughters he had with his new wife, and there was also speculation about whether he'd abused Rask when he was a child as well, a question to which Rask had always responded ambiguously. Rask maintained that he had repressed most of his childhood and adolescence, but that glimpses of a nightmarish past had come back to him when he started studying at the teachers college. One thing that he hadn't repressed were several assaults on children he'd taught, as well as on smaller children when he himself was a boy. The Oslo police had first taken Rask into presentence custody for sexually assaulting a girl at Bryn School in the winter of 1992. It was during these interrogations that Rask quite surprisingly admitted that he'd murdered Kristiane Thorstensen, who had been his pupil at Vetlandsåsen Middle School back in 1986. He'd quickly gone on to confess to the murders of five other girls. During the police questioning he changed his explanation several times, before he finally maintained firmly that he heard voices in his head that ordered him to kill these girls, an explanation he stuck to during the trial.

Bergmann fast-forwarded the cassette up to the reconstruction of the first murder in Tønsberg. The filmmaker had no footage covering the murder of Kristiane, which was a relief. Bergmann never wanted to go back to those woods south of the city, not even on film.

He froze the tape on the image of Anders Rask, who stood bent over some underbrush by a forest road in the heart of Vestfold. It was here that he raped and killed Anne-Lee Fransen the last weekend of August 1978, after she'd visited him at home in the basement apartment he rented from a half-senile elderly woman in Tønsberg. The method of killing in the subsequent cases followed the same pattern. Traces of adhesive were found around the mouth, nose, wrists, and ankles of all the victims, which presumably came from the roll of duct tape that was found at Rask's place in 1992. He had evidently stuck to the same type of duct tape since 1978. Some of Kristiane's belongings had also been found at Rask's place—books, ballpoint pens, and school photos of her—so there was circumstantial evidence that he was the right man. When some of Anne-Lee Fransen's hair and possessions were found in his apartment at Haugerud in Oslo, the case was nearly closed. The fact that they had never found any of the other girls' possessions was largely ignored. Two months after the confession the prosecutor submitted what the press contradictorily called "convicting circumstantial evidence," and everyone agreed that Anders Rask was the worst monster the country had produced for as long as anyone could remember, perhaps ever. None of the autopsies could establish whether the girls were dead before he attacked them with the knife and blunt instruments, because they'd been lying outside too long. Four of them had likely died from loss of blood during the assault.

The prosecutor's so-called convicting circumstantial evidence was based on laboratory tests from Great Britain. Newly developed DNA technology by Imperial Chemicals had already unambiguously revealed in January 1989 that the sperm found in and on Kristiane Thorstensen confirmed that the perpetrator had blood type A and an enzyme profile that excluded 90 percent of all men. The samples from the prostitute who was killed after Kristiane, during New Year's in 1989, showed the same result. When Rask gave his blood samples, he was determined to be among the 10 percent of men with the same enzyme profile, and he also had blood type A. That was enough for the municipal court to decide without a doubt that Rask did not suffer from confession syndrome—despite the fact that he fumbled when asked to describe the injuries he had inflicted on the girls and instead spoke of his compulsion to assault and kill girls and young women.

Bergmann played the film image by image. Anders Rask finally broke into an incomprehensible smile, as if he found something at the scene amusing. He pressed "Play" again, and the film resumed at normal speed. The camera zoomed in on Rask's feminine facial features. There was no denying that Rask had an attractive appearance that was misleading, if you didn't know better.

The voice-over read from Rask's explanation in court. He had agreed to meet Anne-Lee Fransen at his home, in the basement apartment. He then knocked her unconscious in the bathtub, dumped her body into a garbage bag, and carried her out to the car after dark. The assault and the murder took place out in the forest.

Bergmann switched off the TV. He couldn't stop himself from fantasizing about what pain he himself would have inflicted on Rask if he'd had the chance. He wanted to kick him to death, grind his mouth to pulp with iron-toed military boots. No. It would be better to let him loose in the courtyard at the correctional facility in Ila, so that they could tear him apart like hyenas. Or crush his body with a baseball bat or a heavy wrench—first his legs, then his arms, then his torso, crotch, and face. Finally the head.

He closed his eyes. *If you let yourself think along those lines, you're finished.* Rask had gotten the Kristiane conviction reopened, and Bergmann knew that Rask would likely be released. The threshold for getting a case through the commission was sky high, so high that it was overwhelmingly probable that you were convicted on wrong or shaky grounds. And if he was acquitted of the Kristiane murder, he would probably also be acquitted of the murder of Anne-Lee Fransen and the four other girls. Bergmann couldn't waste time on crazy revenge fantasies.

Besides, Rask would get to play a new trump card when the police released the news that Daina, the Lithuanian girl, was killed in almost exactly the same way as Kristiane. The question no one really wanted to ask was whether Rask had established contact with someone on the outside. Was he was actually fooling them all? Perhaps there had been two people involved in the murders from the outset. Or perhaps he was simply innocent.

Bergmann told himself that it was a waste of time to watch the documentary again. He was spinning his wheels. The documentary was based on secondary sources, and Rask himself had never given any interviews, except to Bergmann's contact at *Dagbladet*, Frank Krokhol. He picked up his phone and scrolled down to Krokhol's number. He sat there, staring at the digits. It was too late to call, and besides, he ought to wait until after tomorrow's meeting.

In the bedroom he left the lamp on the nightstand on. He turned over toward the side of the bed that had been Hege's, and prayed that he wouldn't have the dream tonight. The dream he'd had countless times since Anders Rask applied to reopen the Kristiane case almost nine months ago, the dream in which he was walking through the dark rain-soaked forest, as if a hand was pushing him from behind, toward a dark figure up ahead who was repeatedly striking at a shapeless figure on the ground. In the dream, he eventually realized the figure was Kristiane Thorstensen, who was still alive. Bergmann ran the final steps and reached out to the person, who turned around and waved the knife at him. He fell backward and discovered that *he* was the murderer, older than he had been when Kristiane was killed, but just as fully and unmistakably himself.

After trying unsuccessfully for an hour to fall asleep, he got up.

He stood by the living room window and looked out over the apartment buildings on the other side of the square. The white letters of "Blåfjellet Housing Cooperative" were barely visible on the gable wall across the way. He pulled his robe tighter around himself and lit a cigarette. The thick driving snow appeared yellow under the streetlights. The sight made him miss summer, miss Hadja. How long had it been since he'd last seen her? Too long for him to remember. He closed his eyes and tried to picture her, tried to remember her smell, but it was pointless. All he saw in his mind's eye were the last steps he'd taken toward the corpse and Kåre Gjervan leaning down and touching the pendant Kristiane Thorstensen wore around her neck.

In the bathroom he studied himself in the garish fluorescent light over the mirror. The bags under his eyes seemed to have grown larger, darker, and heavier, and his hair was too long. He kept putting off the trip to the barber, perhaps trying to ignore the fact that the gray had begun to extend far above his temples. Fine wrinkles radiated in all directions around his eyes when he squinted, and his eyes appeared more gray than blue, as if they'd never had any life in them. What was left of the man who had found Kristiane Thorstensen so many years ago? He supported himself on the sink and saw himself standing over Hege, who had lain on this very bathroom floor and whispered, as quietly as she could, so that the neighbors wouldn't hear it, "Please, Tommy, don't kill me."

He had promised the dead girl that he would be a good person, and this was the result, sixteen years later. He moved his gaze toward the floor, where Hege had lain sprawled. He no longer had a clear memory of what he had actually done to her—only in flashes was he able to reconstruct small fragments of . . . what? *Assault,* he thought. There was no other word for it.

And there was no forgiving such a thing. An explanation, maybe, at most, but nothing else. If there really was an afterlife, he would be going the same way as the man who had killed Kristiane.

As if to punish himself he sat down on the couch, picked up the remote control, and hit "Play" on the documentary. The flickering images on the screen filled the dark room with a strange bluish light. He rewound to the reconstruction of the first murder in Tønsberg, where Rask stood out in the forest in Vestfold with a sheepish smile. Bergmann froze the image and zoomed in on the feminine face. He closed his eyes and saw himself.

"You and me, Anders," he whispered to the TV screen. "We are nothing but animals."

17

Arne Furuberget went to bed in the guest room a little before three in the morning. His wife's light snoring made it impossible for him to get to sleep. Now he lay there, waiting for the alarm clock to ring. The nearest neighbor had already tried to start his car. It had been snowing heavily all night, and his fool of a neighbor was the only person to break the almost divine stillness that four to six inches of snow could bestow upon humanity. He always left for work at quarter past six and had woken Furuberget every weekday for almost twenty years. Furuberget stroked his beard and almost had to smile at the Schadenfreude he felt when his neighbor couldn't get his car started.

He decided to stay in bed a few more minutes. Finally he dozed off and disappeared down into a dark well of sleep.

His head ached fiercely when his phone's alarm went off. *Five minutes,* he thought. *I got at least five minutes of sleep.*

Just as he set his feet on the cold parquet floor, it clicked. He knew exactly where he knew that name from.

"Maria," he said to himself. "Edle Maria." He noticed the goose bumps under his faded pajamas. He suddenly felt much older, as if he already had one foot in the grave.

Edle Maria. He pulled up one sleeve of his pajamas. The hair on his arm was standing straight up like hog bristle. *I can hear the voice quite clearly,* he thought.

He went over to the window and looked out toward the neighbor's garage. The poor wretch had connected a starting device to the car battery. He stared blankly at the ox of a man for a moment, then ended up studying his own mirror image in the dark windowpane.

It just couldn't be.

And yet.

He was quite sure. Yes, he was completely convinced that he remembered correctly.

He got dressed as if he had the Devil himself at his heels, skipping breakfast, and yes, even coffee. He woke his wife with a light kiss on the forehead, something he hadn't done for years. Fortunately she was too tired to pull him down into bed, even though he thought that was what she was trying to do. *We'll soon be too old for such things,* thought Furuberget, and rejoiced that the car started with no problem, purring like a cat, even though he'd forgotten to put on the engine warmer.

By the time he parked the car at Ringvoll, the gloom had taken over again. He didn't understand where those few minutes of sudden joy had come from.

This is serious, he thought, unlocking the door to the archive in the basement.

He wandered around the windowless room long enough to feel that his body was being emptied of oxygen. He understood little or nothing of these rolling shelves. Oh, he'd grown so old. This business with Rask had been too much for him. He was a psychiatrist, for Pete's sake. He felt his own weakness creeping up on him like an assassin. There was too much of everything—of beige archive letters, numbers, filing codes, and the like. He no longer even remembered what year he was searching for.

At a little past eight o'clock, he heard someone entering the code on the outside of the door.

The administrative director looked at him as if he were a burglar she'd taken by surprise.

"What are you doing here?" she blurted out.

"I'm looking for a case. A patient record."

"Which patient?"

"It was a long time ago. No one you know. A patient that's no longer here."

As she came into the room, the heels of her shoes echoed in his head.

But how? he thought. *How?*

"How long ago?"

"A few years."

"You'll have to go to Brumunddal if the file is more than ten years old."

Furuberget avoided making eye contact. He had to get this cleared up. He simply had to get this taken care of before Christmas. He could not take this mistake with him to the grave, much less admit it to anyone before he was completely certain.

He did not leave until two o'clock in the afternoon. Because of the gathering storm, the drive around Mjøsa took almost two hours, nearly twice the time it normally took. The stationary line across the Moelv Bridge reminded him of the Périphérique, the ring road around Paris. All he could see were the red taillights of the car ahead. The windshield wipers threatened to collapse under the weight of all the snow that had been falling for hours.

The administration building of the Inland Hospital normally looked like a Soviet office block, but in the white inferno that was falling from the sky, it looked more like a stage set from a Christmas story. There were still lights on in most of the windows. Furuberget thought that they should make more of an effort to escape this endless cycle of work and get home to their wives and husbands and kids—and soon, because life would be over soon enough. It was over before you even took a breath. *The only people who should be at work after four o'clock in the weeks leading up to Christmas are those who don't have anything other than solitude to look forward to when they get home.*

Furuberget felt warm, almost feverish, as he got out of the car. He draped his overcoat over his forearm and opened the cuffs under his suit jacket. Either he was coming down with something, or it was the certainty that he was about to make an irreparable mistake gnawing at him from inside. His life had been threatened more times than he cared to remember, but Rask's words had stuck in his mind. His inscrutable smile.

"You're dead," he said to himself, almost spitting it out like one of his own patients on their way into psychosis. No, *slaughtered.* Wasn't that the way Rask put it?

He stomped the snow off his shoes on his way up the stairs.

The wash lights inside the archive blinked a few times, as if to suggest that this was not a good idea. That he should let all this be, that he'd remembered wrong.

"Turn off the lights when you leave," said the young girl who showed him in. "And the photocopier takes a little time to warm up." She smiled as she put on a stocking cap and turned up the collar on her old-fashioned coat—which was probably modern again by now—almost to her ears. She had shown him how the system worked. He hadn't explained what he was looking for—not specifically at least; he simply gave her a time range for a case that "interested him."

"Have a good one, then," she said from the door.

It took him only half an hour to find the right file box. His palms were sweaty as he pulled out the papers, and he started when the old rubber band that held them in place suddenly broke.

He found what he was searching for in week three of treatment.

"I had no other choice."

He then read the caregiver's assessment. Written off as situational psychosis. He pushed his shaggy hair off his forehead. *Psychosis, yes. That was long ago.*

He continued to read. Strong medication. Too strong. Pure anesthesia. And discharged too soon. That was easy to see now.

But the name. It was there. It had been mentioned one Tuesday morning.

> *Asked for her name. Patient said Edle Maria. When I asked again, there was no confirmation until a few minutes later. She is often simply called Maria. But her name is Edle Maria. Her father wanted to name her Edle Maria.*

It couldn't be a coincidence.

He made copies of the pages he needed and put the box back on the shelf, right where it belonged. Rask had caught him making mistakes. He mustn't make any more.

Back outside, he stood on the steps for a long time. The snow was gusting around him, and he was finally blue with cold. The folder holding the patient record was getting wet in the infernal snowstorm. He stuck it under his coat and walked reluctantly toward the car, which now looked like an igloo.

He brushed snow off it with the old snow brush. His movements were slow, as if all this mental illness had suddenly aged him.

He turned on the reading light in the car. He wanted to assure himself just one last time that it really added up.

"The patient says, 'Edle Maria is alive.'"

He took out his phone and started entering the number for information. When someone picked up on the other end, he hung up.

Was that what had been in the letter to Rask?

Yes, he thought. He recalled a fragment. Something about Medusa. Medusa's tears.

Edle Maria.

Had she been a Medusa?

18

It was said that dreams showed your real nature in which nothing was held back, an unvarnished truth held up to the dreamer. When Bergmann's alarm clock went off, he found himself hoping it wasn't true. What had he dreamt? He tried to let it go. Was it the truth about himself?

The wool blanket he'd placed over himself before he fell asleep had slipped to the floor. The room was still warm enough that he could lie there for a few more hours. Through the living room windows he could just glimpse that it was still snowing, even more heavily than the night before. Perhaps that meant the worst of the cold had released its hold on the city.

He turned on his side and saw the same images of Anders Rask pass over the TV screen—the pictures from the woods in Vestfold and his half-cruel, half-infantile smile. A shiver went through him, not because of Rask's face, but because the TV was still on, the VHS tape still playing.

Hadn't he turned it off before he fell asleep?

Maybe not. For a moment he was unable to remember what had happened. If he'd fallen asleep with the TV on, the video must have rewound itself and started to play again.

He got up, found the remote control, and started to fast-forward, but stopped after a few seconds. What was he doing? Could someone have been in the apartment while he was sleeping? He snorted at the outrageous thought, but nonetheless went out into the hall and felt the front door. For a moment he thought it was open, but no. The old door creaked when he pulled on it one more time. It was the original door from when the building was new back in the late fifties. The lock was only a simple spring latch. With a little poking anyone could open it from the outside. Hege had always wanted to replace it, but he'd considered it unnecessary—after all, who did he need to be afraid of in this world? *Maybe that was why she wanted to replace it,* he thought as he settled down in a kitchen chair and fished the last cigarette out of a pack on the table. Because the door was so thin and the neighbors could easily hear them when their arguing was at its worst.

A memory of Hege flashed across his mind's eye—how she'd stood by that very door on the last day. He had been sitting just as he was now, after another night of hell. He knew that she wasn't coming back ever again. Maybe it was her look, which was filled more with pity than hate. And he, of all people, just sat there as if chained to the chair. After she'd left for work, he started crying. *A child's crying,* he thought now.

"Damn," he said out loud. The clock on the stove showed that he'd puttered around too long. He would have to take a taxi to police headquarters in Grønland; he couldn't get there late, not today, not in this case.

Before he got in the shower, he surveyed the apartment. The bedroom was untouched. Living room and guest room likewise—at least, he didn't see anything that didn't add up. He opened one of the drawers in the old dresser Hege had bought at a flea market. The few thousand-kroner bills he had stashed in there, God knows why, were still there. He turned around and scanned the living room one more time, searching for the slightest change. He studied the bookcases and the few photographs he kept there, the coffee table, the chairs by the dining table.

He stared at the TV. He considered briefly whether Anders Rask had slipped out on leave. That was madness, but madness wasn't unprecedented in this country.

He shook himself. Rask had simply gotten one of the cases reopened. For the time being, he was still serving a sentence for all six murders.

Even so, he thought. The TV and the VCR could not simply have turned themselves on.

Had he really turned them both off before he fell asleep on the couch?

19

Elisabeth Thorstensen thought she could sit like this for hours, completely still with her head cocked, and stare at the birds outside the window. They flocked to the birdfeeder that Asgeir had set up—which Kristiane had made in woodshop.

Which Peter made in woodshop, she thought, straightening her head. She lit a cigarette while she tried to remember what the birds were called. She gave up at once. *You can't stand birds, have you forgotten that?* She had once stepped on a bird, a big black devil she'd found on the terrace. It was light as air under her shoe. She could still remember how she'd felt as she poked out its eyes. They looked like buttons on either side of the oblong head, and she had wanted to sew them onto her coat. That would have been something, black bird eyes on the ugly beige coat they'd bought for her.

"Is everything okay, ma'am?"

She shifted her gaze listlessly, noticing as she did so that the movement almost made her lose her depth perception. Valium had that effect on her. She'd taken half a tablet, just to get to sleep, but still woken up after two hours. The pill's active ingredients no longer had any effect on her.

"Don't call me ma'am. You know I hate that."

"*Sorry,* ma'am."

Elisabeth narrowed her eyes.

Rose covered her mouth and walked over to the dishwasher. Elisabeth thought she'd seen fear in her eyes. Had she turned ugly? She put out the cigarette and went out to the hall. She waited beside the mirror for a while before she dared look at herself.

She closed her eyes in sheer delight at the sight. *Beautiful,* she thought. Wasn't that what Asgeir had said to her just this morning? She'd come down from her room to say good-bye to him. For a moment she felt a flash of happiness, the kind she hadn't felt since she was at the hospital with Kristiane at her breast.

"Promise me one thing, Rose." She stood in the doorway as Rose continued emptying the machine. "Never be afraid of me. Never."

Rose set down a glass on the counter. She smiled. It looked sincere enough.

"Of course not."

"If I lose you, I lose everything."

Rose pushed a lock of hair from her forehead. Elisabeth went over to her and took her hand.

"Never."

She put her arms around Rose. Though she tried not to cry, she was unable to hold back the tears.

"Don't be sad," said Rose.

You should have been there, thought Elisabeth. *You should have been there and taken care of me. How old were you then? You weren't even born. Even your parents were still children.*

Finally she let go of Rose and took a step back.

"I don't know what I would have done without you."

Now Rose was crying too.

Elisabeth knew that she would have to let her return to the Philippines someday. Rose had a five-year-old son there, who lived with his grandparents.

But no, she could never let Rose go.

She left Rose to her housework and headed into her office. That dreadful letter was still on the desk. She had let Asgeir read it to her, though she already knew what it said.

We wish to inform you of the commission's decision of December 10, 2004, to grant Anders Rask's request to retry the decision made in the Eidsivating Court of Appeals on February 22, 1994.

She read the words "counsel for the victim" out loud to herself. For the first time since she'd received the letter, she managed to read it without feeling anything. It was only letters on a piece of paper, nothing else, nothing that concerned her.

She looked out toward the fjord as her fingers caressed the sheet of paper, as if it would bring Kristiane back to life. The world seemed drained of color, a palette limited to gray and black. Even the frosty mist that hung over the dark, still water looked gray, not white. How many days was it since she'd last seen the sun?

She closed the office door and picked up the receiver of the old landline phone. She listened for a moment to make certain that Rose hadn't picked up the receiver of the phone down the hall.

She entered his cell-phone number. After three or four rings he answered. His voice was slightly affected, in a way that she knew meant that he was in a meeting. He could have ignored the call, but chose to take it.

It was all she needed to feel happy.

"I have to see you."

He hung up without saying a word.

Seconds later she started to cry.

She lowered her head to the desktop and closed her eyes. Kristiane's face appeared behind her eyelids. "Don't be sad, Mom. There was nothing you could have done." The voice was a child's, a small child's, but Elisabeth was not afraid of it. It was the middle of the day. There was nothing to be afraid of.

She was startled by a sudden sound right by her ear. Kristiane's voice faded, along with the image of her. It took a moment before she realized that the sound was coming from the landline phone beside her.

She held it in her hand and stared at the eight digits. It wasn't him, it wasn't a cell-phone number.

Even through the closed door and from down the hall, she thought she could hear Rose's steps heading toward the hall phone. She carefully set it down and suddenly felt an all-consuming chill. She stood up and opened the door, then walked with quick but controlled steps to the stairs, moving a little more quickly with each step.

Sure enough, though she couldn't possibly really have heard Rose's steps from her office, Rose was leaning over the phone in the hall. Elisabeth stopped on the top step.

"Don't answer it," she said quietly.

Rose evidently didn't hear her because her arm moved toward the phone.

"Don't answer it!"

Rose jumped with fright, almost falling over the writing desk on which the phone sat. They stared at each other until the person on the other end had hung up.

Elisabeth was unable to hold back the tears at the sight of Rose's face.

You promised me, she thought, *that you wouldn't be afraid of me.*

20

Bergmann fixed his gaze on the poinsettia in front of him. He closed his eyes, but regretted it immediately as the images from last night's dream came flooding back, how he had stuck the knife in her again and again, as deep and as hard as he could. The police chief's gentle voice filled the office. She was reading a story from today's *Dagbladet* about the incompetence and tunnel vision of the police. He was still worn out and sweaty after last night, or had he started sweating again in the taxi, on his way down to headquarters? He didn't remember, only remembered having looked at the cross hanging from the rearview mirror—or was it another place, in Tuscany that summer, that summer Hege thought she was pregnant, and he was so happy, for a few days anyway. For a few wonderful days, he was able to forget, to forget how sick he'd been, but when they came home, he'd broken his promise again.

Why?

Bergmann didn't know. He was thirty-nine years old and didn't know a damn thing about himself. He wasn't even able to separate his feelings, couldn't distinguish between how he felt standing in a pitch-dark forest in 1988, looking down at a fifteen-year-old girl who would never age another day and who'd been deprived of all human dignity, and the feeling he got sitting here sixteen years later in the police chief's

office, almost shaking with nausea at the fact that he—of all people—
would get the chance to straighten it all out again.

He rubbed his face hard, almost frantically. Then he observed the
gathering around the table once more. His colleagues were serious,
fake, pathetic, and simply in love with their own careers. Sometimes he
thought they didn't give a shit about the countless victims who'd been
killed, raped, and assaulted; they stepped on them as they climbed up
the ladder. Up, up, that was all they knew, without a thought for those
who were heading in the opposite direction.

Reuter's cheeks were slightly red as he sat beside Bergmann. He
observed Reuter for a moment and felt a pang of contempt for how
the man pretended to be following along as the police chief read. He
moved his gaze to the chief. She adjusted the small reading glasses that
were perched on the tip of her nose, and read the article with feeling.
Bergmann felt as though he was back in the classroom in elementary
or middle school. In fact, if you removed the portrait of King Harald
and Queen Sonja from the wall behind her, her office could probably
have passed for an average classroom, with its light-birch furniture, red
woolen seat cushions, and dull art lining the worn plaster walls that
dated back to the seventies.

But perhaps he was being too harsh. Hanne Rodahl seemed sin-
cerely indignant about *Dagbladet*'s article; it appeared that her desire
to find Kristiane Thorstensen's killer was sincere. And because of the
media's hard-line, the police chief now obviously had a fire under her
to get this solved, ignited by people who stood higher on the ladder
than she did.

That was how the world worked these days, or at least that was how
it had become: the press decided to pursue a case, and headquarters followed like a driverless sled behind a pack of Siberian huskies. *Dagbladet*
had already assumed full reparation and release for Rask and fired off a
broadside almost without parallel in that day's editorial.

"'Not only were they able to get Anders Rask convicted on a completely unsound basis, but the police also ought to ask themselves: If Rask did not kill Kristiane or any of the other girls, don't we have a disturbed child murderer running loose in Norway? And now the police are faced with yet another murder of a young girl, over ten years after he was convicted. PR at police headquarters answered *Dagbladet*'s questions about the case in only the vaguest of terms, which makes it difficult to avoid asking the obvious question once again: Do we have a disturbed child murderer running loose in this country?'"

The police chief stopped reading, took a deep breath, carefully took her reading glasses off her nose, and folded them in her hand.

Silence followed. They all sat there, seven men and one woman, staring at the slightly withered poinsettia, as the clock on the wall seemed to tick closer to a defeat.

"They show as much consideration for the survivors as they always have," said Hanne Rodahl, weighing the reading glasses in her hand.

Bergmann shifted his gaze and stared blankly at the room; there wasn't much to see, but he couldn't bring himself to respond to her half-dejected smile. Besides, he was on the lowest rung of the ladder of everyone in the room. Not that he usually cared much about such things, but he felt a little like the teacher's pet when he thought about why he was sitting here. Reuter had come into his office yesterday and told him where things stood. The attorney general thought he should be ready to take up the whole Rask case again on very short notice, but naturally wanted to wait to make the official decision until it was clear they had something more to go on than they did eleven or twelve years ago, when Rask had cracked under questioning by the Oslo police, was investigated by Kripo, and convicted. This time, said Reuter, the attorney general wanted the Oslo police to coordinate the investigation—if there was a new investigation—but would launch it as discreetly as possible. Oslo had been the district of choice because five of the girls were killed within its boundaries. Or rather, they had disappeared from Oslo. Bergmann had thought the decision was a purely bureaucratic one until Reuter added, "Papa Rodahl is pointing at you, Tommy. She wants you on the case." Reuter often made fun of the police chief behind her back by putting her code name before her surname. Still, that was better than Madame Saddam, as she was referred to in the patrol cars.

"This Rask gives me the creeps," said Rodahl, if only to break the silence. Bergmann sensed that she really didn't want to have this case on her hands. He understood her perfectly. It was like being a freebooter in hell. "Are we quite certain it's not really him?"

"He's going to be acquitted for the murder of Kristiane Thorstensen," said Finneland, who sat at the opposite short end of the table. "Now that he's gotten it reopened, it's over. Let there be no doubt about that. If I'm not mistaken, he'll be acquitted in the next case too. That either means that Rask will eventually go free for murders he actually *has* committed—but that we can't prove he's behind—or that the real murderer, or murderers, is still among us. What I want to know is whether Rask has done what he's convicted of, evidence or no evidence, or whether we should be chasing another man. The same man who killed Daina at Frognerveien. We'll split up, Hanne. We're being attacked on two fronts, and we have to defend ourselves on two fronts. If we find the answer in one of the cases, I think we'll solve both. Sørvaag will continue with the Daina case, regardless of what a dead end that might be, and Bergmann will find gold in the old Kristiane case."

"But why Kristiane?" said Rodahl to no one in particular.

"Exactly," said Finneland. "Why Kristiane?"

"You think Kristiane is the key," said Bergmann, looking at Finneland.

The prosecutor's eyes narrowed, then lit up.

"You think fast, Bergmann. I like people who think fast. Yes, I've asked myself the question why Rask chose Kristiane in particular. Why is she the one he's convinced he didn't kill? Is there something he's trying to tell the outside world?"

"You think he's withholding information?" said Bergmann.

Though Finneland smiled, Bergmann wasn't sure that he liked his expression.

"You can console yourself with the fact that that's exactly what you're going to find out, Bergmann."

Finneland presented this impossible task as if it were the most obvious thing in the world. Though he was officially responsible for the Oslo prosecutor's office, Finneland was also the attorney general's appointee, and, according to rumors, the one who actually made the decisions in the country's highest prosecutors' office. That his nickname in the patrol cars was Pussyland was hardly a surprise to anyone. In addition to being an arrogant bastard, he was known for hitting on all the female attorneys in the department whenever he felt like it. He was good-looking—that could not be denied—and he was in good shape besides. And he had a lot of power, far too much power. *That sort of thing has always worked as a chick magnet,* thought Bergmann. That explained a lot.

"You know what I mean, Svein," said Rodahl. "He's a swine, a misogynistic swine and a child abuser, and he's stark raving mad to boot. I can't escape the feeling that he's fooled—"

"Kripo?" said Finneland.

"Us," said the police chief. "All of us. I really think he's the one who killed all those girls, Svein."

"Not Daina," said Finneland.

"The perpetrator didn't cut off her fingers. And she wasn't as injured as—"

"For God's sake, he didn't have time, Hanne. He was interrupted by a man we're unable to find. We're never going to find the caller, no matter how much money we put up for a reward. When are you going to realize that?"

Finneland sighed dejectedly and steepled his long fingers. A broad wedding ring appeared to have grown into the ring finger on his right hand. In a flash Bergmann was back in the patrol car sixteen years ago; he still remembered the sight of the solitary Christmas star in the window, the dark figure by the roadside, the sound of Kåre Gjervan's wedding ring as it hit the gearshift. *I should have opened the car door,* thought Bergmann, *and run, run, vanished, never come back again.*

A tapping on the tabletop to his left startled him out of his thoughts. Reuter was fiddling with a pencil; his expression suggested he wished this meeting had never taken place.

"You can think what you want, Hanne," said Finneland. "I want to schedule another meeting for next week."

He threw his briefcase on the table, then glanced at the pulse monitor on his wrist. Bergmann knew that if Finneland were to succeed in finding Kristiane's real murderer—whether by producing new evidence against Rask or by finding someone else guilty—the path to the office of the Director General of Public Prosecutors would be wide open. Finneland couldn't care less about Kristiane, or anyone else for that matter. Career was everything to him.

"I'm counting on you to get me something within the week, Bergmann," he said, getting up. "Because a week is all you have."

Bergmann heard Reuter's pencil break. The detective superintendent who sat across from them cleared his throat, as though suddenly allergic to that poinsettia standing between them. Not a word had been said about how this discreet, so-called preparatory investigation would be conducted, but it was now obvious to everyone that the police chief had already given Finneland both the name and number of the man she expected to find water in the desert.

"In a week's time, I want an answer from you to the question of whether there's anything to pursue or not, do you understand? Normally I would have recommended that we fight tooth and nail to defend the old conviction against Rask. But that will be like pissing in your pants to stay warm. One week, that's it. And for God's sake keep quiet about this as long as you can." Finneland talked in a way that brought Bergmann's thoughts back to boot camp in the military, a life that consisted entirely of curt commands and no room for doubt whatsoever.

Finneland continued, "I'd like to see Rask stay locked up for the rest of his life. You can imagine for yourself what a defeat another failed investigation would look like. And sooner or later the dam in the Daina case will break. In the end I'm sure we'll be pressured to open up the whole damned Rask case again, but I want us to forestall the Ministry of Justice from doing that as long as possible. We're already on their backs about that."

Silence. No one appeared to want to speak. The seven others in the room seemed to be relieved that the whole question of whether the old Rask case would be resumed had become a matter between Chief Public Prosecutor Svein Finneland and Inspector Tommy Bergmann.

"Tommy was there when Kristiane was found . . ." said the detective superintendent.

Idiot, thought Bergmann.

Finneland frowned and cocked his narrow head. Bergmann held his hand up in a dismissive gesture.

"Resources?" said Bergmann. *He cut open her belly,* he thought, *and mutilated her.* The sound of the wedding ring against the gearshift, the sound of the plastic bags being pulled apart, the smell of Kristiane Thorstensen, how the birds had hacked at her but let her face be. How could such things happen?

"You'll take Susanne with you," said Reuter, clearing his throat. "The two of you will be able to keep quiet. And she's a bit more organized than you."

Cautious laughter followed. Bergmann caught a few glances being exchanged across the table, but didn't quite understand what was going on. Rodahl smiled sheepishly at Finneland.

"You'll get resources here in the building," said Finneland. "But keep a low profile. People brag about you, Bergmann, you should know that. If you have questions, call me, anytime, day or night. Otherwise, I'll see you next week. Something needs to be on the table by then, something Kripo has overlooked."

Finneland placed a hard hand on Bergmann's shoulder and squeezed.

"Give me something that helps us find that bastard."

21

Elisabeth Thorstensen had not exchanged a word with Rose since the episode with the telephone. She'd been sitting out on the terrace in her wolf-skin fur, looking out at the fjord, the islands Ulvøya and Malmøya, and Nesodden. She was sitting with an unlit cigarette in her hand when she heard a sound from the railway line below the house. Through the leafless hedge she could clearly see Kristiane knocking on the glass with her face pressed against the window of the train. Elisabeth got up and sprinted through the garden, still holding the cigarette in her hand. She tried to push apart the thick branches of the linden hedge, but only ended up scraping the backs of her hands. She brought her face up to the bare black branches and listened to the sound of the train dying away and the cars down on Mosseveien, the endless sounds of traffic, of life, of people who still had something to live for every day.

She sucked up the blood from her hand. The sight of the blood, its sweetish taste and slight scent of iron, made her dizzy. She swayed into the hedge for a moment, then she blacked out.

When she came to, she was lying on her back in the snow. A warm hand was holding hers. When she opened her eyes, the falling snow felt like it was slicing into her eyeballs.

"Oh, Elisabeth," said Rose.

Elisabeth thought the sight was absurd. The beautiful woman wore just an apron, blouse, skirt, and a pair of slippers, her black hair covered with snow. She was so far north of her home.

Go home, she thought, closing her eyes again. She still felt warm. In her fur, she could have lain outside like that for hours.

"You haven't answered the phone?" she said quietly.

"No."

"Will you help me up?"

Back inside, Rose undressed her in the second-floor bathroom.

"Hang on to me," said Elisabeth when she was completely naked. She studied the water in the bathtub, how it whirled under the faucet, foaming as if it were blood pouring out of a stomach. Her legs nearly failed her, and she stumbled into Rose.

"Don't leave me here. I need you to stay here while I bathe."

Rose stroked her forehead, and she sank down into the water. If Rose hadn't been there, she would have simply submerged herself entirely and opened her mouth.

Like in a dream the sound of the telephone rose up from the first floor again. It was like déjà vu from this morning. Elisabeth got out of the bathtub and observed herself in the mirror.

"I'm still a good-looking woman, Rose, don't you think?" She smiled carefully at the housekeeper.

The sound from the phone went away.

It could have been him.

An hour later she reversed the new Mercedes Asgeir had bought for her out of the garage. Fifteen minutes later she drove onto Skøyenbrynet.

She parked a few yards away from the old house, which was still painted red. A thin strip of gray smoke rose from the chimney. The disappointment slowly filled her. She just wanted to walk around the house and look into Kristiane's room. And Alex's. She closed her eyes and saw herself walking around inside the house, up the stairs, across the varnished pine floors of the hall, past the white walls hung with art that Per-Erik said she had spent far too much money on. Down to their rooms, all the way at the end.

It was the strands of her hair. She couldn't have mistaken them.

She opened the car door and stepped out into the snow. The flakes were falling thickly now, and it was impossible to see beyond the neighboring house.

Elisabeth opened the cast-iron gate and entered. After only a few steps she saw movements behind the kitchen window. For a few seconds she pictured herself standing in there. There had been some happy times, no?

A voice inside her said it wouldn't be dangerous to go down into the garden; no one would see her. But she remained standing as if paralyzed. Finally reason won out and she hurried back to the gate and closed it behind her.

She drove away from the house, but stopped again outside the house of her old neighbors, the ones who probably knew what was going on, what Per-Erik did to her.

She looked in the direction of where she lived now. She couldn't see her house from here, but the fact that she lived in the vicinity of the old house was like a rape of Kristiane's memory.

Her wallet lay on the passenger seat. She took out Kristiane's passport photo—the only picture she had of her. Alex had sent it to her last summer, without any warning. "I kept this picture," he'd written.

Had she given it to him?

Why had he kept it, why had *he* kept things from Kristiane, and why hadn't she?

She took out her phone and searched for Alex's number. Quickly, before she had time to think too much, she hit the "Call" button.

His voice was distant, as if he were a different person. His "Hello" sounded more like a question than a greeting.

"Have you seen it?" she said so quietly that she almost didn't hear her own voice. She felt as though someone were staring at her from inside the house behind her. Kristiane, standing at the end of the hall, by the window. She saw everything, heard everything, even this conversation.

Alex didn't answer. She pictured him up there in Tromsø, what he looked like during this dark season, the fine features, the black hair. She had visited him just once when he was in medical school. He lived in a dreadful dungeon of a rented room on the mainland. Everything up there was dark, cold, a nightmare.

"How could you do that?" she said.

Only the static of the connection.

"Elisabeth," he said. Resigned, as if he were her father. The thought made her furious—what did he know about such things, what would he have done in her shoes? Then everything collapsed inside her.

She started to cry, at first quietly, then uncontrollably.

"Why can't you just call me Mother again?"

"Can you promise me one thing?" he said.

She got her crying under control.

"Yes."

"Don't ever call me again."

22

After the meeting Bergmann sat inertly in the office. Outside the window there was only a white wall of snow, as if nothing existed beyond headquarters itself. *Find something that Kripo overlooked back then. In a week.*

Forty percent of all men had blood type A. Bergmann himself had blood type A. Although 10 percent had the same enzyme profile as the perpetrator, only Anders Rask had two of the girls' belongings—hair, notebooks—in his home. On the other hand, no skin was found under the nails of any of the victims before Daina. Maybe he'd tied their hands behind their backs as fast as he could. Knocked them unconscious first, pounded the sense out of them. Apart from Kristiane.

Bergmann knew that he would need a team or two if he was to stand a chance of finding anything at all in a week. But he had only Susanne. And she hadn't been of his own choosing. She was capable enough, but there was a limit to how much the two of them could accomplish in a week. If Susanne had her daughter this week, he might as well just give up now, as it would mean working day and night or more than that. If they only had some idea where to begin. The DNA profile found in and on Daina didn't yield a match in the DNA registry, and all the evidence from the prior homicides had been destroyed. The old profile from the Kristiane case wasn't specific enough to establish anything other than that it *might* be the same man in all the cases. With today's technology, they might be able to get a bit more out of the DNA material. The problem was that the superior, self-righteous democracy of Norway destroyed evidence after a judgment was legally binding. In some cases it was turned back over to the family if they were possessions of the victim. But what family member took an item of clothing with evidence on it? Besides, in Kristiane's case they'd only found DNA in and on her body. Her clothes had never been found.

The words *It's all my fault* suddenly rang in his ears.

Those were the words Kristiane's mother had screamed.

He shook the computer mouse, and the *Dagbladet* website appeared on the screen. The photograph of Kristiane Thorstensen lit up before him. He lowered his eyes a moment, not wanting to stare into her blue irises.

He closed the website and went into the national registry for the justice sector. Kristiane's father, Per-Erik Thorstensen, was registered at Tveita, only a stone's throw from where he himself had grown up. No one else lived at that address. A quick Google search showed that he worked part-time in the IT Department at the Furuset School. He found his phone number on the Yellow Pages site.

Then he slowly entered the mother's name into the search field "current or former names."

Elisabeth Thorstensen.

He'd had her number in his phone, but deleted it after a week.

He could simply not understand why she was at that funeral. Could it be merely out of sympathy? How could she seek out such pain again? He'd eventually decided that she must have her reasons and given up trying to understand.

But now he couldn't avoid contacting her. Regardless of how much pain it would cause.

He pressed "Enter" and stared out at the white wall of snow. The thought that everyone in this building was alone in the world reminded him of a science fiction film he'd seen once when he was in his early teens. Only a few hundred people had survived an atomic disaster, and an endless winter followed, like this one.

He looked back at the computer screen.

So her name was still Elisabeth Thorstensen. Lived on Bekkelagsterrassen in the Bekkelaget district of Oslo. But her phone number was no longer listed. She must have gotten an unlisted number after the episode at the cemetery at Alfaset. She was married to Asgeir Nordli, who was born in 1945. She had two sons: Alexander, Kristiane's brother, and Peter, twelve years old, whom she'd had with Asgeir in 1992.

He found Asgeir's phone number in the Yellow Pages. Two cellphone numbers and one landline number.

Asgeir Nordli. Why did that sound familiar?

He did a Google search and discovered that he ran a real estate company, but that didn't ring any bells. He clicked around on the website, which offered property development and management services. It sounded boring, but based on the annual reports in the Brønnøysund Register, the business appeared to be doing well, and the tax agency confirmed that Elisabeth Thorstensen did not lack for money in her new marriage.

He entered the number for the residence in Bekkelaget before he could change his mind.

It rang for a long time. He expected voice mail to come on at any moment, but it just continued to ring. He looked at the clock. Ten o'clock. They must be at work—though he imagined that Elisabeth no longer worked.

Just as he was about to hang up and try again later, the receiver was picked up on the other end.

But only silence followed.

"This is Tommy Bergmann from the Oslo police," he said, a little louder than he intended.

The person on the other end took a breath, as if about to say something, but then hesitated.

"I would like to speak with Elisabeth Thorstensen."

They hung up.

Bergmann called one of the cell-phone numbers listed for Asgeir Nordli. He answered at once, brusquely, as if the person on the other end of the line was something the cat dragged in.

Bergmann introduced himself, and could almost hear Asgeir change his attitude.

"I would like to speak with Elisabeth," said Bergmann.

"She's on sick leave."

After a few minutes Bergmann finally convinced Asgeir to give him her number. He had to try three times before she finally answered.

"Elisabeth Thorstensen?"

"Speaking," said a female voice on the other end, but so quietly that he could hardly make out the words.

Bergmann braced himself, sensing that he only had one shot. "This is about—" He stopped, as though incapable of pronouncing her name. "Anders Rask, the reopening of the case." He thought for a fraction of a second that he ought to have said it concerned Kristiane instead, but now it was too late.

All that he heard was a half-muffled "Good-bye."

Then a busy signal.

Bergmann closed his eyes. He could still picture Elisabeth sitting on the kitchen floor in Skøyenbrynet, the deep cuts in her wrist, her picture-perfect face distorted by grief, her despairing gaze drained of hope.

He entered the number again, but changed his mind and hung up.

He got up and went to the restroom to rinse his face with cold water. After several minutes, the bags under his eyes had faded somewhat.

Back in the office he called Per-Erik Thorstensen.

"The person you are trying to reach . . ."

He tried the landline, but a voice reported that the number was no longer in use.

He bit his lower lip and studied his hands. Clenched his fists and opened them again. Again and again. Then he took out his phone and found the number for *Dagbladet*'s Frank Krokhol.

Bergmann kept his cards close to his chest. They simply agreed to meet at the regular place.

He looked at the clock for a long time. Eight hours until dinner with Krokhol.

And what should he use Susanne for? "She's a bit more organized than you." Wasn't that what Reuter said? God only knew if he was right.

She was in her office talking on the phone. Her desk was bare, apart from the computer, a perfectly arranged document holder with copies of the cases she was working on, an in-basket, and an out-basket. She emptied the wastebasket at least once a day. Two photographs of her daughter, Mathea, stood beside each other on the desktop, each in a minimalist floating frame. It looked like she was expecting a visit from an interior design magazine at any moment. He didn't understand how anyone could live that way. And she undoubtedly didn't understand how *he* could make it through his days.

He leaned against the door frame and observed her for a while. She must have gotten highlights recently, as her hair was lighter than he remembered. The sight reminded him more of Hege than he liked. He consoled himself with the fact that Susanne was actually dark blonde, borderline brunette, and she had brown eyes, not blue. Besides, he didn't know if he particularly liked her. Or did he? She had worked on patrol for almost ten years, and he liked that about her. Besides, he knew that she was just shy of getting her law degree, with only her master's thesis to finish.

He should have done the same himself, but he never had time. What kind of excuse was that, though? She even had a little girl.

All in all she was probably not that bad.

He knocked hard on the door. She jumped and turned her chair around.

"I'll have to call you back," she said to the person on the other end.

"You know the Kristiane case?"

She fumbled in her hair for her reading glasses, which were about to fall down, but didn't reply, simply furrowing her finely penciled dark eyebrows.

"You and I are going to solve it."

She smiled carefully. Not the usual laugh—the kind that would have made clear to Bergmann that Susanne Bech was too domineering and self-centered to be his type—but a cautious, tentative laugh.

"We have a week."

"Are you serious?" she said gravely, as if only now fully registering what he had said. She pulled on the neck of her thick, tight-fitting woolen sweater, as if it had suddenly become too warm for her.

"Whose idea was that?"

"Finneland's orders. Papa signed off, of course. Reuter said I should use you. He's filling in for me this week. So we'll have to see what we find."

Susanne's frown deepened, and her cheeks looked pinker on her winter-pale face.

"Who, I mean, was it you who—" She stopped.

"What?"

She shook her head.

"Nothing."

"We'll have to split up. Unfortunately I have to give you the shit work. I'll call Kripo, and you'll head up there now and pick up what we need. Put everything else on hold."

She got a slightly strange look on her face and took off the hair band she had around her wrist to pull her hair back into a tight ponytail. Then she put on her brown reading glasses.

"Okay. Just call Kripo," she said.

"How much can you work over the next week?"

"You mean, do I have Mathea?"

"Yes."

"Is that going to be a problem? I have an ex, girlfriends, neighbors, friends, and parents. I'll work it out. You know that."

He held his hands up.

"Fine. Why don't you head up there right now then," he said. "I'll make a couple of calls."

He spent the whole morning on the phone.

First he called the Ringvoll Psychiatric Hospital at Toten, where Anders Rask was incarcerated. The consulting physician, Furuberget, talked nonstop for an hour; he was clearly the sort of man who thought he was God's gift to humanity. When he hung up, Bergmann sensed that he'd been detained with empty talk—as if Furuberget didn't want to get to the heart of the conversation Bergmann needed to have.

He spent the next hour and a half on the phone with the old Kripo investigator who had led the investigation until Rask was arrested. Bergmann understood that he was not going to be of any great help. On the contrary. He was going to do his utmost to camouflage the weaknesses of the old investigation. Chief Inspector Johan Holte had retired as one of the greatest heroes in Norwegian police history; he was known as the man who got the better of Anders Rask. Now he was well over seventy, and Bergmann knew that Holte didn't want to have the myth of his excellence torn to pieces by Rask's new attorney.

If Chief Public Prosecutor Svein Finneland was right, that was exactly what was going to happen.

"So you're quite certain that it's Rask?" Bergmann concluded.

"Certain?" said Holte, almost spitting out the word. He was the type who still thought that was intimidating. "Rask is a shrewd bastard, Bergmann. I'm certain that he's fooled everyone up there at Ringvoll. Mark my words. And do you think he has fond feelings for me?" Holte snorted. "If he ever comes here, I'll personally kill him myself, and *then* drive a stake through his heart just to be sure that he never rises up again."

23

The hands of the clock on the wall had moved ominously fast. Susanne Bech checked her watch just to be sure it was right. She looked over at the head of archives, then averted her gaze from his plumber's crack, which got bigger and bigger as he loaded the final paper boxes onto the cart.

Two hours already.

Two hours still to go.

She imagined an hourglass with sand running too quickly through its narrowest point. She had to get control of this. Her life almost depended on it. *Scratch* almost, she thought. While Tommy *bloody* Bergmann planned to sit at his desk and talk on the phone all day—was that how he intended to resolve this case in a week?—she had to take on what he so tactfully called the shit work. She had to smile at that whole colossus of a man. What was it her mother always said? "If you want something said, ask a man; if you want something done, ask a woman." Not that she was one to complain, but to be reduced to a servant, a mover? She hadn't applied to work in investigations to do that. He could have gotten one of the secretaries up here to do this, then she could have lit a fire under this investigation before the day was over. The only redeeming feature of male dominance techniques was that they were so damned easy to see through.

And Finneland's orders? *Orders my ass.*

She didn't know what to make of that. She hadn't been invited to the meeting this morning; Svein didn't want to grant her that kind of access. But *helping* Bergmann in this case, receiving second-hand information, she was somehow good enough for that. It could only mean that he wanted to pull her panties down again, as he'd done that night after the summer party at Fredrik Reuter's. And five times after that. She had promised herself never again to have anything to do with a charmer with a wandering gaze.

Crafty devil.

She only had two months left in this temporary position and had to deliver like hell now. Otherwise it would be back to patrol duty before she knew what hit her. And ever since the divorce, it was impossible for her to work those shifts. She didn't get the permanent investigator job in the Violent and Sex Crimes Division that she'd applied for last fall, and she knew why. Now he'd evidently decided that he wanted to give her another chance. One last chance. It was almost Christmas; he must get soft this time of year. Part of her wanted to say to hell with damned old faithless menfolk, but another part of her just wanted to wake up beside him. The one who would never be there the morning after. He was married to a woman his own age after all.

It didn't help that she'd gone behind the back of another woman, she'd thought that June night, and blamed it on being too drunk. Good Lord, why should she blame herself? She'd lived like a nun for almost six months after telling Nico he had to move out, that she wanted a divorce, that he'd had enough chances.

But God help her, she'd been so drunk that night.

The next few times with Svein Finneland she'd been stone sober. Just so she could really see if her feelings might be genuine.

The man, who was old enough to be her father, had a stronger hold on her than she liked. Than she was ready for. She'd managed to put a stop to it before summer turned to fall, but that was not to say that she'd stopped thinking about him.

Although he was married for the second time, no doubt notoriously unfaithful and twenty years older than her, she still had the text messages from Chief Public Prosecutor Svein Finneland on her phone. He must have sent her ten or fifteen after she said that she didn't want to see him anymore, each one more ingratiating than the last. In his world it was surely inconceivable that she could reject him like that. She was recently divorced, alone with a five-year-old, while he had all the power in the world and could get her as far as he wanted in the system. She could easily have remarried once the divorce was final, but everyone she met was just like Nicolay. Overgrown boys, virtually incapable of taking on a child or living the way she wanted. Nico always said that he was a playful dad, but there had to be limits to that. That he never set any limits was only the start. It never turned out the way she wanted.

The way I wanted? she thought and involuntarily brushed up against the hand of the head of archives.

She laughed it off and fumbled for her reading glasses in her hair to draw up a receipt for the loan of the documents. He pointed down at the counter between them and slowly pushed the glasses toward her.

She briefly studied her signature. *Susanne Bech.* Though it had improved a bit over time, her writing still looked childish and uncertain. Like her life. Unsteady, with no direction, incapable of standing with legs planted in one place and one place only.

Like hell was Svein Finneland coming back into her life.

The head of archives helped her push the three heavy carts laden with boxes of overstuffed case files down to the loading dock. The sight of the enormous quantity of documents made her melancholy for a moment, similar to the depression she'd felt as a teenager but fortunately grown out of. Or simply suppressed with work. Or Mathea.

Maybe it was just that she dreaded seeing what those cartons contained. She only vaguely recalled Anne-Lee Fransen in Tønsberg, but she remembered the Kristiane case much better than she would have liked. Somewhere deep inside she knew everything in those papers by heart, but she'd repressed Kristiane in her daily life, just as she imagined most women her age had done. She was one year older than Kristiane, and the pictures of a girl who could have been her, in print in the papers every single day that winter, had frightened her so deeply that she hadn't walked alone for a single second before it was spring again and life appeared to return to normal. Her mother had always said she was overly sensitive, and she said as much when Susanne told her that the Kristiane case had almost ruined her entire first year of high school. It wasn't the same with the young prostitute who was killed in February 1989, but Kristiane could have been her. For a while it *was* almost her.

She helped load the cartons into the van, stuffing the last two into the passenger seat.

"Where are you going to sit?" asked the driver, a young guy in his early twenties.

With one box in her arms and the other under her feet, they made their way back down to headquarters. The driver, Leo—South American, Chilean—joked with her all the way down from Helsfyr. She loved men like him—light, carefree, without a worry in the world. Every time he said something she smiled. As if she wanted to forget all the seriousness that lay ahead of her.

"Maybe we could have coffee sometime?" said Leo when he'd parked the car outside the loading dock.

"I'm much too old for you, kid. Will you give me a hand with these boxes, though?" She eased a carton into his arms. He gave her his card anyway, in case she changed her mind.

"You don't need to worry about that," she said.

When all the boxes were stacked in her office, she could barely breathe in there. And Bergmann wanted her to copy the most important files. The *most important*? She didn't even know if she'd brought the most important ones. She felt guilty that she hadn't been able to take the materials covering the three prostitutes. Nine months into this job as an investigator, and she had nothing to show for it but guilt over everything she hadn't accomplished. On patrol they could just pass the problem on to the next shift. Now she had to solve the problem herself. Investigation was the final resting place for all the world's misery.

She spent the rest of the afternoon copying and organizing.

When she was halfway through, she almost gave up and started reading Kripo's summary report as she stood in the copy room. After reading a couple of pages, she was struck by a memory, like one of the lightning flashes from her childhood summers at Hvaler.

Two witnesses, she thought.

She had just started on patrol, and all anyone was talking about was the trial.

The two witnesses hadn't testified in court; it wasn't necessary since Rask had already confessed. But they'd seen Kristiane that Saturday. *Yes,* she thought. One of them had been mentioned in a newspaper, either *VG* or *Dagbladet*, she was sure of it. The headline was "I Saw Kristiane at Skøyen."

Two men had seen Kristiane that Saturday evening. One at Oslo Central Station. The other in the Skøyen neighborhood. Under the railroad bridge, wasn't it?

Anders Rask had said that he had arranged to meet Kristiane in the city, but she had instead come to his place in the Oslo district of Haugerud, where he rented a townhouse. He had never said anything whatsoever about Skøyen. When he confessed, it was suddenly assumed that everything he said was true. No one had been able to catch him make any errors or inconsistencies, so the witness testimony became no longer significant.

She browsed back through the summary report.

"Kristiane observed at Oslo Central Station at 18:30 hours by the witness G. Gundersen," it said on page 12. Nothing else. Could she remember so wrong?

She walked as fast as she could without running to her own office, and bumped into a guy in the corridor without even seeing who it was.

"How about an *excuse me*?" she heard behind her.

"The binders!" she cried, tossing documents to the floor. If she got a head start on Bergmann, he couldn't help but put in a good word for her. She would lay everything out on the table before him and solve this case for him. *Find something Kripo overlooked, damn straight. I'll do just that.*

She paged back through the second of the five binders containing the witness hearings in the Kristiane case. She still hadn't opened the boxes with all the tips they'd received in November and December 1988 and, judging by the quantity, well into 1989. It was no doubt page after page of tips from either disturbed or self-centered persons across the country. She herself had been on the tip line a few times, and there was no limit to what people claimed to have seen. Kristiane had surely been glimpsed everywhere in the greater Oslo area that Saturday. The most publicized cases overflowed with leads from self-appointed mediums and faith healers.

After several minutes she found the interviews with G. Gundersen, who turned out to be Georg Gundersen, an eighty-year-old accountant from Moss. There were two interviews with him: one that took place at the Moss police station on November 30, where Gundersen was "almost certain" that it was Kristiane he had seen; and one dated two days later, December 2, conducted at the Grønland police station by Kripo detective Holte and a man whose name she didn't recognize.

In the second interview the transcript did not say "almost certain." Now Gundersen was "absolutely certain." Gundersen had signed with the same steady handwriting as he had at the prior interview in Moss.

Attached to the interview was a brief note from Holte, who concluded that Gundersen was a reliable witness.

A search in the census registry revealed a setback she hadn't foreseen. Gundersen died in 1998.

It would have been too good to be true if he was still alive.

What about the other witness? The junkie from the newspaper back then.

Near the back of the binder she found the document she was searching for.

According to a detective at the Oslo police station involved in a drug-dealing arrest on Saturday, November 19, Bjørn-Åge Flaten, born March 4, 1964, said that he had seen Kristiane Thorstensen at Skøyen exactly one week earlier. The document was not a separate witness interview in the Kristiane case, but a copy of the initial interview conducted after his arrest for the sale of fifty grams of hash and ten grams of amphetamine in an apartment in Tøyen.

Bjørn-Åge Flaten had been registered in late 1988 at an address in Rykkinn, but was also listed as a tenant in the old workers' quarters of Amalienborg in Skøyen. He said in the interview that he wanted his sentence reduced in exchange for supplying the police with information on Kristiane. Alternatively, as he expressed it, he wanted money, as he expected that Kristiane's family would soon promise a reward.

The only thing he appeared to have to offer was that he had seen Kristiane under the railroad bridge in Skøyen the Saturday she disappeared. When questioned about why he hadn't said anything about this before, Flaten replied that he wasn't in the habit of reading newspapers that often, and it was mostly crap on TV, as he put it.

Susanne Bech chewed on the end of her glasses for a moment. *This may be a simple error*, she thought. So simple and arrogant. And yet so difficult. The investigators had been sure that Kristiane had taken the train to Oslo Central Station, after which she probably took the subway to Haugerud, where Rask waited, according to the plan he had reportedly made with her. It just didn't add up that no one had seen her take the Furuset line out to Haugerud on Saturday evening, especially since it was one of the most heavily used stretches of public transit in Oslo.

She stared out the window at the snowstorm outside. She pictured Mathea at preschool, trudging through the deep snow in the pink snowsuit her mother had forced on her, even though Susanne had bought an almost identical one for Mathea earlier in the fall.

"Mathea?" her mother had said when she visited her at the hospital when her daughter was born. "Mathea? No, you don't mean that, my dear. That's not a name for our family, is it?"

"Mathea," Susanne whispered. Tears welled up in her eyes, which happened occasionally when she thought about her too much.

In her mind's eye, she saw herself open the gate, the last one to arrive at pickup—she was almost always the last. The snowsuit was gone. The door to the drying cabinet was open, but there was no snowsuit there either. The box with a change of clothes was empty. The daycare was empty. She pushed the thought away. That would never happen.

"Bjørn-Åge Flaten," she said out loud, tearing herself away from her own sick thoughts. She held the page out far in front of her, as though to convince herself that she wasn't farsighted and read just fine without glasses.

She put on her glasses again and read the whole document one more time.

There wasn't much substance in it. Bjørn-Åge, who went by Bønna, was a young boy from Bærum who'd started messing around with drugs. Not exactly a breakthrough. Or was it? *Did we just never take you seriously?*

There was no assessment of the credibility of the interview. Perhaps that was unnecessary. Like every other criminal, Flaten had tried to take advantage of someone else's misfortune. Regardless of whether or not that was the case, he was only looking out for himself.

"Bjørn-Åge Flaten," she wrote on a Post-it note.

She left her office before she could reconsider, and walked quickly to Bergmann's office. The door was half-open. She was on her way in when she heard him talking on the phone. The smell of smoke wafted toward her. Someone had to put a stop to that. She would have to bring it up with Reuter, who was the lead representative on all matters related to health and safety. But not until she got a permanent position.

"These are my principles, and if you don't like them, I have others."

Mother, she thought, *my cursed mother.*

It looked like he could be on the phone forever, and she had no intention of interrupting him. As always when men spoke on the phone, it sounded as if it were the most important call ever made.

Back in her office she looked up Bjørn-Åge Flaten in the trial registry, investigation registry, and informant registry. The man had done little other than spend time in and out of prison in the nineties for theft, robbery, and minor narcotics convictions. It appeared that he was no longer active as an informant. Susanne had a suspicion about why. His last known address—the terraced apartments in Sogneprest Munthe-Kaas Vei in Gjettum—was registered to Bjørg Flaten. His mother.

She called Bjørg Flaten in Bærum, but no one answered until the second attempt.

"I have no idea where he is," she said indifferently, as if her son were merely a transient tenant she'd taken in many years ago. "He's not here anyway."

"Do you know where he's living?"

Bjørg sighed heavily. When there was no reply, Susanne guessed that she was crying.

"It's that awful heroin. As long as he . . . we're respectable people. Even sold the house at Rykinn to save him." She had no more to say.

"I understand that it's difficult," said Susanne.

"You? You don't understand a thing."

Susanne remained silent.

"What did I do wrong? I've tried everything. His father, I don't know." She started crying again, then blew her nose loudly, twice.

Susanne closed her eyes.

I understand everything, she thought. *Absolutely everything.* But she didn't say so.

"If he contacts you, I need you to call me right away."

"So what has he done now?"

"Nothing. You must tell him that he's not suspected of anything at all."

"That place at Brobekk," said Bjørg. "They've called me from there a couple of times."

"Brobekkveien? The shelter?"

"They let him in, even if he's high."

After confirming that Bjørg Flaten had her name, along with all the phone numbers, to the switchboard, the office, and cell phone, Susanne pulled up a list of numbers for the shelters.

A tired voice answered at the Brobekkveien shelter.

"No," he said. "He's not here."

She looked at the clock, pulled out the pocket mirror from the new bag she'd bought but strictly speaking couldn't afford, freshened up her eyelashes, and took her Canada Goose jacket from the coat stand.

Someone must know if he's up there. She didn't even bother to ask Bergmann what he thought.

24

When a nurse opened the door to the therapy room, Arne Furuberget was reminded of the words he'd read that morning. He'd stayed up late reading the patient record chronologically. Though his body hadn't wanted to get up when the alarm clock rang at six o'clock this morning, he'd nonetheless gone straight to the office and continued reading.

What was it about this room that made him remember? The room itself? Or perhaps the few rays of sunshine that filtered through the almost impenetrable layer of clouds. Or perhaps the sight of Anders Rask standing with his back to him taking in the view of Mjøsa. His small fine hands that looked like they belonged to a child, like those of the girls he'd killed.

The girls he was *convicted* of having killed, Furuberget corrected himself.

"Leave us alone," Furuberget said. One of the nurses, a burly fellow from Raufoss, looked at him skeptically. The instructions were clear: none of the employees in the security ward were allowed to be alone with the patients, unless the medical director granted explicit permission.

Since Furuberget *was* the medical director, it was therefore up to him to decide if he wanted to be alone with the patients. When the door closed, however, he wasn't quite so sure of his decision on this particular day. Rask had never harmed a fly since he'd been confined in these sixteen thousand square feet of Ringvoll Psychiatric Hospital. Nonetheless Furuberget had recently developed a nagging worry where Rask was concerned. He imagined that a dark fury was building up behind his seemingly unflappable facade. The sort of fury that he'd once taken out on young girls.

But then who had killed the prostitute on Frognerveien?

The words from the patient record fluttered across his mind.

Edle Maria is alive.

He imagined how the conversation might go.

Edle Maria?

Yes, Edle Maria.

She's alive.

Rask stood motionless by the window, as if he were autistic and could not move until he'd registered every single movement outside the windows—the black birds rising from the snow-covered fields, a deer on the ice, the passage of every single cloud across the sky.

Furuberget sat down carefully in the chair he usually sat in. He glanced over at the couch where Rask usually sat. If he wanted to. Furuberget assured himself that he had the alarm on his belt. He brought his index finger over the button he would press if Rask attempted to act upon the threat he'd made last time.

Five minutes later, Rask still had not moved.

"What was it that made you threaten me last time?" Furuberget drew a face on his notepad, then crossed it out.

"I have never threatened you."

"You don't remember?"

Rask shook his head and turned slowly. Furuberget suddenly thought he looked more grotesque than he could recall ever having seen him. The medications had once made him overweight, but now he was thin again, with a child's face on a middle-aged man's body.

"Last time you said that I would die if I didn't get you moved to an open ward."

Rask's gaze remained distant.

"We're all going to die."

"But we won't all be killed, Anders. This is serious. I think you understand that."

Rask did not reply.

"You're ruining it for yourself."

Still no answer.

"Do you think a lot about death, Anders?"

Rask sat down on the couch across from Furuberget and scanned the room. Judging by his expression, it seemed he found the room as repellent as Furuberget himself did.

Without warning Rask stood up and took a step toward Furuberget. He chose to remain seated, but instinctively leaned back in the chair, so that he felt the wooden frame sharply beneath the upholstery. He caught himself breathing out in relief as Rask turned and went back to the window. He brought his hand up to the alarm on his belt and considered pressing the red button.

"Maria," said Rask from over by the window.

Furuberget noticed a faint trembling in his body. Goose bumps started to form on his scalp and around his temples. His mouth felt parched, and his lips parted slightly as he reached for the paper cup of water.

"Maria?"

"Why did you ask me about that name? Maria? And Edle Maria?" Rask had turned around. His gaze was serious, but his mouth held a hint of a sneer, as if he thought he'd caught Furuberget in some kind of lie. Furuberget was unable to conceal that he'd been taken by surprise and knew it all too well.

"Is Edle Maria alive, Anders?"

Furuberget's body shuddered, like the start of a fever. He might as well take the chance.

"Edle Maria . . ." Rask said to himself, dreamily, quietly, as if the memory was about to disappear. He turned back toward the window.

"Maybe we can come to an agreement," Furuberget said.

"Agreement? What kind of agreement?"

"You got a letter. Do you remember that letter?"

Rask laughed, a boyish laugh, as if he were innocence itself.

"I get a lot of letters, a lot more than you."

"Of course, Anders. Of course. If you give me that letter, I'll do what I can to get you transferred. But you can't keep on threatening me. If you do that again, it will be a long time before I can assess transferring you."

"Which letter?" said Rask in a low voice.

"You know which letter I mean."

Rask appeared in front of Furuberget before he even had time to think. Rask's plastic sandals were soundless on the tile floor. He was holding one hand behind his back. Furuberget knew that two wooden ladles had disappeared from the kitchen and a carpet knife from the workshop three weeks ago. The whole place had been turned upside down, but the items were never found. All the patients in the security ward had been stripped down naked to no avail.

Rask leaned over him, his mouth once again distorted into that unfathomable sneer. "You're going to die, you know that?"

He raised his arm slowly toward Furuberget's throat.

No knife.

"Because you intend to let me rot in here. You've probably thought about keeping me locked up here even if I'm acquitted."

Furuberget held his right hand on the alarm.

"Put down your arm. Show me what you have in the other hand."

"What are you afraid of, Furuberget? Dying?"

Rask smelled of cheap soap, and it nauseated him. Rask was holding his wrist, hard, as if he didn't want to let go before it cracked.

He pressed the button.

Rask took a step back.

"Your problem is that you're so pathetic."

By the time the nurses burst through the door, Rask was seated on the couch. Furuberget stared out into the room.

"I just brushed against the button by accident." He could not avoid inhaling sharply. "We're through. Take him to his room."

Down in the office he took off his suit coat and unbuttoned the cuffs on his left shirt sleeve. He tried to massage the circulation back into his wrist where Rask had gripped it. He felt feverish.

The file drawer opened with a sharp crack, and he tossed the old folder containing the patient record on his desk. The sound made him jump. Everything scared him now—the paintings on the wall, the thought that it would never be light again in this country, that Rask would find a way to take his life. And make it back out into the world to meet up with whoever it was he was corresponding with out there.

"Edle Maria is alive," he said aloud to himself. "You must understand that she is alive."

The patient checked for somatic disorders with EEG. Paranoid schizophrenia cannot be ruled out, but transitory nonschizophrenic paranoid psychosis is more probable.

Furuberget read his own notes from the printout. She had improved, and he thought sending her home would help her get better. He thought that the major trauma she had been subjected to had triggered a latent personality disturbance in her, the same one she had shown signs of previously, but that she could be attended to locally at the district psychiatric unit.

He browsed through the copies of her earliest patient records, dating back to her time at the Frensby and Sandberg hospitals back in the seventies. Furuberget himself had worked at Sandberg, but never treated her there.

He studied the pages closely.

June 1975. Patient keeps referring to a female person, Edle Maria, who seems traumatic to patient. Possible persecution paranoia. Schizophrenia less probable. Patient unwilling to talk about symptoms or own illness, reason for hospitalization, attempts at suicide, self-injury, lack of capacity to care for children, panic anxiety, increasing depression.

September 1975. Patient still has had no contact with family. Have not followed up on the person Edle Maria in the treatment. Patient has stopped referring to her. Over the summer patient has developed an apparently strong trust in one of the temporary nurses and seems far more functional than upon admission. Patient has resumed her interest in literature and film and has been accompanied to the cinema on several occasions.

Furuberget vaguely remembered reading the old patient records back then, fourteen or fifteen years ago. He himself had assessed schizophrenia, and more specifically what was previously called multiple personality disorder, but then rejected it. Perhaps because the whole matter had gotten so complicated, and the most important thing at the time was to treat her for the violent trauma she had been subjected to. But she had shown symptoms of dissociative identity disorder, he had to admit that. Her memory lapses were striking, and the way she distanced herself from the trauma, as if she was in a kind of hypnosis, was barely functional.

But that she could have several identities that fought over her personality? Could he really have overlooked something so basic? *Maybe,* he thought. Perhaps he had never really been open to that extreme possibility. He was aware that recent research showed that the dominant personality could actually move aside, even consciously, and that both personalities were aware of the other's existence.

Schizophrenia was a mirrored hall, for patient and caregiver alike.

Furuberget found himself in just such a mirrored room right now—wherever he turned, everything looked the same.

He held the old patient record from Sandberg Psychiatric Hospital between his fingers, carefully, as if it were a newborn baby.

The patient keeps referring to a person, Edle Maria.

But what could that mean fourteen years later?

Edle Maria is alive.

How?

And why did the poor Lithuanian girl say that name?

He had to find her. If it was the last thing he did on earth.

25

Bergmann already felt that things were slipping out of his grasp. Who did they think he was? Jesus? Miracles in a week, forget that. Susanne was still not done with the copies he was supposed to have. Kristiane's mother, Elisabeth Thorstensen, wouldn't talk to him; the father, Per-Erik, couldn't be reached.

All he could do was wait. He should have used Susanne for something else, but that had actually been the best he could think of just then. He needed order.

He opened the window and lit a cigarette. It was early afternoon, but already seemed like it was starting to get dark. He hadn't even noticed that it had started snowing. Again. The snow came blowing in through the open window. A copy of *Dagbladet* by the windowsill grew damp. Kristiane's face, which filled the right column on the front page, looked like it was covered with tears. He picked up the paper and turned to the two-page story. He read it slowly, as if that might give him the answer to whether Rask was guilty or not.

In the bottom right corner of the two-page spread was a facsimile of *Dagbladet* from Monday, November 28, 1988. It showed a black-and-white picture of a short, stocky man with his arms around two girls Kristiane's age. Bergmann remembered the picture now. It was the first time he had ever seen young people gather at the school of a friend who had been killed. Vetlandsåsen Middle School had been open on the evening of the Sunday they found Kristiane. He remembered it all now. Even remembered the man in the picture. He was the handball coach, wasn't he? Yes. What was his name again?

Bergmann tried to read the caption in the facsimile, but the print was so small that it was hopeless. He hurried down the corridor to Halgeir Sørvaag's office, holding the damp newspaper carefully, so that the wet pages wouldn't tear. Sørvaag was on the phone and did not look happy that Bergmann just burst in after a brief knock on the door.

"Your magnifying glass."

Both handheld magnifying glasses and magnifying lamps were part of Sørvaag's standard setup, which had earned him the unavoidable nickname Sherlock back in the day. Hardly any of the new graduates from the Police Academy knew who Sherlock was anymore, though.

Bergmann hurried to one end of the desk, where a large magnifying lamp was stationed. Sørvaag had paid for it himself. The whole thing bordered on autism—it was as if he hadn't registered that the police district had its own forensics unit—but Bergmann needed just such a device right now.

"Careful," said Sørvaag, putting the receiver to his ear again. "What about Frontrunner in the third?" he said to the person on the other end.

Damned gamblers, thought Bergmann. Spending all their free time at the track. Strictly speaking, police employees were no longer permitted to gamble away their salary, but Sørvaag and his buddies didn't give a damn. On the other hand gambling may not have been the worst thing to occupy their time. Occasionally, they even won.

He set the newspaper on the tabletop and lowered the spring-loaded arm that held the magnifying glass. The circular lamp below the glass blinked a couple of times. The faces in the facsimile from the 1988 edition of *Dagbladet* appeared in the diopter at twice their previous size.

"Damn," said Bergmann. The print was still too small for him to be able to read the names of the man and the two crying girls in the picture.

"Try this," he heard behind him. Sørvaag exhaled like a walrus, set the receiver down on the desk, and pushed off with the office chair. He held a smaller magnifying glass with mounted tweezers and a little lamp.

"Five times," Sørvaag said, and rolled back to the phone. "Frontrunner," he said into the receiver again. "Pure gold. The name says it all."

Finally, thought Bergmann. He let the powerful lens glide over the three faces, which were now dissolved into pixels of black, gray, and white. Then he brought the glass down to the caption: "Jon-Olav Farberg, a teacher at Vetlandsåsen Middle School, opened the school on Sunday. Here he is consoling Kristiane's friends, Marianne and Eva."

"Jon-Olav Farberg," he said quietly. He'd turned his face and appeared in profile, so it was hard to see what he looked like. But Bergmann remembered him now from handball. He'd never coached Bergmann's team, but he might have coached Kristiane's. And he was a teacher. He must have known Anders Rask, who taught there around the same time. That was as good a place to start as any.

Jon-Olav Farberg was easy to find on the Internet. He'd evidently given up teaching and was now part-owner of a consulting firm that specialized in recruiting, management, and human resources. The photograph on the company's website showed a man who looked younger than his almost sixty years.

Farberg answered his phone almost immediately. Bergmann studied his features on the computer screen. The voice on the other end was light, almost boyish.

"Many of us are hurting now," said Farberg, "from all these stories about Kristiane. It's like reliving it all over again."

"I understand that."

"I don't know what you stand to gain by talking with me, but by all means. Anything at all to help."

There was a pause. Bergmann thought that perhaps it had been hasty to call Farberg. Nevertheless, it might be worth driving over to his office.

"You knew Anders Rask, right?" he asked.

Farberg did not answer right away.

"Is that what this is about?"

"I can explain when I come out to see you. But yes, Rask has gotten the case reopened, and—"

Farberg sighed heavily.

"Sorry, I don't want to be negative. But being associated with Anders again—the way I, the way all of us were back then—it's, well, extremely unpleasant."

26

He was nearly incapable of leaving the office. Had the threat from Anders Rask rattled him that much? Arne Furuberget closed his eyes and rested his head against the back of his chair. Had he simply been doing this job too long? Committed the classic mistake of not realizing he was too old to handle its challenges anymore? Tomorrow a policeman from Oslo would come to talk to Rask. He barely remembered the name of the fellow who would be showing up here; all he could recall was the look on Rask's face when he took hold of his wrist. For the first time he saw how dangerous Rask really was. He had been at Ringvoll for almost eleven years, and never, not once, had he seen him like today. He was only a patient in the security ward because of the crimes he was convicted of. Nothing in his behavior pattern had ever suggested that he had any reason to be there. Until today. First the death threat yesterday. Today physical contact.

Furuberget chose not to think about it anymore. He'd had far worse patients than Rask, after all. *You can live a whole life in a state of repression,* he thought. Deep down, he knew that no, he had never had a worse patient. He was unable to read Rask, had never been able to.

Quickly, as if it was dangerous to remain in the office for even one more second, Furuberget sprang up from his chair. He rushed past the guard on the first floor without so much as a good-bye. Gusts of whirling snow blew toward him when he opened the heavy steel door. He walked slowly and reluctantly toward the gate and thought for the first time that the fences here in the open ward were too low. The fences at the back of the building—where the security ward was located—were fine, but here? It didn't look like much of a fence at all.

When he held his card up to the reader, his fingers grew instantly numb with cold. Once inside his car, he set the old patient record on the passenger seat. He started the engine, then studied the illuminated windowpanes of the security ward as he brushed the snow off the windshield. The light was on in Rask's window. Just as Furuberget was done brushing off the snow, a silhouette appeared in Rask's window.

This was what was almost supernatural about Rask—that he'd been lying in bed waiting for just this moment when the two dark figures could observe one another from a distance. *Who are you communicating with?* Furuberget wondered. He'd been through Rask's entire mail list, but hadn't found anything of interest.

But how could I have been so dumb that I tried to make a deal with him? Now Rask is going to destroy the letter. Furuberget would have to start all over. He knew that he had to continue to be alone with Rask in the therapy sessions. Rask would never say a word with others present. He could only thank his Creator that he would never be set free. Even if he were acquitted of Kristiane's murder, the five other murders would take time. If only the fools down at the police station had frozen the bastard's sperm.

"Damned fools," he said to himself.

He remained standing and listened to the even humming of the diesel engine while he held his gaze fixed on Rask's silhouette in the window. Rask raised his arm and waved slowly.

Furuberget was starting to feel cold and got into the car with barely controlled movements.

When he parked outside his garage ten minutes later, he realized he could hardly recall anything about the short drive home. He didn't remember having passed a single car as he drove through downtown Skreia, and he hadn't seen a soul out and about. Now everything was dark. Though there had been a last remnant of daylight when he left Ringvoll, it was now completely dark.

He turned off the ignition, and the engine died away. He looked toward the neighbors' house and saw that their outdoor light was on. They'd left on vacation today and wouldn't return until after Christmas. *Thank the Lord,* he thought. It would be like having the entire world to himself here at the end of the street. Only the peace and quiet of the nearby forest and fields. He had no desire to travel to Malaysia for Christmas, but what could he do?

He opened the car door and put his foot in the snow. Then he glanced at the house. It was completely dark. Not even the outdoor light by the steps was on. There was no light in any of the windows. After his wife retired, she always turned on the outdoor light at three o'clock. She wouldn't hear of having an automatic light.

He looked at his watch. It was already four.

She could be out for a walk. But no, she was always there when he came home. Dinner was at four thirty. It had been like that ever since the kids moved away from home.

He left the car door open and pressed the old patient record to his body. He briefly considered walking around the house, but changed his mind. Instead he walked as quietly as he could up the slippery iron steps.

He fumbled for a long time with the keys in his pocket. Then he turned around and looked at the tire tracks from his car. In half an hour they would be gone. Though he had shoveled early this morning, there was no evidence of his work left.

He went back down the steps and past the car. He got on his knees and tried to look for tire tracks from another car into and out of the garage.

It was useless, everything was snowed over again.

It had only begun to snow heavily after noon.

He went back to the house.

Carefully he turned the key in the cylinder lock.

It did not smell like dinner.

A foreign smell?

Maybe.

Someone was here, he thought. He clutched the patient record more tightly, as if he planned to defend himself with it. He remained standing on the entry porch and raised his hand to the light switch, but changed his mind.

"Gunn," he said quietly. An intruder would have heard him anyway. "Gunn!"

Without turning on the light he walked down the hallway. He went past the kitchen, not even hearing his own steps on the runner that covered the length of the floor.

He found her in the living room.

He dropped the patient record at the sight of her. For a couple of seconds his life flashed before his eyes—he was twenty-three again, it was summer, she was three months along and had never smiled so beautifully as that day on the church steps.

She lay on her back on the new couch, facing the ceiling.

He was unable to move his legs.

Suddenly, she sat up.

Furuberget staggered back. Struck his head on the wall.

"Are you home already?" she said dryly. She sighed and lay down again. "I think I'm starting to get sick. How long have I been asleep?"

He shook his head, unable to answer.

Tomorrow he had to tell the policeman everything.

He got two Paracetamol for her in the bathroom and hoped he could hide his frayed nerves. The face in the mirror was not his own.

"I'll fix some food for myself," he said. "Would you like anything?"

She shook her head and fell back asleep almost at once.

He sat there awhile holding her hand, then gathered the documents that had fallen on the floor when he walked in.

As he went into his office, he felt dizzy and there was ringing in his ears, as if he had a brain tumor he'd ignored for much too long. He guided his index finger over the few lines that appeared in the patient record from Sandberg, but did not understand a thing. Nothing other than that Edle Maria had something to do with the Lithuanian girl's murder. And that the news had not come as a surprise to Anders Rask.

He turned on the computer and double-checked the number. He pointed at the four words in the file: "Edle Maria is alive."

He considered calling Rune Flatanger at Kripo, since this was strictly speaking a police matter. But no, she had been his patient during that difficult period, so it would inevitably come out that he himself had done a poor job with her. Though his professional career was coming to an end, he nonetheless did not care to bring such disrepute on himself.

Besides, if he got the cops involved, that would set her back completely. As for Rask . . . He could almost swear that Rask knew something about this. He must be lured out of his hole, not hunted.

He picked up his phone and entered the number.

27

Some afternoons the stairs up to the top floor felt impossibly far. Mathea lay down twice, the first time right inside the entryway. Then on the landing on the third floor. Susanne Bech thought there was little other than uphill climbs in her life right now. The bus down from Vålerenga had been packed, and she couldn't count the number of times she'd cursed herself for not having applied to get Mathea into staff daycare. But it was out of the question to move Mathea now, when she was doing so well.

When she'd made it to the top floor and was waiting for the small feet in their lilac boots to take the last two steps, she couldn't help but realize there were some upsides to her life: she no longer had to clean up after Nico or endure his silence, his distant gaze, the accusations that it was her fault, that he no longer had the energy to have sex that often, that she made too many demands, and his never coming home before 9:00 a.m. after a night out. She had successfully avoided ending up like her mother—a prisoner serving a life sentence in a marriage that had gone stale twenty years ago, that was reminiscent of a carton of sour milk you couldn't bear to pour out in the sink because you were afraid of what was inside.

As she unlocked the door, she remained quite certain that she'd done the right thing. She was reduced to being a damned pack mule, but a pack mule that had done the right thing.

In her left hand she held a bag that was crammed full of all the documents she'd been able to stuff into it. Over her other arm she had a thin garbage bag with all of Mathea's wet clothes. In her right hand she had the takeout bag with their dinner. As she set it all down on the finished pine floor, some of the documents poured out. She glimpsed a few crime scene pictures, leaned down, and put them back in the bag again. She didn't want to know what Mathea would think if she saw them.

She didn't know what would be more productive right now: washing and drying her five-year-old's clothes, or spending the evening searching for a needle in a haystack. She hadn't even finished the job Bergmann had assigned her.

Instead of copying the rest of the material he wanted, she had gone up to the Brobekkveien shelter. It had been little more than pure impulse. She could have called, but she wanted to show up in person. For whatever reason, she thought that Bjørn-Åge Flaten would get paranoid and take off if he found out she was looking for him. Maybe she shouldn't have called his mother. But she had to have something to shove in Bergmann's face. She had to land a permanent job as an investigator; otherwise she would have no choice but to find something else to do.

"I'm so worn out," said Mathea, almost falling over the threshold. The red cap was barely hanging onto the top of her head, making her look like she had just come from Santa's elves' workshop.

"Children don't get worn out," said Susanne. "Only grown-ups talk like that."

"Then I guess I'm a grown-up," said Mathea. She sat on her knees and clearly had no plans to move for a while. "Because I *am* worn out."

She let Mathea sit right inside the front door, picked up the takeout bag off the floor, and placed the two Styrofoam containers of curried lamb from Punjab Tandoori on the kitchen counter. She poured herself a glass of red wine from the box on the counter and had already managed to drink half of it when she heard the sound of the TV from the living room.

The *My Little Pony* opening credits grew louder.

Damned little ponies, thought Susanne. Isn't that the sort of thing you make sausages out of? Nice black sausage we could have on a slice of bread? For a moment she thought about going down to Grønland Square and buying a few sausage slices with as high a content of horse as possible and putting it in Mathea's lunch sack tomorrow.

"Mommy!" she called from the living room, like a princess out of a fairy tale.

The kind that no one could silence. Susanne found herself counting the years until her daughter could move out. Fourteen, fifteen. Nineteen, that was the latest she would leave. If she hadn't begged to be an exchange student before then.

Never, she thought. *Over my dead body.*

"Bath," said Mathea without taking her eyes off the TV screen. "When you're worn out, you should take a bath."

Susanne walked over to the balcony door and opened it to observe the view. From her attic apartment on Mandalls Gate, she still had a view of the fjord, but it would soon be blocked by an impenetrable mass of futuristic apartment and office buildings. That fire that had devastated the Hollender block certainly came at an opportune time for people like her father—property investors, speculators, and vulture capitalists—she'd thought many a time. The fire had laid the groundwork for the building project that was playing out right before her eyes every day; it would take Oslo into the twenty-first century once and for all, transforming the city into something more like Dubai and Abu Dhabi than a capital in the sober-minded north. It was probably ultimately a good thing she wasn't one to cling tightly to the past. Most things hadn't been much better then. Nothing, when she thought about it. But the view—she would never get that back. The only consolation was that the cranes were adorned with strings of lights and a Christmas tree at the top. The light from the Christmas tree that perched above the post office swept by somewhere above her. It reminded her of Paris. She hadn't been there for years, and now she had no man to go there with. You didn't go to Paris without a man.

Svein, she thought and smiled.

In any event not the boy she'd brought home over the weekend.

She didn't want to think about that. It had been so long since she'd cracked. Six months, right before she met Svein.

That was probably what had scared her into sleeping with him. She had truly thought she was done with all that. But you couldn't fool yourself that easily. Part of her just wanted to go back, all the way down into the cellar, or all the way up in the sky, depending on how you looked at it.

She closed the balcony door.

"What did you and Daddy do over the weekend?"

No answer. Mathea braided the thick black hair she'd inherited from Nico and stared into the TV like something out of *Poltergeist.* And why did she really ask? She couldn't recall the last time she'd actually gotten an answer.

What had she done herself?

Don't think about that.

On the positive side, for once she hadn't taken any shifts at Kripo, as she'd done ever since Nico moved out. She couldn't bear any more of Monsen's smutty talk. She had long since given up arguing with him. And given up getting irritated at the way he quite obviously undressed her with his eyes.

She turned on the faucet in the bathtub and observed herself in the mirror. She was used to being very attractive, but she was going downhill fast. The past year had taken a hard toll on her face. She was only thirty-two, but already it seemed as though her mother was forcing her way out in her features; she could clearly see the outlines of wrinkles. *Botox,* she thought. A shot in the forehead at New Year's would save her from turning more and more into her mother. She would do whatever was necessary to avoid being like her, both inside and outside.

Her mother had simply cut her off when Nico moved out. They hadn't spoken since last February. Sometimes it was hard to believe. But Susanne Bech was not one to give in first; she never had been, and she never would be. "Imagine separating from a man like Nicolay" was the last thing her mother had said on the phone, hissing like a reptile. Susanne was the first to admit that she herself had used expressions that weren't fit to print, but cutting your own daughter out of your life? Now it was her father, or sometimes Nicolay, who picked up Mathea if she wanted an overnight with her grandparents. Her only connection to her past was her father. He was a weak and aloof real estate investor, but nevertheless strong enough to defy her mother. He wasn't a man who cut people off, at least not his own daughter.

The phone, thought Susanne. She really was a self-centered little girl, obsessed with how attractive she still was to men. How long had she been standing there looking at herself? The rushing sound of the faucet had eclipsed all other sound, even the idiotic ringtone on her phone.

"The phone, Mathea, have you seen Mommy's phone?" She looked around in the hall, unable to locate the sound; maybe she really was as dumb as her mother made her out to be.

"One moment," said Mathea, appearing by her side. She stood there in a shirt and green tights, her expression looking very grown-up as she held the phone up toward Susanne.

"It's nice to have a little helper," said the man on the other end.

"Who is this?" Susanne said more sharply than she intended. She hadn't looked at the number on the display.

"Don't you remember me from earlier today?"

Brobekkveien shelter. The man in reception. A middle-aged hippie— or outreach worker, as it was now called.

"Has he shown up? Flaten?"

"Bingo."

"I'm coming over," she said before she'd even given a thought to what she would do with Mathea.

"No, you're not."

Susanne said nothing.

"He's in no shape for that."

"In no *shape*?"

"If you come here now, he's not going to respond to a thing you say. His lips will be sealed, do you understand? He's sick, he really shouldn't be here."

"See about getting him admitted to a hospital."

"*I* decide that, not you. Come over here at eight o'clock tomorrow morning. That's going to be your best chance."

Then he simply hung up, as if she was just anyone. Susanne exhaled deeply a few times, then she realized that the guy probably knew what he was doing. His questions earlier today had suggested as much. Is he a suspect, under indictment? She couldn't even say that Flaten had status as a witness. The sixteen-year-old Kristiane case was not officially under investigation. Yet.

They ate in silence. Mathea browsed through an *Architectural Digest* magazine that Susanne had stuffed in her bag a few days ago. She didn't even know why she had bought it. Maybe she just wanted to see gigantic bungalows in California in midwinter. Even if they reminded her of her mother. Most things reminded her of her mother. Winter, Christmas, her reflection, her breasts, her voice.

In the bathroom she could no longer contain herself. She could have gone into the living room to read case documents, but feared that something dreadful might happen if she was gone too long. That Mathea would slip in the tub and strike her head and drown without a sound. Then her mother would be right; then she really would be a bad mother, one who didn't want the best for her child.

She retrieved the bag in the hall and sat down on the warm bathroom floor and started to read. Mathea wasn't paying any attention to her. She was mostly preoccupied with looking at herself in the mirror while she bathed; the rubber ducks she'd kept from when she was younger would have to manage on their own.

She's going to be just as vain as me.

Susanne started with Bjørn-Åge Flaten's witness interview. She didn't know how many times she'd read it, but seemed to think she might find something new every time. She made a note that she had to get hold of any old *Dagbladet* articles on him in the morning.

"Mommy, look now," said Mathea.

Susanne glanced up. She could see a glimpse of the baby her daughter had once been in the little body. Her belly, small hands, and upper arms were still a little chubby. She fixed her gaze on her daughter's chest, where Mathea had made tits of soap foam. Then she sank down into the tub, all the way under this time. She would often stay that way until Susanne couldn't stand it and pulled her up again, half-blue in the face. It had become a game between them, a game Mathea always won.

Susanne took another folder out of the bag.

Oh no, she thought. *Why did I bring this home with me?*

It was a plastic folder filled with 10x15 photographs of Kristiane Thorstensen.

The fifteen-year-old girl lay with her arms out on the autopsy table, her thick curly hair fanned out around the blue-spotted face. She looked like a savior who came in peace.

Susanne held her hand over her mouth.

"My dear girl. There's nothing left of you," she whispered to herself. "I hope your mother didn't see you like this."

The other pictures in the folder simply disappeared in a blur of gray—she suddenly realized she'd been crying for a while now.

She crawled across the bathroom tiles with the folder in hand. In the bedroom she collapsed on the unmade double bed.

She sat up on the edge with her hands covering her face, then heard a sound in front of her.

"Don't be sad," said Mathea.

Susanne still sat motionless with her hands over her face. She cursed herself for having brought new life into the world at all. How could anyone possibly think life had any meaning at all? And Nico, that fucking piece of shit. Why couldn't it just have worked out? She'd wanted it to work out—for the two of them to build a life together.

"Mommy?" Mathea started to cry. "I'm scared."

Susanne got down on her knees and opened her arms. The little heart was pounding at double its normal speed. She was warm and cold at the same time.

"Mommy will always take care of you. Always."

She managed to push away the image of Kristiane lying on a steel bench in the basement at Oslo University Hospital by chanting Bjørn-Åge Flaten's name to herself.

She pressed her child to her as if she never planned to let her go, her sweater drenched by her hair.

28

He puttered around Lilleaker awhile, cursing himself for ever even having the idea of coming out here. Bergmann didn't like this part of town; it was impersonal and cold, full of traffic, noise, and sleek office buildings. The patrol car he'd gotten a ride with to Oslo's western boundary had long since disappeared. He peered at the point where he'd last seen its taillights, feeling like a foreigner, an intruder, in this chaotic landscape of old and new buildings bordering the Lysaker River.

The December darkness had fallen quickly on the way out here, and he could hardly read the signs that were supposed to show the way to the various buildings in the old factory area. At least it had stopped snowing, suddenly, as if someone up there was having some fun by turning the button for snow off and on.

He oriented himself by the illuminated company logos on the ends of the buildings, each name more empty and meaningless than the last. Once this area had been home to real factories and workshops where people actually produced things, back in the day when people actually needed things in this country. Now the newly renovated buildings and newly erected glass palaces alongside them appeared to contain little but office cubicles where the employees sat like slaves in front of computer screens all day—if they didn't find themselves in endless meetings where they outdid each other in using the most complex words possible to package the moronically simple messages they were hired to sell.

Is this what we're living on in this country? he wondered. *Talk and empty words?*

What would happen if there were a crisis, a real crisis, like the atomic winter? Who will save us then?

At last he found the building where Farberg's company, MindWork, was housed. The lobby looked like a flood zone, the slush thick all the way over to the elevator. The second-floor office appeared deserted and abandoned, with only a handful of the company's fifteen employees at their desks. The secretary in reception seemed more preoccupied with hanging Christmas ornaments on a plastic tree than with Bergmann's appointment, and it took Farberg more than five minutes to come down and get him.

Not until he sank down into the visitor's chair in Jon-Olav Farberg's office did Bergmann understand that the man on the other side of the desk had been crying right before he came. His eyes looked red and raw, and his gaze was notably evasive. It appeared to require all his concentration to pour coffee into the cups.

Farberg was a head taller than Bergmann, but despite the fumbling introduction, he radiated a natural authority that made Bergmann feel like a schoolboy again.

Farberg looked down at his hands, letting the coffee cup sit untouched.

"Do you see I've been crying?" he said without looking at Bergmann. He didn't reply.

"It's all a little too much, all this," Farberg said in a low voice. "First the picture of myself in *Dagbladet* today. And now you sitting here in my office."

"I understand that."

"It all came back to me when I saw the picture of Marianne, Eva, and me," he said. "Do you understand? For a moment you let yourself think it couldn't possibly be true; then it all comes flooding back. I couldn't believe it when they found her."

Bergmann brought the cup to his lips. Farberg held his gaze, with a kind of sorrowful smile. Time had been kind to Farberg. He looked at least ten years younger than he was. His fashionable thick hair was becomingly bleached, his skin was lightly sun-kissed—perhaps from a week in the Mediterranean in the fall—and he looked fit under his coal-gray suit. Only the blue eyes appeared to belong to a man who was nearing sixty.

"You quit working at the school?"

"The summer after Kristiane was murdered. I just couldn't take it anymore. Besides, I'd had enough of work in schools. I got a job in the HR department at the old phone company. It suited me well, and that's the path I've been on ever since. I've been running the firm for almost ten years now. Can't say I regret it. I have assignments from your people too, from just a few days ago actually, leadership coaching, you know . . ." Farberg let the sentence die away. He seemed to be study-ing Bergmann's face, searching for something familiar. Bergmann knew what he was going to say. "I know you, don't I? I'm sure I've seen you somewhere before."

"Handball. Oppsal. Many years ago. I think you coached a younger team when I played on the junior team."

Farberg shook his head.

"I'll be damned. I knew I'd seen you before. But the name, no, I don't remember it. You're holding up well, I must say."

You're good at lying, thought Bergmann.

"You too."

Farberg laughed quietly.

"Did you attend Vetlandsåsen?"

Bergmann shook his head.

"I'm from Tveita. The projects."

"Exactly," said Farberg. "The ramp, that is. The original gangsters. Everyone was scared of you guys." He smiled to himself, not condescendingly, but in a friendly way. *It's true,* thought Bergmann. He couldn't even keep track of how many of his old friends had ended up on the skids or dead from overdoses. A few had been killed. He could just as easily have ended up on that side of the fence himself. Been dragged into the Tveita gang instead of getting involved in handball. Coincidence or predestination? He didn't want to know the answer even if he could have found it out.

"You were Kristiane's teacher?"

"Only in Norwegian and some substitute classes. Anders was, well, on sick leave a fair amount."

"And her handball coach?" said Bergmann.

"I took over the team at the end of the spring season in 1988. I was the one who convinced her to keep going. She could have been very, very good . . . yes, she could have gone as far as she wanted."

A silence fell between them. Farberg shook his head again.

"I remember you now. You were good, weren't you?"

"So-so," said Bergmann. "Good, but not good enough."

"But you came here to talk about Anders, not handball." Farberg changed his tone, taking his voice down a notch, so that it sounded darker, not at all like the boyish tone he'd used earlier in the conversation. It tormented him, this thing with Rask, even a child could have seen that.

"How well did you know him?"

"Fairly well. To be fair, he wasn't a person you could get close to easily. A few times he opened up. But he was a curiosity in the teachers' lounge, lacked social antennae. He was capable, though, in some ways very capable, and the kids were fond of him." He glanced down, realizing too late that the expression *fond of him* was inappropriate.

"Did you have suspicions?"

The phone rang almost inaudibly on the desk, and Farberg apologized before answering it. He closed his eyes while he listened to the person on the other end, a woman. *His wife or partner,* thought Bergmann. He let his gaze wander around the room. He thought the office was surprisingly messy for someone in private business. In contrast to how well-groomed Farberg was as a person, the office looked like it belonged to someone in a creative occupation, or perhaps an overworked attorney. Or a teacher, one of the popular ones, the type who got along well with the students and liked to appear at school graduations, had the power of words and made the mothers smile and perhaps think they wanted such a man instead of the boring fellow they were actually married to. Piles of papers were stacked on the desk, and the art on the walls had obviously been purchased by Farberg himself, as the styles were much too different to be part of a company's cohesive program for procurement of art and design.

"Let's talk about it later," said Farberg to the woman on the other end of the line. He hung up without saying good-bye.

"Have you ever been married?" He frowned at Bergmann.

"Live-in."

Farberg nodded.

"Then you know what I'm talking about. Or maybe not. We separated many years ago; she even got my apartment, very close to here, worth a fortune today. And half the money. All the same. There's always something you can be blamed for."

"You're remarried?"

Farberg nodded.

"Why did you take responsibility for the grief work?"

"You mean at the school?"

"Yes. I don't mean to offend you," said Bergmann in an attempt to seem disarming. "But you do understand why I ask? It's often the pyromaniac who's most eager to put out the fire."

Bergmann studied Farberg's expression. He appeared calm on the surface, and his eyes still had the same hint of sorrow. Either he was a good actor, or else he was simply not the type to let himself be drawn out by deliberate provocations.

Farberg nodded.

"The criminal always returns to the scene of the crime, the man who reports his wife missing and drowns himself in sorrow is almost always guilty," said Bergmann.

Still no noticeable reaction from Farberg. He nodded slightly again, his gaze fixed someplace on the desktop in front of him.

"You have a job to do, I understand that, your conclusions, your reality. In my reality, I wanted to help people—children, in this case—who were upset."

"So you opened the school and consoled the pupils out of the goodness of your heart?"

Farberg's palm pounded the table, and Bergmann jumped at the sudden sound.

"For Christ's sake, Bergmann!"

Farberg studied the palm of his hand, as if slamming the table had hurt far more than he thought it would.

"Is this the sort of thing you do now, waltz in and conduct yourself like a sack of shit? I don't have to put up with this." His voice was a little calmer now, but his mood still seemed to be a smoldering fire beneath the surface.

Bergmann leaned back in his chair and felt calmer from Farberg's reaction. There was every reason to suspect people who acted like saviors of the most outrageous actions. A person who showed his feelings was much preferred.

"So tell me again why you opened the school for a pupil who wasn't even one of your own. Why take such initiative?"

"Simply because no one else did it. The Sunday evening she was found, I called the rector. I needed someone to talk to, and she was a good personal friend of mine too. She was completely crushed, almost incapable of talking. So I called the superintendent, who was on a weekend trip to Copenhagen, and just ended up taking on the responsibility myself."

"What about her homeroom teacher?"

"He was a strange character. He'd always been cowardly, but never more so than then. I tried to convince him to take the lead, but he didn't want to, thought it wasn't a school matter. He didn't even show up that evening. It was just me and some of the younger teachers. The young ones always want to help."

Bergmann noted, *Homeroom teacher?*

"What's his name?"

"Gunnar Austbø. An old bachelor from Grenland. Conservative fellow, Christian guy, whom I suspected of being a little right-wing around the edges. Wore a suit, a bit of a character, but a good teacher, somewhat of a math genius. But not an emotional person. And damned conflict averse."

"Do you know where he is today? Do you think he's retired?"

Farberg thought for a while.

"I think he moved to Spain after he quit, but I'm not sure. I can check with some old colleagues, if you want."

"Please do. But back to Rask. Where were we?"

"Suspicions," said Farberg. "You asked whether I had any suspicions. The answer is no. Who can suspect someone of such things? He was eccentric, but I never thought he was capable of something like that."

"What do you think about the reopening of the case? Do you think he'll be acquitted?"

"What should I say? I don't have an opinion about it."

No, thought Bergmann. *Who can blame you for that?* He looked at his watch. He'd killed a little time and gotten a name in his notepad: Gunnar Austbø. Damned peculiar behavior when your student is killed.

"I wish I could be of more help, but there's not that much to say." Farberg placed the business card Bergmann had given him in his jacket pocket and stood up to follow him to the door.

They went down the corridor to the elevator together, where Farberg gave him the same firm handshake as before.

Bergmann tried to turn off his brain and concentrate on the view from the elevator. He could just glimpse the Lysaker fjord in the light from the neighborhood offices.

Dark had fallen. Again. The winter had rarely felt more burdensome than this year. Maybe it was age. Most likely it was Kristiane.

Out in the parking lot he lit a cigarette and took out his phone. He tried to orient himself. E18 hummed a hundred yards farther down; Lilleakerveien went up to the left. How in the hell was he supposed to reach Lysaker station without being run over in this endlessly dark city?

He'd only taken a few steps when he heard someone behind him say his name.

"Bergmann, Bergmann! Tommy!"

He stopped, but didn't turn around. The boyish voice was unmistakable.

Farberg came up beside him. Beads of sweat had formed on his temples. Maybe he'd run down the stairs. His expression had changed. He looked as if he'd just seen a ghost.

"Is something wrong?" said Bergmann.

Farberg wiped his forehead and nodded.

"Or no."

"Okay."

"I just thought of something. It struck me quite suddenly after you'd left. You've reopened the investigation of the Kristiane murder, right? To revisit whether Anders was innocent."

Bergmann didn't reply.

"Otherwise you wouldn't have come here."

Bergmann took a drag of his cigarette. That wasn't something he could admit to Farberg.

"In any event. I'm not sure that it's important, but—"

"But what?"

"Anders told me once about a friend he evidently talked to a good deal."

Bergmann frowned.

"And?"

"No, maybe it's nothing."

"What was the name of this friend?"

"Yngvar."

"I see. Where did Rask know Yngvar from? And what's his last name?"

"Well, I'm sure it's nothing. I don't know much more other than that his name was Yngvar."

"I'm sure you know more," said Bergmann. "Otherwise you wouldn't have come after me."

"Anders said once, many years ago, that Yngvar wasn't an altogether good person. He could get so angry, he said once. He was afraid of what he might do."

Yet another thing to check out when he received the tons of documents from Kripo. It was almost certainly a long shot, but in such a big investigation, vital details could theoretically have been missed.

"I got the impression that Anders and Yngvar had worked together before."

"At a school?"

"I assume so. He never told me that. I'm sure it's not that important, but I just had a bad gut feeling when you left."

"Okay, did you ever tell this to the police?"

"No. No one at school suspected Anders of anything. I was never questioned. And when I hear myself now, I realize it may not be relevant."

"No, maybe not."

Bergmann couldn't say much else. Farberg looked cold standing there without an overcoat. He buttoned his suit jacket with slightly trembling hands.

"It's gotten cold," he said.

It's been cold for weeks, thought Bergmann.

He followed Farberg with his eyes until he'd gone back into the building.

Ten minutes later the Ski train glided into Lysaker station and saved him from hypothermia. He found a vacant seat by the window. The violet cloth on the seatback in front of him had been shredded with a knife, and someone had written a name and a cell-phone number in black marker.

He stared at his reflection in the window.

Gunnar Austbø, he thought. Kristiane's homeroom teacher.

29

What god could have created such a world? Elisabeth Thorstensen asked herself. It was so full of evil, so contemptible and incomprehensible, that its very existence was proof there was no god. She'd known that since the age of nine, but the realization felt a little worse every time.

She had locked herself in the office after dinner and refused to come out, even though Asgeir asked her to several times.

In one movement she swept all the newspapers she had gathered off the desk. Kristiane's face mixed with that of Anders Rask. In one picture, he stood apathetically, his arms by his sides, looking like a shy boy in the forest somewhere in Vestfold.

A shiver passed through her body and a gap opened somewhere inside, as if she'd woken up from a nightmare and only seconds later understood that it wasn't a dream, but reality. The voices outside the door were loud, like the screeching of gulls on a summer day; then they began scraping their beaks against the gap between the door and the floor. The beaks came across the floor now, more and more of them, pecking at the bookshelves, all these books she had acquired, as if they could save her. They had once been her escape, had she forgotten that?

The beaks reached her temples, and she covered her head to keep from being struck. It would be so nice for the family there, not like down here. He would never lay a hand on her again. Never lie down beside her in bed. Never again force himself into her, as he had every night. When had she stopped calling him that name? Daddy? It sounded so foreign, like something from another country.

Everything would be fine, if only girls didn't turn out the way she had.

She jumped at a knock at the door.

"I've made tea for you." Asgeir's voice was gentle, as always. He'd always been kind, much too kind. All the things he'd pretended not to see? She wouldn't be alive today if it weren't for him.

"Just set it in the kitchen. I'll be out soon."

She could picture him out in the hall. First he'd offered her dinner, but she said she wasn't hungry. Then again, after he and Peter had dinner, coffee and dessert. Once again, no. "A cup of tea," she had said, automatically and distant, as if she were an unfeeling grandmother in a British film about upper-crust society.

He was surely standing there deliberating over what to say next, how to persuade her to come out.

But he chose to remain silent.

Finally his steps disappeared in the direction of the kitchen.

Elisabeth sat down in the chaos of newspapers and fumbled through them, as if she believed she might find Kristiane there, the girl's warm hand against her own. There was barely any membrane left between her and the final solution. Tonight, tonight she would do it, she had to do it.

She took the letter from the prosecutor's office and tore it into fine strips. Then she suddenly got up and pulled the curtains back and stared into the dark windowpane.

"Do you see that?" she said. "Do you see?" she screamed a moment later.

Only now did she hear the sound of the phone out in the hall.

Faint steps.

A muffled voice.

Finally the knocking on the door again.

She stood with her face toward the windowpane, the train slashing against her eyes, a row of lights through the hedge. What prevented her from butting her head through the window and simply bleeding to death?

"It's that policeman," said Asgeir. "Bergmann."

Elisabeth smiled faintly at her own reflection. She brought her hand up to her face and stroked her cheek.

"Bergmann," she said quietly. "You said you would save me."

"Did you say something?" said Asgeir on the other side of the door.

"Go away."

He waited.

"You said you would save me. Don't you remember that?"

"But—"

"Go away!" she screamed, so loud that it would be heard all the way into the train cars.

30

Bergmann took the trolley so rarely these days that he felt like a tourist in his own city. He studied a young foreign woman just to his left. She had a white hijab with embroidered silver stripes and was wearing as much makeup as a Western woman. She reminded him uncomfortably of Hadja, just like the prostitute a moment ago had. Occasionally a childish hope rose up in him before handball practice. He hadn't seen her for a year, since before Christmas last year when she was at a few of the matches.

You can't carry on like this, he thought, pressing the "Stop" button before Rosenhoff station. Tomorrow, at handball practice, he would chat with Sara, Hadja's daughter, and ask how things were going for them. Sounded simple enough.

From Rosenhoff he walked almost blindly up to Frank Krokhol's regular Indian restaurant. He stepped gingerly, he had to pee so bad. After taking the train into Oslo Central Station from Lysaker, he'd had two beers for the sheer hell of it at a nearby pub. Not to ruin the evening for the detectives who pretended to be drunk, but simply to observe the drunks, the whores, the pimps' errand boys, old junkies, and the whole hodgepodge of petty gangsters, all those who found themselves at the bottom of the criminal food chain, and who would stay there until they passed away. A Bulgarian whore who he guessed was in her late twenties, and who for some reason didn't realize he was a cop—or maybe didn't give a damn—sat down beside him, so close to him that he could feel her thigh against his, feel her sweet, heavy perfume in his nostrils. She asked if he was alone, and of course he was. Her dark eyes and curly coal-black hair made him think of Hadja. He'd briefly considered asking her to take a taxi up to Lambertseter tonight and stay there until tomorrow. There were worse ways to lose your job.

He'd left when she went to the restroom. He had placed three two-hundred kroner bills in a napkin, on which he'd scribbled, "You're too good for this," and gave it to the bartender, whom he recognized from the old days. "Make sure she gets it, and no one else," he'd said.

As soon as he came in the door of House of Punjab, he gave a signal to the waiter. The gesture for a half-liter beer was the same all over the globe, including at an Indian restaurant in Sinsen. A group of Indians, or more likely Pakistanis, turned toward the open door, but quickly turned back to the big flat screen on the wall behind the bar. They were as interested in him as he was interested in the cricket match on TV.

He made a beeline for the john in a way that made Frank Krokhol laugh like a teenage boy.

"To be honest, Tommy . . . now I'm really curious," said Krokhol when he was back. The old Marxist and chick magnet tore a pinch of Borkhum Riff out of the package, and meticulously filled his pipe. Bergmann studied his companion's careful movements while he mechanically lit his own cigarette. The advantage of an Indian place was that while the owner no doubt wanted to adopt the smoking ban introduced last summer, he would do so when he thought the time was right. Now—in the middle of what appeared to be an important cricket tournament—was evidently not a good time. The gathering of men-folk from the crown jewel of the British empire cheered in unison at something they saw on TV, and they didn't seem to care at all about the two Norwegian men who sat at the very back with their heads huddled together. Krokhol was smart enough to always meet police officers at places where not a soul knew who he was.

"So, what do you think this is about?" said Bergmann.

"Kristiane Thorstensen," said Krokhol while he peeked at the concise menu, which he probably already knew by heart. He tapped his pipe a couple of times, then fixed his gaze on Bergmann.

Bergmann shook his head and smiled faintly to himself. He let his gaze wander around the room, stopping on the TV screen, with its white-clothed men on green grass.

"Tell me about Anders Rask," he said without turning toward Krokhol. "The only interview he's ever given was with you."

Krokhol seemed preoccupied with his pipe. The aroma of the cognac-infused tobacco reminded Bergmann of his childhood best friend's father.

"Well, I never," said Krokhol.

"No leaks," said Bergmann. The rule was simple. During an ordinary investigation involving lots of officers, a leak would have been hard to trace back to him. In a situation like this, however, he was a sitting duck.

"Total radio silence?" said Krokhol.

"I'll give you what I can, but not now. You drive us hard enough as it is."

Krokhol smiled to himself.

"So. It's your job to dig into the Kristiane case?"

Bergmann nodded, then took a hearty swig of his beer, perfectly tapped with a cap of foam, so that the carbonation was well preserved lower down in the glass.

"I have an appointment up in Toten tomorrow."

"That should go pretty fast, I would guess. Well, Anders Rask . . . he's just a simple pedophile," said Krokhol. "A mama's boy with a fondness for little girls and girls with developing tits, as well as stark raving mad with a pathological need to be important . . . When your people started believing him in the interviews, it snowballed, and he started to think he was bigger than Satan himself . . . He was a welcome prey for the prosecutor, Schrøder. There was a hell of a stir back then, and he was the perfect murderer. Though theoretically thousands of men could have killed those girls, he fit the bill a little too well. It's no more complicated than that. Now he's at Ringvoll and gets buckets of fan mail from crazy women all over the country."

"What about the things that were found at his home?"

"He was a teacher to two of the girls, Bergmann. He brought little things home from school. He was obsessed with them. He didn't have any of the whores' belongings. Not Frida's either—because he'd never met them, plain and simple. Besides, I think the whores were too old for him. Almost twenty. Well, the one was sixteen, but by then they're almost fully grown. In the old days anyway. And the duct tape, who the hell doesn't have a roll of duct tape around?"

"Why do you have such strong feelings about him?" said Bergmann.

"One: because I think he's innocent, regardless of whether or not he's a pig and a sexual predator, and two: because the real killer is still running loose among us, assuming he's still alive."

Bergmann didn't say anything.

"And the worst thing," said Krokhol, "the worst thing is that the one who killed Kristiane probably killed all the others too. Don't you think he killed Daina, Bergmann? Why would you be so fucking reserved otherwise? Damn, I've seen the Rask documents a hundred times, but I can't write about it, you know that. I would bet my bottom dollar that Daina was subjected to the same thing. Did he chop off her finger too? What is that? The index finger on the right hand, that was probably where he started this time."

Bergmann's silence was revealing enough.

"Tell me about the Daina case," Krokhol whispered, trying to make eye contact with Bergmann.

Bergmann just shook his head.

"You're on the wrong track, Tommy. Don't tell me otherwise."

"If you write that, we're through with each other," said Bergmann. "How stupid do you think I am? And welcome back. I've been saying all this for years. Damn it, Rask barely managed to explain what happened. You've seen the recordings from Vestfold. He just stands there and points randomly, like any old fool. And the thing with the fingers, he guessed his way to that. Pure guesswork."

"You believe that?" said Bergmann, suddenly overcome with certainty that he had turned off the TV last night. He shook his head.

"Believe?" said Krokhol. "On my mother's and father's graves. There is one man and only one you're searching for, and that man is not Rask. There are too many similarities to be talk of multiple killers, and besides this is a small country, there simply aren't that many crimes here. And if you don't find him soon, he'll take yet another girl. Right now he's reading absolutely everything that's been written about Kristiane and Daina, and he'll eventually feel so much pressure that he won't be able to restrain himself from killing again."

So the paradox is, thought Bergmann as Krokhol laboriously got up to go to the can, *that if you hadn't written so damned much about Daina and Kristiane and blown up those pictures of them all over the newspaper, then maybe he wouldn't kill again.*

And I'll never get the chance to settle accounts.

"Do you think Rask has contact with anyone on the outside?" said Bergmann when Krokhol was back from the restroom.

Krokhol leaned back in his chair. He took hold of the pipe with his right hand and started poking out the tobacco with a matchstick.

"What do you mean?"

"Forget it."

"You think two people may have been involved in the murders, is that what you mean?"

"I said forget it."

Bergmann knew he'd gotten all he would get out of Krokhol. It was time to go.

When Bergmann got back to his office, he found his desk piled high with documents, arranged in a system with Post-it notes.

He spent the next half hour going systematically through the contents of the folders. He could see that Susanne wasn't done. But that was okay. Maybe she should go with him to see Anders Rask tomorrow.

31

"Mommy!" Susanne blinked a few times as Mathea turned over in her sleep next to her. But she had only imagined the scream. A nightmare again, but it didn't usually happen this early in the evening. Mathea woke up every single night these days, without exception.

Susanne looked at the luminous dial on the Tag Heuer watch she'd gotten from Nico as a gift the day after the wedding. It was already eight thirty. The skylight was covered with snow. Had it started snowing again? Or was it morning already?

She turned on the night lamp without caring whether Mathea might wake up. The clock face showed that it was still the same date as when she'd fallen asleep. For a moment she had no concept of time or space.

She turned off the light again and lay in bed thinking about Nico. About his face the first time she saw him. It wasn't dangerous to think about him. No one could know what she was thinking.

It was okay to have regrets.

And she'd rarely regretted what she'd done more than right now.

As she turned toward Mathea to curl up closer to her, images of Kristiane flashed across her mind. She looked at Mathea's thick black eyelashes. She would hardly need mascara when she was a teenager, but that just made it worse: men would look at her, desire her, abuse her, until she would someday have to identify her child, lying in a metal box at the morgue, in a white crepe dress with her arms folded across her chest.

She covered her face with her hands.

The sound of her phone ringing rescued her.

For the first time, it was comforting to hear Tommy Bergmann's voice. There was definitely something wrong with him, but she had never doubted that he was a man who both could and wanted to protect people. She knew she could call him if she was ever truly afraid of anything.

"We should probably keep each other informed of what we're up to," he said. "Besides, I'm going to Toten tomorrow."

Toten? She couldn't help but smile. Then she got serious.

"Anders Rask?" she asked.

"I'm going to see him tomorrow."

She considered asking him why she couldn't go along, but stopped herself. It was hard to escape the feeling that she had been put in the role of the old lady who stayed home and washed up while the men were out having fun. But there was nothing she could do to change that.

She saw herself in the mirror, went out in the living room, and lay down on the couch.

"I didn't get everything done today," she said.

"I saw that."

"I'll get to it tomorrow."

Bergmann didn't answer. *An old dominance technique,* thought Susanne. *But damn if it doesn't work.*

"I did something else this afternoon. I think maybe I'm on to something." She told him about how she'd gone out to Brobekk in search of an old witness.

"Oh?" He sounded surprised. She suddenly felt that she'd set herself up for failure.

"I'm sure it's nothing," she said.

"What are you on to?"

"It's just . . . Remember that there were two people who claimed they'd seen Kristiane the Saturday she disappeared?"

Bergmann did not answer right away.

Damn it all, she thought.

"Yes," he said at last. "I remember that. One of them was Bjørn-Åge Flaten. Bønna Flaten. I've driven that man to jail more times than I care to remember."

She twisted her hair together and let it out again.

"What about him?" said Bergmann. She knew what he was going to say. It had been in the notes, between the lines, all along. He was an unreliable witness who was after money. That was why they'd dropped him from the investigation.

Susanne didn't say anything. She had nothing to say.

"He was never anyone we could count on, Susanne. I knew perfectly well who he was in the old days."

When you and Bent worked patrol, she thought. She was so damned tired of the old stories. The old boys club. The response unit had been nothing more than a bunch of thugs. They beat up criminal immigrants and pushers without papers, wrote "resisted arrest" in the report, and all covered each other's asses.

"I just want to talk to him. He maintained that he saw Kristiane at Skøyen. Why would he say such a thing?"

"Junkies like him are pathological liars. He was just looking out for his own interests. Then he went to *Dagbladet* when we didn't believe him. He just wanted money. He probably got a thousand-kroner bill, but not a penny more. He retracted it all a week later. There was a hell of a stir in the papers, Susanne. It was before your time."

"Mommy!" she heard from the bedroom.

"Well, so I'm going up to see Rask tomorrow. Can't say that I'm looking forward to meeting him."

The hell you aren't, thought Susanne. *Damned men.*

"Why should Bjørn-Åge Flaten lie about seeing Kristiane?"

"Mommy, I peed on myself." Mathea now stood in the kitchen looking into the living room.

She'd simply forgotten to send her to the bathroom after she'd had several glasses of milk with supper. She hadn't started wetting the bed again. She hadn't. Not really.

"Give me a minute," she whispered to Mathea. "No fussing now." The feeling her mother had always tried to impress upon her overpowered her for a moment. She was a bad mother, that was all. A real shit mother. Not the kind of loving mother her sister, Line, surely would have been, if she'd just used a seatbelt and hadn't been killed in a car wreck by her boyfriend almost twenty years ago.

"Route 9," said Bergmann into her ear. "Does that ring any bells?"

"I'm from Asker," said Susanne.

"Route 9 went from Ljabru to Jar. It stopped at Sæter, and it stopped at Skøyen. Actually right by Amalienborg, where our friend Bønna lived at the time. If you were coming from the Nordstrand sports facility and going to Skøyen, wouldn't you just have taken the trolley? I don't think either of those two tricksters saw her, Susanne."

"She was seen at Nordstrand station. She took the train."

"Oh well, maybe she took the train then," said Bergmann. "But we won't get anywhere with this. The old man who saw her at Oslo Central Station is dead. I have no idea why she wouldn't simply have taken the trolley to town, and deep down I still think that's what she did. She could have been sitting with the hood of her college sweatshirt over her head. She could have been wearing a cap for all I know."

"No one wore a cap back then. It was social suicide," she said.

"Susanne," said Bergmann. "Listen . . ."

"But don't you see that this is crucial? Don't you get that?" She heard her own voice. It had risen, just as it had when she and Nicolay used to argue.

There was silence on the other end.

"Sorry. It's just been a bit much."

Why? Why did she apologize? It was so typical of her, raised as she was to excuse herself for the least little thing, especially to men. It was as if she wanted to say, *I'm really just a dumb little girl, sorry, sorry because I'm so dumb and lost control so fast.*

"Maybe she didn't *want* to be seen, Tommy. Maybe that was why she went to all the trouble of taking the train, because there were certainly far fewer people there. Maybe Kristiane was doing something she didn't want the other girls to know about, have you considered that? She was first out of the changing room. She didn't want a ride in the direction of Godlia. Maybe she didn't want to hang around in Sæter and wait for the trolley. No, she disappeared down the dark street and walked all the way down to the train. Because she knew that the train would take her straight to Skøyen."

Bergmann remained silent.

"Okay, I'll give you a chance."

"Thanks."

Maybe I ought to be your boss, thought Susanne. *Just as soon as I'm finished with that master's thesis.*

Bergmann hung up without another word.

Susanne remained standing with the phone against her ear.

"I'm cold," said Mathea behind her. "Mommy."

The child, she'd completely forgotten her child.

I'm cold too, thought Susanne. Her hands were actually shaking a little as she put down the phone. Maybe because she was a little afraid of Bergmann, when it came down to it. Maybe because she'd thought about Line, which was the last thing she wanted to think about. *Maybe because I'm just as miserable a mother as my own mother makes me out to be.* The child was shaking and already smelled of old pee.

I had everything. And threw it away.

After giving Mathea a shower, turning the mattress, changing the sheets, and putting her back to bed, she put on a song by the Motels, the one she almost never dared listen to, the one Line had always played when she had romantic troubles. She played it loud, so loud that Mathea could easily have woken up. Because nothing in this life would ever come back.

She folded her hands and prayed that Bjørn-Åge Flaten could save her.

32

The sound of knocking was unmistakable, though hard to pinpoint. He had tried to ignore it, but could no longer do so. It even drowned out his wife, who was loudly humming an old song in the bathroom. He listened to the sound of the shower water through the half-open door, a splash in the bathtub. Humming.

And once again the knocking.

From downstairs.

One, two, three times.

Then silence.

Either it was the pipes from the furnace, or else there was someone in the basement. A person who was rhythmically striking the pipes below. To lure him down there.

Arne Furuberget lowered the newspaper and fixed his gaze on the doorway out to the hall. The living room was dark apart from the reading lamp by the old Børge Mogensen armchair he was sitting in.

He took hold of the arm of the chair when the faint pounding sound came again.

He counted to himself.

One, two, three.

Exactly the same rhythm every time.

He sat frozen to the spot, incapable of moving. He studied his reflection in the dark living room window. Outside everything was black, but that was to be expected. Beyond the garden there was a field, and beyond the field there was only forest and more forest.

He closed his eyes when the knocking sounds resumed. He got up from the chair and closed the double-lined curtains. He walked quietly across the living room floor. He stopped in the hall and turned toward the bathroom, where Gunn was still humming the same melody. It was melancholy, he'd heard it many times before, but couldn't think of what it was called. It soothed him momentarily. Until the knocking sound came again.

He walked quickly to the entry porch and felt the front door.

Locked.

He exhaled.

Who was he trying to fool?

It was the basement door he was afraid of. The one that led out to the garden at the back of the house.

He turned and reluctantly walked back into the hall.

He stopped at the top of the stairs down to the basement. Everything was dark down there. For a few seconds Furuberget was paralyzed by the same fear he'd felt as a child, when his brother had locked him inside the pitch-dark storehouse.

He snorted to himself and went down the concrete steps.

When he was halfway, he had to hold onto the railing firmly.

The sounds were now right beside him. The pipes to the furnace were attached to the basement ceiling.

The knocking came again.

The pipes seemed to undulate over him; then the metallic sound disappeared.

He could see nothing. The basement was like a black sea below him. Straight ahead was the old bathroom the kids had used when they lived at home. They usually kept the light on in there, but now it was off.

He took the last steps two at a time, nearly tumbling to the floor as he did so. His breathing was heavy now. He hated to admit it, but he'd been scared of this basement ever since they were here for an open house almost thirty years ago. It was narrow and labyrinthine. And at the very back, behind the TV room they rarely used anymore, was the furnace room with the oil boiler he had never been able to understand. The only way out from there was back through the TV room, down the labyrinthine corridor, past the laundry room, which had a door out to the garden, and up the stairs to the first floor.

He found the light switch on the wall.

The fluorescent ceiling light blinked a couple of times.

He thought he saw someone in the laundry room. A face?

No.

"I'm not afraid of you," he said, going toward the laundry room.

It was empty and gray before him. The bare concrete walls and damp air made the room feel like a dungeon. Or an isolation ward. He would feel more confident now if he'd managed to get Rask back into isolation. But that wasn't an option. He didn't want to lose his job, even if he would soon retire.

At the end of the room was the door out to the garden. An old door without a deadbolt. Who needed that out here in the country?

He put his hand on the doorknob.

Just as he was about to check whether it was locked, he heard the knocking sounds somewhere behind him.

One, two, three.

Farther away now.

He knew where it came from. The fiendish black furnace room.

Goose bumps rose on his arms like on a freshly plucked chicken.

Someone must be in there.

"Damn," he said.

He pulled on the door.

It was locked.

Or was it? The old door was sluggish, he knew that. He took firm hold of the doorknob and leaned against the door with all his strength.

It was still locked.

But whoever was knocking on the pipes had gotten in here somehow. The door must have been open earlier in the day, while he was at work. Then the person had locked it behind him.

He took his phone out of his pocket and entered the number to Ringvoll.

"Yes?" said the nurse on duty.

"I dialed the wrong number" was all he said. He couldn't tell whether she believed him. He thought he'd managed to maintain a normal tone of voice.

No, he thought when the pipes started up again. *Now I'm going to get you, damn it.* He walked quickly back through the laundry room without locking the door behind him. The light in the TV room almost blinded him when he turned it on. He grabbed the poker beside the fireplace and almost ran toward the steel door at the end of the room.

Steps, he thought. *Steps.*

He turned around slowly.

"What are you doing?" said his wife. She had slippers on and her old bathrobe loosely tied around her waist.

There was the pounding in the pipes again. Furuberget gestured with his head.

"I'll call the service tomorrow. It's just the furnace, Arne."

He nodded.

She took a few steps toward him. He recoiled instinctively, as if he didn't trust that she was who she claimed to be.

"What's been going on?"

"Nothing."

He was about to say something, something reassuring, but the sound of the phone upstairs caused him to drop the poker.

"Edle Maria is alive," he said. "She's alive."

His wife shook her head.

The phone stopped ringing.

He frowned. He wanted to tell her, *Do not open the door for anyone until Christmas, not anyone,* but not a word came out of his mouth.

33

Bergmann was perfectly fine with the fact that he would probably never figure out Susanne Bech. He wasn't sure whether he would keep her on or not, given the chance.

"Son of a bitch," he said when the census registry's server returned his search on Gunnar Austbø. He was registered as having emigrated to Spain in 1998. *And I won't get any further than that,* thought Bergmann. For Austbø evidently had no family either. He was just an eccentric old bachelor who hadn't wanted to take care of Kristiane's friends that Sunday evening back in 1988.

He considered calling Jon-Olav Farberg to ask him to contact some of his old colleagues, who might know where in Spain Austbø was, but he quickly rejected that. Instead he jotted down a brief note summarizing the conversation he'd had with Farberg, and sent it to Susanne with a message about filing it with the case, if there was a new case, that is.

"Overview," he said to himself, "I need an overview." There was only one place to begin, and that was at the top of the last folder in the mountain of papers Susanne had put on his desk.

After reading for an hour or two, he copied the forensic psychiatrist's report from Anders Rask's trial. He put it in an envelope, which he placed in his outbox along with a note explaining that it should be sent by courier to Rune Flatanger in Kripo's profiling group. Inside the envelope he'd included a Post-it note with a message to Flatanger telling him to read the report as soon as possible. Bergmann had an ambivalent relationship with Flatanger, mostly because he felt that Flatanger read him like an open book. To be honest, he had never liked him. Actually he didn't like psychologists in general. But Rune Flatanger was the most capable one he'd worked with up there, and he needed all the help he could get.

When he got home, he stopped halfway up the steps to his apartment.

Sounds, he thought. *From below.* Sometimes his hearing was too good for his own sanity. Scratching, wasn't it? He went back down to the mailboxes by the entry door and then continued slowly down the basement stairs. He remained standing outside the door to the basement storage compartments for some time. When the entry door opened above him, he hid under the stairs. At first he wasn't able to hear whether the cautious steps above him were on their way down to the basement or headed upstairs.

Up, he thought.

When the sounds of the boots of the person on the stairs had died away, he took out his keys and unlocked the basement door. For a while he stood there, swaying on the threshold. Then he took a tentative step into the big, dark, damp-smelling room. The door closed heavily behind him, and the latch clicked. The stuffy, raw air surrounded him. He felt along the rough brick wall until he found the light switch. He waited.

Someone or something was breathing in there.

A pair of eyes, down by the floor, glistened in the weak glow from the streetlights that filtered through the narrow windows.

He pushed on the light switch and jumped slightly when a black-and-white cat meowed and squeezed into the corner by the farthest compartment. A flood of relief washed over him; unconsciously, he had been thinking it was something quite different than a cat. A moment later, he wondered whether he was losing his grip on reality.

He took a step toward the cat, which scurried in the opposite direction.

"Come here," he said in what he imagined was an inviting tone. He crouched down slowly and reached his arm out toward the cat. "Come on," he said. "You can't be down here all night."

Suddenly, the door behind him was pulled open.

He lost his balance as he tried to get up, and his knee struck the concrete floor. He rose in one movement and spun around.

Whoever had opened the door had still not entered the basement.

His breaths grew uncontrollably rapid and shallow. One thought passed through his head: he *had* turned off the TV before falling asleep last night. He glanced around the room. Right below one window was a snow shovel and a sharp folding spade. With a few steps he would be able to reach the spade.

The person reached around the door frame.

"Oh, it's you?"

Bergmann exhaled heavily. *Good Lord,* he thought. *This can't go on.*

The old woman who lived on the fourth floor—what was her name again? Ingebrigtsen—stepped into the room.

"I'm starting to go batty," she said, shaking her head. The cat bounded over to her and rubbed up against her legs.

"So you got yourself a cat? That's nice."

"Oh yes," she said. "Ever since Trygve died, there aren't as many people to talk to."

He remembered the night the ambulance had come to get her husband.

Mrs. Ingebrigtsen sighed.

"I think I forgot him down here," she said, more to herself than to Bergmann.

"I heard him, and—"

"It's comforting to have a policeman in the building," she said, and smiled weakly. "At least I think so."

"It's nice that you think so."

"But it's too bad it doesn't do us much good down here."

He held her gaze.

"What do you mean?"

She nodded at a spot behind him.

He turned around.

She went past him with the cat in her arms.

"That's your compartment, isn't it?" she asked.

He followed her, almost reluctantly.

The padlock was cut off.

He closed his eyes.

"It was simpler when we just had coal down here," she said quietly. "And people understood the difference between mine and yours."

As he walked up to his apartment, he told himself that these were just coincidences. Someone had just been rooting around in there, even though there was little of interest, mostly empty fruit boxes and old clothes, some schoolbooks he didn't know why he'd kept, and some textbooks from his Police Academy days. *It's just coincidence, nothing else.* One of the sons of a single mother on the third floor was a junkie; it was surely him or one of his buddies with a key who'd broken in. They were dumb enough to try a break-in in their own building, even dumb enough to break into a compartment they knew belonged to a policeman, because that was the only one they hadn't broken into before. He would have a stern talk with the boy next time he saw him hanging around here.

Nonetheless, even though he'd managed to convince himself that these were all coincidences, he had a look around his apartment before he went to bed. He opened all the cupboards and drawers, looked over the bookshelves, studied the photographs, even took a look in the refrigerator.

He opened the refrigerator door slowly, as though expecting to find something repulsive in there. *Idiot,* he thought at the sight of old sandwich fixings and a milk carton he should have emptied and thrown out long ago.

But the feeling didn't go away.

Something was wrong.

Something in the apartment was different, but what was it?

After an hour of lying in bed with his eyes wide open, he got up and rooted around in the medicine cabinet. At last he found a box of valium that Hege had left behind. He took a tablet without checking the expiration date on the box and rinsed it down with water from the tap. The alcohol was probably out of his body now. Mixing benzodiazepines and alcohol was the last thing he wanted to do.

Maybe he would wake up in time to drive up to Toten tomorrow. Maybe not.

He didn't know if a meeting with Anders Rask was what he needed now.

34

Ringvoll might look like an idyllic place, if you overlooked the property's fence, which resembled that of a concentration camp. The snow-covered fields outside the fence sloped gently down toward Mjøsa, and the sky was reflected in the ice on the lake. The facility's entrance, however, could have been taken straight from Treblinka. Bergmann rang the doorbell and pulled the collar of his jacket all the way up. The valium tablet from the night before should be out of his bloodstream in just a few hours. Although the sluggish, confused perception of reality that came with benzodiazepines always depressed him—and he would soon be standing face-to-face with Anders Rask—he felt lighter in spirit for a moment.

He stopped on the gravel path that led to the main building. The rope struck against the nearby flagpole—as if this was a place to fly the flag. Beside the long yellow main building were two lower buildings more recently built, with glass tunnels that connected them with the main building.

It wouldn't be impossible to escape from here, he thought, ringing yet another doorbell. He turned around on the broad granite steps. The fence was of sturdy mesh, but not insurmountable. If you just had a good pair of wire cutters and a car on the outside, it could theoretically be done. The fence was hardly electrified. But maybe there was another reason that those who were confined here didn't need higher security. They probably had enough to do maintaining order in their own heads without hatching an escape plan too. And where would they get wire cutters?

He showed his police ID to the Securitas man, who sat safely protected behind thick Plexiglas in the guardhouse. He slipped Bergmann a sticker with the letter *B* on it through the transaction drawer. While he waited to be picked up, he went through some of the questions he intended to ask Rask, but was still unsure how to approach the matter at hand. Frankly, he was also somewhat unsure why he was even here. But what else could he do? He had six days to present something concrete to Finneland.

A sturdy young man with a mild but direct gaze and firm handshake came to pick him up. *Solid,* thought Bergmann. But his first question destroyed the positive impression.

"Are you the one who's here to talk to Anders?"

Anders, he thought. That sounded too familiar, as if Anders Rask was a person on the same level with everyone else. Bergmann tried to ignore the fact that Rask had killed the six girls. He had to try to see the whole thing from a different angle, like Frank Krokhol. An abuser, but not a killer.

He was shown into a large office adjacent to the nurses' station that had a magnificent view of the country's biggest freshwater lake. Bergmann barely registered the door plaque: "Consultant Physician Arne Furuberget."

The man who received him waved lightly toward the nurse, as if he wanted him out as quickly as possible. Bergmann was surprised when he realized that the man before him was actually Furuberget himself. Yesterday on the phone he'd imagined someone younger, perhaps around his own age, but he turned out to be a great deal older than that. The office décor also suggested that Furuberget was a man from another era. The old hardwood desk and large naturalistic paintings would have been more appropriate back in the late nineteenth century. He even had an inkwell on the desk, two pen points, and a stack of thick stationery on the dark-leather blotter. Only a slender computer screen broke the impression that he'd stumbled into the Victorian era.

Furuberget gestured toward a leather sofa, though he himself remained standing. Bergmann imagined that this was deliberate. Furuberget placed himself in front of the window; the sunlight meant that Bergmann could see little other than his silhouette.

"I think he's going to be acquitted for the murder of Kristiane Thorstensen," Bergmann began, getting right down to business. "That means that the killer is still running loose. If Anders Rask is not wrongly acquitted, that is. If he's acquitted of all the murders, you have a very unpleasant case on your hands. He who is forewarned, is also fore-armed, wasn't that what the Romans said back in the day?"

No response from Furuberget.

"I understand that you've spoken with Rune Flatanger about the Daina murder?" Bergmann asked.

Furuberget nodded and assumed a serious expression.

"Then I'm sure you understand why I'm here."

"I won't take a position on the question of guilt until there is a new judgment. Police work is not my domain." Furuberget averted his gaze and observed his hands.

"How many visitors does he have?" said Bergmann.

"None to speak of. He doesn't want anything to do with his family. They don't want anything to do with him."

"But he has had other visitors?"

"The first year."

"Who were they?"

"I don't remember."

"If he hasn't had any visitors since then, you probably remember who it was?"

"Bergmann, I have thirty patients on the security ward and fifty on the open ward. This is factory work. I can't remember such things, I'm sorry."

"Visitor lists?"

Furuberget shook his head.

"That's not the sort of thing we keep."

"But it must be in his patient record who visited him?"

Furuberget exhaled heavily.

"I'll see what I can find out."

There was a pause. Furuberget went to his desk, picked up a cloth, and started cleaning his glasses.

"What—" Bergmann began.

"It's good you came alone, as I asked you to. Rask gets easily destabilized in situations where he feels pressured. The majority of those with psychoses do."

"So he's still psychotic?"

Furuberget did not answer the question.

"What do you mean? Is he just as sick as when he was convicted?"

Furuberget studied the lenses of his glasses carefully. Apparently satisfied he put them back on.

"More or less equally sick or equally healthy, depending on how you look at it. At times he can appear sparklingly lucid and healthier than you or me. Just between us: the problem is that it may be all an act. He is actually capable of suppressing what we might call his other self for long periods and function well, even socially, during those times. He is also extremely intelligent. But unfortunately the Devil himself may rest just beneath the surface. A science that attempts to capture the human mind will never be exact, Bergmann, it is too labyrinthine for that. I can safely say that Rask's head greatly resembles the labyrinth on Knossos. Who knows if there is any way out? Do you understand?"

Bergmann frowned.

"Once you've worked your way into that type of madness, it's impossible to get out again."

"So he'll never be released, even if he's acquitted of all the murders?"

Furuberget looked at him seriously, then broke into a little smile.

"Not as long as I'm the decision-maker here. But my power is limited. If he's acquitted of all the murders, it will be difficult, maybe impossible, to keep him here on the ward. Besides, I'm retiring soon. Perhaps others will assess Anders differently."

The nurse came back in.

"Then you're ready?" said Furuberget.

The nurse nodded.

Bergmann stood up.

"You're not coming with?"

Furuberget shook his head with a half-resigned smile.

"I'm afraid it will only seem provoking to him. You might say I'm not a favorite of his. On the other hand, he'll probably appreciate you."

"Really?"

"I've seldom seen him so exhilarated as yesterday. Perhaps he sees this as his big chance, what do I know?"

Bergmann stopped on his way out the door to the corridor.

"What if he did it anyway? Didn't you say that he can appear healthy for long periods?"

"If he pulls himself together in court every single time and the evidence is as paltry as it once was, then he'll be acquitted of all the murders. If, as you ask, he did it anyway, well, then he's obviously going to kill again once he's let out. It'll only be a question of time."

Bergmann exhaled heavily out his nose, making him sound more resigned than he was.

"But don't worry about that," said Furuberget. "Anders Rask will be inside these walls until he dies."

Let's hope so, thought Bergmann.

"What do you think? Did he do it?"

"Fortunately it's not my job to determine that."

Bergmann took his hand.

"No, then I guess you'd be in my shoes."

Furuberget let out a quiet, boyish laugh.

"Thanks for the chat, and please keep me posted. I have meetings the rest of the day, but call me, Bergmann, tomorrow perhaps?"

Furuberget remained standing in a strange position. He held his right arm up, his index finger halfway up in the air, like an old schoolmaster who had a thought on the tip of his tongue.

"Is there anything else I need to know?" said Bergmann.

Furuberget lowered his arm and shook his head.

35

Bergmann followed the nurse through a passage with double doors, which made him dismiss any thoughts of escape. On their way down the first-floor corridor, they passed through two more zones with locked steel doors. First access card with code, then keys. The nurse carried a walkie-talkie, and a pager and a small leather bag on his belt. Bergmann guessed it contained a set of straps.

When they arrived at the end of the corridor, they passed a patient accompanied by two nurses. As Bergmann met the patient's gaze, goose bumps formed on his arms and along his hairline. There was something strangely familiar about the wildly wavering gaze.

A modern-looking grate covered the window on the far wall. Bergmann took hold of the metal bars and tried to concentrate on the view of Mjøsa. A series of images flashed before his eyes: a man lying on the floor in a corridor like this, in a fetal position, screaming, like an animal, a wounded animal, white clogs clattering, a cup falling to the floor. He himself alone, abandoned.

He turned and watched the patient and the two nurses. They had stopped a little farther down the corridor; something seemed to be bothering the patient, who was now rocking back and forth on the bottle-green linoleum floor.

Impossible, he thought, observing the confused patient. A muffled scream came from one of the patient rooms.

He closed his eyes.

The images became clearer.

Fragments of another dialect, that cup falling to the floor—he remembered it now. The design on the cup, the coffee spilling across the floor, splashing on his thigh, his mother's relaxed dialect, the northern accent she was never able to drop entirely, which emerged whenever she was really angry. A man lying on a floor like this, in a corridor like this.

When he opened his eyes, the patient and the two nurses had left. They must have gone through the doors to the next zone in the ward.

"Are you coming?" said the nurse who was accompanying him. He stood on the landing up to the second floor with an inquisitive look on his face.

Bergmann nodded.

"So he's not in isolation?" he said.

"No, Anders has a room on the second floor," the nurse said.

Then a loud scream was heard from the first floor. The sound of a door being opened. The scream carried up the stairwell, its echo amplified by the brick walls.

The nurse's walkie-talkie crackled, and the pager on his belt beeped. He stopped entering the code on the door to the second floor and disappeared down the stairs.

"I'll be back," he called out over the sound of the bestial screams.

The screams were draining Bergmann of the last of his energy. He had a memory of a hand stroking his cheek. Soft, warm, a woman's? Or a man's? He didn't remember. Only the words: "Everything will be fine, my dear. Everything will be fine."

He went back down the stairs to the window on the first floor. He took hold of the metal grate in front of the window once again, let his gaze follow the snow-covered earth down toward Mjøsa.

The question was clear: *Have I been here before?*

36

He was shown into a visitor's room on the second floor. The room was on the west side of the building and had a view of a forested area that rose evenly up the hillside. The memories that had flashed across his mind's eye had faded. He was close to telling himself that it was only a dream, a few scattered glass shards of a fantasy that came out of nowhere.

Apart from the grate in front of the windows, the camera affixed to the ceiling, and the signal bell by the door, the room mostly reminded him of an old teachers' lounge. The pine furniture was covered in rough orange fabric, and woodcuts in soft colors in simple white wood frames hung on the pale-green walls. Bergmann imagined that the patients had made the pictures. He touched the glass on one picture as if to assure himself that it was unbreakable Plexiglas. The picture was rather skillfully executed, with grazing horses in a summer meadow and a stoop-shouldered man leaning over a hay-drying rack.

He could just make out the signature: *A. R.*

The door beside him opened.

The same inscrutable sneer.

The man stood motionless in the doorway. It looked as though the sight of Bergmann reminded him of something. Though his gaze was vacant, his mouth showed a sign of life.

Two nurses followed him closely, the one who had first accompanied him and a tall, ungainly fellow. It seemed unnecessary based on Rask's appearance. He hardly looked capable of defending himself if he were attacked. Besides, he had never been violent to anyone other than defenseless girls. On the other hand the violence he was convicted of was so inhumanly brutal that if Bergmann were the head of this hospital, he would never have left Rask alone with anyone.

Anders Rask looked far older than Bergmann remembered from the documentary and the pictures in the newspaper. The years up here had evidently taken their toll. Even his strikingly feminine facial features appeared to have faded after almost eleven years in the ward. He was dressed in an old wool sweater with harlequin patterns across the chest, a pair of worn corduroy pants, and a pair of bright-red Crocs on his feet, no socks. Bergmann tried to imagine Rask as the man he'd once been, a man who had easily gotten the girls at the school to admire him, getting the most impressionable of them to fall in love with him and the most daring to visit him at home, a man so shrewd that he didn't lay a hand on any girls other than those he knew with 100 percent certainty that he could control. Apart from the one girl at Bryn School who dared go to her mother and reveal what Rask was really up to at his place. Or in the cabin at Magnor. The mere thought that he had convinced an eleven- or twelve-year-old girl to go out there with him was enough to make Bergmann think that Rask deserved to rot in a place like this. He did not even want to think about what he would have been capable of doing to Rask if he'd had the chance.

"So do you like the picture?" said Rask, keeping his gaze fixed on a point outside the window. Something up in the forest-clad hillside seemed to occupy all his attention.

"You're a lot more talented than I am, that's for sure," said Bergmann, letting his finger follow some of the lines in the woodcut. "I've only tried linoleum and potato cuts."

Rask let out a strange, snickering laugh.

A middle-aged man in a suit with no tie came limping up to the doorway. He introduced himself as the attorney Gundersen, a trust-worthy-sounding name, from the law firm of Gjøvik, Gundersen, Harboe & Co. So it was this provincial firm that had managed what was assumed to be impossible—what the law firms in Oslo hadn't been capable of: getting Anders Rask's case reopened. Or perhaps more correctly, gaining Anders Rask's trust so they could reopen the case.

Bergmann moved toward the chairs in front of them, as if he was hosting the meeting. Rask sat down without bothering to shake Bergmann's hand. Bergmann was relieved. Something in him resisted the idea; he would prefer not to feel Anders Rask's long, delicate fingers against his own skin.

"This isn't an interrogation, is it?"

Rask raised a trembling hand to his greasy gray hair.

"No," said Bergmann, sitting down across from him. He exchanged a quick glance with the two nurses, who had assumed their positions along the wall. Gundersen cleared his throat, but remained silent as he sat down.

"I'll be honest with you, I've been asked to look into the Kristiane case. I won't ask you any questions about the other killings you're con-victed of, or the assaults. Only Kristiane."

Rask got that sneer around his mouth again. His gaze, which Bergmann believed was affected by the medication he took, grew vacant again.

"Why did you ever admit to a murder that you now maintain you didn't commit?"

Rask looked as if he didn't understand the question.

"I cried the day they found her," he said.

Lies, thought Bergmann. *Damned lies.* He could have told Rask that he was one of the people who found her, but he didn't want to give Rask anything for free.

"Do you know who killed her? Was that why you confessed?" Bergmann leaned forward in his chair.

Something in Rask's face changed. He blinked a few times, and his head rocked a little from side to side, as if the questions were unpleasant to him.

"So," said the attorney. "You said this wasn't an interrogation, Bergmann, isn't that so?"

"Or did you want to be famous, read about yourself in the newspaper?"

"I think that—" began Gundersen.

"Let him answer," said Bergmann.

The man before him—Norway's most despised man—looked like nothing more than a worn-out boy as he sat squirming in his chair.

The room became quiet. The five men waited in silence for about thirty seconds.

"Has he read about the murder that happened a few weeks ago?" Bergmann asked, turning to Gundersen.

"Yes," Rask replied.

"Where?"

"In the newspaper."

"Who do you think did it?"

Rask appeared to disappear into his thoughts again, incapable of orienting himself in the reality outside his head.

"You were Kristiane's teacher?" said Bergmann.

Rask nodded and smiled, once again with that slight sneer. The smile seemed misplaced to Bergmann. In fact, his gaze, hands, mouth, and feet all seemed to have a life of their own; Rask's various parts didn't seem to fit together into a greater whole.

"In which—"

"French and English, a little arts and crafts. I guess I had her in PE too. And crafts. Did I say that?" He nodded at the wall, the woodcut.

"What did you think of her at school?"

Yet another long pause ensued.

"You don't have to answer," said Gundersen.

"Haven't you ever done anything crazy yourself, Tommy? I see it in you. You did something crazy, something really crazy one time." Rask's voice was low, barely audible. "And Tommy. What kind of name is that? And why aren't you taking notes? I don't talk to just anyone . . . Tommy."

This time it was Bergmann's turn to respond with silence.

"Anders," said Gundersen. Then, turning to Bergmann: "I don't know if this was such a good idea."

"No," said Rask, apparently more to himself than to anyone else in the room. "This wasn't such a good idea."

Bergmann nodded. He remembered his thoughts from earlier. What was it he'd seen? Himself?

He felt a cold hand on his own. Rask had leaned over the table. One of the nurses stepped forward.

"It's okay," said Bergmann. He met Anders Rask's gaze. Looking at him now, it was obvious that Rask was heavily medicated. How many diagnoses he had was hard to say; it was at the very least a good cocktail of personality disorders.

"Remove your hand," Bergmann said calmly.

When Rask pulled back his hand, he seemed to collapse.

"He's worn out," said the nurse.

"We can stop." Rask seemed lost to this world. Bergmann looked at the clock. He had plenty of time to make it to handball practice, would even have time to drop by the office for an hour or two. *Handball,* he thought. Maybe that was why he felt doubly connected to Kristiane Thorstensen. It wasn't just that he'd been involved in finding her; she'd also been one of the city's biggest handball talents in her age group. In the fall of 1988 she had transferred from her local Oppsal club to Nordstrand to get higher quality coaching. According to Jon-Olav Farberg he was the one who had encouraged the change of clubs. She had played her final matches at the Nordstrand sports facility on the last evening she was seen alive.

"Yes, let's stop," said Gundersen, getting up.

"Just one last question," said Bergmann. He tried to catch Rask's gaze. "Who was it that visited you the first year you were here?"

Rask only stared vacantly out into the room.

Gundersen cleared his throat. Then he shook Bergmann's hand hard, as if to indicate his gratitude that the Oslo police was taking the reopening of the case seriously. He seemed to want it understood that Rask may have suffered from a transitional mental illness, that he had a sick need to stand out as important.

"Thank you," said Bergmann. "But I think you know more than you're telling me, Anders. Because you're an important person, right?"

He turned toward Rask, but the man just sat as if frozen, holding onto the arms of the chair, and appeared to long for the black forest on the other side of the barbed-wire fence.

"If there's anything we can do . . ." said Gundersen.

Bergmann walked out into the corridor. He was once again seized by the feeling that he'd been here before.

"Tommy!"

Rask's voice resounded from the visitor's room and echoed down the corridor, until it fell silent against the locked door to the next ward zone. There was something desperate in his voice; it was nearly cracking with despair.

Attorney Gundersen shook his head lightly.

"He's . . . worn out." It seemed as if he had run out of things to say about him.

The tall, ungainly nurse appeared in the doorway with Rask by his side.

"You came here to get help," said Rask. His voice had a pompous strain.

"Maybe."

"Let's go over here." Rask nodded toward the window on the far wall. "It's so dark in there. I don't like that side, I've tried to get a room facing Mjøsa for years, but it's never happened. Do you know why?"

"No." So Dr. Furuberget didn't want to give Rask a room with the same view that he himself had, but considered it fine for him to work in the workshop with knives and cutting tools. Bergmann didn't even try to understand the logic there.

Once they had come to the end of the corridor, Rask stood by the window and observed the view through the grate.

"There is so much beauty in this world, Tommy."

Bergmann understood that Rask was not a simple mystery. He suddenly seemed like a completely different person, as if his entire personality had changed in the course of a few minutes.

"It's nice on this side. I can see why you'd want to have a room over here."

"You're a handball coach?" said Rask. "For girls? The same age as Kristiane?"

Bergmann didn't answer; he just looked at Gundersen. Someone must have told Rask what they knew about him. But Rask shouldn't know; somehow that seemed dangerous. Soon he would probably find out where he lived too. *The TV*, he thought. *And the padlock.*

He shook it off.

Coincidences.

"Kristiane was beauty itself. She was strength, truth, and beauty. She could have chosen between piano and handball, you know that, don't you, Tommy?"

"Yes."

"She was a proper girl. I would never have dreamed of doing anything to harm her."

Bergmann said nothing, but couldn't help from having his own thoughts.

"You've seen pictures of her, obviously."

"Yes."

"What do you see in her eyes, Tommy? In the pictures from middle school."

"What do I see?"

"In that picture that appeared in the newspaper when she disappeared."

"I see a girl. An ordinary girl."

Rask smiled again.

"An ordinary girl," he repeated, his expression serious, without so much as a hint of his earlier sneer.

"What do *you* see?" said Bergmann.

"I ran into her at the store a few weeks before she disappeared. I was on sick leave most of that fall. Hadn't seen her since eighth grade."

Or do you mean a few weeks before you killed her? thought Bergmann. He noticed that they were now more or less surrounded by the two nurses and Gundersen.

"Yes?"

"And do you know what I saw?"

The two men measured each other with their eyes; Rask looked as though he'd gotten over the lethargy brought on by his meds.

"She had a glass plate between reason and something else that rested inside her. The madness, Tommy, that rested inside her."

Bergmann slowly shook his head.

217

"What do you mean?"

"Someone had lit a *fire* in her, Tommy. Someone had set fire to the madness inside her that summer between eighth and ninth grade. Don't you understand what I mean?"

"Her boyfriend?"

Rask sneered again.

"He was nothing more than a pimply boy. Besides, they broke up before that summer."

He took hold of the collar of Bergmann's jacket, carefully, not hard.

"Anders." The nurse's voice was calm.

"The fire," said Anders Rask and let go. "Someone lit the fire in her, Tommy." His eyes grew vacant again, and he had to support himself against the metal grate on the window.

37

She'd already been waiting for two hours. She wasn't sure she could bear sitting in this common room much longer, watching junkies and drunks who wondered what the female cop was doing there and thinking they hadn't come here to be brought in. It seemed as though Bjørn-Åge Flaten had just come to town to sleep, rather than to get more money. Though he'd surely had enough dope for today, he would eventually have to go out on the hunt and stockpile for the rest of the week. He would have to leave the shelter to take his next shot, and it couldn't be long until then. Every single one of them was caught in a kind of Robinson Crusoe economy, which only lasted until the next fix and the two days that followed. Over it all rested the dream of the one big break that would save them from the muck.

Susanne drove the short way over to IKEA and had apple cake and coffee like any other housewife. There was not a white person to be seen among the staff. She'd seen most things in this job and lived for ten years in Grønland with the World Islamic Mission as her nearest neighbor, but she was unfamiliar with the sight of an IKEA employee wearing a hijab in the company colors. She told herself she was starting to get old. She'd grown up in a different country than the Norway that was now springing up under her feet.

She had her mouth full of cake and was thinking about the man she mustn't think about when the phone rang.

"He's awake. But he can't take his shot here, so he'll disappear just as soon as he intends to keep destroying his life. He should have gone to the hospital."

"Then send him to a hospital for Pete's sake," she mumbled through the apple cake. "But not just yet. Don't let him get away."

As she ran out through the labyrinthine furniture store, she realized how stupid she was to have gone to IKEA out of sheer impatience. But she was back in the common room only a few minutes later.

About fifteen minutes later, a man came in who looked like the living dead. His face was drained of color and life, more disintegrated than wrinkled. And he was how old? Only eight years older than her. His clothes had obviously been stolen from a discount-store rack many years ago, and hung on him as they would on a scarecrow. His long hair looked freshly washed, but hung lifelessly over his sunken cheeks. He avoided her gaze as he collapsed in the chair in front of her. Judging by his breathing it sounded as if he might die right before her eyes. On one of his wrinkled hands was a simple prison tattoo.

He sat silently and motionless after she had introduced herself. Then something outside the window attracted his attention. She looked, but saw nothing of interest out there, just gray on gray and a long line of cars spewing out white exhaust.

"I've come here to—"

"Is it that case?" he interrupted. He pulled the sleeves of his sweater up and scratched his forearms. First left, then right.

Susanne had not expected him to be so well informed.

"Don't you think I keep up with the news?" he said, smiling carefully. He was missing a few teeth.

Bjørn-Åge Flaten stood up laboriously from the chair. Out of his back pocket he pulled a few bills and coins, which he placed on the table. Then a packet of Red Mix. With his crooked fingers, he pulled off a Big Ben rolling paper, which he filled with tobacco. His breathing grew heavier.

Susanne thought that he could have been used as an extra in a movie. As a dying man.

"You said back then that you saw Kristiane at Skøyen."

Flaten lit the hand-rolled cigarette. He started to cough, first lightly, then harder. She grew almost certain that he was going to die right before her eyes. When he was finally done, he concentrated on his breathing for a long time.

"I should be dead. The heroin makes it possible to live with the pain. Ironic, huh?"

She shook her head weakly. She was scared by the thought of what Flaten could have been today. Or, rather, it was the thought of his trajectory—from an upper-middle-class neighborhood in Bærum to a rooming house at Brobekk—that frightened her. It was the thought that she could end up here herself. The membrane of resistance that had prevented her from tipping over was so thin that she wasn't sure it really existed.

The sight of Flaten was enough to deter her for months to come. The road to heroin was so short that you didn't realize it until it was too late. She could have told Flaten about a girlfriend of hers who had everything she could want, but nonetheless sent the intern across town to buy her single-use syringes. Susanne was the only one who knew about it. Not even her husband knew. She lived her life with dignity, but couldn't live without it. It was all a question of money, nothing else.

"What's wrong with you?" she said.

"It doesn't matter," said Flaten. His eyes looked even older than the rest of his face.

"Did you see her? Kristiane?"

"Why does that matter now? The girl is dead."

"I think it's important, Bjørn-Åge."

His eyes narrowed, and he smacked his lips a few times, as if he despised her for having said his name.

"I needed money." He stared down at the cigarette, which had gone out.

"What do you mean?"

"I made it up. Isn't that what you all accused me of back then?"

"Can't you just tell me the truth?"

"What is truth?" was all he said. "Truth and lies are often two sides of the same thing." His voice seemed frayed at the edges; there was a slight trembling with every word.

She had nothing to say. She felt a surge of disappointment, followed by a flatness she hoped he would not detect, a slight redness in her cheeks. She looked at the clock on the wall. It was too late to drive up to Ringvoll now. She would have to go back to the office and try to get hold of Kristiane's old teacher, the one who lived in Spain. Anything was better than sitting here with an old drug addict who she had naïvely thought was telling the truth, whatever that was, back in 1988.

Flaten gasped for breath.

"I have to go into town," he said.

She spent the rest of the day trying to track down Gunnar Austbø, mostly on the phone with a guy from Kripo, who did his best to help her find a contact in Spain.

The high point of the afternoon was the call from Bergmann. His voice had sounded odd, as if he'd seen a ghost in broad daylight.

"Someone lit a fire in her," Bergmann had said.

"What did you say?"

"Someone lit a fire in her. That summer. In eighty-eight."

His voice had been weak, as if the meeting with Anders Rask had sucked all the energy out of him. *What is it with you?* Susanne had wondered. But what Rask had said gave her hope that something may indeed have been overlooked back in 1988.

Now she was sitting in her office, staring blankly into the room.

She wasn't thinking about Nico.

Or about Svein Finneland.

But about Bergmann.

"Someone lit a fire in her," she said quietly.

God knows that could be dangerous.

But what was truth, and what was a lie?

Should they take Anders Rask's words for truth?

When the clock reached four and Bergmann still hadn't come back from Toten, she punched out, picked up her skates at home, and went to pick up Mathea at daycare. She could read all the papers in the world, but it wouldn't help one bit.

A silly young girl, a temp who was in from time to time, had the late shift at the daycare. Susanne tried to put on a smile. The young girl obviously did not know whose mother she was.

"Mathea," said Susanne, trying to be as indulgent as she could as she set the skate bag down on the floor.

"Yes . . ." The young girl's gaze wandered over the group. Susanne suddenly wondered whether she even knew who Mathea was. What kind of mother was she really? Every day she gave up her most prized possession to people she didn't know, whose names she didn't even know. She felt a shudder in her temples, and her insides turned to ice. She just knew that the young girl's next words were going to be *Mathea is dead, didn't they call you?*

The girl said something, but Susanne was unable to make out what. "She's outside," said a boy Mathea's age. It took Susanne a few seconds to recognize him. Emil, a boy Mathea played with a lot. He had even come over once with his mother.

"So," said the temp. "I—"

"See you tomorrow," said Susanne, taking the bag of wet clothes down from Mathea's cubby. She pretended not to see the drawings on the shelf and didn't even feel guilty.

Mathea was lying upside down on the slide outside.

Susanne went all the way over to her daughter before she noticed her.

"Look, Mommy. I'm dead."

Susanne closed her eyes.

She thought about saying, "Don't say that," but said nothing.

It was almost dark. The lights from the windows in the daycare didn't quite reach her, and none of the streetlights along the walkway outside the fence were lit.

"Do they let you be out here alone?"

Mathea didn't answer.

"Mathea?"

"I got permission."

Susanne went over to the gate in the fence and felt it. It was locked with a sturdy snap lock and a padlock with a carabiner.

She heard slow steps approaching to her left.

A tall figure emerged from the darkness on the other side of the gate. The silhouette seemed to cover the whole walkway. Susanne tried to get a glimpse of the face, but the person had pulled the hood of his bubble jacket over his head, and his face was angled away from her.

Susanne observed the figure, who was now only a few steps from her.

He stopped, still half turned away from her.

She could suddenly hear his breathing, which was deep and heavy, as if he suffered from an illness.

She expected him to turn around at any moment.

"Mommy," said Mathea behind her.

The man with the black bubble jacket motioned weakly with his right arm. Susanne thought that if he turned around, she would find herself face-to-face with Anders Rask.

She turned, grabbed Mathea, and practically dragged her back inside. She was tempted to turn around just to assure herself that the man hadn't followed them back into the daycare. She could have sworn she heard the sound of the snap lock in the gate, the sound of steps following them.

Get a grip, she thought.

The image of Kristiane Thorstensen on the autopsy table flashed before her eyes. The organs, the hair, the cut from the pelvis up to the ribcage, the sawed-off sternum, the missing left breast.

What lunatic would think of going into a daycare center that was still open?

A man who'd spent years at Ringvoll, she thought. A man who had already killed six girls.

The bus felt comforting, heated and light, and Mathea's hand was just so little and warm that Susanne quickly forgot the faceless man on the walkway behind the daycare.

They had Chinese food in Oslo City and looked at Christmas gifts in the big toy store, after which they walked over to the skating rink in Spikersuppa. Every time they passed a junkie under the Christmas wreaths, Susanne wished it was Bjørn-Åge Flaten. And that he would say, *I lied to you earlier. I saw her, I saw Kristiane at Skøyen, and now I'll tell you something no one else knows.*

They skated until Mathea could no longer stay on her feet. In the taxi on their way home to Grønland, she was struck so brutally by a thought that she almost started to cry. The combination of the child by her side, the streets decorated for Christmas, and her overwhelming fatigue all made her think that if Mathea ever went over the precipice, there was nothing she would be able to do to rescue her. Flaten had once sat just like this, holding his mother's hand after skating. Kristiane too. And then one day all that was forgotten, the cord was broken, they disappeared down into the depths, and their mothers never managed to fish them up again.

She took the mittens off Mathea, who blinked her eyes and hung her head. *I'll never let go,* she thought. *I'll never let go of your hand.*

The taxi stopped for a red light at Jernbanetorget, and she fixed her gaze on a group of junkies hanging out by the entrance to the subway. A young good-looking girl leaned toward an older man, a ghost; she recognized him from the old days. What made her come down here the first time?

That thought suddenly shed light on the meaning behind Rask's words.

Someone had lit a fire in her.

Kristiane had fallen in love.

"Obviously," Susanne mumbled to herself.

Fallen in love with someone she never should have fallen in love with.

And it had been the death of her.

38

The warmup was harder than usual. At least it felt that way. His lungs stung as if he'd smoked a whole pack of cigarettes that day. Bergmann acted like he was stretching and pressed himself up against the wall. The truth was that he was having trouble standing up. He tried to regain control of his breathing and get his pulse down to a reasonable level. Either he'd pushed himself too hard, or he hadn't gotten enough sleep lately. This business with Anders Rask was getting to him more than he wanted to admit.

Maybe there was something wrong with him. Had his heart had enough before he'd even turned forty? Every time the doctor asked if he had illness in the family, he simply answered no. The truth, however, was that he didn't know, on either his mother's or his father's side. He knew nothing about his mother's birthplace in northern Norway, which she'd left when she was young. And where his father was concerned, he had nothing to go on. All it said in the census registry was "father unknown." He tried not to give it that much thought, because he knew that "father unknown" generally meant one of two things: in the best case, it meant a one-night stand; in the worst, rape, incest, or code 6, that is, a violent psychopath one must avoid at all costs.

A man like myself, he thought. Those tendencies were usually inherited, he knew that too well from his own job.

But at least he'd left Hege alone after she moved out. That was still something, that he understood when the battle was lost.

"Are you okay?" said a voice behind him.

The assistant coach, Arne Drabløs, gave him a worried look. Bergmann briefly wondered what he was doing here. He'd initially gotten involved to help out his best friend a few years ago; now he had the whole team on his hands, without even having a daughter on it.

He dismissed the thought as quickly as it had come. This team and the coaching work were the closest he got to normalcy. Sometimes it was the only thread that connected him to other people, so that his life was not just made up of death and misery, misery he himself inflicted on others.

"Yes, just get them started for now." He sank down on the bench without his pulse going down noticeably.

A fire, he thought, observing the girls.

Someone had lit a fire in her.

Maybe it was the thought that he would soon have to face Elisabeth Thorstensen again that was sucking the energy out of him. How had she managed to go on living? He'd tried to reach her twice on his way down from Toten. The first time, she'd hung up after he introduced himself; the second call went straight to voice mail. Something in her voice had frightened him. It seemed completely hollow, without the slightest spark of life.

"Hi, Tommy," he heard to his left.

It was Sara coming out of the changing room—late, as always. She'd skipped warmup before almost every practice since last summer. He'd talked to her about it a couple of times, trying not to nag, but she'd fallen into some bad habits on the court. He imagined she was probably going to quit soon, which was too bad because they needed everyone they could get.

Only then did he become aware of two boys Sara's age, perhaps a little older, sitting a few benches away from him. Sara went over to them and tousled one of the boys' hair. They laughed at something or other. The boy stroked her bare brown leg. The movements looked confident. He was clearly used to touching girls. Bergmann stood up, took out his whistle, and signaled that they should gather in the midcircle. He waved to Sara.

"Come on," he said. The boy who had stroked her on the leg smiled in a way that only reinforced Bergmann's initial impression of him. Gangster material. He was too young to have a tattoo on his neck, but had one anyway. And although any number of kids wore square diamonds in their ears like that, it only made Bergmann more sure of it. His cop gaze had never failed him. The boy reeked of trouble from a mile away, and he had Sara deep in his pocket.

Practice went better than it had in a long time, but Bergmann was more preoccupied by Sara's apparent interest in the gangster boy than by the fact that his team was finally living up to its potential. Martine and Isabelle had gotten so good that unfortunately they made him think of Kristiane Thorstensen. For their own sake, he ought to move them to a stronger team, but he'd like to keep them until summer.

After practice he was struck by how different things were now from a year ago. Hadja no longer stopped by the way she used to, supposedly by accident, and these girls were now fourteen or fifteen, no longer just kids. While a few still stood with one foot in a kind of carefree childhood, Sara and a handful of the other girls looked as though their childhood was a thing of the past.

He stayed in the gym for half an hour afterward to watch the women's team practice. He knew they needed a new coach next season, and had surprised himself by saying that he would think about it. There were days when he absolutely did not understand himself. He'd been considering quitting as the girls' coach, and now he might instead find himself responsible for two teams. But he just couldn't bear to see the semidesperate announcements in the local paper every time one of the teams lost a coach. Maybe it was absurd, but the words *Will you be our coach?* always made him sentimental. He'd even called around to some old friends he hadn't seen in years to try to recruit them.

When he came out to the parking lot, he saw something he really didn't want to see. He stood quietly in the darkness, the falling snow soaking into his hair and the shoulders of his workout jacket. A girl who was quite clearly Sara stood nearby, a cigarette burning faintly in her hand, making out with the boy with the tattoo on his neck.

Bergmann bit his lip.

Who did he think he was? Her father?

On the other hand, this would give him a good reason to call Hadja.

He turned away and walked toward his car.

The boy had lit a fire in her. She would soon be fifteen. He supposed she knew what she wanted.

A fire, he thought. Someone had lit a fire in Kristiane.

His phone rang, and he recognized the number at once. He'd saved it earlier in the day.

He remained standing outside the car, as the snow fell harder and harder, but he could not take the chance of missing this call.

"Tommy Bergmann," he said in what he hoped was a tone of both authority and courtesy.

Silence.

A bus passed the parking lot, and he put his hand over his free ear.

"Elisabeth Thorstensen?"

39

Bergmann didn't have time to go home to shower. All he had time for on the short drive over to Elisabeth Thorstensen's old patrician villa was two cigarettes. Her words—"I go to bed early"—made him realize it was now or never.

As he stood on the steps, he hoped he didn't smell like a gym. Even though it was a different house, with a different view, he had the feeling of having traveled sixteen years back in time.

He raised his arm and knocked with the knocker, noticing as he did so that there was no nameplate on the door. He still remembered the childish ceramic sign that had hung beside the door of the red house in Skøyenbrynet: "Here live Alexander and Kristiane, Per-Erik and Elisabeth Thorstensen."

The person who appeared in the doorway must be her new husband, Asgeir Nordli. The slightly long, combed-back gray hair gave him a bohemian look, which surprised Bergmann. The tall body was a bit ungainly, but he was tanned and dressed in an expensive dark-blue cardigan. He had a full-sized foreign newspaper in his hands. The furrow between his eyes seemed to deepen as he studied the big wet man on his steps. Bergmann remembered that he was in workout clothes, emblazoned with "Klemetsrud Handball" and various sponsor logos.

He introduced himself.

The gray-haired man inhaled deeply through his nose before he took Bergmann's hand. Then he turned and closed the outside door.

"I don't like this," he said quietly.

"She called me herself," said Bergmann.

"After you'd been calling her all day."

"I don't think I got your name."

"I didn't say it."

But I know it, Bergmann thought as the man introduced himself.

"Follow me," said Nordli quietly, leading him across the hall. Bergmann glanced around at the abstract art on white walls and the antique furnishings, all vastly more expensive than he could imagine.

Nordli opened a door into what looked like an office or a library. He closed the door quietly behind Bergmann. Outside the window he could see the lights of Ulvøya, but Malmøya appeared to have disappeared in the blizzard. Nordli turned on the ceiling light, illuminating the overfilled bookcases, a desk, and a guest bed. The room was as big as Bergmann's own living room. He fixed his gaze on one of the pictures on the walls. A disturbing picture of a man who appeared to be emerging from a black-and-white vagina.

Nordli could not help but notice Bergmann staring at the picture.

"Ghosts," he said. "Not for delicate souls."

"Your books?" Bergmann said to Nordli, nodding toward the bookcases.

Nordli sighed dejectedly, evidently irritated by the seemingly irrelevant question.

"She's done nothing but cry since you called the first time, Bergmann."

"I'm sorry, but—"

The door behind them flew open, and a twelve-year-old boy appeared, looking at Bergmann as if he were dangerous.

"Peter, go back up to your room," said Nordli.

"Peter," called a female voice somewhere behind him.

Bergmann heard steps approaching across the hall. As his legs buckled a little and his heart raced, he realized that he was insufficiently prepared to meet Elisabeth Thorstensen again.

"I guess we'll have to go meet her," said Nordli. He went almost reluctantly into the hall again and put his arms around the woman who stood there. Bergmann recognized her at once.

Her son stood beside her, looking as though he might burst into tears at any moment. His mother put her hand on his shoulder; her nails were painted red, and she wore a thin wedding band.

Bergmann met her gaze. Her eyes were just as dark as they had been sixteen years ago, but they were vacant and her face had no life in it at all. Not even his odd attire, or the fact that he was soaked through from all the snow, seemed to make any impression on her.

"I'll be right there, just go on in for now. Give him something to drink. Asgeir, will you put on some coffee?"

Bergmann didn't know if he should feel relieved or disappointed that she hadn't recognized him. But how could she have?

As Nordli led him through the house to the living room, Bergmann thought, *This is a good house,* the kind he could imagine living in himself if he just had the money. A house that perhaps had given Elisabeth Thorstensen the peace she needed to go on in life. White walls and broad pine flooring, abstract and colorful art, enough books to last a lifetime, and much more besides. The aroma of spices, likely lingering from dinner, hung in the air, reminding him of Hadja. He nodded to a Filipina woman who stuck her head out the kitchen doorway. He followed the ungainly Asgeir Nordli all the way to the glassed-in porch that was connected to the living room.

"She likes to sit here," said Nordli. "We've put in insulated glass, and, well . . ." He stood by the window. The snow was falling even more heavily than before; it seemed as if it might soon cover the entire city.

Bergmann sank down into one of the wicker chairs. On a low table in front of him were four or five tealights, a half-full glass of red wine, a couple of books, and an old black-and-white passport photo. The ashtray was full of butts, and an empty pack of More was on the table. He studied Kristiane Thorstensen's face, upside down, in the little photo booth picture from the eighties. She was smiling at the camera in a way that suggested she meant to give the picture to someone special, perhaps someone waiting outside the photo booth.

Nordli had disappeared from the glassed-in porch without his even noticing. He carefully picked up the photograph, holding it by the top left corner, as if it were evidence and he did not want to leave any fingerprints. Though she was smiling, her gaze was deeply serious.

Someone lit a fire in her, he thought, and heard Anders Rask's voice in his head. Should he believe such a man, a man he was not at all certain was innocent?

He set the photograph down again, the way it had been. In the nick of time. He heard Elisabeth and Nordli talking together somewhere in the living room. Nordli was clearly trying to keep her from talking to Bergmann, but to no avail.

He stood up quickly when she came out onto the glassed-in porch. He had taken off his workout jacket and hung it over one of the wicker chairs. So he stood there feeling foolish in an old moss-colored Army field sweater, a sweaty microfiber undershirt, and wet workout pants.

"Tommy Bergmann. I'm glad you wanted to see me."

Her delicate fingers disappeared into his big right hand. She raised her other hand up to his cheek. He wanted to avert his gaze, but was unable to.

"To think that it's you."

She stroked his cheek lightly, just as she had sixteen years ago. He could almost feel her blood running down over his skin again.

"I didn't think you would recognize me," he said.

She withdrew her hand, pulled the sleeve of her blouse down. He barely had time to see the outlines of the old scars.

"I would have recognized you in a hundred years."

He studied her as she sank down in the chair behind her and dried her cheeks with the back of her hand. Her brown hair was almost as he remembered it, her face still marked by delicate, symmetrical lines, but she now had wrinkles that radiated out from her eyes and around her mouth. Nonetheless, if he'd seen her on the street, he would have thought she was in her late forties, not fifties. It was strange how well she had held up. Based on what he'd read in the investigation materials, Bergmann had thought that Kristiane's death had taken a hard toll on Elisabeth. He thought that she'd been hospitalized for a long time, though he didn't remember exactly where.

"She resembled him so much." Elisabeth picked up the passport photo.

"Your ex-husband?"

"Per-Erik," she said, staring at the little picture. "I haven't spoken to him in fifteen years. Not once."

"H—" was all he managed to say.

"I've hardly looked at a single picture of her either. I hadn't seen her face since 1988, until *Dagbladet* ran that photograph on the front page recently. I had to lie down in the store when I saw it on the newsstand. For many years I got Asgeir to read through the papers for me. I never watch the evening news. Don't you think they should have called me first?"

She raised her head, her expression leaving no doubt that this was a sorrow she would take with her to the grave.

"I'm sorry" was all he could manage to say.

Elisabeth hid her face in her hands, her tears almost soundless. He didn't know what he should do. Just as he was about to stand up to comfort her, she mumbled something.

"I wish it was him."

"Rask?"

"It gave me peace," she said from between her hands.

There were few reasonable responses to this. Didn't they all wish Rask was responsible for killing Kristiane and the other girls?

He waited until she had calmed down. She lit a cigarette, absently.

"There is one thing I must ask you about. Which I've been thinking about recently."

"Yes?"

"You said something back then, the night we came to talk to you, after we'd found Kristiane. Do you remember?"

She shook her head.

"'It's all my fault,'" he said.

A long pause followed.

"Why did you say that?"

"I don't remember saying that. Why would I say that?" Something in her face closed up. "You were the first one who saw her?" she said instead.

He nodded, even though that wasn't quite true.

"Tell me that she was all right. Please be kind."

"She was in a good place," he said.

Elisabeth put out the half-smoked cigarette.

"You're a handball coach?" She smiled weakly and nodded at the workout jacket hanging over the chair.

He nodded.

Her gaze turned inward again. As if she was thinking the same thing he was. Kristiane had left the Nordstrand sports facility and headed down one of the nearby residential streets, her bag over her shoulder, perhaps strolling, perhaps running to make the train. But why the train? Why not the trolley? It would have been shorter for her. He still didn't understand that, but it was a waste of time to figure it out, despite Susanne's insistence that it mattered.

"We have to decide whether to reopen the case," he said. "But if we do, then we have to have something more to go on, if such a thing is possible now. You know that the evidence against Rask is weak. If there is anything you've thought about over the years, anything you think doesn't add up—"

"I said all I had to say back then."

Which wasn't much, thought Bergmann. She had been in no condition for questioning for several months after they found Kristiane. When a similar murder of a prostitute was committed in February 1989, all resources were transferred to that case. Everyone was convinced that it was the same man, and the newest murder always got highest priority. Cold trails were cold trails. Of the almost seven thousand pages of investigation material against Anders Rask, the interviews with Elisabeth Thorstensen constituted a very negligible portion.

"I must ask you about a name," said Bergmann.

"Name?"

"Maria," he said quickly.

"Maria?" Elisabeth shook her head.

"Or Edle Maria. Does that sound familiar?" It was Sørvaag's track, but there might be something to it.

"No," she said. "That doesn't ring any bells."

Bergmann waited, but she gave no sign of wanting to say more.

"Next I must ask you why you were at the funeral for the Lithuanian girl, Daina. Because that was you, wasn't it?"

Elisabeth grimaced, as if she had to concentrate in order not to start crying.

"Yes," she said quietly. "I decided to go. I even called to be sure about the time. Maybe it was to reconcile myself with my own fate. I wasn't at my own daughter's funeral, perhaps you know that. What mother does such a thing? Not saying good-bye to her own child."

Bergmann didn't know what to say. He could have asked her who she thought had killed Daina, but that was pointless. Besides, he couldn't give her any details about the killing.

"Boyfriend," said Bergmann. "Did Kristiane have a boyfriend when she disappeared?"

Elisabeth shook her head.

"Not that I knew about. She lived her own life. I think she'd broken up with her boyfriend—what was his name? Ståle?—sometime during the summer. I didn't keep very close track, to be quite honest."

"Did you notice any changes in her that fall?"

"No."

"And she hadn't said anything about where she was going that Saturday night?"

Elisabeth shook her head.

"Did she usually take the trolley from Sæter, or the train from the station?"

She closed her eyes.

"Kristiane," she began, then stopped herself. "Usually . . ." She was unable to continue.

"Took the subway from Munkelia," he said to her. That meant that Kristiane normally left the Nordstrand sports facility in the opposite direction.

Bergmann grew annoyed with himself. *Obvious things,* he thought. *We're stuck in obvious things.*

"You weren't home that Saturday? And you didn't see the match?"

"No."

"Neither you nor Per-Erik?"

"He was on a business trip in Sweden."

Bergmann knew that Per-Erik Thorstensen had been no farther away than Gothenburg. Instinctively he thought that Per-Erik was no more than three and a half hours outside Oslo when Kristiane disappeared. He could have made it there and back that night.

"So only Alexander was home?"

Elisabeth nodded, but avoided looking him in the eye.

"We always gave our kids great freedom; I often didn't know where they were, or where they'd been, before they came home in the evening. Freedom with responsibility, it always worked fine."

Bergmann knew that solid police work had been done in the case. Everyone's alibis and movements were charted, apart from Elisabeth Thorstensen's. The two circles around the victim—first the immediate family, then friends, acquaintances, and the expanded social circle—had all been accounted for. Her ex-boyfriend, Ståle, had an alibi and was questioned and checked out. None of those questioned had given any sign that would suggest they were a likely candidate. And five other girls. All the usual lunatics—semipsychotic rapists, of which two were convicted of murder from before—had alibis in place. On the other hand, the killer could be a person who was able to conceal his madness. Wasn't that what Dr. Furuberget had said? That Rask could appear healthy for long periods of time. That probably was true of any number of people in this world.

Like me, thought Bergmann.

"My life was as good as it could be," said Elisabeth.

He acted as if he hadn't heard what she said, and asked instead, "Where were you that evening?" That was her weak point, which no one had ever bothered to dig into after Rask was arrested. Maybe it was nothing, but he had to try.

"I was in town. You don't need to know more than that, Tommy."

Her voice was firm, but not unfriendly. She met his gaze. There was nothing more to say. Not for the time being anyway. They stared at each other for a few seconds. He couldn't help but think that she was attractive. More than attractive. She could have wrapped him around her little finger if she wanted.

"Oh well."

"But one thing you *must* know, Tommy. My life had been a living hell up until 1987. Then suddenly my life became better than it had ever been. And a year later Kristiane disappeared."

"I don't understand."

"Sometimes he hit me with oranges wrapped in a wet towel."

He didn't understand the meaning behind what she had said right away. Then her words slowly sank in. Bergmann felt the glassed-in porch begin to spin; it felt as if the wickerwork in the chair beneath him was unraveling.

"Per-Erik," he said quietly.

They stared at each other. She seemed to see right through him—it was clear she knew men like him. Then they regained a kind of equilibrium. Elisabeth fumbled with the cigarette pack on the table. Faint jazz music was heard from the living room. Bergmann closed his eyes, thought that he hadn't been as bad as Per-Erik Thorstensen. *Lies,* he thought a second later.

"There's nothing about that in the old investigation."

She blew the smoke right toward him.

"That was always our little secret. Ever since the year after I met him. The bit with the oranges was his little specialty. You don't get any bruises from that, but minor internal bleeding. It was so dreadfully painful, you wouldn't believe it."

He said nothing. He felt an urgent desire to get out of there, but he had no choice but to finish.

"For almost all those years, Tommy. Even when I was pregnant with Kristiane, he thought I flirted with other men. I was pregnant, *pregnant,* Tommy. I could have lost her."

He felt a strong wave of nausea rising up from his stomach.

"Aren't you going to ask me why I didn't leave him?"

Bergmann couldn't take any more. He closed his eyes, but all he saw was Hege. He inhaled deeply through his nose.

No, he thought, *I won't ask you why you stayed.*

He was barely able to coax a cigarette out of his Prince pack. Then he rooted in the pockets of his workout jacket, tried to look as if he was searching for his phone, just to have something to do, to avoid answering her question. It wasn't there; he must have left it in the car.

"Is there something wrong?" she said.

"No," he said.

She smiled at him and looked as if she meant it.

"But the last year before Kristiane was killed, everything got better. It was like a miracle. He joined one of those men's groups, you know, a kind of anger-management course, completely on his own initiative. I don't know how he did it, but he suddenly seemed to get ahold of himself."

Bergmann said nothing.

"Can you imagine what it's like to lose your child just when everything seems to be resolving itself, after such a marriage?"

He nodded tentatively.

"Can you imagine that?" she repeated. "Right when you think your life has gotten as good as it can get. Then you lose your child." Elisabeth pulled up the sleeve of her blouse and exposed her left forearm. The scars were still thicker and whiter than the thin skin around them.

"By the time I came home from the hospital—or the nuthouse, I knew perfectly well that's what it was—Per-Erik had already moved out. It seems that Kristiane had to die for that to happen. I threw away everything of hers, absolutely everything. Then I got this picture from Alex last year." Elisabeth held the little passport photo between her fingers, lightly stroked it with her index finger. She remained quiet, disappeared into herself again.

"Who ran that group?" he asked suddenly.

Elisabeth studied him a long time.

"What do you mean?"

"The men's group Per-Erik joined. Anger management."

She took one last puff of her cigarette. Bergmann looked at the city below them. The snowstorm had let up, and it was once again possible to see beyond the next house.

"I don't know."

"Try to think back."

"Is it that important?"

"Did he have any friends in that group?"

What was it Farberg had said? That Rask had a friend? Someone who got so angry that he was afraid of what he might do.

"I don't know. I really don't."

"Do you know where the course was held?"

"Can it be that important?"

"Try to remember."

"I think it was on the west side somewhere."

"The west side?"

"Yes. I think Per-Erik mentioned that, but I don't remember exactly where."

"The west side," he wrote on his notepad and looked up. He was no longer able to concentrate. They studied each other. He should have averted his gaze, but didn't want to. She smiled carefully, as if she were a girl Kristiane's age and not a woman nearing sixty.

"And you still don't know why you said, 'It's all my fault'?"

Elisabeth opened her mouth to speak, but stopped herself at the last moment.

"Why can't you tell me where you were the evening she disappeared?"

It was the most obvious hole Bergmann had found in the previous investigation. Maybe it wasn't all that strange that the question hadn't come up again when she returned from the hospital in the winter of 1989. Maybe it was nothing, but he wanted to make sure that all was in order with regard to the case. He had to find something for Svein Finneland, almost regardless of how insignificant it might seem.

"Why is that so important?"

She was close to tears again.

Asgeir Nordli appeared in the doorway.

Elisabeth hid her face in her hands.

"I think you need to leave," said Nordli.

"No," she said, without taking her hands away. "Go, Asgeir. Please."

She sat with her hands over her face until Nordli had closed the door behind him. He remained standing in the middle of the living room, as though deliberating over whether to leave. Finally he disappeared out of view.

Bergmann nodded at Elisabeth.

"I was with another man," she said.

A sense of relief seemed to come over her face. She touched her hair, rearranging it a little. Bergmann cursed himself for enjoying the sight of her. The delicate hands, the dark features, the glistening eyes.

"The Saturday she disappeared?"

She nodded.

"We were at the Radisson hotel until Sunday morning. He was married then."

Bergmann felt a faint stirring in his body. He tried to look as nonchalant as possible as he took notes.

"What was his name?"

She sucked in her cheeks, stared past him.

"Morten Høgda."

His pen stopped on the paper.

"So you had a relationship Per-Erik didn't know about?"

"Lord help us, yes. He had only himself to blame. He drove me into Morten's arms. Literally beat me into his arms. If you'd been me, you would have done no differently."

Their eyes met once again, but neither of them spoke.

Morten Høgda was a kind of investor, if Bergmann remembered right. One of those semifamous rich people who popped up in the newspaper from time to time.

But there was something else about that name, wasn't there?

"Was that why you said that?"

"Said what?"

"'It's all my fault.'"

"I don't understand . . ."

"You were with another man the evening she disappeared . . ."

Elisabeth clenched her teeth, then took a deep breath and held it for a while before releasing it.

"You know what," she said calmly. "I think we're done now."

40

He couldn't find a snow brush in the car, only an old ice scraper. It wasn't ice that was the problem, but the crazy amount of snow. He sighed dejectedly as he dragged the thick layer of snow, too heavy for his near-failing wipers, off the windshield.

He could clearly see Elisabeth Thorstensen's silhouette through the kitchen window. She hadn't even come close to showing him out, had barely let a "good-bye" cross her lips.

What was the name of that interim pastor? He would have to call the Oppsal church first thing tomorrow.

Had she really said that? Screamed it.

"It's all my fault."

Oh well, he thought. He'd gone too far. But he only had five days left, and at least he had one new name on his pad. He was just relieved to get out of that house. For a moment, it had seemed as though Elisabeth saw right through him, he was sure of it. After having gotten out of her marriage to Per-Erik Thorstensen, she was certainly on her guard for any sign of men like him.

Morten Høgda.

Though he'd written it down, he made a point of committing the name to memory.

Before getting in the car, he brushed away the worst of the snow that always fell from the car roof onto the seat because he was either too lazy or too distracted to clear it before he opened the door.

His phone was on the passenger seat. He picked it up to call down to Dispatch. If they were having a quiet evening, they could do a search on Morten Høgda. The name "Høgda" rang a bell.

He cursed quietly. His phone was dead. It must have died right after Elisabeth called earlier that evening. How long ago was that? He checked the clock. Two hours? Three?

Though only a short drive, the trip home felt like a mountain expedition. He could barely get up the hill on Lambertseterveien because of all the snow. He may have to spend money on new snow tires. *Then again, maybe not,* he thought as he realized that he wasn't going to slide down the hill. Just before the shopping center, he almost ran into a monster of a snowplow, narrowly avoiding its enormous blade. The orange light was still burning in his eyes when he finally found a parking place.

As soon as he got home, he threw himself at the old landline in the hall. He dialed the number to Dispatch and asked them to do two searches. The one on Morten Høgda and the other on the interim pastor from the Oppsal church. Bergmann had remembered his name on his way from the car to the apartment. Hallvard Thorstad.

While he waited for them to call back, he sat down on the couch in the living room and lit a cigarette. As soon as he turned on the floor lamp in the corner, he sensed that something was wrong. Really wrong. He stood up and surveyed the room. Then he went into the bedroom, turned on the light, and studied the bed that he and Hege had once shared. He had a feeling that someone had just been lying in it, but quickly dismissed it. *Craziness,* he thought as he went over to the bed. He crouched down and held his hand that was holding the cigarette up above the bed, so that he wouldn't set fire to the bed linens.

The phone rang out in the hall. He leaned down quickly and checked under the bed. Only dust bunnies. He cursed quietly.

"Morten Høgda," said Johnsen down at Dispatch, "has been charged with rape three times. Each one of the three different women who called it in withdrew the charges. According to the pussy police he's also a regular with the street prostitutes. Income last year: forty million, assets a hundred and ten. Nice guy. Just a bit of a violent sexual drive."

He closed his eyes, and an image of Elisabeth Thorstensen flashed across his mind's eye. Her dark eyes, the new husband. She'd finally found herself a good man, someone she could count on. Asgeir Nordli seemed like a decent guy. Maybe a little too nice, but how bad could that be for a woman who'd been through what she had?

"Okay, thanks," he said as a question formed in his mind. Knowing what lengths women were willing to go to for men, what had Elisabeth been capable of doing for Morten Høgda once upon a time?

"And do you have the number for Hallvard Thorstad?"

"There's only one Hallvard Thorstad, and he lives in a little settlement in Vestlandet."

Bergmann jotted the number down on an old newspaper.

"Thanks a lot."

"By the way, things are boiling over a bit over at Dispatch in Oppland right now."

"Yeah?" said Bergmann absently.

"Haven't you heard?"

"Heard what?"

Bergmann tried to open the top dresser drawer to pull out his cellphone charger.

"Anders Rask has escaped."

He had his hand halfway into the drawer.

"What did you say?"

"Anders Rask escaped from the hospital, along with another crazy. Two nurses were killed. There's talk about deploying the SWAT team to find them. The helicopter's in the air. They won't get far, the camera will probably track them down soon."

"Hell," said Bergmann. He turned around in the hall. Scanned the living room. The couch, table, carpet, pictures, knickknacks, and bookcase all appeared to be okay. Nonetheless, he couldn't shake the feeling that something inside the apartment was very wrong. The news that Rask had gotten out of Ringvoll didn't help. The question was how he'd done it. And where he was now. *Here in the city,* thought Bergmann.

"How long ago?"

"A couple of hours."

There was a short pause.

A couple of hours. It wouldn't have taken them more than an hour and a half to get into Oslo. Change cars on the road, maybe, drive into some quiet residential area and find an old car they could hotwire. *Two hours at most,* he thought. *They're already here.* The easiest place to hide in all of Norway.

"No, they won't get far," he said to Johnsen. "Thanks for the info."

He set the phone carefully down in the cradle and plugged his phone into its charger.

Eight unanswered calls. All from Reuter.

"Where the hell have you been?" said Reuter when he answered. He was short of breath, and Bergmann figured he'd just gotten off his treadmill.

"Forgot to charge the phone."

"Forgot?"

"I was at Elisabeth Thorstensen's."

That information seemed to soothe Reuter a bit. His voice calmed down.

"Did you find anything out?"

"Yes."

"We'll deal with that tomorrow. Finneland wants to have a meeting at his office at seven o'clock sharp, not a second later. I'm guessing that we'll end up handling Rask's escape. He wants to find him quickly, but I'm sure he also wants you to carry on with your investigation, though I'm guessing you have less time than you did earlier this evening. Do you think Rask is our man?"

"Didn't he kill to get out?"

"I don't know if he was the one who did it. Another psycho escaped along with him who's capable of just about anything. One of them, if not both, probably had a relationship with a female nurse up at Ringvoll. She gave them her card and keys and God knows what else. That fucking cow is at Gjøvik now, it's just a matter of finding the thumbscrews, milking her for all she's worth, and then burying her. Can you beat that, Tommy? Two men dead up there tonight. My God."

What could he say? He'd been in this game too long to be surprised by anything anymore. Almost.

He went straight to the shower after hanging up with Reuter and let the hot water scald his skin for several minutes. He wrote "Morten Høgda" in big letters in the condensation on the shower wall. Then he drew a line and wrote "Rask."

He thought he heard the faint sound of his phone, but it could just as easily have been the doorbell or the landline. He turned off the shower and stood there, his body covered with soap, his hair full of shampoo. He had locked the door to the bathroom for the first time. He didn't want to be surprised if Rask decided to pay him a visit.

No, he thought. *Just my imagination.*

No phones ringing, no sounds.

He turned the water back on. As he was rinsing the shampoo out of his hair, he realized what he had reacted to.

Even in the hot water he got goose bumps on his arms.

It was gone.

The photograph.

He stood in the shower, as a kind of stoic calm settled over him. Or paralysis. He was barely able to turn off the water.

He wrapped a towel around his waist and unlocked the bathroom door.

He went to stand, dripping wet, in the middle of the living room. A pool of water formed beneath him on the parquet.

He fixed his gaze on his IKEA bookcase. It was half-full of books, some magazines, two dried-up cactuses, some knickknacks Hege had left behind, and five or six framed photographs from old times. A ten-year-old picture of himself and Hege that he left there only to torment himself. An old class picture, a portrait of himself.

Half-hidden behind a framed postcard of Alice Springs, Australia, from an old classmate who was no longer alive, he'd placed a small photograph of his mother in a silver frame. It dated back to when she was in nursing school, at the Red Cross in Tromsø, sometime in the midsixties, right before he was born.

But now it was gone.

He walked slowly backward into the hall.

"He's found me," he whispered. "He's been here and he's taken the photograph of her."

The phone was still on the dresser in the hall. Bent, his old colleague, answered almost at once.

"I thought you'd be sleeping at this hour," he said.

"Gun," Bergmann said. "I need a gun."

PART THREE

DECEMBER 2004

41

The view was nothing like what it had been the day before. Though it was almost ten o'clock in the morning, there was barely any daylight and a dense snowfall largely concealed the main building at Ringvoll Psychiatric Hospital. The wind was so strong that the flag line whipping against the flagpole sounded like a snare drum. The flag was soaked through and hung at half-mast, whipping around in the wind one moment, then collapsing again the next.

He assured himself that the small pistol Bent had brought him the night before—a Raven MP-25—was well concealed in the glove compartment. He hadn't slept a wink. He'd spent half the night in the basement with the Saturday Night Special pistol stuck in his back pocket. He'd stored a few of his mother's boxes down there after she died. The ruined padlock two days ago was clearly no coincidence. He didn't know what was in the boxes, so he couldn't tell if anything was gone, but he'd spent several hours searching through her papers to find traces of who she'd been, and who she'd known. Eventually, he'd had to give up. There was nothing of interest, mostly letters and postcards from girlfriends and what he assumed was an occasional fly-by-night boyfriend. Otherwise it was mostly old receipts, budget lists, and a jumble of notes that suggested they barely had enough food to survive at times.

What the burglar had been searching for in his basement compartment Bergmann didn't know. But he was sure of one thing, and that was that the man who'd killed Kristiane Thorstensen and the other girls—if it was only one man—had been in his apartment. At least twice.

The car door blew shut. He pulled the hood of his bubble jacket over his head and jogged over to the steel gate. *Damned Svein Finneland,* he thought. It was his idea for Bergmann to go up to Ringvoll again, mainly to search through Anders Rask's room and that of the other escapee, Øystein Jensrud, a psychotic thirty-five-year-old who had killed both his parents seven years ago. Bergmann thought it would have been more useful to have a talk with Elisabeth Thorstensen's old lover, Morten Høgda, but he'd kept his mouth shut about that.

The brief morning meeting with Finneland—as well as Reuter and Kripo psychologist Rune Flatanger—had been stormy enough. Flatanger had spent the night before going through the material Bergmann had sent him, and rather quickly come to the conclusion that Rask had never killed anyone at all. According to him, Rask was in all likelihood just what Frank Krokhol maintained he was—a pedophile, but not a serial killer. Finneland, however, thought that the escape and the killings at Ringvoll indicated something quite different, and with that they were off. Bergmann mostly sat on the windowsill of Finneland's office and stared at the morning traffic flowing through snow-covered Pilestredet. For a while he was convinced that it was his own father who was back. His mother had escaped from something awful, that he was sure of, and it couldn't be anyone other than his own father. For where had his own craziness come from? Besides, who else would break into his apartment and take a photograph of his mother?

A wild thought struck him: Was it his own father they were searching for?

For a few seconds Bergmann saw himself as a child, someplace in northern Norway. It was the middle of the night, and he and his mother had run away. She had packed their clothes in an old sailor bag, and a car picked them up. She cried the whole way, hiding her face from him, even though it was dark in the car. Had a man driven them? The howling from a psychiatric institution flashed through his mind.

But was it a real memory, or just something he'd constructed after the fact?

Bergmann waved away some reporters who had jumped out of their cars as he approached the gate. It was snowing horizontally now, and Mjøsa was invisible, buried in whiteness.

"No comment," he barked as he showed his ID to the two uniforms standing guard at the gate.

It was not Arne Furuberget who met him at the guardhouse, but a man who introduced himself as the hospital's second-in-command, Thorleif Fiskum. His face looked like a death mask.

"Where's Furuberget?" said Bergmann.

"He left an hour ago. He said that his wife wasn't feeling well, she called and asked him to come home. Besides, he'd been here all night and was exhausted. He's coming back this afternoon."

"So he's at home?"

"This is terrible," he said quietly and shook his head. "Betrayed by one of our own, Bergmann."

He nodded. There wasn't much he could say.

"She regrets it, naturally. Rask had promised her that no one would be harmed. She was stupid enough to believe him."

Fiskum sank down in a chair in Furuberget's office. Another man was already sitting there; he introduced himself as the investigation leader from Gjøvik. Bergmann thought that it wouldn't be long before this man was no longer investigation leader of anything at all in this case.

They spent a few minutes discussing *how* Rask and Jensrud could have managed to escape, which Bergmann could only bear to spend time on out of politeness. The most important thing now was that they *had* escaped. Whether Jensrud managed to make a knife out of materials in the workshop, or whether one of the female employees had been in love with Rask, was of no interest to Bergmann. The only thing he cared about was finding Rask. In principle they could be anywhere at all, maybe even Sweden, but Bergmann was pretty sure they were in Oslo. And either Rask had been in his apartment, or another man had been there. The killer they were searching for. His own father? Bergmann almost snorted at his thoughts. *Pull yourself together,* he thought. But it couldn't be Rask. Someone had broken the lock on his basement compartment a good day *before* Rask escaped. That couldn't be a coincidence, could it?

"I'd like to see Rask's room," said Bergmann.

"We've already gone through the room," said the investigation leader from Gjøvik.

"I'd like to see Rask's room," Bergmann repeated, as if he were autistic.

A few minutes later, a psychiatric nurse came by to get him. His eyes were red-rimmed, and his gaze evasive. It was clear that he'd been crying.

Bergmann walked calmly behind the nurse, keeping his eyes fixed on the bottle-green linoleum, and had the exact same thought he'd had the day before: *I've been here before, or a place just like this.*

They passed the security passage into the security ward. He stopped midway through the corridor when he heard the steel door close behind him and turned around slowly.

He'd been in a place like this with his mother.

Maybe not right here, but a place like this.

But where? And when?

The guard held him back when he had opened the door to Rask's room.

"I promised not to say anything," said the nurse. He lowered his eyes.

"Say what?"

"Furuberget was in here a few days ago."

He waited, clearly assuming that Bergmann understood the significance of this revelation.

"Yes?"

"He was searching for something while Rask was in the workshop. A letter. I've never seen him so desperate. He carried on for almost two hours."

"A letter Rask had received?"

The nurse nodded.

"Did he find it?"

"No. He searched everywhere. I stood outside here and watched him for the last ten minutes. Things were all over the place, he'd even taken the cover off the mattress and taken half the bed apart." The nurse demonstrated how he'd observed Furuberget by pulling open the viewing hatch in the door.

"Okay. Shut the hatch again," said Bergmann, closing the door behind him. He had no need to share his thoughts with the nurse.

He spent a few minutes getting oriented in the sparsely furnished room. There were few places to hide anything in there. The bed had tubular legs, but Furuberget had already searched there. Apart from the bed, the bookcase was the most obvious hiding place.

Bergmann looked at the clock and thought he should call Furuberget, rather than start turning the room upside down himself. But there must be a reason he wanted to keep the search for the letter secret. If Bergmann didn't find the letter himself, Furuberget would certainly deny the whole thing.

On the top of the bookcase at the very back was a kind of photo album. Bergmann pulled it out and set it on the desk by the window. It turned out to be a bizarre scrapbook of clippings, which Bergmann could not fathom that Furuberget had allowed Rask to keep.

On the first page Rask had pasted a newspaper clipping from *Tønsbergs Blad* in August 1978—now old and yellowed—about the murder of Anne-Lee Fransen. The following pages contained several clippings about the same girl from other newspapers. Anne-Lee had evidently bicycled home from the house of a girlfriend who lived in another part of Tønsberg; it was dark when she left, but she had a dynamo and a light and often got around that way. The bicycle was found a year later, on a forest road not far from where Anne-Lee's body had been found. In a newspaper story later that year, Kripo speculated that the murderer had retrieved the bike in Tønsberg after he'd killed Anne-Lee, and brought it to the vicinity of the murder site. Bergmann remembered that Rask had said in court that he went back and retrieved the bicycle after he'd killed her out in the woods. Then followed a series of clippings with pictures of Anne-Lee. The next pages were filled with clippings of the three young prostitutes who were killed, but since they were prostitutes, there wasn't much information about them. The press didn't used to print in-depth stories on sixteen- or seventeen-year-old street girls who were killed. Two of them were also known in the heroin community and therefore were of little interest to the press. If it had happened today, they probably would have dug up a dysfunctional family and some old class pictures of a pretty elementary school girl from someplace in western Norway. But back then they were nothing but incipient heroin-using wrecks who staggered over to a car on Stenersgata one night in June, in too-short denim miniskirts and high-heeled cork shoes with needle marks up their arms. It was the three schoolgirls—Anne-Lee, Kristiane, and a girl by the name of Frida from Skedsmokorset, who was killed three years later—who had been the object of popular sympathy.

Most of the clipping book, fifteen to twenty pages, consisted of newspaper clippings covering the killing of Kristiane Thorstensen. The newspapers had somehow found their way to Ringvoll Psychiatric and into the room of the very man who was convicted of killing her. Bergmann thought that Rask had collected all this right after the murder; perhaps it was formerly confiscated material that had been returned to him after the judgment was legally binding. The final clippings, of Frank Krokhol's stories about Kristiane and the reopening of the case, were only a few days old.

Bergmann tried to get over his irritation that Rask had been allowed to sit in here with this memory album, and instead concentrate on the places Rask had underlined in the articles. He found no particular connection between them, no pattern in what had caught Rask's attention. He slammed the album shut and spent the next fifteen minutes searching for hiding places where Rask could have tucked away letters or small scraps of paper. He checked the bookcase for holes, whether the flooring was loose anywhere, whether there was room to slide a sheet of paper between the wardrobe and the wall.

"Nothing," he muttered. At last he took out the little Swiss army knife he kept in the pocket of his bubble jacket. He'd gotten it on a trip to Bern with the police association one time, and it came in handy sometimes. Like now, for example. He guided the knife blade into Rask's mattress and sliced along one side lengthwise. He pulled off the top part of the mattress and looked down into every single spring.

He turned back toward the bookcase.

A final attempt, he thought. One by one he pulled out the ten or twelve books and held them by the spine, so that he could flip the pages. "Nothing," he said. "Not a damn thing." He picked up the thick red book titled *The Book of the Law*, as an absolute last resort. The name of the author seemed familiar.

As he started browsing through the thin pages, he became aware of the thickness of the book cover between his left thumb and index finger.

259

He sat down at the desk and set the book down carefully, as if it were the most fragile object in the world. He ran his index finger along the edge of the yellowed end sheet inside the front cover and pulled it away from the cardboard underneath it. And there it was. The letter was tucked between the end sheet and the cardboard in the binding.

Anders Rask must have somehow removed the glue from the thin sheet, stuck the letter under it, and then glued it all back in place.

Bergmann stared at the letter, motionless, for a few seconds. He unfolded the paper carefully, taking hold of it at the very top edge so as not to destroy any fingerprints.

He skimmed through the text. An undated letter. Neat handwriting, perhaps a fountain pen. But who had written it? Was it Rask himself? Bergmann held the stationery up toward the ceiling light between his thumb and index finger. It looked quite new. The paper was nowhere close to being yellowed. He walked backward toward the bed and read the letter more slowly this time, word by word.

> *By the time you read this, I may already be dead.*
> *I have always known that it must be you. Just as Jesus himself chose the man who would betray him, perhaps I picked you back then.*
> *This Devil's gift that I have received will be my curse, but that's nothing you know anything about. No one can know anything about it, perhaps not even me?*
> *A gift is a gift, it's not something either of us ever asked for. Only the giver can control a gift, and if the giver is God himself, what can the rest of us do?*
> *You have a gift yourself, my boy, did you know that?*
> *Like me, you never asked for it.*
> *The way no child has ever asked to be born.*
> *Oh, child . . . why did I write that?*

When I was little—it doesn't feel like very long ago—I went to have my fortune told by a gypsy woman in a traveling carnival. She stared at my open palms, then folded them again. "You don't need to pay," she said, and shooed me out. She told my mother that I was too young for such things, too young to get my fortune told. She had made a mistake when she took me in. Think how unhappy this made me, my boy, that this gypsy woman wouldn't tell my fortune.

From where I live, the sea looks black, no foaming waves . . .
I tore the newspaper to bits when I saw her face again.
What do you think that fortune-teller saw in my hands?
That everything had a meaning?
That her tears were only Medusa's tears?

Who wrote this?

It must have been Rask.

Or had someone written the letter *to* Rask?

Bergmann shivered at the thought. Had Rask hidden the letter there so that he would find it? Did he know Rask from before?

He read the text again. "What do you think that fortune-teller saw in my hands?"

A woman, he thought. *Is that a woman's handwriting?*

He folded up the letter and left Rask's room as quickly as he could, as though suddenly afraid of being locked in there himself.

The nurse was still standing outside.

"Where does Arne Furuberget live?"

"Don't know."

"Get me out of here."

He read the letter again in the security passage: "From where I live, the sea looks black."

Now he was quite sure. This must be a woman's handwriting. And Medusa? Wasn't that also a woman?

He refrained from showing the letter to the second-in-command and the investigator from Gjøvik. They had to focus on the escape, and it seemed that was more than enough for them.

"Where does Furuberget live?"

He got the address and directions, and the second-in-command drew a crude map of how to find it on the back of an envelope.

In the car he set the envelope containing the letter in the glove compartment, on top of the unregistered Raven pistol.

The letter must have been written by someone who knew Anders Rask from before.

A name appeared in his mind.

Jon-Olav Farberg. Rask's colleague at Kristiane's school. What was it he'd said? A cryptic story about some friend of Rask's, Yngvar.

But no, Yngvar was no woman. And this had to be a woman's handwriting.

Bergmann snorted as he drove through downtown Skreia. He barely noticed the wreaths and store displays on the main street all decorated for Christmas.

After seven or eight minutes he turned onto a forested road. Two houses were off by themselves. There were no lights on in any of the windows. The house to the left, where Bergmann had been told that Furuberget lived, didn't even have an outdoor light on.

He turned off the car radio and the engine, and the car glided soundlessly over the fresh snow on the gentle downhill incline. He put on the brakes when he was a dozen or so yards from the house. Over at the neighbor's the outside light was on, and a car was snowed in in front of the garage.

He stayed in the car for several minutes looking for movement in the windows. First in Furuberget's house. Then the neighbor's. He opened the glove compartment and fumbled his way to the Raven pistol, keeping his eyes fixed on the Furuberget house as he did so. Then he turned his headlights back on.

Fresh tire tracks on both sides of the road led to Furuberget's house. He turned off the lights, opened the car door, and got out of the car, watching the dark windows the entire time. He released the safety on the pistol and took a couple of steps between the four tire tracks. The tracks on the right side were more snowed over than those on the left.

Damn, he thought. He'd passed a car on his way up here, but didn't remember what kind it was. He started to walk quickly toward Furuberget's house, running the last few feet. The steps were slippery, and he took hold of the railing so as not to fall, nearly dropping the pistol as he did so.

He paused for a few seconds, then took hold of the door handle with the sleeve of his bubble jacket to avoid destroying fingerprints.

The door was unlocked and opened with a creak on the poorly oiled hinges. He stepped quietly into the entry with the pistol in position and turned on the light switch.

A pair of slippers stuck out of a door down the hall, and a pool of blood ran toward the kitchen on a floor that must not have been quite level.

Bergmann stayed close to the wall as he brought the pistol up and turned his head from side to side.

Arne Furuberget lay on his stomach with his legs over the threshold of the doorway. His head was turned to the side and resting in his own blood. His throat was slit up to his ear, and his blazer was dark with blood. In front of him on the floor were broken coffee cups, a silver carafe, coffee grounds, and a crushed cookie.

Bergmann leaned down and felt Furuberget's hand. It was still warm.

Damn. What kind of car did he pass? A passenger car, that was all he remembered. Midsized.

He went back through the hall. *I wonder if the wife really was sick,* he thought.

He opened the first door to the left, then pushed it all the way open with his foot as he held the pistol in a two-handed grip. A guest room. Empty.

The wife was in the next room, her throat cut as well. But she was in much worse shape than her husband. Her face was almost gone. He couldn't bear to turn on the light. Instead, he lowered the pistol, took out his phone, and called the emergency number. After a brief conversation, he called Fredrik Reuter and told him about the letter he'd found in Rask's room.

"Strictly speaking, this is not our case, Tommy. I have to talk to Svein. He's trying to—"

Bergmann hung up.

He jumped at a knocking sound coming from the basement. Three knocks.

He went over to the stairs that led down to the basement and told himself that it was just the oil furnace. Then he took a seat halfway down the stairs with the pistol aimed toward the darkness below.

When he saw a blue light rotating in the windows on the first floor, he stuck the Raven pistol in his inside pocket, went outside to greet the officers, and took one of them down with him to the basement.

It was empty, and all the doors were locked.

Up in the living room the sheriff made the same observations as Bergmann.

"The visitor killed him. He would never have made coffee for Anders Rask, don't you think?"

Bergmann shook his head.

The investigator from Gjøvik eventually arrived, along with Furuberget's second-in-command at Ringvoll.

"It's Rask," said the investigator.

"Would you have made coffee for Rask?" asked the sheriff. Bergmann felt like giving the man a pat on the shoulder.

"What kind of car did Rask and his buddy escape in?" he asked the investigator.

"A Nissan Micra." The investigator gave him a small, sad smile. Two madmen in a tin can of a car.

"I passed a car on the way up here."

"Yes?" His eyes widened.

"It was no Nissan Micra. It was starting to get dark and hard to see, but I'm sure it wasn't a Micra."

"So what kind of car was it?"

"I don't know." Bergmann frowned. "It was too dark to tell. Maybe a Focus or Astra, you know, medium class. Not a station wagon, I don't think."

The investigator opened his mouth, but evidently changed his mind and remained silent.

"Did Furuberget ever talk about any letters Rask had received—a letter he was searching for in Rask's room?"

The second-in-command shook his head. He had fallen to his knees in the entry.

42

Bergmann did not manage to break away until an hour later.

The afternoon traffic was heavy, and he crawled along in an inferno of white snow and red taillights. He could barely see the landscape around him, but what little he could seemed familiar—a little valley, a patch of forest. He caught sight of the sign for the old hospital, Frensby, and worked his way into the exit lane.

Was it here? he thought, turning on the brights as he curved onto a winding country road lined with bare black trees. The highway lights disappeared quickly in the rearview mirror. He somehow knew that Frensby Hospital was up ahead. So was that where his mother had worked when they first moved to Tveita? Yes, he remembered that now as he got closer.

After a few minutes of driving on a country road with no street-lights, he came to the closed hospital. It stood like a Gothic monument over a time he hardly recalled. The dark windows gaped at him as he walked across the plaza toward the main entrance. He set his feet carefully on the slippery granite steps and peered in the window. A wash light that was on at the far end of the corridor cast an intense glow over the green floor and row of doors on either side.

He put his hand on the door handle. It was freezing cold. He knew he should have released it, but he couldn't resist. Fortunately the door was locked.

He exhaled. If the door had been open, he would have gone in. A secret hung over this old hospital. A secret he didn't know if he wanted to find out. His mother had worked here once upon a time, he was sure of it.

Was this where he'd seen Elisabeth Thorstensen before?

No, no. He shook his head. It was only his imagination.

He had just gotten back on the highway when his phone rang. He assumed that it was either Svein Finneland or Fredrik Reuter, and decided to let it ring.

It rang again as he approached Gardermoen. He picked it up and studied the number. *Damn,* he thought, *it's Elisabeth Thorstensen.*

"Are you going to find him?" she said without preamble.

Bergmann got into the right-hand lane, feeling how tired he was after his sleepless night. He planned to stop at the Shell station at Kløfta and buy himself some coffee, have a smoke, and get a little fresh air.

"Yes," said Bergmann.

"I have a terrible feeling," she said. Her voice sounded distorted for a moment, as though a child was living deep inside her.

"What do you mean?"

"That he's coming here."

Elisabeth did not elaborate.

"Do you want police protection, is that what you're trying to say?"

She did not reply.

"Has he ever contacted you?"

"No."

"Then he's not coming."

"I don't want a guard. No, I don't want that," she said, more to herself than to Bergmann.

"Was there anything else you wanted to tell me?" he said after a long pause. He was almost at the exit to Kløfta. He was about to tell her that he was sorry he'd pushed her too hard yesterday, and that he was glad she'd called, but he didn't.

"That part about my relationship with Morten is—" She stopped.

"Well, I don't quite understand why you're so preoccupied by that."

You seem fairly preoccupied by it yourself, thought Bergmann.

He turned off toward the Shell station.

"I'm just trying to close up any holes I can find in the investigation. You're welcome to call me nitpicky."

Elisabeth took a deep breath.

"Oh well," she said as she exhaled.

Bergmann parked the car and got out.

He walked through the slush to the back side of the station and lit a cigarette. He'd once sat back here with Hege, after a trip to Rena, where they'd spent the weekend with friends who had a cabin there. It was one of the nicest trips they'd had together. It was summer; he was happy—as happy as he could be; and she was happy, too, for once. Said that she wanted to have a child with him. Didn't she? Yes. He stared up at the gray clouds blowing across the black sky. He moved his gaze to the cab of a parked truck. A small Christmas tree shone in the front window. *On Christmas Eve I'll be alone.* Then he stopped, refusing to let himself wallow in self-pity.

"I'll call you if anything happens," he said to her.

"Alex is his son."

He took a deep drag on the cigarette.

"His son?"

"Per-Erik isn't Alex's father. Morten is his father. Morten Høgda."

There was silence on the other end.

He waited.

"I don't know why I'm telling you this. It has nothing to do with Kristiane. It's just that I've repressed her since 1988. And so much else too. I can't go on like that. I can't live a life full of denial. Do you understand what I mean, Tommy?"

He didn't reply.

"Do you understand?" she said again.

"Yes. I understand," he said quietly, the words drowned out by the roar of the highway nearby.

"Only you and one girlfriend of mine know this. I want it to stay between us for the time being. Not a word to Per-Erik."

"No. I can't get hold of him anyway. The school told me he's in Thailand."

"No surprise," she said, not without a certain coldness in her voice. "Thai women make no demands."

He ignored her. There were more important things to worry about.

"So no one else knows that Høgda is Alex's father?"

She paused.

"No."

"Not even Morten Høgda?"

She did not reply.

"I'll take that as a yes," said Bergmann. *I don't like people lying to me,* he thought, but didn't want to provoke her.

"And Alex?"

"No, God forbid."

"I think I'd like to talk to Høgda myself."

"Oh well." The answer came quickly.

"Are you friends?"

"We talk sometimes. Not often. He probably doesn't understand why, but I have to take things one day at a time. Besides, I can't understand that he would have anything to do with this."

"He's Alex's father," said Bergmann. "And he was with you the night Kristiane disappeared. Maybe the night she was murdered."

She was silent.

"Tell me a little more about him."

"He was a friend of Per-Erik's. They were business partners. They shared everything, actually. Before Morten took over the whole firm."

She stopped there.

They shared everything, thought Bergmann. *Including you.*

"Another thing," he said, "about Alexander, *Alex* . . . I'll ask you flat-out: Could he have lied during the questioning? He claims he was alone that whole afternoon and evening, until about ten, when he left for a party. But no one can recall seeing him at the party until around midnight."

"I don't recall," said Elisabeth. "Why would he lie about that?"

Either you don't understand, or you don't want to understand, thought Bergmann.

"But Alex and Kristiane were both left alone almost all day that Saturday when she disappeared?"

"Yes, I think so."

"Could he have picked her up somewhere, or perhaps driven her someplace? After handball practice?"

"What do you mean?"

"Alex maintains that he was alone until ten o'clock on the Saturday Kristiane disappeared," Bergmann repeated, "when he left to meet friends at a private party. But no one there remembers him arriving before midnight, if we can rely at all on witness statements from half-drunk high school kids. Did he usually drive her places? What was the relationship like between them?"

"I don't understand where you're going with this."

"Do you think he could be holding something back, that he knows something, but didn't want to speak up, out of fear of getting dragged into it?"

She waited a long time.

Too long.

"No. No, I could never imagine such a thing."

"Does he still live in Tromsø?"

She didn't say anything.

"I—" she started to say.

"Yes?"

"I have to go."

When he got back in the car, he picked up the envelope with the letter to Rask. He felt like his head was in a vise. He needed more time, a lot more time.

Alex was not the son of Per-Erik Thorstensen.

And who the hell wrote this letter to Rask?

A woman.

43

The last person she wanted to talk to just then was Halgeir Sørvaag. Susanne Bech had spent most of her time after lunch falling into what she knew was a transient depression, one of the countless mood swings Nicolay said he couldn't live with.

So why didn't he leave me? she wondered. *Why was I the one who had to leave him?* She'd been trying to read through documents systematically since eight o'clock that morning, with only one thought in mind: *Kristiane had fallen in love with someone she shouldn't have.* Before lunch she'd even gone over to *Aftenposten* and sat in the text archive to find something about Bjørn-Åge Flaten's attempts to sell his story. But now she felt just black inside, and that damned Halgeir "I'm undressing you with my eyes" Sørvaag was standing in the doorway, shifting from one foot to the other.

She turned her chair around slowly and hoped that Sørvaag couldn't see that she'd been crying. Ten minutes ago she'd been on the verge of calling Nicolay to ask him to drop the girl she knew he was consoling himself with and come home for Christmas. Instead she had raced into the restroom and cried as quietly as she could. She had washed off her mascara after she had no more tears left, and it looked like Sørvaag didn't recognize her at first.

"Yes?" she said, putting her reading glasses on, in the hope that it would make her look like a serious thirty-two-year-old and not a sulky teenage girl who regretted her choices. Anders Rask had escaped, two nurses had been killed, and the head doctor at Ringvoll and his wife had been stabbed to death, and here she was, hiding in the restroom and crying about how she'd left Nico and was going to be alone with Mathea on Christmas Eve.

"Have you seen Tommy?" Sørvaag asked, perhaps more acidly than he'd intended.

No, I haven't seen that nutcase, she thought, but managed to keep her mouth shut and just shook her head.

Sørvaag grunted a kind of "Oh well" and gave her a strange look.

"Can I help you with anything?"

He shrugged, which pulled his shirttail out of his pants. He didn't even bother to tuck his shirt back in again, but just fiddled a little with his knit jacket, as though he were an insecure schoolboy and not a man who was rapidly approaching the state's required retirement age.

"It was just that thing about . . . perhaps you remember . . ."

Remember what? thought Susanne. That he'd put his hand on her ass when they danced together at the summer party? That she'd ended up with Svein Finneland? Damned men, she was so fucking tired of the whole lot of them.

"That thing with Maria. Edle Maria. The who—" Sørvaag stopped himself, and Susanne felt her eyes narrowing. She was about to get up and slap him. If he called that poor Lithuanian girl a whore one more time, he would have only himself to blame, and she could find a place in line at the employment office.

"What about her?"

"The girl said only one understandable thing, and that was Maria. Do you remember that I said I'd heard that name somewhere? The word the girl said first, Edle, and then Maria?"

I remember that Fredrik Reuter made you look foolish, thought Susanne.

"Yes."

"Old Lorentzen, my first boss, once told me about a case from many years ago. Something about Maria, from a place he'd worked. Edle Maria. Somewhere up north."

"And you still think there's a connection?" Susanne took her glasses off, and any thought of Christmas Eve alone with Mathea, or Nicolay between the legs of a twenty-something blonde, disappeared. Sørvaag was no favorite of hers, but he'd never been stupid.

"Where was it Lorentzen worked?" she asked.

"It may be a coincidence."

"It's worth checking out."

"The problem is that his personnel folder has been destroyed. He's dead, and his wife is dead."

"Yes, but we can get hold of someone who worked with him, his kids. There must be someone who can tell us where he worked."

Sørvaag nodded.

"He only told me about it once, one night we were working together. The first time I saw a murdered person. He told me that there was a young girl up north, where he worked, who'd been found after several months. Killed with a knife, slaughtered according to the autopsy, and devoured by animals. Her name was Edle Maria. I'm quite certain of it now."

His phone rang. He stood there, looking at it like an idiot.

"I'm sure it's just a coincidence," he said again, then disappeared down the corridor.

It's no damned coincidence, thought Susanne, looking up the number for Kripo.

"Do we have a list of persons killed in the sixties? In northern Norway?"

The man on the other end laughed cynically. "No, that system hasn't been invented yet. The file is probably still located where it was investigated, or more likely in the National Archives up there. If the record still exists at all, that is. Listen, I have another call."

She was put on hold.

It was almost four thirty.

She cursed as she sat there looking at her own reflection in the window.

She could picture Mathea, lying upside down on the slide on the daycare playground, the dark-clothed person standing motionless on the walkway observing the little girl. She hung up. Her child was far more important than waiting for men who laughed at her.

She had just gotten her bubble coat down from the coat stand when her phone rang.

"You have to go out to Malmøya," said Bergmann without so much as a hello.

"Hello to you too. Bad day?"

"The worst. I passed the car of the person who killed Furuberget. But do you think I remember what kind of car it was? Hell no. I can only remember what kind of car it *wasn't*."

"Cryptic," said Susanne. She was already on her way down the stairs; she didn't have time to wait for the elevator. With any luck, she would make it to daycare before it closed. Mathea would undoubtedly use it against her one day that she almost always got picked up last.

"Regardless. Furuberget was searching for a letter that someone had written to Rask. There's got to be a connection there, don't you think?"

Susanne shook her head.

"Tommy . . ."

"I think Furuberget was killed by someone he'd met before. He was about to serve coffee when he was killed, do you understand? Perhaps by the person who wrote the letter. But I think it's a woman. That confuses me."

"I don't understand a thing," said Susanne.

She jogged across Grønlandsleiret, looking out for a taxi in the absurd chaos of Christmas wreaths, tandoori restaurants, round-cheeked elves, and women in hijab. Bergmann filled her in on the letter Furuberget had been searching for, the letter he was convinced was written by a woman. Medusa's tears.

"Jon-Olav Farberg is the only one we have who knows Rask. I think he's holding something back. Read the report, go out to see him, and decide for yourself."

Susanne had already read the report from the first interview with Farberg. She knew what Bergmann was getting at. Who was Rask's friend, Yngvar? If Farberg said *A*, he would have to say *B*.

"I think it's a woman who wrote to Rask. And I think he's on his way to meet her. Question Farberg. I have to go talk to someone else tonight. It's urgent."

"Okay, I'll get a babysitter," she said.

He sighed on the other end, as if he'd forgotten that she had a child. As if he thought, *Oh good heavens, that kid, always the damned kid.*

There's no way in the world he'll ever recommend me for a permanent position. If she didn't pull this off, it was all over.

"It might have to be this evening."

"It has to be this evening. Check him out, understand? You're good at this. Read the report I wrote after the interview with him out at Lysaker. His number's in there. Ask him about Rask. Use that as a point of entry. He knows Rask. Rask has escaped. Got it?"

"But why do you find him so interesting?"

"He's the only person who knows Rask, and I think he's lying about something. Shouldn't that be reason enough?"

She got hold of Torvald on the first try. He still had a meeting at work before he could leave, and said he couldn't pick up Mathea on such short notice. But of course he could watch her this evening.

Again. If Mathea had been two years younger, she probably would have thought that the gay man from the floor below was her father.

Susanne felt a tingling down her spine. She just had to print out that damned report. Mathea would be standing by the entry with a grumpy daycare teacher by her side when she arrived.

She stopped on the sidewalk and keyed to Bergmann on the contact list on her phone.

"Why—" she began, but just got a busy signal. *Why can't you go out there?*

She turned around and went back the same way she'd come. Police headquarters stood like the Ice Castle among the trees in the park, as if she were on her way to see the Snow Queen in the Hans Christian Andersen story.

The Snow Queen.

The evil witch.

A woman had written a letter to Rask, wasn't that what Bergmann had said? *Medusa's tears?*

Susanne turned on her PC and looked at the clock. She called the taxi dispatch and ordered a taxi for ten to five; it would just have to do. She entered "Medusa" in the search field and skimmed the text.

> *A monster from Greek mythology. Living poisonous snakes as hair. Anyone who looked her right in the eyes would turn to stone. Medusa was originally a strikingly beautiful young woman, "the jealous longing of many suitors," but when she was captured and raped by Poseidon, "the Lord of the Sea," in Athena's own temple, the furious Athena had Medusa's hair transformed into snakes and made her face so ghastly that no one could look at her without turning to stone.*

"I don't understand any of this," she said to herself.

Edle Maria. Medusa.

No. She would have to check the report Bergmann had written from the interview with Farberg.

She found the file in the common area, but the printer in the copy room was out of paper. On the corkboard there was a postcard from Mombasa, a notice about Christmas lunch, and a thank-you card featuring a bridal couple, a younger female colleague. Someone had printed out an e-mail from his wife about a Christmas celebration at Stabekk School. She read the text surreptitiously and sat down on the floor with an unopened ream of paper in her hands.

"Have a nice day. Love you," it said at the bottom.

She guided her index finger over the last two words.

"Love you," she whispered. "I still love you."

44

Even on the easy listening radio stations, there was hardly anything but reports about Rask and Jensrud's escape, interspersed with the customary talentless commercials, so poorly executed a person would do almost anything to avoid hearing them. He turned the dial to NRK on the old Blaupunkt radio. Vestoppland was still responsible for the search, which suited Bergmann fine. The newscaster reported the same things Fredrik Reuter had summarized on Bergmann's voice mail while he'd been with Flatanger up at Kripo: The dark-blue Opel Corsa the two escapees had used for their flight from Ringvoll had been found burned in the Sørum municipality. The nurse who had now been named Anders Rask's lover had probably placed another car in the vicinity of the isolated forest road in Sørum. But as long as she stubbornly denied having helped the two men with even one car, Rask and Jensrud were now in flight in an unknown vehicle. The dilemma was obviously to not create panic, while making what the police's PR people called "the general public" aware that Rask and Jensrud were dangerous and perhaps armed. The police chief in Vestoppland therefore had no choice but to advise everyone in Østlandet to exercise caution and not open the door to strangers.

Brilliant, thought Bergmann. One and a half million people now wouldn't open the door to strangers. He parked the car in one of the few vacant spaces on Munkedamsveien and took the Raven pistol out of the glove compartment. If Rask and his companion were even thinking about visiting him, he would blow both their craniums from here to eternity.

The idea that Rask might have been in his apartment nagged at him. It couldn't be him; in any event, he couldn't have been the one to break into his storage compartment. He needed to get hold of the neighbor's drug addict son, though he already knew it wasn't him or any of his buddies. They would have taken what little there was of value down there—some bottles of wine and old silverware Hege had left behind. Whoever had been in the compartment had been after something very specific. Or maybe whoever it was had just wanted to scare him. If that was the case, he'd succeeded fairly well. Better than Bergmann cared to admit. He couldn't stand enemies he couldn't see.

He was irritated at himself as he stood in the elevator on his way up to the top floor of the building in Stranden. He put his hand on the pistol and checked that he'd closed the zipper on his pocket. Maybe it was silly, but he didn't like people breaking into his place, or, more specifically, not people like this. People who had slaughtered seven girls and let them bleed to death.

Morten Høgda answered the door himself. Bergmann's shoes had already made a wet pool on the Persian rug in the hall. Høgda's gaze shifted to the puddle, as if Bergmann were just another servant. *Good thing there's wood flooring under it,* thought Bergmann, disliking the man instinctively. *The richer, the greedier.*

They went through a hallway lined with graphic art. Bergmann didn't have time to study the motifs; he only caught random brush strokes in pastel colors. Høgda showed him into the living room, if you could call it that. The room was bigger than his own apartment.

"You can hang your coat up here," he said in a condescending tone and pointed at a coat rack, certainly from some designer Bergmann had never heard of.

He had to smile. Høgda's efforts at adopting an Oslo dialect were not particularly successful. But he'd landed one of the city's best apartments for himself, he had to grant him that. The apartment had a maritime character; Bergmann might just as well have been on a boat. One side of the living room ended in an angle with an open 180-degree view of Rådhuset, Akershus fortress, Bunnefjorden, and Nesodden. The postcard-like view of the fortress and the sparkling lights from thousands of buildings had a hypnotizing effect on Bergmann.

"Something to drink?"

Høgda was standing over by the open kitchen. It did not smell of food or look as though the spotless kitchen was ever used. But that was hardly a surprise. He was the type who had household help come in twice a day and ate dinner out every evening.

"Whiskey, cognac, or something nonalcoholic?"

"Coke would be fine."

"Coke it is then." Høgda had evidently gotten over his initial peevishness and now seemed to be trying to pour on what Bergmann often thought of as West Side charm, though he knew Høgda wasn't from the West Side at all, but a little village in northern Norway. *You don't fool me,* he thought. Either you had the laid-back self-confidence that financial security, education, and upbringing in the right postal codes gave you, or you didn't. Not even a hundred million kroner on the tax form could change that. That was the weakness of the nouveau riche. Bergmann knew that Høgda was nothing but a simple fisherman's son who had earned his first money by cleaning cod on the pier. If Høgda was smart, he'd realize that himself and put an end to his ostentatious overtures.

"Where in northern Norway are you from again?" said Bergmann as Høgda set the glasses on the coffee table.

"Kvænangen." The answer came almost reluctantly.

"Right," said Bergmann. "So you're not an Oslo boy? I don't know where I got that from." He smiled like the yokel he was pretending to be.

Høgda appeared to shrink a little on the couch on the other side of the table. He took a drink from the whiskey glass, which was probably of the finest crystal. Here he'd spent his entire working life trying to make himself as refined as possible, with handmade shoes and razor-sharp creases in his trousers, and then an East Side slob like Tommy Bergmann plops down on his couch and the first thing he asks is which fishing village he's from. He almost had to smile at himself. He considered revealing that his mother was from northern Norway to show him that they weren't so different when it came down to it, but decided that could wait for another time.

"Elisabeth told me that you know . . ." Høgda stared distantly down into his glass. It was already empty.

"I just need to fill in a few holes in the investigation." Høgda invited him to get right to the point, and Bergmann liked that.

"Did you socialize much with Per-Erik and Elisabeth?"

"To be quite honest, Bergmann . . ." Høgda stood up and went slowly to the kitchen, retrieved the bottle of Bushmills whiskey, and sat down again. He poured the glass half-full again. "I don't understand why you need to talk to me. Elisabeth asked me to, and I'm doing it for her sake. Yes, we had a relationship for many years, behind the back of one of my very best friends, Per-Erik, and yes, I'm Alex's father. He doesn't know that, of course. I didn't even know it myself for many years. But I don't understand what any of that has to do with Kristiane. She was Per-Erik's daughter, and God knows he adored her. She was everything to him, Bergmann, absolutely everything."

Bergmann had to think. Høgda was obviously not a coward—there was little doubt of that. He looked Bergmann in the eye with a serious expression on his face. His eyes were green, almost turquoise; those eyes had likely made him a bit of a ladies' man in his prime. Now just over sixty, he looked drawn and worn, but he could probably still get the women he wanted. If not, he probably just took them anyway.

"As I said," said Bergmann, "we don't need to talk for long. But I'd like to fill in the blank spaces in the investigation. Rask has got the case reopened, as you know, and now he's escaped—"

"Unbelievable," said Høgda. "When you find him, you can just shoot him as far as I'm concerned. In fact, I hope they put up some resistance. That will give you solid grounds for getting rid of those two lunatics." He took a big gulp from the whiskey glass.

"Sure. But back to my question, you were a friend of the family?"

"Definitely. Including both my first wife and my second wife."

"Even after Kristiane was born?"

"Until she was killed, Bergmann, until Per-Erik called me that Sunday night and told me she'd been found. I've never heard a grown man cry like that. I would have done anything at all to lighten his grief, but there was nothing I could do. It was a double tragedy. He had behaved like a total swine to Elisabeth for many years, but pulled himself together to a degree I didn't think he was capable of. And then the apple of his eye was killed. I thought he might kill himself. That was before I knew that Elisabeth had tried to."

He searched Bergmann's gaze. Perhaps he knew Bergmann had been the one to stop the blood that was streaming from her wrist so long ago.

"So you were together the night she disappeared?"

"From two o'clock in the afternoon until eleven the next morning, Sunday."

"You were together the whole time?"

He nodded.

"What were you doing?"

Høgda sniffed.

"We were doing what people usually do when they're unfaithful. I guess we were trying to fuck each other's brains out."

Bergmann didn't say anything.

"Isn't that what you do when you betray your respective spouses?"

"I guess that's it," said Bergmann.

"I was only one in an endless series of men." Høgda appeared to be lost in thought. "For many years Elisabeth could have anyone she wanted. I guess it was a kind of consolation for her. Per-Erik was no angel."

"So you knew Kristiane well?"

Høgda emptied the whiskey and stared into the glass awhile, as if the answer could be found at the bottom of it.

"What are you suggesting, Bergmann?" His almost-turquoise eyes narrowed.

"I just want to have a third party's view of her, someone who could see her from a bit of a distance, and at the same time knew the family."

"I'm hardly a third party. Wouldn't you agree?"

Høgda poured himself another glass of Bushmills and fell silent.

"I'm trying to form an impression of Kristiane for myself."

"And what the hell is the point of that, so many years later? Do you think that will bring her back to life, Bergmann? Do you think that will help Elisabeth find peace in the years she has left on this earth?"

Høgda got up and walked away, taking the whiskey glass with him. Bergmann stared down at his own hands, the little notepad, the blank page, the pen lying on the glass coffee table.

The sound of a sliding door being opened broke the silence.

Then a low sound came out of some unseen speakers. Probably built-in. An opera he'd heard before, a tenor he recognized.

A cold draft passed over the living room floor, followed by the odor of cigarette smoke. Bergmann went back to the entry to find his own pack. As he passed through the corridor, he stopped and studied one of the prints. Now that he had time to look at them, he saw what they depicted. In one, a young Asian woman, probably Japanese, was hanging from the ceiling in an almost dark room, bound by her wrists with rope. Judging from her expression, she appeared to be writhing in pain, but it was difficult to tell. The body may have been covered with bruises, but it was hard to be sure due to the pastel red color laid over the surface of the picture in three apparently random brush strokes. *But yes,* thought Bergmann, feeling the nausea rise in his throat. He had to stop staring at the graceful body. Several of the other photographs depicted humiliated women in black and white with their hands tied behind their back, overlaid with slashes of yellow, pink, and green. The last picture Bergmann looked at before he went back to the living room was of a young woman, presumably also Japanese, lying dead in a casket—or perhaps just acting the part—strewn with orchid petals. Her face was purple with postmortem lividity.

He tried to suppress the images from his mind as he went out to join Morten Høgda on the balcony. It was snowing more heavily now, and he could barely see the fortress. He still felt queasy after viewing the collection of . . . *Of what?* he thought. It was hardly art. It reminded him too much of something else. Of himself.

"You have a few pictures on the wall."

"They're beautiful, aren't they?" said Høgda, staring out at the city. He barely seemed to notice that Bergmann had come out onto the balcony. "Akira Nobioki. Paid a small fortune for them. People from across the globe have been collecting his work for years. From Tokyo to New York to Cape Town to Buenos Aires."

"You don't have many visits from your grandchildren?" said Bergmann.

"I don't have many visitors. I'm not overly fond of people. And I don't have children," said Høgda.

"You have Alex."

He laughed quietly.

"Those pictures are in a class of their own. Nobioki has his own aesthetic. He puts out a couple of photo books every year, at reasonable prices, if you're interested. Around ten or fifteen kroner, I think."

"Do you have any interests of that type?" said Bergmann. "Torture?"

Høgda frowned.

"Call it torture if you want. You're no liberal, I'm guessing. What happens in the bedroom, stays in the bedroom, I say. It's art, Bergmann. Art."

Bergmann lit a cigarette and smiled to himself. He thought he should have left, but he didn't want to give Høgda that satisfaction. They stood there and smoked in silence. The snow dampened nearly all the city noise; only the faint rumble of a Nesodd ferry broke through the quiet music coming from inside the living room. Bergmann knew he'd heard that opera somewhere before. Høgda appeared to notice that Bergmann was trying to think of what music he was playing. He put out his cigarette, a filterless Camel, and took a new one from a pack on the weatherproof teak balcony table.

"Why is Iago so evil?" said Høgda, lighting the cigarette. "You're a policeman, can you answer that?"

Othello, thought Bergmann. The music was Verdi's *Othello.* Where had he heard that opera before? Once again he saw himself standing in the corridor at Ringvoll, meeting the eyes of the patient. A glass had fallen to the floor, he remembered that. A penetrating scream. *Something I experienced as a child.* That was clear to him now. But where?

Suddenly it came back to him.

His old neighbor in Tveita. He was one of the few men that his mother trusted.

Høgda cleared his throat, then said quietly, "What satisfaction does he get from destroying Othello's life? Othello, who trusts him so blindly? Who exploits other people's blindness so damned deliberately, Bergmann?"

"I don't know." Bergmann barely remembered the story of Othello just then, but pretended otherwise.

"Iago leads Othello to believe that his wife has been unfaithful with the man he has promoted, the man Iago believes got the advancement he himself deserves. But why does he do that? Did he want Othello to kill the woman he loved more than anything on earth? Did that give him satisfaction?"

Bergmann did not answer. They smoked another cigarette in silence. Høgda took a few more slugs of whiskey. Bergmann knew he would have to come see Høgda another time. He wanted to read the rape reports to him personally, but pressuring him about them now would be foolish.

"Kristiane was a great girl," said Høgda. "What else can I say? She could have been anything at all, had whatever she wanted. Just like her mother. Lived a good life. Better than mine, God knows."

Bergmann nodded.

"What about Alex?"

Their eyes met. Høgda looked away.

"What about him?"

"Do you have any contact with him?"

He shook his head.

"He knows that you're his father," Bergmann tossed out, testing the assertion.

"What does that have to do with the case?" said Høgda. His expression did not change.

"Nothing." *Nothing other than that Elisabeth Thorstensen is lying to me,* he thought.

"Okay. Yes, he knows it. We've met a few times."

"I don't like it when people lie to me."

"That was stupid." Høgda was holding something back.

"Did she ask you to lie? Elisabeth?"

"No."

Bergmann didn't pursue the matter. He didn't believe Høgda, but he decided to drop it. What else could she lie about, or get others to keep quiet about? He noticed he had an incipient weakness for her, an impulse that would excuse why she was capable of telling a lie right to his face.

For some reason, Høgda started talking about one of the boats tied up to the pier below them. Some Americans who had no doubt anchored there for the winter.

"Free people. They just do whatever they want. Wouldn't it be something to live such a carefree life?"

"Sure."

Bergmann decided it was time to go. As Høgda followed him out, they stopped by a large Modernist painting.

"There you have my boat," said Høgda, pointing. The painting was of a summer house by the sea. The boat was a short distance from land. Bergmann just managed to make out the painter's notation in the lower left corner: "Hvasser 1987."

As they passed by the bizarre pictures of bound, tortured women again, Bergmann wondered whether it was the thought of Elisabeth Thorstensen that made the sight of these photographed women so unbearable. Did she like that sort of thing? The thought tormented him—and the fact that it did tormented him even further.

Høgda gave him a firm handshake. He even placed his other hand over Bergmann's, as though they knew each other well. His hands were big, with well-groomed nails and soft, warm skin, like a woman's.

"Call me if I can be of any help. And find those two lunatics."

As Bergmann walked down the street, he put the hood of his bubble jacket over his head, whether to protect himself from the snowstorm or from a couple of lovebirds walking toward him, he didn't know. They walked close together, the man laughing at something the woman had said. Bergmann thought they were roughly his age, hovering around forty. Either they'd found each other quite recently, or they'd managed to keep the flame alive without the one destroying the other.

He stood looking at the Nesodd ferry that was putting out from land until its sparkling lights disappeared in the increasingly heavy snow.

He was struck by a sense that he'd been misled. Had he let himself be led to the target, only to be fooled at the last moment?

He had disliked Høgda when he arrived, but liked him by the time he left. He'd almost forgotten that he'd been charged with rape several times and presumably was a regular in the red-light district.

It was something Høgda had said or done that he had instinctively reacted to.

As he parked in the police station garage, it came to him.

Morten Høgda had had a cabin in Hvasser since the late seventies.

To get to Hvasser, what town did you have to drive through?

Tønsberg.

The first girl was from Tønsberg.

45

She didn't know how many times Torvald had come to her rescue. Susanne slipped quietly out of Mathea's room, a last remnant of warmth from her little body still lingering in her sweater. Torvald had been leaning against the door frame for the last few minutes watching them. Susanne put her hand to his cheek.

"I often dream that you're hetero," she whispered in the hallway. "You should know that."

He was very handsome, and her age. But God had decided that he was lost to the women of this world.

"Are you going on a *date* in *that?*" he said as she pulled on an old wool sweater.

"Not a *date,*" she said, giving him a hug.

"Good Lord, such an exciting life you lead."

"I said it was work, Torvald."

He shook his head. "Life is no dress rehearsal, my girl."

Tell me about it, thought Susanne.

She put her bubble jacket under her arm and headed down the stairs. On her way down, the sight of the brass molding on each step reminded her of the courtyard on Frognerveien. Though she hadn't been there in person, she'd seen the crime scene photos.

The perpetrator had walked off just like this. Calm, collected. As if none of the slaughter had happened. What could he have been thinking? Or was it a she?

Raped by Poseidon. Put the blame on herself.

During the short taxi ride she tried to read the text of the letter Bergmann had found in Rask's room. He had dictated it to her on the phone, and she'd written it down on the back of an old issue of *Elle*, over the face of a Lancôme model: "A traveling carnival . . . a gypsy woman . . . You yourself have received a gift . . . From where I live, the sea looks black." Bergmann was certain that a woman had written the letter to Anders Rask. Susanne shook her head. A woman, why a woman?

As the taxi turned sharply onto Ormøya, she gave up and turned off the reading light in the ceiling. She took in the sight of the old houses decorated for Advent. Maybe when her parents died, she would buy an old house out on Malmøya—that is, if her mother didn't convince her father to practically disinherit her and only give her the minimum the law required.

"Was it my fault that Line died?" she mouthed, as if she were talking to God himself. *Maybe,* she answered herself. Then, *Good Lord, what am I thinking?*

As the taxi glided slowly across the bridge to Ormøya, she thought that life must be good out there on one of the city's own Greek islands.

"I could've lived with this," she said to herself as the taxi parked in front of Jon-Olav Farberg's house.

She put the expensive bag Nico had bought for her last Christmas over her shoulder, and the taxi disappeared from sight. She felt strangely abandoned. Though she wasn't far from home and Mathea, she felt a flash of fear that she'd never see her again.

The moon had broken through the cloud cover and cast a strip of light across the water right below the old Swiss chalet. Susanne stopped in the graveled yard and assured herself that the plastic folder with the copy of the letter to Rask was tucked well down in her bag.

She looked up at the sky again. The cloud layer had almost completely broken up; for the first time in a long while, they might have a cloud-free sky. She studied the stars for a while. It was darker out here, and she could see them more clearly. The only constellation she was able to recognize was as usual the Big Dipper. She was clearly no astronomer. Not to mention astrologer. Like that gypsy woman.

The doorbell gave off a quiet ring on the other side of the door. Then all she heard was a faint lapping of waves.

She put her ear to the door. Had she heard wrong? Maybe the doorbell didn't work.

No sound.

Though the outside light wasn't turned on, there were lights on in the windows on both the first and second floors.

She checked her watch. It was only five to nine.

Steps approached. A woman's voice. She was talking to someone, perhaps herself. She sounded crabby, maybe cursing the fact that someone saw fit to ring the doorbell at that hour.

The woman who opened the door initially looked shocked when Susanne held her police ID up and asked whether Jon-Olav Farberg was at home.

"Has he done something wrong?" she asked quietly. She had thick gray hair tied up in a bun. Susanne wondered whether she was a teacher, or perhaps an artist, with a studio at home.

The door to the entry porch was closed, but she could see into the front hall through the glass in the door.

Susanne shook her head.

"Not at all. I'm hoping he can help us with a case." She smiled warmly, and the woman smiled back.

"Sorry, I'm just so surprised."

She introduced herself as Birgit Farberg. Susanne imagined that the house had belonged to her family, though she wasn't sure why.

"Jon-Olav is in the shower. He's been out running."

"I can wait."

"I'll let him know." She looked at her watch, an expensive one. "And then I just have to watch the news. It's appalling, what's happened with those escapes. I almost don't dare to go outdoors with that sort running loose. What if Rask were to show up on our doorstep? Jon-Olav used to work with him after all."

She led Susanne into the library. From the windows, she could see out to the sea. The moon still shone, and the waves refracted the light, giving it a dreamy, dance-like quality.

She heard rapid steps up the stairs to the second floor.

The sound coming from the TV meant that she couldn't hear anything else going on upstairs. A commercial for something to do with Christmas. She could picture the commercials, Americanized, with the mother and father, each more photogenic than the other, two children, maybe three, all in pajamas, opening presents on Christmas morning.

This was not reality. Not even an illusion of reality.

The news began. Unsurprising, the escape was the lead story. The newscaster took pains with the dramatic, serious tone of voice. Who could hold that against him? This was serious. Two of the country's craziest men had killed two nurses. They could be anywhere at all.

Susanne tried to shake the feeling that Rask knew who she was. That Bergmann had said something about her. That they were on their way to get Mathea. Right now.

She took her phone out of her bag. No one had called. But why should anyone have called?

How she hated the vulnerability Mathea subjected her to, the fine layer of tiny needles she felt all over her body. If something ever did happen to Mathea, all the needles would be pressed into her skin and slowly drain her of blood, burying her for all time.

She got up from the wing chair and walked around the room, studying the spines of the books. As a former teacher Farberg had plenty of books. Perhaps his wife was a teacher too. Then her thoughts quickly snowballed. Susanne had grown up with endless shelves of books too. Her mother was a teacher, even though she never had to work. How could someone who had read so much about people be so damned cold?

Between two of the bookshelves was a series of older lithographs or etchings. Susanne recognized the Zorn motifs—naked, voluptuous women in black and white. Next to them was a black-and-white photograph of a balding man with a long bushy beard staring intensely at something next to the photographer. The man's crazed expression reminded her of a mixture of Strindberg and Rasputin. The guy could not have been in his right mind.

At the bottom of the photograph it said in white script: "Goodwin. John Norén. Uppsala."

"Hello there." The voice behind her overpowered the sound of the TV in the adjacent room.

Jon-Olav Farberg was standing in the doorway. He was barefoot and dressed in blue jeans and an unbuttoned pale blue Oxford shirt. He was drying his hair with a towel.

Susanne was surprised at how well preserved he looked. She would have guessed him to be at least ten years younger than he was. Judging from his expression, he looked like he'd just had sex—but not with his wife. She had seemed too crabby and unapproachable for that.

He walked toward her and introduced himself.

"What happened to the other guy, Bergmann?"

"He's busy."

Farberg smiled and gestured toward the leather couch behind her.

"Rask has escaped." Susanne tipped her head in the direction of the TV room. "The doctor has been killed. You know all this, of course. You knew Rask from before, back when Kristiane Thorstensen was killed."

"I wonder what Anders is thinking now," he said, nodding toward the double sliding doors that led into the TV room.

"Just so long as they don't think about doing something stupid," said Susanne. "Something even worse than what they've already done. If that's possible."

Farberg buttoned his shirt. His forehead gleamed with perspiration. He had probably showered too soon after his run.

"It's impressive to go jogging in this weather."

"Physical fitness is a perishable commodity. It's all about willpower: nice weather, bad weather, you can't let yourself be ruled by that sort of thing." Farberg threw the towel over the back of the other wing chair and sat down. "I'm not getting any younger. Do you exercise, or is it just an all-out effort before a physical?"

Susanne did not reply, just smiled, albeit unwillingly. *That's enough now,* she thought.

"Sometimes I drive up to Ekebergsletta," he said after a while. "Or up to Rustadsaga. Nice to run out there with a headlamp."

"What do you think is going to happen? Where could he conceivably go? You know Rask better than any of us." Susanne nodded toward the sound of the TV again. The police chief in Vestoppland had a deep, booming voice, in stark contrast to the police commissioner's, whatever she might have to do with the case. The Minister of Justice had probably forced her to make an appearance.

"I don't know," said Farberg. "I never really knew him. None of us did."

"Do you think that Rask is the type to look up people he knows and try to hide with them, maybe even kill them?"

Farberg looked skeptical. Susanne held his gaze—a little too long. She felt like an amateur.

"He's not coming here anyway." He started to smile, but then appeared to change his mind, as if he suddenly realized that might indeed be a possibility.

"It must have been the other guy who killed the two nurses," said Farberg. "Anders could never have killed two grown men. What's the other guy's name?"

"Jensrud. Øystein Jensrud."

A little shiver passed through Farberg's body. He buttoned the cuffs on his shirt absentmindedly.

"Jensrud," he said to himself.

"Someone you know?"

Farberg did not reply.

"The fact that he escaped suggests that he killed those girls, don't you think? What about the doctor? Do you think Rask could have killed him?"

Farberg shrugged.

"To be honest I don't think Anders is capable of killing anyone at all. I'm sorry, I was supposed to get you the number for Gunnar Austbø, wasn't I? He was Kristiane's homeroom teacher. Did Bergmann tell you that?"

Susanne nodded.

"He's not easy to find," she said.

"I'll get on it first thing in the morning."

"I came here to talk with you about the man you mentioned. Rask's friend."

"Friend?" Farberg looked uncomprehending.

Susanne leaned forward.

"Oh, yes." Farberg appeared to grasp what she meant.

How could you forget such a thing? Susanne wondered. A moment later, she cursed Bergmann for not having taken Farberg seriously until now. Why hadn't he asked Rask about this Yngvar when he had the chance? Regardless, they wouldn't get far. *Maybe,* she thought, and was uplifted for the first time in a while, *maybe Rask would try to go to this confidante.*

There was a knock on the door, and Farberg's wife appeared in the doorway.

Susanne could not understand how the two of them had ended up together. Farberg looked much too good for her and seemed far more lively and social than she did. His wife may have been pretty once, but her looks had faded. Susanne thought she knew exactly what this marriage was: quiet and empty, interspersed with occasional outbursts of bitterness and recriminations.

"My sister's picking me up. I might just spend the night there," she said, avoiding Susanne's gaze.

"Okay," said Farberg without turning around. He looked as if he wanted to add, *Don't ever come home again.*

The wife closed the door. Farberg looked at Susanne, frowned, and shook his head.

"It won't be easy," he said.

"That friend," said Susanne. She looked down at her notepad, if only to avoid his blue eyes. The front door slammed, and the house became quiet.

"Yngvar," said Farberg. "I'm not sure—"

"It may be worth pursuing." *It may be a critical clue,* she thought. She wrote in big letters on her notepad, "Yngvar."

"You think they may have worked together?"

"As I said, I think so, but I'm not certain of it."

"Can you remember anything else about this Yngvar? When did Rask mention him for the first time?"

"I think it was at a summer staff party at the rector's house. He'd been drinking a little, he rarely drank—"

"Yngvar didn't work at Vetlandsåsen in any event," said Susanne.

Farberg shook his head. As he got up from the chair, it seemed for a moment as if he was going straight for Susanne. Instead he brushed past her, his pant leg barely grazing the shoulder of her wool sweater. He took another few steps, then it was quiet.

"I don't know how many times I've stood here like this since I moved out here."

Susanne turned halfway around on the couch. Farberg stood with his back to her, staring out toward the garden, which appeared to incline gently down toward the sea.

"Now I could never live any place other than right here."

Susanne imagined for a few moments what it would be like if she lived here herself. If his wife never came back. In a few minutes Farberg would be lying on top of her in one of the cold bedrooms. Then he'd light the tile stove after sleeping with her. She'd wake up late the next morning. Mathea would have her own room.

Idiot, she thought a moment later. *Fucking amateur idiot.*

Farberg turned and went back to the sofa. Susanne felt that she was blushing, as if he could read her sick thoughts.

"I can see if I can get you the staff lists from the schools where he's worked. I know that Laila, the office manager, keeps track of everyone who's worked there since she started. She must still have Anders's folder at the office. Or she can get it from Bryn, which was the last place he worked. This can't go on much longer. I mean, they're on the run. Something frightful could happen."

"Great," she said. "Please ask her to say that the police have asked for it, but that we obviously insist on their discretion."

"Do you have a number where I can reach you? Or should I call Bergmann?"

Susanne picked up her bag and rooted around in it. She felt his eyes on her while she fumbled for a business card, which was on the bottom.

"Women and handbags," he said. "It never ends." His smile was warm. His eyes looked gray in the weak light, though she knew they were blue.

"Susanne Bech," he said. "Are you related to Arild Bech?"

She ran her hand through her hair, unsure what to do for a moment.

"He's my father."

Farberg made a quiet whistling sound.

"I thought there was a resemblance."

Susanne stood up. She hadn't come out here to talk about her father. If she were honest with herself, she could barely remember why she'd left Mathea in the first place. Because Bergmann had asked her to. *Ordered her to,* she corrected herself.

"Thank you for all your help. You have my number. Call me anytime."

This house is just a dream, she thought as they walked down the hall.

She happened to think about his wife. Where had she gone?

When they reached the entry porch, Farberg said, "He had a cabin." He touched her forearm and held his hand there a moment. Their eyes met. He smiled and took her hand.

"Cabin? Who?"

"I remember it now." Farberg looked right at Susanne and started nodding to himself. "I'll be damned. Anders said that."

"Cabin, this Yngvar had a cabin?"

"Yes." Farberg ran his hand through his hair, evidently absorbed in thought. Finally he exhaled heavily out of his nose, resigned. "But I can't remember where. Impossible."

"Try."

"Yngvar lives in a cabin."

"He lives in a cabin?"

Farberg nodded slowly.

"That was what he said."

He opened the door for her. The cold air struck her in the face, made it easier to think clearly. She pulled the hood of her Canada Goose jacket over her head. Nico had always said that she looked like a little girl with that coyote pelt around her face.

She walked carefully down the slippery steps.

"I'll call if I think of anything else. Or if Anders calls."

Farberg smiled to himself.

"Just one last thing," said Susanne. She waited to turn around. It was dark in the neighboring house and all around her. For a moment she was scared. Scared to turn around.

"Maria," she said, turning around.

Farberg cocked his head. It was freezing cold out, but he was in his shirtsleeves, as if he had a woodstove inside him.

"What did you say?"

"Does the name Maria say anything to you? Or Edle Maria? Did Anders Rask ever mention a girl or woman whose name was Maria? Or Edle Maria?"

Farberg did not reply.

"It doesn't ring any bells?"

"I don't think so."

Susanne waited. *We're searching for a woman,* she thought, but she couldn't say that. A woman who has written letters to Anders Rask, who he might be going to meet right now. Though she wanted to go in and call a taxi, she had an overpowering feeling that it wouldn't be a good idea.

"Where do you live?" said Farberg. "Don't you have a car?"

"I'll walk."

"I can drive you home."

She stuck her hand down into her Louis Vuitton bag and wrapped her fingers around her phone.

"My boyfriend will pick me up."

Farberg didn't say anything.

"Policeman?"

She nodded.

"Or taxi driver?" He laughed quietly to himself.

She started walking away from the house.

"I'll call you about Gunnar Austbø," said Farberg. "Agreed?"

46

Something felt different as soon as he entered the entry of his building. He couldn't pinpoint what exactly, but Bergmann sensed that something had happened there after he left early that morning. He pulled down the zipper on the right pocket in his bubble jacket. The little Raven pistol had only one bullet in the chamber. He would shoot through the jacket if necessary. He turned and started back down the stairs to the basement storage compartments. When he came to the bottom, he pressed on the light switch and spun around to face the hollow space under the stairs.

He unlocked the door to the basement and turned on the light, keeping his hand on the pistol. He entered the room, looked left, then right, and saw nothing but a few snow shovels and three or four bicycles. He scrutinized the doors to the compartments, the rows of roughly planed planks, and the padlocks.

He hadn't bothered to get a new padlock for his own compartment, just left the old one there so that the door wouldn't swing open. But now it looked as though there was a small gap, as if someone had removed the broken padlock without putting it back. He walked quickly over to the compartment. Two steps from the door he pulled the Raven pistol out of his pocket. The padlock had been removed from the fitting, and the door was open. He tore the door completely open. The blood was pounding in his temples, and he could hardly hear because of the roaring in his ears. He quickly swung the pistol around.

It seemed like all the air in his lungs was suddenly released. *Fortunately nothing,* he thought. Fortunately? What was he doing? Nothing in the compartment had been touched. Maybe someone had simply bumped up against the lock and didn't put it back properly.

On his way back up the stairs, he got that same feeling again that something had happened in the entry. He stopped at the mailboxes by the front door and studied the cork bulletin board. Something about a Christmas market, a stroller for sale. A copy of the summons to the general meeting in January. Information from the property management company, Property Services.

He took the key ring from his pants pocket and checked that he'd closed the zipper on the pocket of his jacket, so that the pistol didn't fall out. He turned the key carefully in the mailbox lock, which made a dry creaking sound. A solitary window envelope. For once he was relieved to be getting a bill in the mail.

No.

A folded piece of paper was tucked deep inside the mailbox.

He stuck his hand into the narrow opening and fished out the paper. At first the letters just danced around on the white paper, refusing to form complete sentences. When he finally understood the message, he had to brace himself by taking a step to the side and leaning against the wall leading down to the basement.

He really has found me. He couldn't stop the thought. It seemed like the only possibility. He fumbled for the pistol. It was safely in his bubble jacket. Then he turned slowly around.

No one. He was alone.

Even the TV in the closest apartment was quiet. Everything was still. He read the page again, his hand still firmly on the pistol.

In Whitechapel, they said it could have been a midwife, did you know that? A woman. Why not? She could have walked around in public with a blood-soaked apron; she knew female anatomy; and she tolerated the sight of blood so very well. Why did it take them so long to think of that? When it was too late to find him. Or her.

Tommy, my friend, what do you think?
Could it have been a woman?

Do you remember me?
I came close to injuring her for life. And you too.
She reminded me of her.
Everything was about her.

If you understand this—that we two are the same—I will be dead before Christmas.

But don't fear for me, my friend, for I have already seen Hell open standing.

He stood there a long time, just shaking his head. "If you understand this—that we two are the same—I will be dead before Christmas." It was less than two weeks until Christmas. And "we two are the same." Was that true? *We two are the same.* The missing photograph of his mother. And now this.

He retrieved the copy of the letter he'd found in Anders Rask's room. The letter that Furuberget had searched for.

It wasn't the same handwriting.

The letter to Rask was written by a woman, he was quite sure of that. This letter was written by a man. They were searching for two people. A woman who had contact with Rask. And a man. A man who knew Bergmann?

Bergmann turned around slowly. With careful movements he folded up the paper and stuck it in the inside pocket of his jacket. He didn't care whether he put fingerprints on the paper. Whoever had come in through the front door and placed that sheet of paper in the letter slot of his mailbox would have used gloves anyway, he was sure of that. He waited a few seconds on the stairwell before heading quietly back down to the dark basement. It was so quiet in the entry that he could hear himself breathing through his nose.

How had he gotten in?

The door out to the street had a lock that used the same key as the basement door. No legal enterprise in the city would have copied a master key; it would have been game over for that business. It had to be ordered, and the housing association and the property owner kept a list of all the keys and their owners.

He must have come in with some other people, unless he just rang the bell of a temporary resident who had let him in. He must have used the same technique when he took the picture of his mother. But how the hell did he get hold of the keys? Bergmann only just now realized that he had to get the lock changed on his front door.

He started by ringing the doorbell of the Pakistani family who lived right across from his apartment. After ringing three times and knocking on the door several times, he gave up. He heard the TV on inside and saw that the peephole was dark. They probably decided not to answer when they saw it was him. He had quarreled with them several times, and even gotten the mother to go out on the lawn in front of the building and pick up meat scraps that she had thrown out the window. "This is no country village in Punjab," he'd said. Her husband had come to the door and accused him of racism, upon which Bergmann had slammed the door in his face. You could call him many things—most of which were probably true—but he'd never been a racist, and he wasn't going to start now, even though he'd certainly seen enough in his line of work to be drawn into the semifascist muck that characterized far too many of his colleagues. He was unsure whether the father of the family had even been hit by the door, but if he had been, it would have been no worse than a little nosebleed. Given all that, perhaps it was no wonder the family simply ignored him when he stood there pounding on the door.

On his way up to the second floor, he took the letter out of his pocket again. He stopped on the landing and read it again, slowly, letting the words really sink in this time. His spine still shivered at the words "we two are the same," but that wasn't what he noticed. It was the strange formulation at the end of the text.

But fear not for me, my friend, for I have already seen
Hell open
standing.

I have already seen Hell open standing, thought Bergmann as he rang the door to the left on the second floor. Why didn't he write—for it must be a *he*—"I've seen hell *standing open*"?

The young couple on the second floor hadn't heard or seen anything when Bergmann asked them if they'd opened the door to a stranger, either earlier that day or the night before. The third-floor tenants didn't know anything either, but did say they would ask their daughter if she'd let any strangers in this morning when she came home from school.

His last hope was Mrs. Ingebrigtsen, who lived on the top floor. Before he rang the doorbell, he opened the stairwell window and looked down toward the entrance four floors below. The awning over the entryway made it impossible to see who was ringing, but it might be possible if she looked out the bedroom window.

He rang the doorbell and waited. The TV was on loud enough inside that he knew she was home. He checked his watch. Of course she could have fallen asleep in front of the set.

He rang the bell again. She was his last chance. If no one had opened the door or let in a stranger, it could only mean that this savage had access to the main key. Unless it was the mail carrier or a visitor?

He kept his eyes on the ancient peephole, which must have been installed sometime in the seventies. The kind with clear glass and no wide angle. The little eye turned black, and he knew that Mrs. Ingebrigtsen was standing on the other side of the door.

He heard the lock being turned, then the deadbolt a few seconds later.

"Is that you again, Bergmann?" said Mrs. Ingebrigtsen, sounding half-frightened through the narrow crack that the chain allowed. It was old and decrepit, some cheap shit her husband must have bought forty years ago. He could have kicked in her whole front door if he'd wanted to.

"I was just wondering if you've opened the front door for any unknown person today, or sometime last night."

"Up here?"

"Downstairs. If you've buzzed the door open with the entry phone or let someone in with you that you don't know, someone who said they were going to visit one of the other tenants, you know."

She shook her head and slipped off the security chain, as if she wanted to show him that he was worthy of her trust.

"Well, wait a moment," she said, opening the door halfway. It struck Bergmann that she was starting to get forgetful. Her behavior seemed odd. Either she had a guilty conscience, or she was simply sinking gradually into the darkness of dementia. "Someone was delivering flowers to you."

Bergmann felt his eyes widen, though he tried to look as relaxed as possible.

"Flowers for me?" He tried to smile, but didn't know if he succeeded. She nodded.

"Yes, a man said he had flowers for you."

"Do you remember when that was?"

"Today, sometime in the middle of the day, eleven or twelve maybe, my memory isn't so good anymore, you know. Maybe it was this afternoon."

"And you let him in?"

Mrs. Ingebrigtsen paused before answering.

"Was that wrong?" she said in a low voice. Bergmann held her gaze. The deep-blue irises were encircled by a dense network of broken blood vessels, and her eyes were moist, as if she was about to start crying.

"Not at all. Flowers are always nice," he said, smiling at her. This time he did so properly.

Mrs. Ingebrigtsen smiled back and brought her hand up to her hair, the way old ladies do, to check that her hairdo was still in place. She appeared not to have noticed the surprise in his voice when he'd said, "Flowers for me?"

"Maybe they're from a secret admirer?" she said inquisitively, half teasing.

He shook his head.

"Doubtful, Mrs. Ingebrigtsen. But you didn't happen to see who the man was? The flower deliveryman."

"No, I went over to the window, but I couldn't see him."

"And you didn't see a delivery truck from Interflora or another flower store parked in front?"

"No. But he had a very nice voice, he was a polite and friendly sounding man. You don't encounter them too often these days."

"No, you can say that again. What kind of voice did he have?"

Mrs. Ingebrigtsen frowned. Perhaps she was starting to get confused, but the lady wasn't stupid; she seemed as clear as she had ever been just then.

"Why are you asking me that?"

Bergmann tried to put on a disarming smile, with some success, he thought.

"No special reason. Just curious about who it might have been."

"Who?" said Mrs. Ingebrigtsen.

They'd clearly come to the end of the road. He tried a couple more questions, but her moment of lucidity seemed to have passed.

He wished her a pleasant evening. As he walked away, he thought that if Mrs. Ingebrigtsen ever found out who she'd let in, it would surely be the death of her.

He walked slowly back down to the first floor, as if he expected the man who had placed the letter with the strange phrasing to be waiting for him on each step.

We two are the same.
Hell open standing.

His head ached. Like so many times before, he felt he was not smart enough for this job. Had he been waltzing around blindly yet again? Morten Høgda was from up north, from Finnmark—why hadn't he thought of that before? Bergmann's mother was also from up there, he just didn't know exactly where. *I don't know a damn thing about myself,* he thought again and again, until there was nothing left to take hold of inside his cranium. Was it Høgda who'd been in his apartment and taken the picture of his mother and called Mrs. Ingebrigtsen today? Why should this lunatic want a picture of his mother?

As he put the key in his front door, he was struck by something.

He turned around slowly and looked down the stairs at the mailboxes. His gaze fell on the bulletin board by the door.

He walked slowly down the six steps and tore off the page describing snow-removal procedures.

Property Services.

Asgeir Nordli's company.

Elisabeth Thorstensen's husband.

Bergmann took out his phone and keyed in her number.

"The subscriber cannot be reached," said the voice on the other end.

He picked up the copy of the letter to Anders Rask.

Medusa's tears.

A woman's handwriting.

Where have I seen Elisabeth Thorstensen before?

47

She thought she felt his arm under her head. But no, it must be her own.

"Torvald?" she said into the dark room. There was still a faint trace of his cologne in her nostrils. Susanne lay back down in bed and wished he was still lying there, holding her and stroking her hair. For some reason she'd felt unsafe after she came back from seeing Jon-Olav Farberg. Her phone call with Leif Monsen over at Dispatch a few minutes after she got home hadn't improved her mood. She wanted him to cross-check the name Yngvar with cabin owners in Vestfold, but he'd given her such a tongue-lashing that she hardly dared mention it to Bergmann. As occasionally happened, she simply collapsed and was utterly incapable of taking care of herself, much less Mathea.

What could be more reassuring than falling asleep in the arms of a gorgeous gay man?

She raised her arm and focused on the luminous dial. Two thirty. Torvald must have slipped out a few hours ago. The sight of the watch reminded her of Nico. And his girlfriend. And her own sick need for older men. As old as her own father.

She lay there for a few more minutes staring up at the ceiling. The street noise coming through the skylight almost lulled her to sleep again.

Right before she nodded off, she thought, *Why did I wake up? Was I dreaming?* But she didn't remember. Not until she heard her phone ringing somewhere in the apartment.

"The phone," she whispered. That was it. She'd been woken up by her phone. And now it was ringing again.

She pulled the duvet around her, even though she'd gone to bed fully clothed, and headed into the kitchen, where the phone was glowing green on the counter. She prayed that it wasn't Farberg. What signals had she given him? Men like him never gave up, she knew that all too well.

She picked up the phone and studied the number. An unknown Oslo number. Keeping her gaze fixed on the Christmas star Torvald had hung in the window earlier that evening, she brought the phone slowly to her ear.

"Susanne Bech?" said a female voice.

"Who is this?"

"I'm very sorry that I woke you up."

The woman paused. Susanne felt herself frowning. A strange feeling came over her—that someone was in Mathea's room. Had Torvald closed the door properly? The deadbolt wasn't locked.

"Who is this?" she said sternly. She let the duvet drop to the floor and turned on the Poul Henningsen lamp over the kitchen table.

"I'm calling from Lovisenberg Hospital."

Mother, thought Susanne. But no. They would have called from Bærum. Besides, she certainly wouldn't have been told if her mother had died.

She went to the front door and checked it. *Thank God,* she thought. It was locked. She turned the deadbolt and walked down the hall to Mathea's room.

"We have a patient here who insists on speaking with you."

Susanne stopped outside the door to Mathea's room. She put her hand on the colorful princess drawing that was taped to the door.

"Can't it wait until morning?"

"I'm not sure he'll be alive in the morning."

Susanne felt goose bumps form on her arm.

"Is it Flaten? Bjørn-Åge Flaten?"

"Yes. He refuses to talk with anyone but you. He has some information, he says. The doctor has agreed to let you come."

There was a pause. Finally Susanne heard herself saying, "Don't let him die. I'll be right there."

She had no choice but to take Mathea with her. Torvald had already done more than enough this evening.

She opened the door to Mathea's room. Mathea was talking in her sleep.

"Ma . . . ," she said. "Ma . . ."

"Mommy is here," said Susanne.

Mathea turned toward the wall without waking up. Her breathing was heavy, so heavy that Susanne hesitated for a moment. She looked at the watch, thought of Nico, and promised herself that she would sell it before Christmas.

Ten minutes later Mathea was standing fully dressed by the door waiting for Susanne. She'd been allowed to put on exactly what she wanted, so long as it was winter clothing. It was almost three o'clock in the morning, and the girl looked like she was going to the Theater Café in a green velvet dress from Fru Lyng with a white bow that was much too small, white wool tights, and a blue duffel coat. On her head she wore a hat that would have been better suited for Pippi Longstocking.

Good Lord, what a pair we are, thought Susanne as she was struck by a cold wind out on the street.

"This is fun," said Mathea.

"Do you think so?"

Fortunately there were two taxis outside the bus terminal.

"Don't ask," said Susanne to the taxi driver, pushing the swanky Mathea onto the passenger seat.

"What are we going to do?" Mathea asked.

The taxi picked up speed as it headed down into the tunnel.

"I'm just going to talk with a man." Susanne took her little hand and squeezed it. *A man who's going to die,* she thought, clearly hearing the voice of Flaten's mother. *But first I'm going to hear his confession.*

When they emerged from the tunnel, she was almost overwhelmed by the sight of the Trinity Church. A homeless man had settled down for the night next to the church wall, a bundle of blankets and cartons. The taxi shifted gears and swerved on the slippery surface up Ullevålsveien. Susanne stroked Mathea's hand. Æreslunden at Our Savior's cemetery disappeared in the darkness. *It's not likely Flaten will be put to rest there,* she thought.

"I'm here to speak with Bjørn-Åge Flaten," Susanne said to the nurse in the emergency psychiatric ward. The nurse entered some commands on the keyboard and glanced at Mathea.

"Hi," said Mathea.

"Can you keep an eye on her for a while? Just give her something to draw on."

"Do you like cocoa?" the nurse asked Mathea. Her name tag said Jorunn, and her relaxed Vestland dialect gave Susanne a sense of security that made her feel calmer than she could remember feeling in a long time.

"He shouldn't have come here," said Jorunn to Susanne. "You know how it is—he has a transitory psychosis, and a patrol car dumps him on our door."

"Where should he have gone?"

"To hospice. We'll get him transferred tomorrow. If we have him that long."

"If he's psychotic, then—"

"He's taken his medications. See it as his last wish."

Mathea remained with Jorunn in the nurses' office, so trusting that Susanne was almost afraid for her. One day her trust in other adults might be her undoing.

Susanne opened the door to Flaten's room slowly. A scream from the adjacent room startled her, and she looked over toward the nurses' office. Strangely enough Mathea didn't appear to be scared.

What kind of mother am I, waking her up in the middle of the night and dragging her to an emergency psychiatric ward?

She entered the room.

The light coming from a mounted wall lamp gave Bjørn-Åge Flaten's face a mild sheen. He must have been sleeping lightly, because he woke up when she'd taken two steps into the room.

"I just fake my way in here," he said in a quiet, hoarse voice. "If I need a decent place to sleep."

Susanne took off her jacket and set it on the floor. She sat down in the chair near his bed.

"You're sick," she said.

Flaten closed his eyes, and she saw how old he looked.

"You're the only one who knows I'm here. Not even my mother knows. She's given up on me. You know that."

"I haven't given up on you," said Susanne. She took his hand and squeezed it as if she were his girlfriend.

"I've let everyone down. Everyone who wished me well. I didn't want to let you down too."

"What do you mean?"

"You never would have believed me. No one believed me."

"So tell me the truth."

"I just want you to find who killed Kristiane. Who killed all those girls."

Susanne released his hand, and he reached for it with all the strength he had.

"I saw her under the railroad bridge at Skøyen."

"The Saturday she disappeared?"

"Yes."

"She was just standing there?"

"I'd come in on the train from the city center. I was the last one off the platform. Stepped down on the sidewalk and was going to light up a smoke."

"And then?"

"There was a girl standing a few steps away from me, under the bridge. Her Nordstrand bag was on the sidewalk. She didn't quite seem to know what she was doing there. 'Do you have a smoke?' she said."

"Yes?"

"So I gave her a smoke. I said I was going up to Amalienborg, told her she could come along if she wanted. That I wasn't dangerous."

"Did she say her name?"

"No. But I saw the picture of her the week after. In the paper, when she was reported missing."

"So did she go with you?"

"You don't believe me."

She stroked his hand.

"Yes, I do."

"It turned out that she was going the same way as me. I asked her if she was going to a party."

"What did she say?"

"That she was going to visit someone."

"She didn't say who?"

He slowly shook his head.

"We went our separate ways at Amalienborg."

"Did you pass anyone on the way?"

"An old lady with a dog. She just looked down at the ground, probably hated people like me—a junkie in Skøyen, you know. Amalienborg was full of riffraff like me."

"And then?"

"'Don't get into trouble now' was the last thing she said. It looked like something was bothering her, but I didn't want to ask. A boyfriend, I guessed, but how could I know?"

"And then?"

There was a knock at the door. Flaten's gaze barely moved toward the door. She was still holding his hand, stroking it with the other.

The nurse, Jorunn, stood there with Mathea.

"Is that your kid?" he whispered.

She nodded.

"I didn't know you were single. You don't look like you would be."

"No one probably looks like that."

She thought that Mathea might be afraid of Flaten, the way he looked closer to death than life.

He had closed his eyes. A tear trickled down from each eye.

"What's her name?"

"Mathea," whispered Susanne.

"Never say this to yourself . . ."

"What's that?"

"If I only had one more chance."

She took his hand again. It seemed as if life really was ebbing out of him.

"What did you do when you parted ways?"

"What?"

"What—"

"I pretended like I was going in a door . . . then I waited ten or fifteen seconds. And I stood and watched her."

Susanne tightened her grip on his hand.

"Where did she go?"

"You won't believe me."

"I will."

"She turned left, toward the terraced apartment buildings."

"The terraced apartments?"

"There's a courtyard there with terraced apartments, the kind that Selvaag built back then."

"You think she was going there?"

"Yes. If she was going someplace else, she would have continued straight ahead up Nedre Skøyen Vei. The street where she turned dead-ends at those apartment buildings."

"Mommy," said Mathea from over by the window, "I want to go home."

Bjørn-Åge Flaten smiled slowly.

"Take her home. Just promise me one thing."

"I promise."

"Believe me."

48

Nothing in the apartment had been touched. He opened the refrigerator, cleared away the worst of the old vegetables and cheese and some other shit he couldn't identify. He found two bottles of beer he'd forgotten about at the back of the middle shelf. He pried open one of them and took a couple of swigs before mounting the door chain he'd bought on the way home. Solid stuff, according to the seller.

A little too solid for this door frame, thought Bergmann as he tightened the screws with the screwdriver. The old frame creaked, and he noticed a substantial crack up the middle of it. It had been so long since he'd done anything practical that he forgot to use an awl first. *The whole thing will probably just fall out,* he thought. He finished the beer and figured it would have to do. Just let him come. Or let them come. If it was Rask, he would probably have his friend Jensrud with him. Tomorrow he would call the locksmith.

He stood in the middle of the living room and studied the bookcase. He should have reported this missing photograph, but what was the point? A break-in without a trace. Whoever had entered must have had a key.

He took an old photograph of himself from the shelf. It was a portrait from seventh grade. It had been raining that day. Rain and autumn, that was his clearest memory from his school days. Wasn't it always rain and autumn? *If I haven't repressed the rest,* he thought. What more did he recall? Dry leaves blowing along the apartment buildings, a dusty spring day, the aimless emptiness of suburban life in springtime, his longing for summer to be over, the sun baking the little apartment, broken windows at the subway station, the sound of glass on the ground, sneakers running along the platform, over the electrified rails, a junkie on his knees, some glue-sniffers lying on the steps, a warm summer night, a couple having sex in the underpass below Tvetenveien, carrying on like dogs.

He shook his head, and put the 1970s version of Tommy Bergmann back on the dusty shelf.

He lay down on the couch, pulled a wool blanket over himself, and read that satanic letter over again.

He should have called Reuter, but he was too tired.

Hell open.

If you come here, I'll kill you.

I'm ready was his last thought before he fell asleep. The sight of the Raven pistol on the coffee table became part of his dream. After that his army boots got wet, a flashlight swept over black spruce trunks somewhere in front of him, and the image of a figure working with a shiny tool flickered somewhere up ahead in the forest. He tried to pick up the pace, but couldn't, was unable to move his legs fast enough—the moss, mud, and water underfoot made it impossible. He fumbled for the pistol in his pocket, but it fell out and disappeared into the earth. When he got there, the figure with the shiny tool was gone, and a bundle of a girl lay on the ground. It was too dark for him to see her face clearly. She was holding her stomach, slashed from the neck on down, crying quietly, her face white like a doll's. He leaned over, and she turned toward him and screamed, spasmodically, a howl so loud that he fell back, landing in the wet marsh.

He sat up on the couch. He had goose bumps on his sweaty skin.

That sound, he thought.

Her screams.

The entry phone was buzzing.

The sharp sound of it penetrated the entire apartment. The room was ice cold, as if someone had turned off the heat.

It buzzed again.

Bergmann took the pistol off the coffee table. The display on the DVD player showed 03:40.

He threw off the blanket and put his feet on the floor. For a moment he was afraid that the ground would be wet moss and marsh, that this was a mixture of dream and reality, a labyrinth he wasn't going to get out of.

The entry phone buzzed again.

It couldn't be him. Not like this.

He nonetheless crouched down as he passed through the living room into the hall. He noted that he'd had the foresight to pull the curtains in the guest room, whose window was right by the entryway to the building.

He paused by the entry phone, looked at the safety chain, and placed his index finger on the cold curved steel of the trigger.

When it buzzed again, he picked up the receiver.

First just a sigh.

"Tommy?"

A few seconds passed before he recognized the voice.

A woman's.

It was different than he remembered, slurred, dulled by alcohol or drugs.

He pressed the door button to let her in, but kept an eye on the stairwell through the peephole in the door.

Elisabeth Thorstensen let the entry door glide closed behind her. She looked lost in her big fur coat, as if she were from another era and didn't understand anything she saw around her. Bergmann saw that she stopped by the mailboxes for a moment. Then she started the few steps up to the apartment.

Property Services, he thought. Did she have her own set of keys to the building? Or did her husband? Could she have given keys to someone else?

He opened the door to the closet beside him and dropped the loaded pistol on the floor in there. Then he observed her for a few seconds through the peephole. He was unsure how to interpret her expression—unsure whether it was sorrow or madness, or perhaps both. He unlocked the door and removed the safety chain.

"I've taken some pills," she said quietly. She was standing in the middle of the entry, looking like a baby bird in that massive fur coat. Her dark hair was wet with snow, and her mascara had run down her cheeks. "Something I got from a doctor one time. He was in love with me." Though she laughed quietly, her eyes remained sorrowful. "After Asgeir went to bed . . . and then I started drinking."

"Please come in," he said.

Elisabeth tried to get out of her coat, and he gave her a hand with it.

"I can't bear to go on living anymore. I don't know . . . I thought of you."

She brought her hands up to his face. Her head fell against his open shirt front.

"You saved me once before."

He put his arms around her.

"I'm just so tired."

He tried to push her gently away from him, but she didn't let go.

"Don't leave me," she said.

She started to cry. But a minute later, her tears turned to laughter.

"I don't know why I came here," she whispered.

I think I know, thought Bergmann, but he didn't say anything.

"You must always be kind to me, Tommy," she said into his ear. "Promise me that."

He had a forbidden thought—that he'd desired her that first time in Skøyenbrynet, when she sat on the kitchen floor with the knife in her hand—but he pushed it away. Thoughts like that weren't allowed.

"How late is it?" she said.

"Almost four."

"Can I sleep here?"

Bergmann shook his head. Her expression suggested that she shouldn't be left alone. She blinked, and the tears trickled down her cheeks.

"I miss her. I can't live without her, Tommy."

He took a deep breath and knew that he was doing something stupid.

"You can sleep on the couch."

"Then you have to sleep beside me."

"I—"

She put her hand over his mouth.

"I don't want to die," she said.

He put his arms around her.

"You won't die."

He woke up to the sound of the building's entryway door slamming shut.

Elisabeth Thorstensen lay partially on top of him on the couch, sleeping heavily. He thanked the Creator that they still had their clothes on.

Nothing happened, he thought, feeling the onset of a pounding headache. He slid off the couch without waking her up, checked the closet to make sure the pistol was still there—it was—and then headed into the bathroom.

When he came back into the living room, she was awake. Had she only been pretending to be asleep?

"She's the first thing I think about every day when I get up, and the last thing I think about before I go to bed."

Her face was barely visible in the faint glow from the streetlights outside the living room windows.

"You must never believe anything else about me."

"I don't."

"Kristiane would have liked you. You're a good person. Do you know that, Tommy?"

He closed his eyes and thought that was the nicest thing anyone had said to him in as long as he could remember.

He studied her body as she stood up. She pulled her hair back and smiled at him in a way that filled him with an inexplicable calm.

She went up to the bookcase. The feeling of calm was replaced by a spike of anxiety.

"You looked so good together," she said suddenly. She must have been talking about the picture of him and Hege. God knows why he had left that there.

Oh well, he thought. *Maybe we did.* Then he remembered the missing photograph of his mother. There was a sudden awakening. What was he getting mixed up in?

"I think it's best that you leave now."

Elisabeth set down the photograph of him and Hege. She pretended to frown.

"Oh well."

She brushed past him, into the bathroom.

He went into the living room and picked up his phone off the coffee table. There was a text from Susanne. It must have come during the night. He wondered why he hadn't heard it: *Kristiane was going to the terraced apartments on Nedre Skøyen Vei. More tomorrow.*

He was still staring at the message when Elisabeth came out of the bathroom.

"Call a taxi for me. That's the least you can do."

"Maybe."

Elisabeth stood in the entry with her coat on. Bergmann leaned against the door frame into the living room, a lit cigarette in his hand. She had quickly applied two or three brushes of mascara and a little lipstick. It was quarter to six in the morning, God only knew why she'd gone to the trouble.

She stroked the sleeve of her coat a few times. Then she stepped toward him, took the cigarette out of his hand, gave it a couple of puffs, and handed it back to him.

"Come here," she said.

She kissed him quickly on the mouth, then put her head against his chest. He heard a car brake outside the bedroom window, the low-frequency sound of a diesel engine.

"It was like Kristiane was sent from heaven, Tommy. She saved Per-Erik. I'm sure I sound crazy, but I truly felt that way. Can you understand that?"

"Yes."

"So it is possible to become a better person. He did anyway."

Bergmann pushed the thought of himself away; he should have been lying on his therapist's couch, not standing here with his arms around a witness.

He pushed her away.

"I've seen you before somewhere. Before Kristiane was killed. I won't have any peace until I find out where it was."

"I have to go," she said.

"Where were you hospitalized after Kristiane was killed?"

"Frensby."

He felt a stab in his stomach. That was where his mother had worked.

"Before that," he said.

"I've been hospitalized several times. My father . . . he . . . I can't bear this now."

He must have seen her there many years ago. Sometime when he was with his mother at work.

"Can I see you again? Before Christmas?"

"I can't do that," he said. "You understand that."

"I . . ." she began. They looked at each other for a long time. Her eyes appeared to fill with tears, but somehow she pushed back the sorrow.

". . . nothing."

She opened the door, stood there uncertainly a few seconds, then closed it again.

This was what you came for, thought Bergmann. He took a final drag on his cigarette. She came over and put her arms around his waist.

"I thought I was going to take this with me to the grave," she said.

"What's that?"

"I think she was in love with him."

"Who?"

She closed her eyes.

"Kristiane. He can be unbelievably manipulative, and he has the same magnetic quality that his father does. I almost didn't make it out of that relationship with him, Tommy. Once Morten has his hold on you, he doesn't let you go."

"What do you mean? That she was in love with Morten Høgda?"

She shook her head.

"Alex is just like him."

Bergmann took a step back.

"What are you trying to say?" he said.

Elisabeth took a breath, then held the air in a long time before she exhaled through her nose.

"I think Kristiane was head over heels in love with Alexander. *Alex.*"

He slowly shook his head.

"With her brother?"

"Half-brother. Yes."

Elisabeth closed her eyes.

"Oh God," she said. "May she forgive me, my child."

He waited.

"I think he used her," she said so quietly that he barely heard it.

"What do you mean?"

"I found strands of her hair in his bed. You've seen her hair yourself. It was unmistakable."

He heard the voice of Anders Rask in his head.

"She changed that summer. She broke up with her boyfriend and—"

Someone lit a fire in her.

His head filled with Rask's voice. His wild gaze. The energy that ebbed out of him after he'd tried to convince Bergmann that Kristiane had changed that summer.

"Did Alexander also have Anders Rask in school?" he asked.

She had a desperate look on her face, as if she were reliving Kristiane's death all over again.

"Don't tell this to anyone, Tommy."

"I can't promise you that. This turns everything on its head, Elisabeth, do you understand that?"

She followed him into the bedroom.

"But answer me one thing: Did Alex have Rask in school?"

"Yes."

His phone rang. The taxi driver asked whether anyone was coming out soon, the meter was running.

"And promise me," he said. "You must tell me if you still have anything to do with Morten Høgda."

She shook her head.

"You have to promise me."

"I promise."

He squeezed her hand.

"Call me," she whispered. "Can *you* promise *me* that?"

"What is it you're not telling me?"

She shook her head.

"You're protecting someone."

"Who?"

"Who have you told about this? The thing with Alexander and Kristiane?"

"No one."

"She really was going to Skøyen that Saturday, Elisabeth."

She put her hands over her face.

"Who lived in Skøyen?"

"I don't know," she whispered.

"Was it Morten Høgda? Did you ever tell him about all this? Or Per-Erik?"

"No," she said. "No."

She crumpled to her knees and hid her face in her hands.

"Not Morten," she whispered. "It can't be Morten."

For a moment he considered calling an ambulance. It seemed as though all the life had drained out of her, as if she'd given up. He crouched down beside her, held her wrists, felt the scars from the kitchen knife.

"I have to talk to Alex. You understand that. He works at the hospital in Tromsø?"

"Yes," she said into his shirtfront.

"Go home now," he said. "I'll call you this evening."

"Do you promise?"

He nodded.

When he saw the taxi disappear behind the KIWI store, he was quite sure that he had just made an enormous mistake.

He had spoken with the investigators up at Toten the night before. In Furuberget's house the crime scene investigators had found two different pairs of shoeprints that didn't belong to either of the people who lived there. But they didn't belong to Rask and Jensrud either, who were both wearing running shoes when they escaped from Ringvoll.

Arne Furuberget had been visited by two people when he was killed.

Bergmann was quite certain that the letter to Rask was written by a woman—regardless of what Kripo's analysis might show.

So they weren't searching for Rask and Jensrud.

They were searching for a man.

And a woman.

PART FOUR

DECEMBER 2004

49

Susanne Bech waved to Mathea and tried to forget that the little girl had only slept a few hours the night before. Mathea seemed half-drunk with exhaustion as she stood leaning against the window. It was five past seven, and for once they'd been the first to arrive at daycare, even showing up a minute or two before the director.

She took the subway to Oslo Central Station and wandered around aimlessly for a while, the way she imagined that Kristiane had done that Saturday in late November 1988. The departure hall was a swarm of morning commuters. She walked against the flow, down toward the old East Line hall, which was now connected with the new station. The big Christmas tree reminded her that Christmas Eve was getting closer by the day. It would be nice, just her and Mathea—did they really need more than each other?

She pretended that she was Kristiane, walking through East Line hall, now renovated into a shopping center, past all the stores and out the doors, where she was last seen. She stood in the middle of the square, the way she thought Kristiane had done, in the December darkness. Straight ahead of her was Karl Johans Gate, decorated with green wreaths and shiny Christmas lights that gave badly needed light to the city.

She had changed her mind, she thought. Kristiane stood here just like this. She took the train from Nordstrand because she didn't want her teammates to see her. And because she was actually going through the city. To Skøyen, where she ran into Bjørn-Åge Flaten. She stood just like this. And changed her mind when she got off at Oslo Central Station. This was not where she was going. After that she went back into the East Line hall and took the next train to Skøyen.

Susanne turned around sharply and did exactly what she thought Kristiane had done.

She saw herself as Kristiane as the train from Ski glided in on platform 9. Her hands trembled for a moment as she sank down in one of the vacant seats and the train disappeared into the tunnel under the city. She opened the bag where she had her notepad and a printout of a brochure about the Nedre Skøyen Vei condominium association. *I have to believe him,* she thought, closing her eyes.

She woke up suddenly when the train stopped at the National Theater station. She had goose bumps on her arms; she'd had a dream during the short trip in the tunnel. Mathea had been standing in the window at daycare waving, just like this morning. An ominous shadow had slipped up behind her. But it wasn't someone who worked at the daycare. It was impossible to see the face. Just a shadow behind Mathea. A hand on her shoulder.

As she got out of the train at Skøyen station, Susanne shook her head. She simply hadn't gotten enough sleep, and the visit to Lovisenberg had further drained her of energy. *That's all it is,* she thought, starting down the stairs from the station.

Halfway down she stopped. She let the other passengers go past. Then she turned around slowly, as though expecting the person from the dream to be standing right behind her on the dark stairs.

Without a face, with a hand on Mathea's shoulder.

She exhaled deeply.

"No one," she said. "No one."

She continued down the stairs and stopped on the sidewalk. She peered over at the railroad underpass where Flaten had seen Kristiane that Saturday evening. She took a few tentative steps toward the bridge until she was standing beneath it. The traffic was almost constant, but she barely noticed it. It was as if they were standing before her now: Kristiane in her blue Millet bubble jacket and the young junkie Bjørn-Åge Flaten.

"Who were you going to see, Kristiane?" said Susanne.

She started to walk up toward Amalienborg following the same path Bjorn said they'd taken. She felt as though Kristiane was walking beside her. As if she could put her arm around the young girl and say, *I'll find him, I promise I'm going to find him.*

Suddenly, the feeling came over her again. The faceless person she'd dreamed about on the train. She slowed her pace. At last she stopped completely.

Take me, she thought. *Take me. But let Mathea live.*

50

Fredrik Reuter looked at the clock with an affectedly purposeful expression. Then he aimed his index finger at Bergmann. "I assume you have control of your lady."

Bergmann shrugged. It was five past eight in the morning, and Susanne was nowhere to be seen. He'd tried calling her, but only got her voice mail.

"I don't know where she is. We'll just have to start without her."

Svein Finneland sat across from him with a strange look on his face. Bergmann had seen his expression change just when Reuter uttered the words *your lady*.

Oh well, he thought. *So you're jealous because I'm her boss. Be my guest. Or are you afraid that she's been sleeping with some other guy?*

"Oh well," said Finneland in a way that made Bergmann think he'd been reading his thoughts. He straightened up. "Then it will be the five of us. You can update *your lady* later today, Bergmann. Whenever she might see fit to show up."

Halgeir Sørvaag caught Bergmann's gaze. He had a slight, wily smile in the corner of his mouth, and Bergmann imagined he was thinking about what Susanne looked like with no clothes on, lying in his bed in the place of his lifeless wife.

Kripo psychologist Rune Flatanger sat with his eyes glued to the letter Bergmann had received in his mailbox the day before. It looked like he was mouthing the words "hell open."

"I got a cryptic text message from Susanne last night," said Bergmann. "Something to the effect that Kristiane was going to Skøyen." He shook his head. Just as long as she hadn't talked to Bjørn-Åge Flaten again. He'd probably wanted money from her; for all Bergmann knew, she might have paid him out of her own pocket.

"Last night?" Finneland's face darkened.

Bergmann nodded.

"Shall we begin?" said Reuter. He was going to the police chief's meeting in an hour, and Bergmann knew that Reuter had his eyes on her job.

"So," said Finneland. "As I understand it, we have an enhanced picture from the surveillance camera on Cort Adelers Gate."

He took a folder that lay in front of Reuter, opened it, and passed out three copies of the photographs across the table. Bergmann got up from his chair and eagerly seized one. It took a few seconds for his brain to connect the face in the photograph to a man he'd recently met. But it didn't necessarily mean anything that he had been at Porte des Senses the same night that the Lithuanian girl was killed. Or was he fooling himself? He needed time to think and chose not to say anything just then.

"And," said Finneland, pausing for effect, "Anders Rask and Øystein Jensrud stopped for gas at the YX station in Oppdal last night, with a credit card belonging to Rask's *lady*." Again the prosecutor looked at Bergmann.

You could use a good punch in the mouth, thought Bergmann, giving him a crooked smile.

"That particular bit of news won't be released, so keep your mouth shut about it," said Reuter.

"What about getting the night shift at YX to keep their mouths shut?" said Sørvaag, savoring the words a little.

"We'll have to trust our Lord to arrange that," said Reuter. "Besides, YX is unstaffed. It was the credit card that triggered the alarm."

"Fools," said Bergmann. He didn't quite know if he meant Rask and Jensrud or Reuter and Sørvaag.

"That's just the start of it," said Finneland. "It's crucial that they not know that we know where they are."

He set out new photographs that clearly showed the license plate on the car. Now that the police knew what car the men were driving, it was only a matter of time before they were caught. One picture showed Jensrud as they were filling up. Rask was turned away from the camera. It looked like he was smoking a cigarette. If he'd been a little smarter, he would have stayed in the car. But he probably knew that the card would be monitored. The female guard at Ringvoll could have given them cash, but then they would have had to pay at the register. Rask probably knew that they were as good as lost.

If I could just talk to you now, Bergmann thought, studying Rask in the photograph. This Yngvar fellow Jon-Olav Farberg was talking about—did he really exist? Was that who Rask was on his way to see? And what about Alexander Thorstensen? Could Rask be on his way to Tromsø? That was a wild thought, but not entirely out of the realm of possibility. Rask knew that Kristiane had fallen in love with someone she shouldn't have: Alexander, her own half-brother.

"Let them keep driving," he said.

Finneland took off his reading glasses.

"I must not have heard you correctly."

"Let Rask and Jensrud drive for a while. Follow them, but don't arrest them, do you understand?"

Finneland shook his head.

"It's not up to me, but I've got to say that must be the dumbest thing I've heard this year."

"They're headed north. That makes no sense if they don't have a specific destination in mind, do you understand? Someone on the outside has been writing letters to Rask." Bergmann held up the copy of the letter he'd found in Rask's room at Ringvoll. "Maybe they're going to meet the person in question?" He kept quiet about the rest. He would not allow these clowns to destroy this case.

Finneland shook his head.

"You'll have to convince Kripo, they're running point on Rask and Jensrud."

Flatanger yawned loudly, as though trying to impress upon them that this was one of the least interesting conversations he'd ever had in his life.

"To be honest I think Rask only cares about getting away. The problem is that he doesn't have anywhere to go. What is of real interest here is the letter to you, Tommy. Didn't you get it yesterday?"

Bergmann nodded. The original had been sent to Kripo for fingerprints and handwriting analysis, but he had the copy in front of him.

"So you think that the letter to Rask was written by a woman, while the letter to you was written by a man?" Flatanger asked, looking right at him. Bergmann sensed that he knew that he had therapy sessions with Viggo Osvold—and that he had skipped the last two sessions. If Reuter found that out, his career would be over.

It hardly mattered.

"Yes, I think so."

Flatanger placed the two letters side by side.

"At least I think that they were written by two different people."

"What makes you so sure?" Flatanger was leaning over the letters. "It looks as though the text could have been written by the same person."

"But look at the handwriting in the first one. And 'Medusa.' The writer's referring to a woman."

Flatanger nodded.

"True enough."

"What are you thinking?" said Finneland, standing up suddenly from his chair and walking around the table until he stood behind Bergmann.

"I think that the letters may have been written by two different people in one mind."

Bergmann held his hand up.

"What do you mean? Two people in one mind?"

Flatanger drew his hand across his face.

"Or two minds in one person."

"But how . . ." said Finneland behind Bergmann. He continued around the table toward Flatanger.

"I think the tone is markedly similar in both letters, but the hand-writing is clearly quite different. Nonetheless, I think we're looking for one person, not two."

"And you think we're looking for two people, Bergmann?" Finneland had returned to his seat. Bergmann studied his thin face awhile, the obvious veins on his hands.

"I think a woman wrote to Rask, and a man wrote to me." It was as if another person were speaking for him. *To me,* he thought. *To me.*

"This last person knows you, that's fairly obvious."

"Or," said Flatanger, "the person in question thinks or imagines that he knows you."

"Why are you so sure that it's a woman, Tommy?" Reuter's voice was low and hoarse. He kept his fingers on the letter, then let go and tapped his finger on the table.

"Doesn't that look like a woman's handwriting to you?"

"Maybe," said Flatanger. "We'll figure that out."

"And this thing with the girl on Frognerveien. Why did she say 'Maria'? There must be a woman involved in all this."

"That's right. Sørvaag?" Finneland turned to him. "Did you get any further? Didn't you have some lead on that?"

Sørvaag took a breath and shook his head.

"Just as I thought."

It was quiet for a long time. At last Flatanger broke the silence.

"I'm quite certain that we're searching for just one person. I think that Arne Furuberget was searching for an old patient."

"How do you know that?"

"I just think so. He told me that he'd been to Brumunddal. The Ringvoll archives are there."

"What if it's a man who thinks he's a woman?"

"A man who thinks he's a woman?" Reuter shook his head and looked at Bergmann as if he had completely lost his faith in him.

Bergmann just sat there, holding his coffee cup. He set it carefully aside and held up the surveillance picture. He was not in the slightest doubt about who was in that picture.

"A man who thinks he's a woman?"

"A man by day. A woman at night," said Flatanger. "I understand where you're headed."

"Like this man?" said Bergmann. He held up the surveillance image from Cort Adelers Gate. He had held back long enough. "This is Morten Høgda," he said. "He had a relationship with Elisabeth Thorstensen in the past. And I'm quite certain that he still does."

He kept quiet about the rest of it—that he was Alexander Thorstensen's father. And that Kristiane had evidently fallen in love with him, her own half-brother.

"Morten Høgda," said Reuter. "Morten Høgda?"

Høgda would have some explaining to do.

"Inconceivable," said Finneland. "Is that really Høgda?" He picked up the photograph and held it up to his face.

"We won't call him in for questioning yet. He mustn't know a thing about any of this ahead of time, okay?"

"Call him in for questioning?" said Finneland.

"Good Lord, we've been looking for this guy for days—our only lead—and he couldn't be bothered to report in. That's almost grounds for indictment."

Bergmann stood up. He didn't have time for this. He had to get up to Tromsø during daylight hours, and he wanted his arrival to be a surprise for Alexander Thorstensen.

"Høgda's owned a cabin on Hvasser since the seventies. Do I need to remind you where the first girl was killed?"

"Tønsberg," said Flatanger. "I'll check if he's ever been admitted to Ringvoll."

"Be careful," said Reuter. "I don't want Høgda's lawyers on my back. Owning a cabin there doesn't automatically mean that he's the country's number-one maniac. Okay?"

"Fine. So I guess we're through?" said Bergmann.

Reuter opened his mouth, but nothing came out.

Bergmann left the room without a word.

He walked quickly to his office, opened the browser, and entered "Morten Høgda" in the search field. Høgda was evidently media shy, but one of the few pictures that came up was good enough that he could print it out.

On his way to the copy room, he asked Linda in reception to book a flight to Tromsø around noon.

When he came back to his office, Halgeir Sørvaag was sitting in his chair.

Bergmann set the picture of Høgda on the desk and put on his bubble jacket. He had no intention of telling Sørvaag where he was going or why he was taking the picture with him. The worst thing would be if Høgda was abroad, got a phone call about coming into Oslo for questioning, and hopped on the first flight to Cambodia.

Sørvaag stared out the window without saying anything.

"Enjoying the view?" said Bergmann. "I'm short on time, so get to the point."

"I got hold of one of old Lorentz's kids last night. Damned if I couldn't stop thinking about the Maria stuff."

"Maria?"

"Edle Maria. What the girl said at the hospital."

Bergmann stuffed the picture of Høgda in an envelope.

"I have to go, Halgeir."

"No one believes me."

Bergmann stopped in the doorway.

"What do you mean?"

"Maria, Tommy. It's no coincidence that the girl said that at the hospital. Maybe someone called her and scheduled a time with her. Someone who called themselves Edle Maria. But we can't find her damned phone."

The images flickered past Bergmann's eyes. How she'd sat up and screamed. How scared he'd been.

"It may only be a coincidence," said Sørvaag.

"Maybe."

"Nordreisa," said Sørvaag.

It took a few seconds for Bergmann to understand what he'd said.

Then, in the blink of an eye, he felt the turning of the earth quite clearly. His feet disappeared into heavy marshland, and his head was pressed as though in a vise.

"What did you say?" Bergmann said, so quietly that Sørvaag didn't hear him.

"Old Lorentz was a deputy sheriff in Nordreisa. That girl, Edle Maria, was killed there. The son confirmed it. I remember him telling me that, but I didn't remember the place. They never found the killer."

"Nordreisa?"

Bergmann had to support himself against the door frame.

He unfolded the copy of the letter he'd received in the mail. "Can you remember me?"

He'd always told himself that he didn't know where his mother came from. But he just didn't want to know, didn't want to know anything about her, without ever knowing why.

She was from Nordreisa.

And Morten Høgda was from the neighboring town.

51

Her fingers were frozen to the bone; her skin cracked under her thin mittens. Susanne cursed herself for this fool's errand. She was standing outside the fourth terraced apartment building in the Nedre Skøyen Vei condominium complex. The sun had climbed over the horizon, blinding her as she approached the doorbells with their nameplates. She had already filled ten pages in her notepad with names and addresses, but it all seemed pointless.

It had been sixteen years since Kristiane had been here. The person she was searching for probably didn't even live here anymore. Even if she looked up everyone who was registered here, some of them were renters and the name in the register didn't always match the address. In fact they seldom did.

She quickly jotted down all the names on a blank page; she was up to a hundred and ten names and needed a new pad.

Stop, she thought. The feeling that something had happened to Mathea had been growing with every passing minute.

She took out her phone, nearly blacking out with panic as she entered the wrong PIN code twice in a row. When she finally remembered it, she closed her eyes while the phone searched for a network. She felt certain there were several missed calls from daycare.

No. Four missed calls from Bergmann, that was all. She'd turned off her phone specifically to avoid talking to him since she was certain he would try to talk her out of what she was doing. And who could blame him?

She jumped when the phone rang while she was staring at it. "Tommy Bergmann's mobile" it said on the display.

The door to the entry opened with a bang. An elderly man looked at her suspiciously. *Damned two-front war,* she thought. *Damned men, young and old. They're all alike, every one of them.*

"And what are you up to?" he said, buttoning the top button on his cardigan. "I've been watching you, young lady."

Thanks for the compliment, thought Susanne.

"I'm from the Census Bureau," she said, smiling as disarmingly as she could. Her phone stopped ringing. A text message arrived a moment later. She could almost hear from the sound that it was Bergmann. And he was angry.

"Census Bureau? What nonsense."

She would have to play the role of serious patrol officer. She opened her jacket and held out her police ID, which hung around her neck.

"I'd like to work in peace, if you don't have anything against that."

"I'm sorry," the man said. "May I ask—"

"No. Unfortunately you can't ask anything. Have a nice day."

The man's expression changed immediately, and he suddenly appeared subservient and afraid of her. He closed the door and disappeared. If she'd told him what she was really up to, he would probably have laughed at her. Search here, sixteen years after Kristiane Thorstensen had apparently been on her way to one of these five terraced apartment buildings—and all this according to a dying junkie? It was folly.

Her phone rang again. Bergmann. She had no choice but to answer it.

"Where have you been?" he said, but not sounding as angry as she'd imagined he might.

"Working on a lead."

"Would've appreciated it if you'd informed me. We have to talk." He paused. "But I have to go to Tromsø today. I need you to go straight over to the National Library. Find out what the newspapers up north—*Nordlys*, or whatever they're called—wrote about the murder of a girl by the name of Edle Maria in Nordreisa. Sometime in the early sixties. It's urgent."

"Edle Maria?"

Susanne walked around in circles a few times.

Maria. The name the Lithuanian girl had screamed at the hospital. And Edle. Wasn't that the name Sørvaag had mentioned?

Susanne had over a hundred names on her pad, sixteen years after Kristiane had been at the apartments. And Edle Maria. Nordreisa. She shook her head, felt like sitting down and crying. How could this possibly all add up?

"Oh well." Her voice was submissive.

"This may be important. Do you understand? I need you now, Susanne. What are you really up to?"

Susanne waited a moment.

"I was at Lovisenberg in the middle of the night. Bjørn-Åge Flaten is on his deathbed. He saw Kristiane at Skøyen. Saw where she went. I believe him, Tommy."

He took a deep breath on the other end.

"Okay," he said simply. "Okay. But I need you at the National Library. Maybe you can just make a few calls about the other stuff?"

Susanne leaned against the concrete wall by the doorbells. She wanted to tell him that if he was already going to Tromsø, he could stop by *Nordlys* and check their archives himself for Pete's sake. But she didn't dare.

She looked down at her notepad filled with names. This was worse than a needle in a haystack.

Sixteen years, she thought. *This is hopeless.*

52

It was easier to find a parking space than he'd thought it would be. Bergmann didn't have time to drive around the block endlessly. As he squeezed the old Escort in between a BMW and a Mercedes, he told himself that he was fortunate to be an underpaid policeman.

Self-deception was undervalued as a survival strategy. He smiled for a moment before he was again overcome by gloom.

Edle Maria. Nordreisa. He got shivers at the thought. He tried to recall what his mother had told him about herself, but he'd never really paid attention the few times she'd done so. He'd only remembered a kind of quiet fury in her when she spoke of the past. That it would have been for the best if the little woman who called herself his mother had been dead. That he ought to have killed her himself. He remembered thinking he might be crazy. That this was just the way his father must have been. That was why she'd escaped here, to the south. That was exactly what Osvold had been getting at—it wasn't Hege he'd beaten up, but his mother. It just felt so damned distasteful to admit that everything Hege did reminded him of his mother, that the blazing rage he'd felt had nothing to do with Hege at all. Paradoxically, he was relieved that she'd managed to get away from him.

Osvold, he thought. Tomorrow he would have to get around to going to see Osvold again. He was just a phone call away from getting fired. Besides, he needed someone to talk to. And could he trust that Susanne would do what he'd asked? The fact that he hadn't reprimanded her for believing Bjørn-Åge Flaten suggested that he was getting soft in the head.

He walked over to the entryway of the building where the Lithuanian girl had almost been killed. The young couple in the neighboring apartment knew more than they'd told them, he was sure of that. The wife did, in any case. She was home with a six-month-old baby. With a little luck, he would catch her before she went out to push the stroller in Frogner Park with her girlfriends or slipped away to one of the many coffee shops on this side of the city. She was concealing something. And it was best to come when she wasn't expecting him, like now.

He pushed the doorbell.

"Hello?" crackled the loudspeaker.

"Tommy Bergmann, police."

She didn't answer at once.

"It's not a good time."

"Then I'll have to ask you to come down to the police station later today."

She sighed in resignation.

He looked at his watch. He'd miss his flight if she was going to be difficult.

"Okay, then."

He pushed open the entry door. Just as the killer had done.

You? wondered Bergmann, taking the surveillance-camera picture of Morten Høgda out of his pocket.

She was waiting for him with the kid on her arm when he arrived on the fourth floor. He hardly recognized her without makeup.

"I just have a few quick questions for you."

Her face was serious, the child's eyes wide. She smiled, then started to cry.

Who can blame you? thought Bergmann, taking a look at himself in the mirror in the entry.

The woman set the child down under a baby gym in the living room, and she stopped crying. The light streamed in through the windows, making the room look even whiter than it already was.

"Would you like something to drink?" she said, avoiding his gaze.

Bergmann shook his head.

"Is your husband at work?"

She nodded and scratched her forearm with her artificial nails. He took out the enhanced picture of Morten Høgda from the surveillance camera. Then he took out the print of the picture he'd found on the Internet.

"Have you seen this man before? In the entry?"

Therese Syvertsen pushed her blonde hair behind her ears and studied the pictures for a long time. Much too long. She closed her eyes and took a few steps away from him.

"Have you?"

"Yes," she said.

"The night the girl was attacked?"

She shook her head.

"He's been here a few times. I've seen him through the peephole in the door. I ran into him down in the entryway lobby. He looked at me as though he thought I was like her. As if I could be bought."

"But you didn't see him through the peephole that night?"

"No."

"Are you sure?"

"I was asleep. I didn't see anyone."

"What about your husband?"

"Nothing wakes him. Not her, at least." Therese nodded toward the child who lay babbling to herself on the floor. She reached for the toys that dangled from the baby gym.

"Do you know who he is? Have you seen him anywhere else?"

She shook her head.

"I'll need you to come down to the police station tomorrow. Nine o'clock, can you manage that? Feel free to bring the child with you. You'll have to sign some papers."

Therese stared vacantly at him, as if there was something more she was withholding.

"Has your husband asked you to keep your mouth shut?" he said. It seemed as if that struck a chord in her, as she straightened up immediately and her expression changed.

"No, what makes you think that?"

"It's important that you tell me everything, absolutely everything. You'll also have to look through the photo registry down at the police station." The person who called Dispatch when he found the girl upstairs could be her pimp. With any luck, he was in Kripo's digital photo registry.

Bergmann called Reuter on his way to the car. It was so cold that the patches of snow on the sidewalk crunched. It reminded him of his childhood. Of his mother.

He explained the situation to Reuter. Reuter responded with silence.

"Put surveillance on him, okay? I don't want him to know yet, or everything is shot. Make sure he doesn't leave the country."

"The lady was quite sure she'd seen him in the entry?"

"Yes."

"Doesn't have to mean anything."

"No," said Bergmann. "But there's something wrong with him. Something he's hiding from me." Of course, Reuter didn't know that Alexander Thorstensen was Høgda's son. Or that Høgda was from the town next to Nordreisa. Had Høgda been acquainted with his own mother up there? Could he possibly be his father?

The thought almost made him vomit.

"Hell open," said Reuter suddenly, out of the blue. "That's one hell of a strange word order the lunatic chose in the letter to you, don't you think?"

Bergmann didn't want to talk about that letter. It made him feel as though he was being slowly suffocated, as if someone had tied steel wire around his throat and was slowly, slowly winding it around. Someone who knew more about him than he did himself. Someone who had taken the life of these girls, or at the very least knew who had.

"Yes, it's strange. 'I have seen Hell lying open' sounds more natural. What does Flatanger have to say about it?"

"He agrees. He thinks it's deliberate. I'm not so sure."

"I'll mention it to my wife," said Reuter. "She should have my job. Does nothing but read and think."

"What do you think of what Flatanger said? Two persons in one mind. Or the other way around?"

"A man who thinks he's a woman," said Reuter. "Man by day, woman at night?"

"Yes."

"Just find that confused bastard, then I won't give a shit if there's one or two or three people in his head, or if he parades around in skirts at night, okay?"

"Just find Høgda. Then I think we have him," said Bergmann.

"For that matter, Kripo is planning to capture Rask before they get to Trondheim. They flew the SWAT team up there too, it's getting to be a real circus."

Bergmann did not answer. He thought they were making a mistake. But maybe not. He no longer knew up from down. Could Rask be on his way to see Alexander Thorstensen? Bergmann no longer thought so.

To be on the safe side he called the university hospital in Tromsø from a concealed number at Gardermoen Airport.

"Alexander Thorstensen? He's on his shift. One moment, I'll see if I can transfer you."

He hung up and ordered another pint, wondering how many times he'd sat like this before.

He fell asleep before takeoff and dreamed that Elisabeth Thorstensen was holding him. That the case was solved, that she was living with him.

That she was sitting in his hallway with a knife to her wrist saying, *It's all your fault. Your fault, Tommy.*

53

The National Library reminded her of an old asylum, though she'd never actually been inside one. Susanne assured herself yet again that her phone wasn't turned off, just the sound.

She got help from one of the librarians. *Nordlys*, early sixties? *There better be something there*, Susanne thought, smiling as innocently as she could. A tired smile was all she got in return.

An hour later, her eyes were so tired from skimming the cursed microfilm that she was about to give up. It was noon. She should have been searching through the census for that needle in a haystack.

She worked fast, checking just the front page and the first few news pages, figuring that's where a murder story would appear. She didn't have time to sit and study the Christmas sales or the washing machine and liquor ads from 1961.

At one o'clock, she realized she hadn't eaten anything all day.

When she got to October 1962, she thought that enough was enough.

She left the reading room and went over to sit down on a sofa with a view of the beech trees and Hydro Park on the other side of Drammensveien. She entered Torvald's number.

"Is everything okay?" he asked. Once again she wished that he had been born with different genes. That he liked someone like her.

"Are you busy this evening? I need childcare."

"Oh?" he said. "Hot date, I hope?"

"I'm going to look up a hundred and ten names in the census registry."

Torvald was silent.

"I've got a customer. I'll call you back," he said without managing to conceal a certain disappointment in his voice.

A few minutes later a text message arrived: *All fine with Mathea, darling. But didn't we have a deal that you would get yourself a life . . . life after Nico?*

I will, thought Susanne. *Just let me find this lunatic who's been killing these girls.*

She checked the clock on the wall and sat down at the microfilm reader again. Foolish chore. From a man who was just then walking around Tromsø.

She opened the newspaper for October 2, 1962.

The words in the right-hand column made the hairs on her neck stand up.

16-Year-Old Girl Killed in Nordreisa

A black-and-white picture of some buildings.
An introduction.

Sixteen-year-old Edle Maria Reiersen was found murdered in Storslett yesterday morning. The police have no leads in the case. The circumstances around the killing are unknown, but according to what Nordlys has learned, the girl was badly disfigured.

54

Few places in the world had more beautiful light than Tromsø in the middle of December. It was the middle of the dark season, but even so, the landscape appeared to be painted in blue, white, and pink. The Arctic landscape worked like a sedative and told him one thing: maybe he felt more at home up here than in the south. He got off the bus at the university hospital almost reluctantly, disappointed that the trip hadn't been longer.

In the reception area there was a Christmas tree—not a plastic one like at the police station in Oslo, but a stately, genuine spruce that smelled and glistened with authenticity and strength, more or less like the landscape itself. Bergmann introduced himself at the counter and said he wanted to speak with Alexander Thorstensen, even if he had to wait until his shift ended at midnight to do so.

He told himself that it couldn't be Alex. He was eighteen when Kristiane disappeared. But he was a surgeon. He couldn't ignore that.

The woman at the reception desk didn't seem to notice the slight absurdity of his inquiry; she simply referred him to the waiting room and said that Thorstensen was very busy, but she would call him.

Bergmann repeated that he had all day. He got no reaction other than a half-raised eyebrow.

He had only been browsing through *Nordlys* for a few minutes when he heard someone clear their throat behind him. He turned and jumped at the sight.

The slightly feminine features were unmistakable. He so closely resembled Elisabeth Thorstensen that he probably could have been taken for a girl in his younger years. The idea suddenly seemed plausible. He was only Kristiane's half-brother, and he had the kind of appearance that teenage girls always fell for. Why wouldn't Elisabeth Thorstensen tell the truth?

"Alexander Thorstensen." He extended his hand, large with well-groomed nails and a broad wedding ring. The white coat gave him an air of authority, despite his unlined face. Bergmann felt like a ravaged old wino alongside Elisabeth Thorstensen's picture-perfect son.

"You're not from the department up here," said Alexander, releasing his gaze.

"It's—"

"Kristiane," Alexander completed the sentence quietly. For a moment he was so like Elisabeth Thorstensen that Bergmann almost felt a surge of longing in his belly for her. He was really sinking into the quagmire now; he would look up Viggo Osvold as soon as he was back in Oslo.

He tried to detect a resemblance to Morten Høgda in Alexander's face, but found none.

"I just have one question."

"Which you couldn't ask on the phone?"

"I prefer to see who I'm talking to. Besides, a little fresh air does me good."

The pager in Alexander's coat pocket beeped. He sighed and walked quickly to the phone on the counter.

"You'll have to wait," he called to Bergmann, trotting down the corridor. Bergmann followed him with his gaze until he disappeared behind a double door.

He sat down in the cafeteria and read all the newspapers he could lay his hands on and smoked five or six cigarettes outside the entrance. The woman who'd been at the reception desk earlier finally came into the cafeteria with a message for him.

"Telephone," she said.

"Meet me up in Anatomy," said Alexander when he picked up the receiver. Then he tried to explain how to get there.

"I'll find it."

Bergmann finally found the right staircase. On the landing he stopped and looked out the window. He just caught the last remnants of daylight. A slalom hill on the other side of the sound looked like an overgrown glowworm in the twilight.

"Come with me."

He turned and looked up the stairs. Alexander stood on the top step. He appeared to have aged in the few hours since Bergmann had last seen him.

They walked in silence to a door marked Anatomy Hall. Alexander exchanged a few words with two young women walking toward them, apparently students. They glanced at Bergmann, then disappeared down the stairs. At the bottom he heard quiet laughter, the kind of girl laughter that men would never understand.

He stopped in the doorway to the enormous room. Alexander walked on in, clearly unfazed by the sight of the twenty or thirty glass display cases showcasing different body parts in formaldehyde.

The first thing Bergmann saw was a fetus that appeared to be floating, its thumb in its mouth, its neck bent. Then an amputated arm, and alongside it a torso. He took a few steps into the room and studied the fine cut where the arm had been attached to the body, then moved his gaze to the throat. The head was nowhere to be seen. He thought of the girl on Frognerveien. Of Kristiane.

This is all a person is, he thought, standing behind the showcase that contained the torso and studying the back of the man who had donated his body for medical research and ended up in the Anatomy Department as a monument to human perishability, cut up like an ox, each body part frozen in time and space.

"Why didn't you study in Oslo?" he asked Alexander, who had sat down at a table at the far end of the room.

"What do you mean?"

"Did you want to come up here, or did you not get accepted to medical school in Oslo?"

Alexander held Bergmann's gaze for a moment, then fixed his eyes on the weightless torso floating in formaldehyde in front of him.

"I had to get away. I was suddenly nothing more than the brother of the girl who was killed, do you understand?"

Bergmann studied the man before him. Yes, Kristiane could certainly have fallen in love with him, once she had crossed the threshold between right and wrong.

"Was that why you came all the way up here?" said Alexander. He laughed quietly, underscoring the faint hint of sarcasm in his voice. "To ask me about my studies?"

Bergmann shook his head.

"You know as well as I do that Anders Rask has escaped, even though he got Kristiane's case reopened."

Alexander nodded. "A paradox, don't you think?" he said. "He escapes even though he maintains that he didn't kill my sister."

"Was he one of your teachers in school?"

"Yes."

"Did you have any contact with him after you finished school?"

Alexander snorted.

"What do you think?"

There was a pause.

Alexander supported his hands against the tabletop, pushed himself up, and started walking toward the glass showcase with the torso. He leaned his head against the glass, his face distorted through the liquid.

"When did you find out that Morten Høgda is your father?" said Bergmann.

"Right before I turned eighteen."

"The spring of 1988?"

"Yes. But I'd suspected it for many years. It showed, somehow. And on Dad too."

"What did you think about that?"

"About what?"

"That Morten Høgda is your father?"

"What would you have thought?" Alexander pushed himself off the display case. He walked with his hands behind his back between the many cases, as if he were an old schoolmaster walking around among his pupils.

"What do you think of your mother?"

Alexander smiled.

"What are you? My psychologist? Mom has always been nuts. Really nuts. It's just that no one is able to see that."

Bergmann followed Alexander, who appeared to be intensely preoccupied by the contents of the various cases.

"Did you ever tell Kristiane that you were only her half-brother?"

Alexander opened his mouth to say something, but evidently changed his mind.

"What kind of question is that?" He ran his hand over the case with the sawed-off torso. "I've always liked it in here," he said. "It tells you so much about life, don't you agree?"

"Did you ever tell her? That you were only her half-brother?"

"Yes."

"When?"

"Once."

"When?"

"That last summer."

"1988?"

Alexander was now looking at the case with the dead fetus. It must have had its thumb in its mouth when it was removed from its mother. *Imagine seeing something like that,* thought Bergmann. A stillborn child with its thumb in its mouth.

"This is the most beautiful one," said Alexander. "I often think about this little guy when I'm alone with my son. The boundary between life and death is so thin."

He stopped talking, as if he had run out of words. He stared at the dead fetus for a long time before he opened his mouth again.

"We were alone at the cabin one weekend, and—"

"At Hvaler?"

He nodded toward the glass.

"Mom and Dad were gone all weekend. The weather was nice, Kristiane was off from handball for once. I said she could bring a girlfriend along, but she didn't want to. She'd had some trouble with a boyfriend or something."

"So you were there alone?"

He didn't reply.

"Did anything happen at the cabin that weekend?"

"What would have happened there?"

"Your mother said she thought Kristiane had fallen in love with you."

Alexander's expression did not change.

"A lot of girls were in love with me. But they weren't interesting."

"But your fifteen-year-old sister? Was she interesting?"

"She knew what she was doing."

"So what your mother said is true?"

"What did she say?"

"That you slept together. You and Kristiane."

Alexander laughed quietly.

"Didn't you hear what I just said? My mother is not in her right mind, Bergmann."

The door behind them flew open. Two students almost fell into the room, a boy and a girl.

"Oh, sorry," the boy said. The girl started to laugh, at first tentatively, but increasingly hysterically as they left.

An alarming silence settled over the room when they had gone.

Bergmann and Alexander Thorstensen studied one another. Alexander turned his head slightly to the left. Bergmann had to concentrate not to do the same.

"You were alone the evening she disappeared? Did you pick her up anywhere?"

"Listen here," said Alexander. His voice was still controlled, but under the superficial coolness of it something quivered that Bergmann thought was fury. "What exactly are you insinuating?"

"I just want to know if it's true that you slept together and where you were the night she disappeared. No one can remember seeing you before midnight at the party you claimed to be at."

"Are you saying that I killed Kristiane?"

His voice cracked, as though he were an adolescent, but it wasn't fury, only a kind of defeat—as if he'd been cornered and knew that there was no way out.

"Were you going to meet her somewhere that evening?"

Alexander shook his head.

"The party was in Nordstrand, Bergmann. She took the train *from* Nordstrand, didn't she?" He smiled faintly. "You ought to focus your attention elsewhere," he said. "Such as on the fact that my mother needs help. You mustn't believe everything she says. Haven't you realized that? She's not healthy. She's been hospitalized before, don't you know that?"

Bergmann took a deep breath. Who's the one who's crazy here?

"Did your mother tell anyone else about it? Per-Erik? Morten Høgda?"

Alexander turned on his heels and walked toward the door without a word.

Right before he came to the last display case, he stopped. For a moment Bergmann thought that he was going to knock over the one with the sawed-off leg, shattering the glass and spilling the leg and formaldehyde out over the green linoleum floor.

He seemed to regain control over himself, but when he came to the door, he struck his hand against the frame so hard that Bergmann feared he'd broken it. A surgeon with a broken hand was worth nothing. Then he was out the door and disappeared from sight.

Bergmann waited a little while before starting after him. When he came out into the corridor, Alexander Thorstensen was gone. There were three ways he could have gone: straight ahead through a double door, to the left down the stairs that they'd come up earlier, or to the right through an emergency exit, which would have triggered an alarm if he'd opened it.

Bergmann decided on the stairs, but it was already too late. He trotted over to the reception desk and had the new receptionist call Alexander Thorstensen.

Damn, thought Bergmann. *Where the hell has he gone?*

"I'm just getting voice mail. He's gone off shift, so—"

Bergmann nodded silently.

He took a taxi to Skolegata, where Alexander lived in an old Swiss chalet. All the windows were dark; not even the Christmas lights were on. He rang the doorbell several times, then took a walk around the house. His shoes filled with snow, and he cursed Alexander and everyone he'd ever known. He tried to see in through the windows, but to no avail.

No one's home, he thought. *Unless they're hiding on the second floor.* He walked backward through the snow until he was standing in the middle of the yard. There were no shadows visible in the windows, though it was hard to see from that distance. He stood there motionless for a few minutes, but no faces appeared behind the windowpanes.

His phone pinged with a text message.

Susanne.

```
Found the girl. Edle Maria, killed in
Nordreisa October 1962. But won't be any
wiser until I find the case.
```

Oh well, he thought. And then, *Damn.* That didn't get them much closer to the truth. They had to find the case. *And I didn't even get to ask Alexander Thorstensen about Edle Maria.*

But he had to get back to Oslo. He had to talk to Morten Høgda again. The best thing to do would be to get him indicted, if for nothing else than for not reporting what he witnessed to the police.

He cursed himself in the taxi out to Langnes. He'd gone all the damned way up to Tromsø for nothing.

At the airport he bought some new socks. He walked over to the departure hall in stocking feet and enjoyed the funny looks he got.

As he sat napping in one of the chairs at the gate, his phone rang.

"Think the old lady cracked it," said Fredrik Reuter.

"What are you talking about?"

"Hell open, have you forgotten about that?"

The truth was that he'd almost forgotten about the letter.

"Not really."

"The only thing she could think of was Fröding. Majored in Nordic languages, can you believe that, she's half-autistic besides. Never play Scrabble with her."

"Fröding. What the hell is that?"

"You mean *who* is that? Or who *was* that, rather."

"Well?"

"Gustaf Fröding, Swedish poet, a real lunatic, spent most of his life in a mental hospital. He once wrote a poem called *A Vision*. One of the lines is 'Hell I saw open standing.' That is, 'Hell open standing.' Do you understand?"

Bergmann sighed.

"No," he said. "A bit esoteric for me."

"I'm siding with the old lady," said Reuter. "She's smarter than me. And if she's smarter than me, then she's definitely smarter than you."

"We'll discuss it when I get back."

"Listen," said Reuter. "What I'm about to tell you, keep your mouth shut about it for now. It'll be released in an hour or two."

"I'll be on the plane then."

"A thirteen-year-old has been reported missing in Kolbotn," said Reuter. "One Amanda Viksveen."

"She's probably just on her way home."

"She was coming home from the Sofiemyr gym, Tommy."

"How long has she been gone?"

"Two hours."

"Two hours, age thirteen. Please. Are they panicking in Follo?"

"No doubt a well-behaved girl. Credible parents. They had an agreement that she should come straight home."

"Well-behaved girls are always the worst."

"The parents want to file a missing-person report. They were going to take her to the mall to go shopping. She's disappeared without a trace, Tommy. Was just going to take the shortcut through the woods."

Damn, thought Bergmann. He'd been in those woods a thousand times. It was pitch black there in the winter. There was one spot between the gym and the soccer field that was like being in a black hole.

"I'm an optimist."

Reuter hung up. He was not an optimist.

Bergmann was just thinking that the thirteen-year-old Amanda would surely show up sometime over the course of the evening when he became aware of something happening somewhere to his right. It was an argument over by security.

Bergmann thought he heard someone say his name.

No. He closed his eyes. *Fröding,* he thought. What could that possibly mean?

"Bergmann, can Tommy Bergmann report to security?" came through the loudspeaker. It took him a minute to realize they were calling his name.

Alexander Thorstensen was standing like a dog on too tight a leash on the other side of security.

"You have to believe me," he said.

Bergmann looked at his watch. Then he looked at Alexander Thorstensen again. The security guard by his side appeared eager to put the young surgeon in cuffs at any moment.

He was going to miss his flight, but there was another one in an hour.

"Meet me downstairs," he said to Alexander.

He was standing outside the doors by the arrival hall when Bergmann walked up. They walked in silence toward a bench.

"You have to believe me. I didn't do anything with Kristiane. I was alone all evening until I went to the party in Nordstrand." He drew his hands over his face, then ran his fingers through his hair.

"But she was in love with you?"

He shrugged.

"I don't know."

"Tell me the truth."

"Maybe."

"Why would your mother tell me such a thing? Do you think she really believed it? That she found strands of Kristiane's hair in your bed?"

"Maybe Kristiane slept there sometime when I wasn't home. I have no idea." He opened his mouth to say something more, but changed his mind.

"Well?"

"Mom was obsessed with incest. It was like she was actually encouraging me. 'You can get married,' she said to me once, and then smiled in a way that frightened me. 'You would have such good-looking children,' she added. She said things like that to me all the time when we were alone. 'You're so beautiful, Alex.' Sometimes I was almost afraid that I'd find my own mom lying in my bed. Do you understand?"

Bergmann shook his head.

"Not really."

"She still needs help, Bergmann. Why do you think I came all the way up here? I wanted to get away from her. And away from Morten too. I think he's almost as crazy as she is."

"Your mother was at Frensby, right? I think I met her there once myself, actually. When I was a kid."

"Frensby? I didn't know that."

"Oh?" said Bergmann. "Didn't she ever tell you where she was?"

Alexander just stared at him. Bergmann felt the recognition slowly wash over him.

Somewhere along the way, he had made a trivial error.

"I have to go," said Alexander.

Bergmann shuffled after him.

They went their separate ways at the exit. Bergmann headed straight to the SAS counter and said he needed to borrow their computer. He flashed his police identification in the face of the young woman behind the counter, and she let him in. He opened the browser to *Dagbladet*. Anders Rask had been shot by a police patrol in Trondheim. It must have just happened.

Sure enough. His phone started vibrating. Reuter. Bergmann ignored it and entered "Gustaf Fröding" in the browser's search field.

A series of black-and-white pictures came up. And sure enough, the bald man with the big beard looked like he was a haunted soul.

But it didn't actually ring any bells. He clicked on the most striking picture, a yellowed black-and-white photograph. Something was written in white script in the lower left-hand corner. Bergmann read it, but was none the wiser.

What the hell kind of guy is this?

And why couldn't Susanne finish the job he'd asked her to do?

He looked at the clock. He could have gone down to *Nordlys* himself, but he had to get home this evening.

Frank Krokhol, he thought. *I'll owe him a big favor.*

The old *Dagbladet* doyen answered his phone almost immediately.

"I told you. It's not Rask, you know. Old Anders has driven into the police barricades in Trondheim, and a girl disappears over three hundred miles away in Kolbotn. I told you that, didn't I?"

"How do you know that?" Bergmann blurted out. He should have known better.

"Dear friend," said Krokhol. "I had better sources before you were born than you'll ever have."

"So do me a favor. You're from Tromsø, aren't you?"

Krokhol didn't reply.

"That case. Edle Maria. Do you remember I asked you about that?"

"Sorry, Tommy. There's been too much lately."

"Get me the obituaries from *Nordlys*. October 1962. Mainly that one."

"I grew up with that paper."

"In that case you remember it well."

"I'm not that damned old."

"Pull a few strings. Quickly. I need everything they have on the case. Who, what, where, do you understand?"

"Good Lord, I thought you had a certain sense of order, Tommy. Let me escape to a warmer country before Christmas, huh?"

"Just do it. You'll get the scoop first, you know that."

Bergmann could hear Krokhol tapping his cigarette on the other end of the line.

"Edle Maria. October 1962. What the hell will you do with the obituary?"

I don't know, thought Bergmann. *I don't know if I can bear to find that out.*

55

Should she feel guilty about letting Torvald pick Mathea up at daycare? Yes. Definitely.

Susanne Bech sat with the phone receiver squeezed against her ear while she entered names in the census registry. She'd been at it since four thirty and was just finished with the inhabitants of the first apartment building. This was no doubt a completely idiotic way to proceed, but it was all she had right now. And she had to hurry and finish before Bergmann got back from Tromsø. If she didn't get any results, she was through. He might well believe that she was coming unglued.

She studied her own reflection in the window while Mathea's voice filled her head.

"So you and Torvald are having a good time?"

"Yes."

"What are you watching on TV?"

"Something about old things."

"Old things?"

Torvald spoke up in the background. "Some antiques show or other. Mathea's the one who wanted to watch it," he said.

Like I believe that, thought Susanne.

"Torvald makes better pancakes than you," said Mathea.

"I have no doubt about that." Susanne looked at the clock. Her daughter should have been in bed long ago.

"But aren't you tired?"

Susanne printed out the information on the ex-husband of Randi Gjerulfsen, who lived on the third floor of the first building. Rolf Gjerulfsen had two convictions for assault.

Good Lord, she thought. *This is madness.*

Torvald took the phone.

"Listen," he whispered, "if you were to ever die, God forbid, I'll take her, just so that's clear. Do we have a deal?"

Susanne breathed heavily.

"Then you'll have to move in with Nico."

"Anytime."

"Put her to bed, please. If she doesn't want to brush her teeth, don't worry about it. As for you?"

"Yes."

"I'm very fond of you, do you know that?"

"Hugs and kisses."

The dial tone filled her ear. She hid her face in her hands and thought that she mustn't cry. She was just so worn out. But she had to do this. Bergmann didn't like her much, she was sure of that. But if she could do this, if she found a decisive lead, he would have no choice but to give her a permanent position, or at least extend her temporary position. Or so she hoped.

She heard Fredrik Reuter's voice down the hall and straightened up.

Pull yourself together, she thought. *You're blubbering worse than an old lady. Worse than when Line died.*

"I thought you had your daughter today?" said Reuter, waltzing into her office.

She mumbled something unintelligible.

"Jensrud is dead from gunshot wounds," he said. "Keep that to yourself for the time being."

"And Rask?"

"Hopefully he'll die in the course of the night."

"But they didn't kill Furuberget and his wife," said Susanne. "And then we haven't made much headway."

Reuter refrained from commenting. Instead he took a toothpick out of the chest pocket of his shirt. Susanne shuddered. He used the same one all day until it splintered. She had nothing against Reuter, but that toothpick alone was enough to make her think, *Not if you were the last man on earth, Fredrik Reuter.*

"And you're working on what?"

"Skøyen," she said, continuing to enter names into the registry, then into an Excel spreadsheet, and finally, cross-check them against all the registers.

"Exactly," said Reuter, poking thoroughly between his molars. "Tell me," he said finally. "Have you ever heard of Gustaf Fröding?"

"Fröding? No, why is that?"

"Just a question. And check the news sites in an hour. I'm sorry to have to tell you this, but I think Christmas is shot for all of us."

He disappeared from her office. She closed her eyes and knew exactly what he was thinking: Susanne Bech was a silly brunette who wasted the taxpayers' money, spent her years as the parent of a small child getting divorced, and entered stupid names into a stupid form.

She was just getting ready to leave at 10:00 p.m. when Bergmann called. It was surprisingly comforting to hear his voice. She told him about the Edle Maria search at the National Library and took the opportunity to say that she was still working on the Skøyen lead.

She took the fact that he didn't bawl her out as a compliment. That said, he didn't seem particularly interested either.

"Did you check the obituary?" he said.

"The obituary?"

"Edle Maria. There may have been an obituary in the paper after she died. Worth seeing that before we find the case."

You could have spent the night in Tromsø and gone to Nordlys *first thing in the morning,* she thought, but kept her mouth shut.

"See you tomorrow," he said, and hung up.

The hell I will, thought Susanne. She checked the clock and turned the computer back on.

She picked a random name from the third apartment building and entered it in the search field in the census registry.

Anne-Britt Torgersen, born in 1947.

Susanne clicked on the details.

A child, born in 1985.

It took a few seconds for her brain to register that she'd seen the name of the child's father before. She fumbled with the mouse for a few seconds. It couldn't be a coincidence. Did he live there then?

In a moment of clarity she remembered a fragment of the brief report Bergmann had written. She went into the folder labeled "Kristiane reopening" and read, "Ex-wife called. He said he'd given his ex the apartment. Very close to here. Worth a fortune today."

A quick search made her stomach sink. Her fingers stiffened against the keyboard. He'd reported moving away from Nedre Skøyen Vei in 1990.

That couldn't be right.

Suddenly Reuter's words popped up in her mind: "Check the news sites in an hour."

She went to *Dagbladet.*

Amanda (13) Missing in Kolbotn

Oh God, she thought. *It can't be him.*

She flipped back through her notepad and found his telephone number. She looked at the page in the census registry. He'd lived in

Skøyen in 1988. He really had. She entered the first four digits of his number, then changed her mind.

She went down the corridor to see if Reuter was still in his office, but no. The lights were off. She looked at her watch. Who worked this late in the evening without extra pay?

But I must, she thought. She entered Bergmann's number into her phone. She closed her eyes when she got voice mail.

She had to tell Bergmann.

Was that really what had happened?

56

Susanne ran out into Grønlandsleiret without looking, and a bus going by barely managed to brake for her. She remained standing on the sidewalk for a while afterward, trying to register that she'd almost been run over. That she'd just had a narrow escape.

Like I did out there?

She supported herself against the window of a Thai restaurant. The gaudy Christmas lights strung along the window frame momentarily confused her. Was it already Christmas?

She'd been alone with him. But it simply couldn't be true.

The slush reached over the tops of her short boots as she turned onto Mandalls Gate toward home. Those poor parents in Kolbotn. She hadn't been able to read past the introduction; that alone had almost made her throw up.

On her way down in the elevator at police headquarters, she had once again been overpowered by a feeling that something dreadful had happened. That Torvald had been killed in the apartment, that Mathea was not dead yet, but dragging herself bleeding toward the door while screaming, "Mommy, Mommy."

Her hands shook as she unlocked the front door of the building. She slammed the door behind her and ran halfway through the court-yard before she stopped.

The Christmas lights strung from the kitchen windows on the floors above her made her feel more secure. It was Christmas. It really was Christmas. It couldn't be that bad. Or could it?

The stairs in the entry made her think of the building in Frognerveien. She hadn't been there herself, thank God, but she'd seen the pictures. And she'd seen the pictures from Kristiane's autopsy and knew that she would never be able to erase them from her mind.

Her pulse was racing by the time she knocked on her own front door. She simply didn't have the energy to take the key out of her jacket pocket.

"Good Lord, what is it with you?" asked Torvald. He looked more handsome than ever, and she couldn't help but smile.

"Nothing. Just a little tired. Did it go okay?"

"Like a dream. I want a little one like that, you know?"

"So marry me."

He took her jacket, held the coyote fur up to his face, and studied himself in the mirror in the hall.

"Watch it, Liberace. Will you have a glass of wine with me before you go downstairs?" Susanne squeezed out of her boots and headed to Mathea's room.

She pushed the door open quietly. In the faint glow from the skylight, she saw her daughter lying on top of the duvet. One leg hung over the edge of the bed.

She sat down at the foot of the bed and stroked the little bare leg. *I love you,* she thought. *I really love you.*

Torvald appeared in the doorway with a half-full glass of wine in his hand.

"Has something happened?" he whispered.

"No." She stood up and took the glass from his hand.

She lay down on the couch with her head on his lap while the TV hummed in the background. A rerun of some English talk show Torvald had missed over the weekend.

Ten minutes later she was fast asleep. She was soon trapped in a nightmare she hadn't had since she was a child. Alone in the cellar of an old house. Raw, damp air and rough concrete walls. Everything was dark, and she fumbled along the wall, her hands bleeding. Mathea's voice was barely audible as she called to her. Occasionally, she screamed like she was being tortured, then cried out like an infant—"Mommy!"—as if she'd just learned to talk.

She gasped for air and opened her eyes.

Torvald placed one hand on her forehead.

"What is it, Susanne? It's something to do with work, isn't it?"

She got up without answering him and picked up her phone. It was already eleven thirty.

"I have to get some sleep, my friend. I'll call you tomorrow, okay? Eternally grateful." She kissed him on the cheek and pulled him up off the couch.

He picked up his shoes and took hold of the doorknob. For a moment he stood there, looking at her as if he wanted to say something.

"What is it?" she said.

"We'll talk tomorrow." He walked out the door, and Susanne watched him, even though he was only going down one floor.

Eleven thirty, she thought, making sure that the safety chain on the door was fastened.

She studied herself in the entry mirror. The incipient wrinkles around her eyes, the furrow on her forehead—all inherited from her mother. *To hell with her,* she thought. *To hell with everything.* She gripped the phone in her hand. *Can I call him now? Don't I have to?*

"Very close to here." It must have been. Or was Kristiane going to see someone else? Susanne knew that she'd gone through less than a third of the names, much less looked up everyone who was related to the residents or had once been part of the family.

She went back to the living room and flopped down on the couch. The last remnants of warmth from Torvald could still be felt in the fabric.

Audience laughter burbled quietly from the TV. She looked around the big loft apartment. It had been too big for the three of them, Nicolay, her, and Mathea. Now it seemed absurdly large. Cavernous. And dark.

She picked up the glass of red wine and brought it to her lips.

Her phone rang out in the hall. She'd set it down on the old dresser. She went to grab it, taking her glass with her.

I have to call Tommy, she thought.

It was Torvald.

"Had you gone to bed?" he said.

"No. Soon. You're not mad at me? I'm just tired. Nothing more than that."

He didn't answer.

"Torvald?"

"I just have to tell you this. I almost forgot."

His voice sounded different, as if he was nervous about what he was about to say. Susanne felt the hairs on her neck standing up. This was not good, this could not be good.

"What?" she said, more sternly than she intended.

"Mathea told me tonight, right before she was going to bed . . ." He stopped.

Susanne tightened her grip on the wine glass. The gaze that met her own in the entry mirror was hollow; she hardly recognized herself. "Calm down," she mouthed to herself. Don't get hysterical, wasn't that what that cursed mother of hers always said to her?

"What did Mathea tell you?" *That the new daycare teacher, a pleasant young man, had touched her,* she thought. *I'll kill him. Cut off everything.*

"No. I'm sure it's nothing."

"Tell me. Now."

"She said she was alone in the playground today, she likes to go out there . . ."

Susanne's hands and arms had gone numb. Her head felt white, blanked out by a snowstorm.

"Said she started talking with a lady outside the fence. A nice lady, but Mathea said she was a little startled. She said she would come back one day, but Mathea must promise not to say anything to anyone."

"Who would come back?"

"The lady. That Mathea talked to. She thought Mathea was pretty." Torvald's voice was barely audible.

"Why the hell didn't you call me, Torvald? Are you aware of—" She stopped herself. Her eyes filled with tears.

"Don't be angry, Susanne. Please. I forgot."

"Forgot? You can't forget that kind of thing!"

"I'm sorry." He sounded like a child now.

"Okay." A sudden calm came over her. She didn't need two kids. "It's all right."

The sudden calm disappeared as soon as Torvald started talking again. He said a word—only a single little word—but she was unable to understand what came after it. Then he said two words and Susanne almost dropped her glass.

"Edle Maria," he said. "It sounded so strange, I just—"

Susanne stared at herself in the mirror, watching her face grow gradually more distorted. Now she was the one who was crying like a child.

"Susanne. Say something. Say something, anything at all."

She didn't even notice the wine glass slipping from her hand, just heard the sound of shattered glass. Her gaze shifted apathetically down to the floor. The red wine looked like blood on the floorboards, splashed up over her pant legs.

"Say it isn't true," she whispered.

"What?"

"Maria. Edle Maria. Say it isn't true."

"But that's what Mathea said. That the lady said her name was Edle Maria."

57

Only nice-looking girls smoke Marlboro Lights, thought Bergmann, reaching behind the books on his bookcase. He'd run out of Prince cigarettes and searched the entire apartment for an emergency smoke he'd hidden away for moments such as this one.

There. His hand felt a soft pack. Something Hege had left behind. Duty-free, he didn't remember which trip. One of those disastrous times. Weren't they all? No, not all.

He had just lit the all-white filter cigarette when his phone rang. He looked at his watch. *Alexander Thorstensen,* he thought. Or maybe the guy in Surveillance, who had Morten Høgda in his sights. You could have wiped your ass with the first report. Høgda had been at the office until eight o'clock. Then he'd walked right across the street into his building. Five minutes later the lights went on in his apartment. He was still there.

He didn't manage to answer it in time, but it started ringing again at once.

Susanne, he thought. *Now?*

As soon as he'd pressed the green "Answer" button, she started shouting, "You have to come. You have to come."

"If you calm down, I'll think about it."

She fell silent. He could hear that she was crying.

"She wants my child, Tommy."

He shook his head.

"What are you talking about?"

"Maria," she whispered. "Edle Maria."

"Edle Maria?"

Susanne said nothing.

He held the phone to his ear while he worked his left arm into the sleeve of his bubble jacket. The Raven pistol pressed against his chest. He had a feeling that he was going to have use for it.

"Are you at home?"

He heard a barely audible "yes."

"Hurry," she said. "Just hurry."

The trustworthy Escort started on the first try. He double-parked in front of her building. A man answered the entry phone.

"Who are you?" said Bergmann.

"A friend," said the voice. It sounded as though he was crying too. Bergmann shook his head. There were some things he didn't understand.

Susanne answered the door. She pulled him to her as if she'd been waiting for him her whole life.

"Edle Maria," she whispered. "Edle Maria was at the daycare center."

Bergmann became aware of noise coming from inside the apartment. The TV was on. A children's movie.

Susanne told him what had happened. How her daughter had talked to a lady by the fence at the daycare center who said her name was Edle Maria, and who said she thought Mathea was so pretty.

He went into the living room and nodded to the good-looking man who was sitting there.

"Torvald," said Susanne. Bergmann shook his hand. "Neighbor and friend. My best friend. Mathea," she said. "Can you tell Tommy what happened?"

Her daughter didn't answer. She was lying on the other end of the couch, staring at the TV with eyes as big as saucers.

Bergmann took the remote control from the coffee table and turned off the TV.

"I think you have to help us, Mathea."

"She was nice."

"Good to hear."

"I'm going to talk to her tomorrow. At daycare."

"What color was her hair? Do you remember?"

"I want to watch the movie."

"Was it light or dark?"

"Don't know."

"Mathea," said Susanne. "You have to—"

"Let her watch the movie," said Bergmann. He got up from the couch and pointed toward the kitchen. Susanne poured red wine into a glass, but he shook his head. She drank it herself in two big gulps, as if it were juice. "Did you print out the articles about the Edle Maria case?"

She nodded. "But they're at the office."

"I'm going up there."

"I just don't understand. She's supposed to be dead."

"What did you do today?"

"She was going to Skøyen, Tommy. I think I know who she was going to see too."

"Who?"

"I think he was the one she was in love with."

Bergmann frowned. This was too cryptic for him.

"Farberg. Jon-Olav Farberg. He lived in Skøyen then."

"Are you sure? Impossible," he said. "One of the people we're searching for knows me. Or my mother. It can't be Farberg."

"What do you mean?"

"Do you have a computer?"

She pointed down the hallway.

"In Nico's old office."

"Edle Maria is dead," said Bergmann. "She must be dead." *She was killed in the same town my mother was from.* That was an unavoidable fact, a fact that almost made him physically ill.

He opened the web browser and entered "Gustaf Fröding" in the search field. A series of pictures came up on the screen. He clicked on the picture he'd noticed before, the yellowed black-and-white photograph. At the bottom in white script, it read, "John Norén. Goodwin. Uppsala."

"Reuter thinks that the person who wrote the letter to me referred to one of this guy's poems. And Elisabeth thinks that Kristiane was in love with Alexander, her brother. She never said a word about Farberg."

"Oh, good Lord," Susanne said quietly, standing beside him.

He turned toward Susanne. She pointed at the screen.

"That picture."

"What about it?"

"It's him. It's him, Tommy."

"Who?"

"Jon-Olav Farberg. The teacher. Her coach. I was at his house. He could have killed me, Tommy. I think he thought about it while I was there. That he wanted to kill me. We were alone in his house. All alone."

Bergmann stood up and grabbed her by the shoulders.

"Start at the beginning, Susanne. What are you talking about?"

"That picture is hanging in his library."

He went out into the hall without a word, and Susanne followed a few steps behind.

"Get a towel," he said.

She looked perplexed, but did as he said.

He took the pistol out of the inside pocket of his bubble jacket and wrapped the towel around it.

"No questions," he said. "If he comes, don't think. Aim for the stomach."

58

He crashed through the turnstile on the first floor. The Securitas guard called out something behind him, but he was already halfway up the stairs.

Farberg, he thought, while his blood threatened to burst his temples. Did he dress up in women's clothes? Was he two people in one mind, as Rune Flatanger had suggested?

He yanked on the glass doors after holding his identification up to the card reader. Locked.

Once again. A click in the door. He waited two seconds and opened it slowly, then pressed on the light switch.

"Fucking door," he mumbled as he jogged down the corridor to Susanne's office. Fluorescent lights came on one by one above him. As if that would help him think clearly. Jon-Olav Farberg? What did he have to do with Edle Maria? Because Edle Maria was the key. She must be. And Farberg had a picture of Fröding at home.

It was him. It really was him, the pig that had fed him that line about Anders Rask's presumed friend, Yngvar.

I'll bash your skull in as soon as I find you. But first you're going to tell me about Edle Maria.

Susanne had placed all the printouts on the Edle Maria case in a separate folder. He skimmed the text in the first printout. *1962*, he thought. They'd written almost nothing about the case. That was back when the press kowtowed to the authorities, and no one asked critical questions about the obviously miserable investigation.

He took out his phone and called Fredrik Reuter.

"This better be fucking important."

"It's barely midnight, only children have gone to bed by now."

"Well? Have you found the thirteen-year-old in Kolbotn?"

"Call Papa. I need weaponry and two active patrols."

Reuter did not answer.

"We've found him."

"Where?"

"Malmøya. Jon-Olav Farberg. One of her teachers. Colleague of Rask's."

"Malmøya. Give me the address."

Bergmann heard from his voice that Reuter was not far from heading down into his basement and unlocking his own gun cabinet.

It's only a question of which one of us is going to kill him first, thought Bergmann as he got into one of the patrol cars. He unholstered the old Smith & Wesson revolver as they headed down Tøyenbekken, past Mandalls Gate. He looked over his shoulder past the World Islamic Mission, toward Susanne's apartment.

59

As they approached the driveway to Farberg's house, the patrol cars turned off their lights and continued with only their parking lights on. Bergmann raised his service revolver and tried to get an overview of the house. The car slid across the snow like a glider. The house looked abandoned. Just one light was visible on the second floor, besides the outdoor light.

He edged carefully out of the car with the revolver in ready position. His bulletproof Kevlar vest felt like a straitjacket, and he wanted to tear it off. He was going to kill Farberg before he even managed to go on the attack. Taking Farberg alive—if he did attack—was never going to happen.

Gesturing with his arms, the operative commander sent one of his four men to the side of the house and another to the front, down toward the water. At least they had MP5s with red-dot sight and light, not an old, almost scrap revolver like Bergmann's.

Bergmann had a brief discussion with the commander in the cover of the big Dodge van and decided to follow the officer who'd gone behind the house. He edged his way through the snow, his shoes getting colder and wetter with every step. The officer was already up on the patio on the sea-facing side of the house. Bergmann was quickly by his side. The lights were off on this side of the house too. The officer placed himself behind the nearest wall and shone the rifle light through the living room windows. Bergmann placed himself on the other side of the living room window.

He saw the officer shaking his head.

"Can't see a thing."

There was a crackle in the walkie-talkie.

"We'll ring the doorbell," said the commander.

"Received," said the officer. He raised his machine gun and aimed at the porch door. The red-dot sight moved across the living room floor. A couch. Bookcases. Fireplace.

A glimpse of someone.

A person.

The thirteen-year-old, thought Bergmann. He hasn't hidden her here in the living room, has he, or killed her here?

"Wait," he said out loud. The officer jumped.

"No one's answering," said the commander.

Bergmann placed his hands on the windowpane and tried to see into the living room. He had to hold his breath so as not to fog up the glass, but that only worked for a few seconds. His pulse was pounding so fast that he was unable to manage without oxygen. If Farberg was standing somewhere deep inside the living room, he could easily have used Bergmann's face as a target.

He detected the faint sound of a car in the distance. Or not. A gust of wind passed through the trees behind them. Then silence, darkness.

And a car. Pulling up in front of the house.

He pressed his face against the glass again.

A person lay on the couch that faced the windows toward the sea. It might be Farberg.

He banged on the window.

"Open up, Farberg!"

He pounded the window so hard that it almost broke. The bundle inside the living room showed no signs of moving.

"Give me the machine gun," he said as a car door slammed on the other side of the house. He struck the butt into the glass of the porch door, three times in a row. The air filled with the sound of splintering glass. He stuck his hand in through the opening and turned the lock, then the doorknob.

A red light went on in the living room. One of the security system sensors had been triggered. Somewhere in the city a silent alarm was notifying a security company.

Bergmann gave the revolver to the officer and moved carefully across the shards of glass. He turned the machine-gun light on. The red-dot sight and the sharp light swept across the walls. The sound of crushed glass and the front door opening at the other end of the house confused him for a moment. He pointed the light at the sofa arrangement in the middle of the room, then up the wall to his left, illuminating a picture he'd seen before. *Gustaf Fröding,* he thought. Susanne had said she'd seen that picture right here.

The ceiling light in the room was turned on, blinding him. Then his gaze fell on the woman who lay on the sofa—or what was left of her. She lay on the beige leather couch, which was soaked with blood from countless stab wounds. Her face was almost gone. Bergmann didn't know who she was; he could only assume that it was Jon-Olav Farberg's wife or partner.

"Oh shit," he heard the officer say behind him. It sounded like he was going to break down at any moment.

"I don't understand," Bergmann said to himself, lowering the MP5 toward the floor.

His phone rang in the pocket of his bubble jacket. He tore it off and loosened the Velcro on the Kevlar vest. He felt as if he couldn't catch a breath. "Frank Krokhol" it said on the display.

He studied the dead woman's body. The commander stomped around while he called for an ambulance on the portable radio, even though it was too late.

Bergmann went out on the patio.

Krokhol called again, though Bergmann had no idea why.

"Yes?" He looked in through the living room windows.

"Has something happened?" said Krokhol. He could smell news simply from the tone of Bergmann's voice, which he was unable to control.

"What is it?"

"That obituary. They found it right away up there."

"And?"

"'Our dear Edle Maria,'" Krokhol read. "'Edle Maria Reiersen. Born on May 3, 1946. Died October 1, 1962.' Then Gunnar and Ester. And one more name."

Bergmann felt as if all the blood drained from his body. For a moment he was unable to make out the name Krokhol said into his ear.

He was not even able to answer when Krokhol asked, twice in a row, "What is this supposed to mean, Tommy?"

60

An inexplicable calm almost always came over her when they brushed their teeth. It was so late that they really should have skipped it.

But just then, it felt delightfully ordinary, a necessary little ritual for her peace of mind. Torvald had gone down to his place to get a bottle of red wine since she didn't have any left. And she simply could not let herself get so damned hysterical. The doors were locked, both to the courtyard and out to the street.

A little wine, Susanne thought. *A little wine is all I need.*

God help her, she'd drunk so much this autumn. She would have to change her ways after Christmas.

Just so long as she'd remembered to lock the door behind her.

Of course. Of course she had.

The music from the living room was barely audible. The door to the bathroom was half-open.

"Nice Mommy," said Mathea. "Nice, pretty Mommy."

Susanne shook her head a little at her child, surprised by these out-of-the-blue compliments. She put water on the toothbrush and straightened up. She felt that she'd been crouched down too long, and her head was getting too little oxygen. She felt lightheaded for a moment, as though she was going to faint. All went black before her eyes for a few seconds.

When she recovered, the sound of running water sounded unnaturally loud, like a waterfall. Her gaze moved along the surface of the mirror.

A face. White. At the very edge of the mirror.

In the doorway.

Susanne breathed deeply through her nose. The sound of the water drowned out every thought. She closed her eyes for a moment.

The face was gone.

Susanne opened her eyes and focused all her attention on turning off the faucet. The apartment was completely quiet.

"Mommy?"

Susanne stared down at the tiles on the floor.

"Why are you breathing so funny?" Mathea tried to take the toothbrush out of her hand, but she wouldn't let it go. She was unable to let it go. She looked up again in the mirror.

The face was gone.

But it had been there.

White face. Dark hair. A woman.

"Be quiet," she said. "Torvald?" she called.

"Mommy, what is it?"

"Nothing." She smiled, and could tell from Mathea's expression that her attempt to calm her was successful. "Let's play a game," Susanne whispered. "Can you count to a hundred twice in a row?"

"I think so."

"I'll go out and lock the door to the bathroom. You sit down on the floor and count. If you can do that, you'll get a prize. Then I'll unlock the door, and tomorrow we'll go to the toy store in Oslo City and buy anything you like. How does that sound?"

"Anything?"

"Anything."

"That's a funny game. But okay."

She opened the medicine cabinet and found the key that she kept hidden there, so that Mathea wouldn't lock herself in the bathroom.

Mechanically, as if she'd done it a thousand times, she found the metal nail file.

Had she been seeing things?

No.

She heard a sound coming from the apartment. From the kitchen. A glass being knocked over.

"I'm sure it's just Torvald," Susanne whispered. "Start counting now." She kissed Mathea on the cheek.

Bergmann's pistol was hidden in the inside pocket of her jacket in the hall. Another sound, another glass, from the kitchen. She had a chance.

Miraculously Mathea had sat down on the floor. She was already up to twenty.

Susanne took a deep breath. She was trembling as she exhaled.

She opened the door with the nail file in one hand and the key in the other and looked out into the living room. She closed the door behind her and tried to regain control of her hand. It seemed as if the key didn't fit. She turned and turned, glancing around as she did so.

Finally.

She put the key in her pants pocket.

Torvald, she thought. *Has something happened to Torvald?*

She backed down the hall toward the entry, turned and looked into the living room. No one there. No Torvald. The woman with the white face must have caught him on his way downstairs. She bumped into the wall in the entry. Her front door was halfway open, and she saw Torvald's shoes on the landing. A movement. She heard a gurgling sound and peered out the doorway, saw that it was coming from his mouth. Blood was pouring out of him, but he was alive. He whispered something, but she couldn't understand what it was.

"You must be Susanne."

At the kitchen door stood the woman with the white face. She held a knife in her hand, a kitchen knife, which hung limply alongside her body.

An icy chill coursed through her, and she suddenly felt colder than she ever had before.

She took a step to the side and fumbled for the little pistol Bergmann had given her, which was still in the inside pocket of her jacket. Her hands were calm as she released the safety.

"Shoot me," said the woman, coming toward her. She resembled an injured predator in her big fur coat. She must have once been a very beautiful woman, but her face was now drained of color, of life itself.

"Mommy," Mathea called from the bathroom.

The woman stopped outside the bathroom.

Just as Susanne raised the pistol in a two-hand grip, she recognized the woman.

This can't be true, she thought. *Please, say it wasn't you.*

"Shoot me while she's listening. If not I'll take her. You know that. Edle Maria is bad. Elisabeth has told me that I'm bad. My name means *noble*, isn't that strange?"

"Edle Maria is dead," said Susanne.

"No, Elisabeth made me."

"No, you're Elisabeth. Put down the knife, then I'll help you. You need help."

Elisabeth Thorstensen must have absorbed the personality of her dead sister, Edle Maria. She was no longer Elisabeth. She was Edle Maria.

"I'm coming soon, Mathea," said the woman. Mathea fell silent.

"I'll kill you if you try to take her," said Susanne. "Do you understand that? I'm going to shoot you."

"Daddy never touched me. Never. Elisabeth was so much prettier than I was. I hated her for that. That fucking bitch." Her voice changed to a thin whine. "He was our father. Do you understand?"

"Who killed you? Who killed you, Edle Maria?"

The woman came closer.

"Jon-Olav told me about you. That fool. You asked him about me. He's Elisabeth's best friend. She told me that he read for her at the hospital in Sandberg during the summer. She told him everything. That whore told him everything. No one else, just him."

"Mommy!" Mathea called. She pounded on the door, just inches from the woman.

"Come out," said the woman. "Come, my girl."

"Mathea, don't answer her," said Susanne. She took a step closer, lowering the weapon.

"Elisabeth asked me for help, but I never helped her. I knew about her and Daddy, do you understand?"

Susanne almost dropped the pistol.

"He abused her? Is that what you mean?"

"Mommy. Mommy." Mathea's voice was so desperate that Susanne considered wounding Elisabeth Thorstensen just so that she could get her daughter out of the bathroom.

"Don't be scared," Susanne called. "I'll be there in just a minute."

She tried to get her phone out of her back pocket, but wasn't able to.

"Is Jon-Olav a friend of Elisabeth's?"

"Yes."

"So he's Elisabeth's friend? Is he the one who gets you to do the bad things?"

She nodded.

"He said to Elisabeth that if I do bad things, then maybe Elisabeth will get healthy. He just wanted to help Elisabeth get better. I'm the one who did those things, not Elisabeth. I lured them to me. Jon-Olav said no one would ever suspect a woman."

"Why did you take Kristiane? You know that she was Elisabeth's daughter?"

Elisabeth Thorstensen stared at her with a look Susanne knew that she would never forget, as if her real personality was trying to get out, but was unable to.

Susanne's hands were sweaty on the pistol stock. She didn't know what she could say to get Elisabeth to set down the knife. And she had to get to Torvald.

"But Jon-Olav is dead now," Elisabeth said.

"Where is he?"

"In an oven," she whispered.

Mathea was crying quietly inside the bathroom. Susanne tightened her grip on the little pistol.

"In an oven?"

"He didn't want to make Elisabeth healthy anymore. So I killed him."

"Where?"

"An old factory. You'll figure it out. We went there occasionally."

Susanne shifted her grip on the pistol with both hands and held it up in front of her.

"You want to know who killed me? Elisabeth killed me," said the woman, barely audible. "She crushed my face with a stone. He'd moved us north. But he didn't stop touching her. She had a girlfriend, but she didn't help her either. Elisabeth told me that it was the mother of your husband, Tommy." The woman smiled.

"He's not my husband."

"He is your husband. And then she crushed my face with a stone. She held me by the jaw and struck my face until it was completely gone." The woman crumpled to the floor and let go of the knife.

"Stop talking," said Susanne.

Mathea's crying grew louder, but Susanne hardly heard it. She went slowly toward the woman, who sat with her head bowed like a child, like Mathea. The knife was within reach. *I can do this,* she thought.

She heard boots in the stairwell. Several people. A portable radio. A command.

"I'll help you," she said. "Elisabeth, I'm going to help you."

"Elisabeth killed me!" the woman screamed.

At first Susanne didn't feel anything. It moved so fast that she didn't understand what had happened. A shudder passed through her leg, then a pain so sharp that she feared her leg might have been severed. She fell to the floor, onto the hand that held the pistol. The woman stood up, looming over her with the knife in her hand.

That's my blood, thought Susanne. Then she passed out.

"I'm so sorry," the woman whispered, raising the knife. "But your child is going to be like Elisabeth. Haven't you realized that? I can't let her live. Jon-Olav said that. You mustn't let her live."

Susanne came to and twisted to the left. All she heard was her own pulse—not Mathea, not the boots on the stairs—only the pounding in her temples and chest and throat. She thought she might have broken her arm when she fell, but she was able to raise it.

After the shot, there was silence. The woman's right eye disappeared. A geyser of blood struck Susanne in the leg and stomach. She fired again, this time the way Bergmann had told her to, right in the stomach.

The woman dropped the knife and fell. Susanne felt her ribs crack as the woman's head struck her body.

Then everything was quiet.

There were no boots on the stairs.

No Bergmann.

Mathea started crying again.

Susanne tried to push the dead woman off her, but was unable to. Her left leg burned with pain, and her right arm was unresponsive.

"I'm coming," she whispered. She tried to call out, but no sound came out. Her clothes were soaked with blood, the woman's head lay in her arms, and all she could manage was to whisper, "I'm coming, Mathea, I'm coming."

Torvald, she thought. *He's still lying out there on the landing.*

She tried to call out again, but only a thin, wheezing sound came out.

A door opened. A shout in another language, Punjabi, she thought. Several voices.

61

Five days later

One of the girls put the ball in the crossbar. It must have been the reaction from the small crowd that woke Bergmann up.

First rejoicing, then disappointment.

The sound of the ball against the wood and the cheers of the parents in the stands finally reached him, as if reality was being sent with a two-second delay.

He got up from the bench. He was still confused and pretty out of it, but now he was at least following along. He looked up at the scoreboard and remembered seeing Hadja before the match. She was there with her new boyfriend. It had set him back for a moment, but what about it? Could he even call whatever they'd had a proper relationship? It had been almost a year and a half ago. Whatever. He was an idiot.

It didn't matter. Something else had made him numb and detached.

He called out some words—"faster ball tempo"—then signaled for a play. Seconds later Martine slammed the ball into the goal. He gave the assistant coach a high five and sat back down on the bench, nearly tipping over and landing on his back like a drunk.

He'd arrived on the last flight from Tromsø yesterday and lain awake all night, then gone to a therapy session with Osvold at eight o'clock. Maybe it wasn't all that surprising that he hadn't been able to sleep.

"Maybe I should have been admitted to Ringvoll or Sandberg myself," he'd said to Osvold. The psychiatrist had not replied, and Bergmann interpreted the silence the way he wanted.

The second meeting with Alexander Thorstensen in Tromsø had not told him much more than he already knew. Bergmann knew that he should have checked whether Elisabeth had been hospitalized at Ringvoll, not Frensby, after Kristiane was killed. And at Sandberg as well, back in the seventies. The healthcare reforms in this country had sent her and her presumed schizophrenia over half of eastern Norway. Alexander said he wasn't surprised his mother never got the help she needed, the liability disclaimers in the healthcare system being what they were. Besides, it may have been impossible for anyone to correctly diagnose her. There was little doubt that she had developed a split personality. For a long time it was believed that schizophrenia was linked to split personality, but today that was known to be incorrect. Patients with split personalities could in the worst cases be aware of the existence of the various personalities and could be capable of concealing them under the guise of a psychotic condition. Alexander thought his mother was probably a mystery to those treating her.

"But Jon-Olav Farberg must have been able to read her like an open book," Bergmann had said.

Alexander said that Farberg was probably the first adult his mother had ever trusted—the first person she had ever been able to reveal her true self to. With her upbringing and pattern of illness, she was easily taken advantage of by someone like Farberg.

The personnel records at Sandberg showed that Farberg had worked at Sandberg Psychiatric Hospital as a summer and vacation replacement while he was studying at the teachers college in Hamar. And every time there was a full moon, they had to call in extra staff.

Alexander told Bergmann that he assumed Kristiane had fallen in love with Farberg, and that she went to his apartment in Skøyen to see him. Elisabeth must have somehow found out. It seemed to be an enormous relief to him to learn that his mother was dead; she had killed all those girls, even his own sister. Who could blame him for that?

Martine pounded in yet another goal, a forearm shot from nine meters. Bergmann saw it without seeing it. He clapped, but it was as if his hands weren't his own.

Bergmann had spent the rest of the day questioning Morten Høgda.

Høgda had finally broken down in the interview room. He said that Elisabeth had once told him that her father had started abusing her sexually when she was eight or nine years old, but that he mustn't tell anyone. She told him that her father had never touched her sister, that she felt so dirty, that all girls were dirty little whores like her. They didn't deserve to live, as she herself didn't deserve to live.

"And you made her even dirtier yourself," Bergmann said, "instead of trying to help her."

Høgda said that he'd occasionally been afraid of Elisabeth, that she had something frightening and indefinable behind her eyes, that she had another face he never clearly saw. She got furious when he tried to bring it up once and suggest that perhaps she should be hospitalized again and tell the doctor everything. Høgda thought he'd been fooled— he wasn't the one who had exploited Elisabeth all those years, but the other way around. She had tried to lure him into a trap. He wasn't the one who'd arrived late to their meeting at the Radisson hotel the night the Lithuanian girl was killed.

"Two days later she called me and asked why I arrived so late," Høgda said. "I told her she was the one who was late—over two and a half hours late. Then she just started crying, like a child. She'd always been a little wacky, but this . . ."

Bergmann just shook his head. Then he got Høgda to write a four-page letter by hand, just to rule out the possibility that he had written one of the letters. When he came back into the interview room, he took one look at it and confirmed what he already knew, then just wadded up the pages and threw them in the wastebasket.

Elisabeth Thorstensen was dead. Jon-Olav Farberg was dead. And Anders Rask was still in a coma in Trondheim. But they still hadn't found Farberg's body. An old factory, Elisabeth Thorstensen had said. Where should they start?

The match was finally over. Bergmann barely registered that it ended in a tie.

He left the assistant coach in charge and tried to leave the gym as quickly as he could. Unfortunately he was held up by some of the parents who wanted to thank him for the season and wish him a merry Christmas.

Hadja and her boyfriend managed to catch up with him.

"It's been a long time," she said. "I'd like you to meet Thomas."

Bergmann extended a hand. He was young, good-looking, and slender, with clothes that fit him well. Not like Bergmann, a mastodon in rough-hewn granite, in an extra-large blue workout suit that was still too small.

He felt nothing, and that was probably good. She hadn't meant anything to him, had she?

She gave him a hug when they came out of the gym. Her hair fluttered in the snowstorm, just as it had that summer.

"I hope you're doing well," she said. "Merry Christmas."

Thomas put his arm around her as they turned up the steps to the shopping center. Bergmann remained standing in the blizzard with an unlit cigarette in his hand. He stared at the many buses parked by the subway station, the throngs of people on the platform.

Christmas, was it Christmas?

If only Susanne could have shot Elisabeth in the leg. But what kind of wish was that?

He threw away the unlit cigarette and headed into the parking garage. The image of Hadja with that young guy was burned into his mind's eye. *I hope you're doing well.* What did she mean by that?

The sound of his phone ringing in his pocket rescued him from falling into what he knew would be a deepening depression that would last all through Christmas.

"Tommy?" It was Leif Monsen from Dispatch.

Bergmann stopped on the stairs of the parking garage. A weak light settled over him. His gaze followed a falling snowflake.

"I'm in Frysja, at the old brickworks."

Bergmann walked quickly up the last few steps. He knew exactly what Monsen was about to say.

"I think you should take a little trip up here. Two Polish workers found a little suckling pig in one of the kilns about an hour ago."

"Suckling pig?"

"No matter how hard you try to burn a dead person, it doesn't work, you hear what I'm saying? The remnants resemble a suckling pig, albeit one with a shrunken human head."

Fifteen minutes later Bergmann parked his old Escort outside the gate to the closed factory in Frysja. A young uniformed officer held up the barricade tape for him, just as he himself had done for experienced detectives back in the day. A solitary work lamp hung over the old entryway. The sign labeled "Høgda Property Development" was barely visible.

Apart from the young officer at the barricade, only Monsen and the CSI Georg Abrahamsen, who lived right up the road, were in the big factory hall. The doors to the kiln were wide open. Bergmann nodded at the two Poles and Monsen. He went over to the kiln, where Abrahamsen was busy rigging up a lamp.

"Hold this," he said, giving Bergmann a metal rod he guessed was part of a stand. A cold wind blew through the cavernous room from one of the broken windows up under the roof. *Elisabeth Thorstensen must have known about this place,* he thought. Maybe Høgda told her about this project.

But how could she possibly have arranged everything? She couldn't have had enough time. First kill Farberg's wife, then Farberg himself, then kidnap the girl in Sofiemyr, assuming that's what happened, and finally show up at Susanne's apartment?

Completely impossible.

Abrahamsen stuck his head into the kiln.

"You have to get the body out," said Bergmann.

Abrahamsen remained silent.

Bergmann studied the kiln and imagined how Elisabeth had gotten him in there on her own. She could easily have rolled Farberg in through the open doors. The mechanism by the doors seemed quite simple. A power switch, a thermostat. Like a kitchen oven.

Abrahamsen had found a spade that resembled the kind used at Italian pizzerias.

When the shriveled figure finally lay in front of them, it seemed inconceivable that it had once been a human being.

"It's going to take some time to get that identified," said Abrahamsen, crouching down. Bergmann thought the little body was more reminiscent of an incinerated extraterrestrial than a suckling pig, but the sight was still unpleasant.

"Not a good smell on this Farberg fellow," said Abrahamsen, taking a pinch of snuff. "But I think his teeth are knocked out." He pointed the flashlight at what had once been the person's face.

"So it could be anyone at all," said Bergmann. "But you don't knock out someone's teeth unless you want to make the identification process as difficult as possible."

"It's not impossible, but it's going to take a hell of a long time."

"Why would Elisabeth Thorstensen knock out Farberg's teeth?"

"To buy herself time."

"But why would she need time? She told Susanne herself that she'd killed him."

"Could it be the girl from Kolbotn?" said Abrahamsen, apparently more to himself than to anyone else.

"The girl?" Bergmann heard somewhere behind him. The door of the building slammed shut, and a draft made Bergmann raise the hood of his bubble jacket over his head. He lit a cigarette without asking for Abrahamsen's permission.

"So this is Jon-Olav Farberg?" Fredrik Reuter looked like he'd intended to kick the burned carcass with one shoe.

"She knocked his teeth out," said Bergmann.

"That's Farberg. I'm certain enough to write his death certificate myself, Tommy."

"Just as long as it's not the thirteen-year-old from Sofiemyr," said Bergmann. "Amanda."

Reuter's facial color was about to change from white to red.

"Don't ruin Christmas for me, okay?"

"Has it occurred to you that Anders Rask let himself be exploited, Fredrik? And that he wasn't the only one?"

"Never let facts ruin a good story. By the way, merry Christmas, Tommy."

Bergmann knew that nothing he said would get through to Reuter just then. Reuter wanted to celebrate Christmas in peace, and perhaps he'd like that too, when he thought about it.

After spending an hour in the old factory, there was nothing more Bergmann could do there. Abrahamsen and his colleagues could manage alone. Reuter had refused to talk to him about anything other than Christmas.

Nonetheless, he could not let the thought go. Who had Georg Abrahamsen scooped out of the kiln?

No, thought Bergmann as he parked the car in a rare vacant space outside his apartment building. *I don't believe it.*

He checked his mailbox. It was empty.

"Fortunately," he said quietly.

Inside his apartment he found a knife in the kitchen and went from room to room. At last he kicked open the door to the bathroom. Just as damned empty as it had been since Hege left. At least as damned empty as it had been since he got the new safety lock mounted.

You're being misled, just like Anders Rask and Elisabeth Thorstensen.

He sat down at the computer to read about the thirteen-year-old girl in Kolbotn. "Amanda (13) Missing" read the headline. A school portrait filled the screen. He pictured Amanda walking through the forest. She was barely over five feet tall and slightly underweight. What resistance could she have put up, paralyzed by fear? Maybe she never even realized what happened. Half a minute, that was all it would take. That was all she'd needed.

She?

Elisabeth? Bergmann tried to draw a kind of timeline on a piece of paper, but gave up almost before he'd started.

Elisabeth alone?

Inconceivable. Why didn't Reuter realize that?

Bergmann stared at the face of the young girl on the screen for several minutes. She had a heart-shaped face, teardrop-shaped eyes, and almost perfect teeth. Elisabeth must have been spying on her for a long time. She was going to be pretty as an adult. She was already pretty. In a way that had provoked Elisabeth. Because men would soon start desiring her—perhaps they already did.

Bergmann didn't know why, but he suddenly felt sure that Amanda was still alive.

The drive down to headquarters took ten minutes. He grabbed the keys to Farberg's house in Malmøya and tried to think as little as possible.

62

He drove in a trancelike state. Gradually, it all began to make sense. As he drove over the bridge between Ormøya and Malmøya, everything seemed settled.

He sat in the car with the reading light on for a long time. He tried once again to draw a timeline in his notepad. They should have done this a long time ago, but this case had been cursed by a series of false conclusions, and they didn't seem to have exhausted them yet.

Had they killed all those girls together? What had Elisabeth said to Susanne—he didn't want to anymore?

He turned off the reading light and lit a cigarette.

Where was Amanda?

Asgeir Nordli had an empty cabin in Nesodden. Jon-Olav Farberg had two cabins, one in Geilo and one in Hvaler. Both equally empty.

The girl must have a boyfriend, thought Bergmann, tossing his cigarette out the car window. One that she hadn't wanted to tell anyone about.

It was no worse than that.

He sat for a long time outside the house and studied the windows one by one. He had a feeling he wasn't going to be alone in there. It was completely irrational, but nonetheless, he couldn't let the thought go. Should he ask for firearms? He was in trouble enough as it was, but he didn't regret giving Susanne the gun. It had saved her life. So it was worth it, even if it cost him his job.

He walked around to the back of the house, just as he'd done the week before. When he put his face up to the living room window, he was afraid for a moment that Farberg's wife would still be lying there.

He walked back around to the front, removed the barricade tape from the front door, and broke the seal on the lock plate with the key.

In the entryway, he put on a pair of blue shoe protectors and pulled a hairnet from a box by the door. He'd only taken a few steps into the hall when one of the wallboards creaked.

"Damn," he said to himself. He swept the MagLite through room after room—the kitchen, the library, across the picture of the crazy poet Fröding, the office, and the living room.

He went back to the office and sat down in the chair behind the desk. The flashlight's beam cut through the darkness, making it almost impossible to see the outer edges of the room. He flashed the light beam over a photograph of Farberg's son that rested on the table. He was maybe twelve or thirteen years old in the picture. How old was he now? Bergmann thought he'd give him a call tomorrow. He'd spoken with Farberg's ex-wife several times already. She hadn't been home that Saturday when Kristiane was in Skøyen. They'd quarreled earlier in the day, and she'd taken her three-year-old son with her and gone to her mother's in Holmestrand.

This is hopeless, he thought, turning on the green library lamp. He didn't even know what he was looking for.

Unless. Of course he knew.

He turned off the lamp and walked carefully upstairs to the second floor, without turning on the light. The steps creaked under his weight, and he stopped midstep and turned around. Silence. He had locked the front door behind him, hadn't he?

In the bathroom on the second floor he turned on the fluorescent light. It blinked a few times. He observed himself in the mirror and remembered how Susanne had seen Elisabeth's face in the mirror.

He opened the medicine cabinet. A comb and a hairbrush with what looked like Farberg's hair. He put both in a Ziploc bag. Then he emptied the dirty clothes out of the laundry basket onto the floor, picked up two of Farberg's underpants, and put them in another bag. Tomorrow he would get Abrahamsen to send all that up to Kripo for analysis, even if he had to do it behind Reuter's back.

He had just pulled out of Farberg's driveway when his phone pinged. He pulled over and adjusted the rearview mirror. For some reason he wanted to have the darkened house in view while he talked. He had a feeling that a light might suddenly go on in one of the windows.

Susanne? he thought. It was ten thirty at night.

Are you sleeping? the message said.

No, he answered.

She called half a minute later.

"Everything okay with you?"

"I don't like being here. But I didn't like the hospital either."

"I understand that. Just let me know if you need anything."

She didn't reply.

"How's Torvald doing?"

"He'll survive. He'll have to learn to walk again, but he'll make it. Will you go out there after Christmas to visit him with me?"

Bergmann waited before answering. Not because of the question in itself, but because of the tone in her voice. It sounded as if she really wanted him to go with her. Like she wanted them to be together.

Fool, he thought.

"Yes," he said at last. "Of course."

"What are you doing the day after tomorrow?"

"The day after tomorrow?"

She laughed. Not the usual attention-seeking laughter. Something more gentle, tentative. A laugh he could live with.

"Christmas Eve, hello?"

She knew perfectly well he didn't have a family.

"I'm going to . . ." He tried to pull a lie out of his sleeve, put on a poker face. But he'd never been a poker player. "Nothing."

"You can't sit at home alone. You don't have my permission to sit at home alone, Tommy."

He didn't reply.

"Mathea likes pink. Anything pink."

63

It turned out to be a better Christmas Eve than he could remember having had in years, at least since he was a kid himself. Susanne was funny, and she could cook. Bergmann had a strange feeling that he was wanted there, and not just because he didn't have anywhere else to go.

For some reason the girl, Mathea, appeared to have an almost frightening trust in him. Maybe she was that way with everyone—he didn't know—but for the first time he considered the possibility of having kids. *Me? Forget it,* he thought a moment later.

Mathea had fallen asleep with her Christmas dress on, and he carried her to her room. He just stood there and watched the sleeping girl for a while. A few minutes in the presence of such pure innocence did him good. This job easily ruined a person. The world wasn't all bad. Not all.

Susanne was standing in the kitchen with an unopened bottle of wine when he came out. He saw from her expression that it was time to go home.

"Svein's coming over in a little while. We'll have to have that second bottle another time, Tommy." She tried to smile.

He shook his head. "Svein?" he said. Then he understood. "Finneland?"

She nodded and frowned. Her body language indicated that she didn't want to talk about it. "They've argued. I—" She stopped.

"I should be going anyway."

She laughed. "It was really nice of you to come."

"It was nice of you to invite me. And I don't usually say such things."

She followed him out to the entry, her gait steadier than he'd thought it would be.

"That cast really suits you."

She laughed again. He hated to admit it, but he liked that laugh. And those eyes.

"To be honest I thought he was married, Susanne."

She put her arms around him and hugged him for a long time. "How old are you?"

"Forty next year. In two months, actually."

"Perfect." She stroked his cheek. "We would have been perfect together, don't you think?"

He frowned, shrugged.

"But life isn't perfect, Tommy."

"Exactly." *And I shouldn't drink anymore now,* he thought.

"Svein Finneland," he muttered as he fumbled with the key in the building door. He stopped in front of the bulletin board. A new copy of the notice from Property Services was hanging there. Elisabeth had worked there. Why hadn't he ever followed up on that?

He put the key in the mailbox lock and opened the little hatch.

Two advertising flyers. And several white envelopes.

All were postmarked Lillehammer December 20, four days ago. Twenty of them altogether. Second-class mail, which explained the delayed delivery. The handwriting was exactly alike on all the envelopes. He'd seen it before. Of course he had.

He tore open the first envelope with his key. Inside it was a Christmas card, the cheap kind you can buy in any convenience store. He opened the card. A slip of paper fell out and landed on the dirty floor. It was a copy of an old black-and-white picture of a young man with glasses, in white tie and tails. *Gustaf Fröding*, thought Bergmann. He read the densely written text on the inside of the card.

I am so excited about how that went. Susanne, wasn't that what she said her name was? I know that act. Elisabeth never killed anyone other than Edle Maria. But she watched every time. I said it would make her healthy, and she believed it. She thought that Edle Maria would disappear from her body, that she would never haunt her again. She brought cassettes to me with their sounds. It was our music, Tommy. She called me from Tønsberg and said that she'd found a girl, a girl she wanted us to kill. She was with Morten at the cabin. She had seen a girl in town one day and followed her home. She soiled her with Morten, she knew that herself. Knowing that Elisabeth did everything I wanted . . . ? It gave me a power you will never understand. Do you think she killed me, Tommy? Maybe she hated me from the first time I came into her room at Sandberg. Maybe because I convinced her that Kristiane must be sacrificed too—she would become exactly like Elisabeth. A whore for her brother. Or no, for me. Just as Elisabeth had been for her father. These frivolous women. They destroy the world. No, women destroy the world. At last they're all like that. That is all you need to understand. There is nothing else to understand on this earth. And that idiot Furuberget. He barely remembered me from the job at Sandberg. No surprise that Elisabeth fooled him. Maybe he didn't want to see the

truth when she was admitted after you found Kristiane.
If you find me, you'll find her patient record. As if that
would tell you anything at all.
I can tell you more. If you search in the right place.
Trust yourself.
Then you'll find me. At last.

Bergmann read the text over again. He shook his head. Some of it was incoherent, disconnected. Other parts made sense, though. If any of it was true, that is.

He folded up the Christmas card and stuck it back in the envelope. Then he opened the next envelope.

It was empty.

The next seventeen envelopes were also empty.

He paused before the last one. Another Christmas card, identical to the one in the first envelope, featuring a red wax candle in front of a Christmas wreath. The same handwriting.

The Devil's features.
Where was I?
Soul in flame, blood in dance.
Where was I, Tommy?

64

Bergmann called Susanne. He closed his eyes and felt her next to him. The scent of her in his nostrils. And he'd never even liked her.

"Yes?" she said a little sharply. Svein Finneland must have been there. Oh well. To each his own.

"Never mind."

"Has something happened?"

He thought about the Christmas card. The writing wasn't the same as in the letter he'd found in Anders Rask's blood-red book. It was like the writing in the letter he'd received. He understood just then that Elisabeth had written that letter to Rask, but Farberg had dictated it. The letter to Bergmann must have been written by Farberg, but dictated by Elisabeth. Unless he'd put the words in her mouth.

"No. Talk to you later," he said. *And lock the door securely for once*, he thought, but he chose not to say anything. Farberg wasn't obsessed with Mathea. But what about Susanne herself?

After checking all the rooms in his apartment, including the storage compartment in the basement, he sat down at his computer and did a search on Gustaf Fröding. "In the early 1890s Fröding was admitted to the sanatorium at Suttestad in Lillehammer, Norway," he read. He clicked on the link to Suttestad. A kind of hotel was operated on the property, which was located a couple of miles outside the city. It had six large rooms, with a view of Lillehammer and the waters of Lågen.

He took the stairs in two bounds and was out the door before he'd even thought about what he was doing. Not until he reached the Shell station at Skedsmokorset did it occur to him that he was unarmed. *If I die tonight, there's probably a reason for that,* he thought.

It was almost Christmas morning, and there was virtually no traffic on E6. Bergmann easily flew down the road at eighty miles per hour, as fast as his old heap of a car could tolerate.

It was three thirty in the morning when he turned into the Suttestad estate. Bergmann parked by the storehouse. Large mounds of cleared snow towered up around him. The snow crunched under his feet, loud enough that anyone who was awake would have heard it through a closed window.

Three cars were parked by the large white building, all of them with Lillehammer plates. He walked carefully up the steps to the main entrance and pounded hard on the door several times. Then he rang the bell that hung down from the balcony. The sound echoed between the old buildings.

Bergmann tried not to think as he started pounding on the door again.

Thirty seconds later, he heard muttering from somewhere up on the second floor, then steps on the stairs.

"This is one heck of a note," the voice said on the other side of the door.

The lock slowly turned in the door.

"What the hell is this?" he said, staring at Bergmann with a haggard look on his face.

Bergmann held up his police identification.

"Have you had any overnight guests here in the past few days?"

"Honestly," said the man, "is this something worth waking my kids up for?"

"I drove here from Oslo. It's important."

The man tightened the belt around his bathrobe and shook his head.

"I've been in London on a soccer tour with my boy, but no, I don't think so. You'll have to ask my old lady."

He closed the door. Bergmann remained standing outside on the steps. After a while he heard steps on the stairs again. The man returned with a woman who looked a few years younger than her husband. She looked cold standing in the doorway in a kimono.

"No," she said. "Hasn't been anyone here. Not many people this time of year."

"Sorry," said the man. "We would have liked to be of help."

Bergmann held the woman's gaze as she closed the door. He'd been doing this job long enough to see that she was lying. And that she was scared to death.

He walked slowly back to the car. He lit a cigarette and got in. It was still warm enough inside that he could keep the engine turned off. After a second cigarette, the hall light came on, and the door opened.

He got out of the car and took a few steps toward her. She pulled up the hood on her bubble jacket and jogged across the yard. Her breath steamed as she got into the passenger seat.

"Fortunately he falls asleep quickly again."

She pointed at the pack of Prince cigarettes sitting on the console. He lit a cigarette for her. She smoked half of it in silence.

"There was a man here. Vidar Østli, he called himself. Paid cash." She stared stiffly ahead of her and talked in a low voice.

"When?"

"Two days ago. He said he was separated, thrown out of his house. Needed time to think."

Bergmann could not help inhaling deeply. She turned toward him.

"Who is he?" she said.

"Which room did he stay in?"

"The big one. The corner room."

"You have to show me that room."

417

She shook her head.

"Why not?"

"I can't say. He'd kill me."

"What do you mean?"

"You mustn't mention this to anyone. If I show you the room, you must never say that you've been here."

Bergmann opened the car door, and he studied her when the interior light came on. She was young, perhaps in her early thirties. They got out.

Everything was dark around them. The city lights sparkling in the distance seemed like another planet. She led him to the gable end of the main building, where there was a separate entrance to the guesthouse.

"This was a sanatorium at one time?" he said as they went up the stairs to the second floor.

"Yes. It's a little disturbing to think about that, though. Sometimes I think I hear sounds at night."

They walked down a dark corridor. She turned on the light in the room at the end. It was a large room with windows on two walls.

"I was just going to change his bed. He paid for two nights."

"Yes?"

"He came into the room. Slipped in, I didn't even hear him come in. He said to me, 'If you ever say that I stayed here, I'll come after you.' Then he just stood there in the middle of the room."

"Who have you told this to?"

"No one."

"Not even your husband?"

"No. He's so hot-tempered, I'm sure he would have tried to find him. Good Lord, I have three kids. I can't even sleep at night anymore."

Bergmann put his hand on her shoulder.

"He's not coming back."

She closed her eyes, unable to hold back the tears.

"What kind of car was he driving?"

"I think it was blue, but I don't remember exactly. Maybe gray. He frightened me so. At the same time he was so calm."

"Blue?"

He looked away and stared out at the city. It would be hopeless if he didn't get a search under way tonight. He had a feeling it wouldn't do any good.

"In the morning on the second day the dog barked so much at his car that I had to bring him in."

"What kind of car was it? You must try to remember. Model, size?"

"A delivery van," she said quietly. "It was a delivery van. Pretty big. The kind that tradesmen use, you know."

The girl, thought Bergmann. *Amanda. She's alive.*

He opened the window and put on the catch. Cold air poured in and made it easier to breathe. It was as if the room had threatened to suffocate him. He leaned out of the window and looked out at the city lights blurred by the cold fog like brush strokes.

"And the dog barked at the car?"

"He never does that. But he was marking, somehow. Like during a hunt."

Bergmann only needed to search for a few minutes. In the top drawer of the nightstand, under a worn tourist brochure, was yet another Christmas card, just like the ones he'd received in the mail.

Bergmann recognized the handwriting.

Soul in flame, blood in dance.

Where am I, Tommy?

ABOUT THE AUTHOR

Photo © 2014 Charlotte Hveem

Gard Sveen is an award-winning crime novelist who divides his time between writing and working as a senior adviser to the Norwegian Ministry of Defense. *The Last Pilgrim*, his debut novel, was originally published as *Den siste pilgrimen* in Norway and is the first in the series featuring troubled police detective Tommy Bergmann.

The novel was an instant hit with critics and readers, and it went on to win the Riverton Prize in 2013, the prestigious Glass Key in 2014, and the Maurits Hansen Award, also in 2014. Sveen is the only author to date who has received all three honors for a first novel. The only other author who has managed to win both a Riverton and a Glass Key for their debut novel is Jo Nesbø.

ABOUT THE TRANSLATOR

Paul Norlen is a translator based in Seattle, Washington.